Tre

A Po ___a Day novel

by

Ruth Saberton

Edition 3

Copyright

Also by Ruth Saberton

Escape for the Summer

Escape for Christmas

Dead Romantic

Hobb's Cottage

Weight Till Christmas

Katy Carter Wants a Hero

Ellie Andrews Has Second Thoughts

Amber Scott is Starting Over

The Wedding Countdown

Runaway Summer: Polwenna Bay 1

A Time for Living: Polwenna Bay 2

Winter Wishes: Polwenna Bay 3

Writing as Jessica Fox

The One That Got Away

Eastern Promise

Hard to Get

Unlucky in Love

Always the Bride

Writing as Holly Cavendish

Looking for Fireworks

Writing as Georgie Carter

The Perfect Christmas

Chapter 1

"That'll be eighty-eight quid and ninety-five pence. Is there anything else? Pork scratchings? Crisps? Better say now, because you won't want to queue again and it's only going to get busier between now and midnight."

Adam Harper, landlord of The Ship Inn, leaned against the real-ale pumps. The tone of his voice conveyed an interesting alchemy of greed, stress and genuine concern. At least, Issie Tremaine assumed this was Adam speaking. The rotund figure stretching a cupped hand over piles of empty glasses bore a resemblance to the pub's landlord, and he had the same sort of thinning hair. Still, it was hard to know for certain who was behind the highwayman's mask and costume. Equally, the plump Wonder Woman stacking the dishwasher could have been the landlord's wife Rose; the rowdy crowd of pirates necking tequila at the furthest end of the bar might well be a group of local fishermen; and the moth-eaten Wookiee feeding the juke box could be local chip-shop owner and *Star Wars* fan Chris the Cod.

"Talk about stand and deliver," grumbled Issie's brother-in-law Ashley Carstairs, peeling notes from his wallet and passing them over. Even though half his face was covered by his *Phantom of the Opera* mask, it was clear that he was looking puzzled. "Just how many people did I buy drinks for again?"

"Pretty much everyone in here," replied Issie's sister, who was dressed as the bride of Frankenstein and sporting green hair. Mo Carstairs' red curls peeked out from under the wig as she shook her head despairingly. "Seriously, Ashley, even you don't have enough money to keep this lot in beer."

Ashley dropped a kiss onto Mo's painted nose. His lips already had an emerald tint to them, probably because he and Mo never seemed to be able to go more than five minutes without snogging, Issie thought fondly.

"I've got a lot to celebrate this year," he was saying, and his tone was serious now. "I should be buying champagne, not just a few pints here and there. Tonight is a night I didn't always think I was going to see."

Mo reached onto her tiptoes and wound her arms tightly around his neck. "This is just the start," she promised. "Things are only going to get better from now on. I promise. The next twelve months are going to be even more wonderful."

"Gross! Cut it out, you two, and get the beers sorted! Some of us have got some serious partying to do, unlike you old married folk!" said Issie's twin Nick, abandoning his fishermen mates and, on the lookout for beer, joining them. Clad in full Jack Sparrow gear, Nick drew admiring glances from just about every girl in the place – and didn't he just know it! Issie was filled with amusement; she wondered if the same girls would be quite so admiring if they knew that Nick had taken at least four hours to get ready and used more mascara than her and Mo put together? Or that he'd shrieked like a scalded cat when Tara Tremaine had waxed his eyebrows?

Deciding to save this arsenal of embarrassing sibling information for a more useful time, Issie passed Nick a foaming pint of Pol Brew and glanced around thoughtfully. It was New Year's Eve and the low-beamed pub was rammed full of drinkers, all in party mood and – as was the tradition in Polwenna Bay – wearing fancy dress. The thirty-first of December was a highlight in the village calendar and locals and holidaymakers had flocked to The Ship, all determined to outdo the previous year's costume and drink as much alcohol as possible before midnight struck. As always it was a wonderful excuse for alter egos to emerge. Issie often thought a psychologist would have a field day analysing who had chosen to come as what. So far tonight she'd spotted an entire Marvel comic's worth of superheroes, plus a number of fairies and several dodgy attempts at Ross Poldark – which would fool no woman, no matter how much mulled wine she'd knocked back. On her way to the pub Issie had been caught up in a crowd of marauding Vikings, chatted to Dracula and smoked a sneaky cigarette with Cruella de Vil.

And all this before she'd even had a drink! Anyone who thought life in a small Cornish fishing village was dull had clearly never visited Polwenna Bay.

While her brother-in-law put his depleted wallet back in his pocket and teased Adam about ordering a new Range Rover with the night's takings, Issie glanced across the pub to the quayside, which was bustling as though it was peak season. Everyone was in high spirits, filled with a potent cocktail of optimism and alcohol. The trawlers were all lined up against the harbour wall while their crews celebrated, the steep valley sides were starred with the lights from cottage windows, and beneath the marina's Christmas tree a young couple were kissing as though they never wanted the embrace to end.

Issie bit her lip and looked away from them, concentrating hard on the bright slice of moon floating above the harbour and the reflections of Christmas lights dancing in the inky water. The moon was so beautiful and so lonely that her throat tightened. Would this deep unhappiness stay with her forever?

The idea made her heart twist. Issie turned back to the bar and focused her attention on the glass of cider Adam was passing in her direction. She took a big gulp to stop it from spilling, felt the kick of the alcohol hitting her taste buds and closed her eyes with relief. A drink: that was all she needed. In fact, forget *one* drink. She needed several, and what better place to get them than right here in The Ship and on New Year's Eve? After a couple of pints she'd be having fun and not in any danger of thinking about… about…

Issie almost swore out loud, annoyed with herself for being so pathetic. It was New Year's Eve, for heaven's sake! This was no time to be dwelling on the past and all the stupid mistakes that had gone before. This was a night for new starts and new adventures. There was no point mourning what she'd lost.

He clearly wasn't.

She tightened her grip on her glass until her fingertips were putty-coloured.

Don't think. Don't think. Don't think.

Thinking was deadly; it was the first footstep onto a rickety bridge that would eventually splinter and send her plummeting headlong into the darkest chasm imaginable. No, dwelling on how stupid she'd been would be fatal. What she needed was a distraction. And fast.

Issie took another gulp of her drink and flipped her blonde braids back from her face with a practised toss of her head. It felt a little like flicking a switch into another mode, from contemplative to autopilot maybe, or perhaps from self-destruct to totally combusting. Who knew?

Who cared?

Glancing across the pub and catching the eye of a suave 007, Issie leaned forward, raised her glass and curved her lips upwards into an expression of promise. It was almost too easy – and by the time Ashley's round was distributed, Bond's jaw was swinging open, partly because this was a move that never failed and partly because Issie's pirate-wench outfit had given him more than an ample glimpse of her scarlet Wonderbra.

"Stop it," said Mo sternly to Issie, as the sisters elbowed their way through the crowd to the window seat where the rest of their friends and family were gathered.

"Stop what?" said Issie, wiggling a little so that her dress slipped seductively off her shoulder. Bond was making a beeline towards her, with a bottle of Bolly and two glasses; she waved at him merrily.

"Giving Teddy St Milton the green light when you're not in the least bit interested in him."

"I don't know what you're on about," fibbed Issie. "I'm not doing anything."

"Don't give me that bollocks, Isabella Tremaine. I know you, remember? It's not fair to encourage him just because you're bored."

"Who says I'm bored? Maybe I actually like Teddy?"

Mo snorted, sounding just like one of her horses. "Yeah, right."

"And what's that supposed to mean, exactly?"

"It means that I know you're not at all interested in Teddy, or not in any way that really counts. There's no challenge for you there," her sister said. "You need a man who's going to keep you on your toes and make you think – an intellectual equal – and Ted's never going to offer you that. You'd die of tedium in minutes. Don't screw your nose up at me like that. You know it's true."

Issie did know, but she wasn't about to admit this to Mo. Right now a spot of no-strings, no-intellect sexy tedium was *exactly* what the doctor had ordered.

"It's just a bit of fun," she protested.

Teddy, whose journey across the pub had been interrupted by a burly-looking Batman who reeked of Old Spice, glanced over and gave her a wink. Issie couldn't help herself; she winked back.

Mo shook her head so hard her green wig nearly flew off. "And *that* is exactly what I mean! Issie, you are *totally* encouraging him. Unless you were actually winking at Mickey Davey? In which case there really is no hope."

Issie almost spluttered her drink everywhere. Mickey Davey, aka Batman, was a relative newcomer to the village with a florid face and a penchant for loud shirts, gold chains and slip-on shoes. He delighted in telling all and sundry how he could *get a deal* on anything. Not long ago he'd bought the Mermaid Beach Café, which he'd promptly renamed Davey's Locker. Apart from selling pasties and the odd cup of coffee, not a lot of business seemed to go on there; how he afforded his big gold Bentley was anyone's guess.

"I'll take that as a no," Mo said, slapping Issie on the back. "But think about what I'm saying, yeah? Messing with someone like Teddy St Milton is asking for trouble."

"Jeez, Mo, I'm having a laugh, not looking to marry the guy," Issie grumbled as she placed her drink on the table and nudged her brother Jake to move up a seat. "Like I said, it's just a bit of fun."

"To you maybe, but are you certain Teddy sees it that way?"

Issie couldn't look her sister in the eye. All of a sudden the beer rings on the pub table seemed endlessly fascinating. Oh look, they were making the Olympic pattern. How amazing.

"Issie?" Mo said darkly, when her sister didn't answer.

"There's nothing going on," Issie muttered mutinously. For God's sake! She'd only snogged the guy a couple of times, and maybe had a bit of a fumble after a few drinks. It was no big deal. What was it with Mo these days? Since she'd hooked up with Ashley she'd become so serious about everything. Of course, Issie understood the reasons why, but privately she thought life had been easier when all her sister had cared about was horses.

"Be careful, Issie; he's a lot more like Ella than you might think," Mo said. "This is a bit of a gypsy's warning, but I've a feeling Teddy could be very bad news if you upset him."

Not many people could pull off giving a stern lecture while dressed as Frankenstein's bride, but somehow Mo managed it. Issie, now sitting in between Jake and Caspar Owen, the village's resident writer (who'd come dressed as himself, as far as she could see) pretended to listen to the conversations ebbing and flowing around her – but, inside, she was wondering whether Mo was right.

Was she being unfair to Teddy? Surely not. Mo was just overreacting. It was New Year's Eve and Issie was only letting her hair down a bit. Like her, Teddy was single and up for a laugh. So what could possibly be wrong with just having a few drinks with him? After all, he was loaded. He was good-looking too, if you liked the public-schoolboy thing – which personally Issie didn't (dark, brooding and slightly edgy being more her style). Anyway, the point was that Teddy had always enjoyed more than his fair share of female attention, so there was no reason to think she was anything special to him. He was as game for some no-strings New Year's fun as she was. No, Issie decided, Mo was just overdoing the older sister role. Besides, her sister had her own axe to grind with the St Miltons, having been enemies with Teddy's sister Ella practically since the dinosaurs had roamed Polwenna Bay.

"Who do you think should get the prize for the best costume, Issie?" Jake's question interrupted her thoughts, and it was with some relief that she turned her attention to the fancy dress. Each year Adam and Rose awarded a yard of ale to the person with the best costume, based on a pub vote, and the villagers usually got more competitive as the night wore on.

"Well it won't be you," she said to Caspar. "You haven't even bothered."

He looked outraged. "Yes I have! I've come as a writer. Me! Besides, I can't imagine Hemingway dressing up to go to the pub."

Caspar wrote racy bodice-rippers and was to Hemingway what Justin Bieber was to classical music – not that this stopped him from taking his "art" very seriously indeed. When he had writer's block everyone knew about it, and heaven help whichever woman he'd decided was going to be his latest muse. "Death by bad sonnet" was how Tara Tremaine had described it.

"I bet Hemingway would have dressed up if there was a yard of ale in it for him," teased Jake's girlfriend, Summer. She was dressed as the Princess Leia to Jake's Han Solo, complete with the Chelsea-bun hairdo; she'd certainly pulled the stops out. As had Tara Tremaine and the local doctor, Richard Penwarren. Clad only in their *Baywatch* swimwear, they might be chilly but they were certainly giving The Hoff and Pamela Anderson a run for their money. Big Rog and Little Rog

Pollard, the local father-and-son builder duo, had come as Fred Flintstone and Barney Rubble, and primary-school teacher Tess was rocking the naughty fairy look so completely that several pirates had jumped ship and joined the Tremaine table.

"I've been flat out editing," Caspar said indignantly. "Burning the midnight oil. Wrestling the muse. Searching for inspiration. Anyway, Issie, talk about the pot calling the kettle black! You've dressed as yourself too."

"I have not!" Issie protested. "I'm a sexy pirate wench."

"I rest my case," grinned Caspar. He pointed to her necklace. "I especially like the medallion."

Issie's fingers rose to touch the heavy gold coin hanging from her necklace. Although it was technically her grandmother's, this was Issie's most treasured item.

"That's wrecker's gold, you philistine! It's the last of Black Jack Jago's loot!"

"Black Jack Jago?" Caspar leaned forward, his author's antennae on full alert. "Like Betty Jago from the village shop? Is there a story here?"

"Don't get her started, mate," Jake advised. "Issie's been obsessed with this story since she was a kid. I can't remember how many times Granny Alice had to tell it, or," he grinned at Issie, "how many nightmares she then had about it."

"I did not!" Issie said.

"She did too," Mo told him. "She screamed the place down. I should know – I had to share a bedroom with her and it drove me mad."

"You scream the place down too sometimes," Ashley remarked softly, his dark eyes glittering as they swept over his wife. "I don't think it's because you're *scared* though."

Mo walloped him on the arm and Issie could see that she was blushing, even beneath her green face paint. "Ashley! Stop it!"

"Don't keep me in suspense: tell me all about this Black Jack character," begged Caspar. "I love all the legends and myths here! I never need to go far for a plot."

Issie's fingers curled around the coin; the metal felt warm and curiously alive from the heat of her skin.

"Black Jack Jago was an ancestor of Granny Alice, and a wrecker," she said, repeating the familiar words that her grandmother must have told her a thousand times. "His heart was as black as the dark nights when he and his henchmen would lure ships onto the rocks. Once the ships had foundered the wreckers would wait for the cargo to wash up on the shore – after they'd finished with any survivors, that is."

"Ah. A bad Ross Poldark type. Excellent," said Caspar, whipping out a notebook from his flowing black cloak and scribbling something down. His eyes were bright with excitement and the reflected glow of the log fire. "I love it. Go on."

"Careful, he's going to pinch your story! Make him give you the copyright on this, or at least a cut of the royalties," Tara Tremaine teased.

Issie shrugged. "It's not my story. It's all history anyway. There are tonnes of documents about it all."

"And Issie would know; she studied history at uni," Jake told Caspar.

Issie downed her drink. "Until I quit." There. She'd say it for him. Save them all a job. Issie Tremaine, disappointment and screw-up. The family member who'd won a place at the prestigious University of Westchester, and then thrown it all away to fester back in the village.

Bar work. Seasonal shifts. Living back with her gran. That was her. Issie Tremaine. Failure.

"There's plenty of time to pick that up again if you want to," said Jake gently.

Issie raised her chin. "No thanks. I'm never going back to Westchester."

There was an awkward pause. There was no way Issie wanted to talk about what had really happened at university. She was far too hurt and ashamed to tell anyone the truth. It was better that her family just thought she was a flake.

"Anyway," she said, trying to steer the conversation away from all that, "there was a Spanish treasure ship called the *Isabella* that was carrying gold coins and maybe jewels as well."

Sensing Issie's discomfort, Mo picked up the narrative. "Legend has it that the treasure was cursed. The ship was blown off course and her captain headed to Plymouth to shelter. That was the last anyone heard of it. The story goes that Black Jack wrecked *Isabella* somewhere off Polwenna Bay, hid the treasure in a cave and then made his way home through the smugglers' secret passage."

"A cave? Like the beach cave? The one near Davey's Locker?" asked Caspar, making even more notes.

"That's the one," nodded Mo. "It's utter rubbish, of course. Can you think of a more obvious hiding place?"

"The cave itself wouldn't have been the hiding place, though. That secret passage you mentioned runs under quite a lot of the village, or so I've been told," said Summer. "My dad says the smugglers used it all the time."

"Yes, I think it's the same secret passage that Jonny St Milton said he went through as a boy," Issie agreed. "It's blocked now, though."

"Or else it never existed," Jake winked.

"Jonny St Milton?" said Caspar. "The elderly gentleman who owns the hotel?"

"That's the one. Teddy's grandfather," Mo replied. "He's lived here forever and his family used to be big landowners."

Caspar's fountain pen hovered over his notebook. "So what happened to this Black Jack Jago?"

Summer took up the tale. "It's said that he was returning to the cave through the passage when the curse of the treasure struck and the tunnel collapsed."

"And that was the end of him," Jake concluded, smiling at her. "Black Jack Jago was never seen again, and neither was his loot. The wreck was never found either – but they say that on a stormy night the galleon can be seen out at sea, and that Black Jack's ghost haunts the cave, guarding his ill-gotten gains."

"And the necklace?" demanded the author. His eyes were glued to the coin around Issie's neck. "What's the story there?"

"This is just a family myth, so don't take it too seriously, no matter what my little sister would have you believe," Jake laughed. "The legend goes that although Black Jack was never seen again, a handful of gold coins mysteriously appeared in the family home on the night he vanished. Over the years they've been spent, but allegedly we still have one left as a necklace, which Granny inherited. That's what Issie's wearing. I can't imagine it's worth much, though. I doubt it's all that rare."

"It wouldn't be, would it, if there were thousands of them in a treasure chest!" Issie snapped, feeling protective of her necklace. She hated it when Jake dismissed the family legend. Issie was convinced there was truth in the old tale. Quite how she would ever prove this she wasn't yet sure, but she was determined that one day she'd find a way.

And then let Jake and Mo tease her!

"True or not, it's a great tale. I love the idea of secret passages under the village," Caspar was saying thoughtfully as he tucked his notebook away. "I can really picture the shadowy streets and the smugglers spiriting the contraband away. With the rocky coast and the caves, Polwenna Bay must have been perfect for them."

"It hasn't really changed much over the centuries," Dr Penwarren said. "I bet a whole lot more goes on around here today than we'll ever know."

Jake raised an eyebrow. "Like the *gardening* up on the cliff allotments, you mean?"

The doctor shrugged. "I wouldn't know about that, but when I've been out late on call I've seen the lights of boats that seem very close to the shore, far too close to be our local trawlers. If you want novel fodder, Caspar, you should walk up on the cliff path at two in the morning."

"Talking of walks, where shall we head to tomorrow?" Summer asked Jake. "I quite fancied a walk to the next bay. After all Alice's cooking, I need to burn a few calories."

Issie tuned out at this point. There was no way she was setting off on a New Year's Day route march over the cliffs. No, she decided as she finished her cider and joined the now five-deep queue at the bar, tomorrow was going to be spent in bed nursing a huge hangover. In fact, if she didn't even see New Year's Day then that would suit her just fine.

Issie was trying to catch Adam's eye, the bar digging into her hip and her head wedged into the armpit of someone dressed as Iron Man, when the vibration of her mobile tucked deep into the bodice of her costume announced the arrival of a text.

"I can help you with that," offered Barney Rubble, peering hopefully over her shoulder as Issie delved for her phone beneath the Wonderbra padding.

"In your dreams, Little Rog," said Issie mildly, turning her back on him and pulling out the phone.

"Can I buy you a drink then?" he asked, ever the optimist.

Ignoring him and concerning herself with her phone instead, Issie felt her heart thrill at the sight of a familiar number on the screen. And then reality rushed in, as cold and as unstoppable as the icy waves that crashed against the harbour wall. Not trusting herself to read the message, Issie deleted it with a trembling finger. But it was too late; the damage was already done. There was no way she could undo this sudden and unexpected knowledge.

Dr Mark Tollen was thinking about her on New Year's Eve. On the very night when the past should be left behind and new starts should be made, he was sitting in his study with a glass of whiskey held loosely in those long fingers, and remembering all that they'd once been to one another. Right or wrong didn't come into it as far as the heart was concerned; what mattered was that she was still in his thoughts all this time later, just as he was in hers.

Maybe it would always be this way?

Issie couldn't bear it. The heat and the noise were suddenly pressing down on her with such weight she thought she would pass out, and there was a rushing in her ears as loud and relentless as the tide.

There was only one thing for it.

"Do you know what?" she said, turning to Little Rog and treating him to a high-beam smile. "I think I will have that drink after all."

Chapter 2

Alice Tremaine was having a quiet New Year's Eve at home, or as quiet a New Year's Eve as was possible after a day spent at Seaspray with her grandchildren and their partners. They'd all been working on their fancy dress for the evening, and had needed endless last-minute adjustments. A veteran of many such thirty-firsts of December, Alice had retrieved her elderly hand-powered sewing machine from its semi-retirement under the stairs and, with a mouth full of pins, had spent several busy hours altering old costumes and helping create new ones. She'd lost count of how many times she'd done this over the years. It was a tradition that went back to the days when she and her husband Henry had celebrated in the village – and then she'd helped her son Jimmy with his New Year outfits, before turning her hand to sorting out costumes for his children. Goodness, how was it possible that so many decades could have flown by in a heartbeat?

By the time eight o'clock arrived and the house was finally empty, Alice was shattered. So far today, she'd made a frilly pirate shirt for Nick, dyed some shorts and a swimsuit red for Richard and Tara, turned a moth-eaten wartime blackout curtain into a cloak for Ashley, and persuaded Issie that her dress needed some extra lace around the bodice if she didn't want to run the risk of giving Eddie Penhalligan another heart attack. In between all this, she'd made a stew, done two loads of washing, walked Mo's terrier Cracker, and done some cyber-stalking around her son's Facebook page in the vain hope that she might discover the identity of Jimmy's secret woman. Her search had drawn a blank: Jimmy had either done an extremely good job of erasing his virtual footsteps (unlikely) or there wasn't a woman at all (even more unlikely, if she knew her son). Perhaps the mystery American wasn't on Facebook?

After shutting the laptop lid with a frustrated thud, Alice had then walked down to the village shop to buy more milk and extra potatoes, in case there might be unexpected dinner guests, before trudging back up the cliff path to the house to finish the supper and serve it up to everyone. She was probably making far more work for herself than was strictly necessary, Alice had reflected while ladling stew and dumplings into bowls. Jake was forever telling her to take it easy and that they were all big enough and ugly enough to sort themselves out, but Alice could no more sit back than she could fly to Mars. Looking after her son's brood was second nature after twenty years – and besides, experience had taught Alice that it generally paid off to line the youngsters' stomachs before they headed to the pub for a night of heavy-duty partying.

Now, as she sat at the table in Seaspray's kitchen with a cup of tea and the celebrations from London playing on the television, Alice's eyes were growing heavy. She wondered whether Jake had a point. Alice was so tired that she wasn't sure whether she would even stay awake long enough to hear Big Ben chime in another year. What would the next one hold anyway, that would merit waiting up to celebrate its arrival? She sighed and sipped her tea. It would be just another year without her Henry, and twelve more months of the aches and pains that were starting to make the daily climb back up the cliff path an ordeal rather than a pleasure. And no doubt it would be full of even more worry about her family. Tears blurred her vision.

"Oh, snap out of it, you silly old fool," Alice scolded herself impatiently. She should count her blessings. Wasn't that what Jules, their vicar, would say? After all, Alice might be nearly eighty but she was still as sharp as she always was, and for that she was glad. It was just that recently her body couldn't quite keep up with her mind – something that always came as a shock, just as looking in the mirror sometimes caught her out too. That old woman with long grey hair and a lined face bore no resemblance to the Alice she saw in her thoughts.

Maybe this was the curse of growing old: to remain forever sixteen in your head, while the passing years and unforgiving looking-glasses told another story.

"And here I go again, being daft," Alice said to Cracker, who thudded his tail in agreement from his place by the Aga. "And I'm talking to a dog, not to myself," she added, just in case clarity was required here. There were plenty of good things to look forward to and be thankful for. Her health for one and her family for another. Yes, her grandchildren might drive her to distraction, and most days she lived in fear that Jimmy would place all the family savings on a "dead cert" horse, but Seaspray was always full of life and laughter, which was exactly how it should be. Being alone on New Year's Eve was only to be expected at her age, and it was hardly surprising that sitting here by herself at the close of another year made her reflective.

"Get a grip, Alice Tremaine," she told herself sharply. "Just be thankful you didn't let Issie talk you into dressing up and joining them! Then you'd be wishing you were here in the peace and quiet rather than stuck in a crowded pub."

It was five to midnight now. On the television screen, scenes of excited crowds along the Thames radiated excitement as the countdown grew closer. Alice glanced across the kitchen and out over the village, where she could just make out the lights of the pub pooling into the trembling waters of the harbour. Inside it would be hot; revellers would be pressed shoulder to shoulder as they jostled their way to the bar to buy drinks for toasting the New Year in. Meanwhile, on the village green crowds would be gathering around the Christmas tree, linking arms and singing *Auld Lang Syne*. Alice didn't need to be down there now to picture the scene: all she had to do was close her eyes. After all, hadn't she spent many such evenings there herself? All things had their time, and hers had long since passed. It was only right that her son and his family were out enjoying themselves while she took things easy at home, listened to the ticking of the clock and sipped her tea.

Logical arguments aside, there was also a huge part of Alice wishing she were in the village and joining in the revelry, even if it was just to keep an eye on her wayward son and her grandchildren. Of course, Jake and Mo were old enough to look after themselves, Symon would be busy working in his restaurant and Danny was looking after his son, so Alice was confident these were all fine.

Her musings then turned to Zak. Just thinking about this middle grandchild, with his fallen-angel looks and more than his fair share of his father's charm, was enough to make Alice smile. Zak was like sunshine on a grey day; no matter what he got up to, he did it with such sweetness that everyone instantly forgave him anything. He was still abroad at the moment, ostensibly recording an album, and hopefully keeping out of trouble.

But then came thoughts of Nick and Issie. The idea of those two on the loose in the village worried Alice terribly. The twins were so wild and never seemed to think about the consequences of anything they did. Just look at Nick's behaviour this year, constantly going to sea hung-over and almost losing his crewing position. And Issie had so carelessly abandoned her place at Westchester University, only to come back to the village and a series of dead-end jobs. Yes, when it came to her two youngest grandchildren, Alice was in despair. They played and drank far too hard, and she had no idea why. Her anxiety that maybe this was down to something she'd done wrong was enough to make Alice reach for the dregs of the Christmas sherry.

If I had one New Year's Eve wish, Alice reflected as Big Ben began to chime and woolly-hatted Londoners counted down with huge excitement, *it would be that Issie and Nick would have a happy year this time*. There was nothing Alice wanted so much as to see them both settled. Who knew how much longer she might be around to look out for them?

"We are not now that strength which in old days moved earth and heaven; that which we are, we are," Alice quoted aloud. Wasn't it funny? Those lines from Tennyson where as fresh in her memory as the day she'd learned them a lifetime ago, sitting on a hard wooden bench in the old primary school, with the fear of an equally hard schoolmistress etching them into her nine-year-old's mind. And yet some days she had trouble recalling what she'd eaten for lunch – although that could well be because she was usually so busy that sometimes she didn't even stop to eat.

Telling herself that she was being ridiculous, Alice was busy filling the kettle for another restorative cup of tea when a sharp rap on the front door made her jump. Who on earth would be knocking on Seaspray's door at midnight? Apart from the fact that everyone she knew would either be celebrating or tucked up in bed, Seaspray was a steep climb up the cliff path. People didn't tend to just drop by. Whoever was knocking must really want to see her. Intrigued, she opened the door.

"I'm here for the first footing," announced Jonny St Milton – or at any rate, Alice thought that was what he said. He was wheezing and gasping so much that she could hardly hear him. Beneath his jaunty tweed cap his face was the same hue as his snow-white hair, and he was doubled over clutching his side.

"You didn't walk up here just for that daft tradition did you?" Alice asked, taking him by the arm and guiding him out of the sharp, frosty air into the warmth of the kitchen. "Jonny St Milton, you silly old fool. Whatever were you thinking?"

Jonny St Milton, the owner of the Polwenna Bay Hotel and grandfather to Teddy and Ella, was eighty years old and more accustomed to enjoying a brandy by the fire in his own bar than hiking up the cliffs, especially since a stroke two years ago had left him with a limp.

"I couldn't risk another suitor getting here first, could I?" puffed Jonny, sinking onto the old sofa by the Aga and not seeming at all perturbed that his canary-yellow cords would soon be covered in pet hair.

Alice rolled her eyes. "I think at my age I'm a bit beyond suitors, and if I wasn't then I'd prefer them not to arrive half dead, thank you very much."

"You'll never be beyond suitors. You're every bit as beautiful now as you were in your teens," Jonny said gallantly.

She snorted. "Well then, there's proof that your eyesight's going. Anyway, if it's first footing you've come for, isn't that supposed to be a dark-haired man bearing coal and whatever else? Not somebody with white hair and not a lump of coal in sight?"

"My hair used to be black, remember?"

Alice did remember. A vision of that just-too-long hair, glossy and dark as a blackbird's wing, was seared forever in her memory.

"Coal would have at least been useful," she said, jolted by the unexpected blush rising in her cheeks.

"Your Aga's wood-fired," Jonny pointed out mildly. His breath was less ragged now, she noticed with relief, and the heat of the house was bringing the colour back into his drawn face. "Anyway, bugger coal! I've bought a bottle of fizz. Far more fun."

He held out a bottle of champagne which even Alice, who didn't know much about wine, could see was extremely expensive.

"As if I can drink that on all my medication!" she said, shaking her head.

"Come on, Ally. Live dangerously." Expertly, he eased the cork until it gave a whisper-soft sigh of release. Then he reached into his overcoat pocket and pulled out a pair of plastic champagne flutes, which were soon overflowing with bubbles. He held one of the flutes out to Alice and winked. "If you really want to go with tradition I'll even take the ashes out for you after we've finished these?"

"Wasn't that *my* job, young master?"

He sighed. "Can't we move on from all that? It was a long time and another world ago."

Alice blinked. Maybe the fabric of time wore a little thinner on evenings like this, when the days were so short they seemed to finish before they'd even begun and the nights that followed were inky dark. To her, the old hurt seemed just as fresh as though it had all happened yesterday. Besides, it was easy for him to say this. Jonny wasn't the one who'd been humiliated, was he?

He patted the seat beside him and his eyes crinkled up at her. They were deeply lined now and faded too, but nevertheless they still contained the mischievous glint she remembered. Oh dear, thought Alice. She'd never been able to resist him then either.

"Oh, go on then," she said irritably, taking the glass but ignoring the empty seat next to him and leaning against the kitchen table instead. "It's New Year's Eve, after all. Who knows how many of them we've got left?"

"How cheerful you are, dear Mrs Tremaine. But since you've pointed it out, then yes, we're both old and who knows how much time we've got to enjoy ourselves?" He grinned. "So, what do you say, Ally? Let's not waste any more time, eh? Your place or mine?"

Alice felt her face grow even hotter. Jonny had always had that effect on her and it seemed that the intervening decades hadn't changed much. To cover her shock at this discovery, she said coldly, "And whose fault is that? Whose decision was it that we wasted an entire lifetime? Not mine!"

He stared at her and his teasing vanished in a heartbeat.

"Is that how you feel? That we wasted a lifetime?"

"Yes. No." Alice was flustered. She set the glass down and pressed the heels of her hands against her forehead in an attempt to stop the sudden thudding there. "I loved Henry. He was everything to me and we had a wonderful life together. I could never regret that."

He nodded slowly. "I know, Alice, and I understand. I can't regret marrying Milly either. We might not have had the happy marriage that you and Henry enjoyed, but we built a family and a legacy. I'm looking forward to the day I hand the business over to Teddy to lead it into the future."

Privately Alice thought the only place Teddy St Milton was likely to lead a business was into receivership. To her mind the shrewd and sharp-as-a-tack Ella was a far more worthy recipient than her feckless younger brother. She could only suppose Jonny was old-fashioned in the respect that he wanted the St Milton name to carry on. In any case, he certainly had a huge blind spot where his youngest grandchild was concerned.

"Alice, our spouses have been gone for a long while now. Please let me prove I'm not the idiot schoolboy I was back then." Jonny rose creakily to his feet and took a step towards her – and then lurched dangerously as his foot caught on a flagstone. "Oh! Bloody leg!"

"Careful! The floor's uneven!" Alice grabbed his arm, shaking her head despairingly, and guided him back to the sofa. "Jonny, sit down and rest, for heaven's sake! The climb up's really taken it out of you. Don't worry," she added once he was seated again, "there's no danger I could think you're still a teenager."

But Jonny wasn't laughing. "I still see the girl I fell in love with all those years ago. You must remember how it was with us? Remember when we went to St Wenn's Well?"

Alice couldn't look him in the eye. Of course she remembered. How could she not? A girl – a woman – never forgot a moment like that.

"Not really," she fibbed.

"Liar," said Jonny fondly. "You remember it as clearly as I do." Then he flashed her his old rascally grin, the one that still made dimples dance in his cheeks and wicked promises glitter in his eyes. "Otherwise, how else would Lord Blackwarren have a birthmark in a very cheeky place? Unless of course my whippersnapper grandson is more your type these days?"

"Oh, blast that book!" exclaimed Alice. Honestly, her self-published novel was causing her all kinds of headaches that she'd never imagined when she'd innocently typed it on the family laptop. A romp of a read, it had taken Polwenna Bay by storm as villagers had tried to guess both who'd written it and who the sexy hero was based on. As the author, Alice knew the truth – but she wasn't telling.

"I enjoyed it," Jonny said. "Brought back some very happy memories. I'm flattered. My stock's gone right up in the pub."

Alice put her hands on her hips. "You think you're Lord Blackwarren?"

"Well, aren't I?" Jonny hauled himself out of the sofa again and, stepping forward, took her hand. "Oh, Alice, I can't waste any more time apart from you. I—"

"Granny! Fetch a bowl! Quickly!"

The kitchen door burst open as Nick and Ashley half carried, half dragged a staggering Issie into the room. The green tinge to her face was almost a dead match for Mo's bride-of-Frankenstein make-up. A cut above Issie's eye was bleeding freely and the contrast of her clammy skin and the scarlet blood made Alice's own stomach lurch.

Instantly she and Jonny sprang apart like guilty teenagers. They needn't have worried, though; the new arrivals were too busy trying to manoeuvre Issie to the sofa to notice anything else. Besides, two old people having a quiet chat in the kitchen wasn't nearly as dramatic as fetching a saucepan for Issie and holding her hair back from her face as she retched.

Alice's heart plummeted. You didn't raise seven children through their teens (eight, if she counted her own son) and not recognise when one of them was blind drunk.

"I'm sorry, I'm sorry," Issie kept saying, her eyes crossing with drink as she stared wildly round the room. "I'm so sorry."

Then she buried her face in the saucepan and threw up.

"Happy New Year," Mo said to Ashley, who was now retreating in revulsion. "Sure you want kids?"

"Is Issie up for adoption then?" he asked.

"She will be if she keeps this up," said Alice grimly. What was it with her granddaughter? Why did Issie keep doing this? Horrified, she rounded on Nick. "How on earth did your sister get in this state?"

Nick pulled a face. "The usual way, I'd guess. One minute she was necking shots with Little Rog and the Penhalligans and the next she was snogging Teddy's face off."

"Oh dear," said Jonny. "That doesn't sound good."

"I don't think he was complaining," Nick said. "To be fair, neither was Issie until she fell over and walloped her head on the floor."

Alice sighed and went to fetch the first-aid box from the cupboard. Was there ever going to be a time when she could stop worrying about her grandchildren and actually think about her own life?

Somehow she doubted it.

"Happy New Year," she said to Jonny as he made his excuses and backed out of the room.

"Happy New Year, Ally," he replied, blowing her a kiss and adding, "Please don't worry. I promise things are going to get better."

As she dressed Issie's cut, then helped to get her upstairs and into her nightclothes, Alice could only hope Jonny was right. She couldn't bear to think what the year ahead might hold for her damaged and very troubled youngest granddaughter if he wasn't.

Chapter 3

The slap of waves against the pier, the warm evening breeze straight off the Gulf of Mexico and the buzz of Key West on New Year's Eve all lifted Luke Dawson's spirits. Hell, it was pretty damn impossible to be down anyway when you were in Mallory Square just before sunset, with the sky streaked pink and gold. Here street traders juggled flaming torches, and tanned girls sauntered by in tiny hot pants and even tinier bikini tops. Their sun-kissed hair, peachy butts and jiggling breasts went a long way towards cheering a guy up, Luke decided as he necked his ice-cold Bud. A couple more drinks, followed by a trawl of the bars on Duval Street, and it would be as though the last few weeks had never happened.

Maybe.

Although it was only early evening, with the sun still a fat gold coin balancing on the horizon, the streets of Key West were thronging with visitors and the air thrummed with a party vibe. This southernmost tip of the USA, where Uncle Sam dipped his toe into the beginnings of the Caribbean Sea, already enjoyed a year-round carnival atmosphere, but tonight the locals had really upped their game. Floridians loved to party and Luke was certainly in the mood to sink a few cold ones and join in. Once the sun had fully set he figured he'd head over to his next bar and start the rest of the night as he meant to go on. With any luck, by the time the New Year rolled in he'd be mellow enough not to care about anything else except grabbing another bottle of Bud and joining the flood of revellers as they pushed on through until dawn.

He'd intended to have one more beer here first, but with the sunset hour fast approaching, Mallory Square was filling up with tourists keen to see the famous green flash as the sun slipped into the sea. Well, he'd seen enough glorious sunsets to last a lifetime, Luke decided, and being jostled while waiting for another wasn't doing it for him. Time to move on.

So, where next? Down to the pier for the fireworks display or over to the Schooner Wharf Bar to see if any of the guys were there? Somewhere with some air con, that was for sure. The humid air was thick; even though his shirt had been fresh on only twenty minutes earlier, it was already sticking to his skin, and the too-long chestnut hair that fell over his collar was coiling into ringlets. Not a good look for the start of the night. Maybe a quick one in the hotel bar down by the pier? He could check *Casadora* on the way, make sure her moorings were still good and that she was fuelled and ready for the next trip. Save the old man a job.

Luke shook his head. Christ. Old habits certainly died hard. He didn't need to do any of that anymore, did he? Not now he was no longer a part of the family business. Mal Dawson could check his own goddamn boat and spend the rest of his years scouring the ocean floors for lost galleons without Luke by his side. His father had made it perfectly clear just how much respect he had for his son's opinions.

Luke downed his beer and wiped his mouth with the back of his strong, tanned hand. Screw the Dawson family business. He didn't need it and he didn't need his father. From now on Luke was going it alone. Setting off towards the hotel bar, he couldn't help smiling at the irony of thinking he'd go it alone on a crowded New Year's Eve in the Conch Republic. You could hardly move for sequin-clad drag queens sashaying through the thong, and the press of bodies on the sidewalks was five people deep.

Still, crowds aside, he was cast adrift from the Dawson clan and very much on his own. If he wanted to prove himself to his father, then he'd need to find a way and some serious greens. Being a professional treasure hunter didn't come cheap: without a proper dive boat and a generous sponsor, Luke had no hope of showing Mal exactly how attuned his instincts were. As his father had contemptuously suggested, Luke might just as well go and crew a boat for one of the plethora of water-sports companies that littered the Keys. Days on from their colossal argument, Mal's words still rang in Luke's ears. *You'll come crawling back*, his father had sneered with his trademark confidence. *You'll never make it without me.*

Luke's fingers tightened on the empty bottle. He damn well would make it on his own. There was no way he was going to ask Mal for help. He'd rather give up all hopes of a career as a professional treasure hunter and run jet-ski tours round the island. *That* was how much he was prepared to do in order to not come "crawling back", as his father put it. He'd sell his own boat too, the small Boston Whaler that was his pride and joy, and plough any funds from that into setting something up. No matter what it took, Luke Dawson was on his own now.

No sooner had this thought flickered through Luke's mind, as bright and as unmistakable as the green flash that made the tourists gasp, than the sun slipped beneath the horizon. It felt symbolic. With the dying of the light also passed his old life as the son and right-hand man of Mal Dawson, dive master and treasure hunter.

Exactly one year ago, Luke had stood on Sunset Pier and watched the sky flame. The same place, the same atmosphere, the same relentless heavy heat as though somebody had thrown a hot wet towel across his face. But there had been one major difference: last year he'd been with his family.

Having been Key West residents for six generations, the Dawsons were as well known in the town as conch fritters or Key lime pie. They drank harder than Hemingway, raced fast boats on Miami poker runs and were a splash of colour in an already vibrant community. The family home was an old clapboard house, slumbering in the heart of the Old Town behind high vine-smothered walls. Much of the time its purple louvred shutters were closed, as though the house was having a siesta beneath the shady casuarina trees while the burning sunshine beat down on the deck. Inside, the rooms were welcome pools of shade where ceiling fans ticked lazily and the worn floorboards were cool beneath bare feet. This beautiful and historic home had been as much the realm of Luke's mom, Beth, as the deck of *Casadora* was Mal's. Luke and his sister, Mia, had been equally at home in both places, happy whether they were diving in the Gulf of Mexico or curled up reading on the veranda while twilight seeped across the garden, with the hurricane lantern flickering in the warm breeze and crickets serenading nightfall.

They were a family. His mom and dad and Luke and Mia. A tight unit. His father, Mal, was single-minded and a risk taker, known for having a nose for treasure and a taste for danger. His mom, Beth, strong and calm, was as happy to take the *Casadora*'s helm as she was to barbecue supper for twenty people. Then there had been Mia, a skilled diver and one of the best he'd ever worked with. As for him? He was the youngest of the bunch, with a love of history that had taken him from searching the seabed to becoming a history major at UCLA. They were the Dawsons. Legendary. Successful and unbreakable.

Or so he'd thought. Funny how one tiny, almost imperceptible crack could suddenly force something apart that had once appeared so strong. Like a boat that was slowly letting in water, nothing had seemed wrong at first until the bow split and the vessel foundered. For Beth Dawson the final crack had been when Luke had announced over lunch on New Year's Day that he'd quit college to follow in his father's footsteps. She'd not even finished her lunch but instead had quietly put down her cutlery and headed upstairs to pack a case. By the time the meal was cold and Luke had realised what was happening, a cab had pulled up to take her to the airport.

"Mom?" Hearing the blast of a car's horn outside and the opening of the front door, Luke had pushed his chair away from the table to find a taxi driver lifting his mother's case into the trunk. "What's going on?"

Mal, who'd followed him, had placed his hand on Luke's shoulder. "She's leaving, son."

"Leaving?" He might have been twenty-one years old and over six feet tall, but hearing this had felt like a blow to the solar plexus. "Mom? That's not true, right?"

"It's true, honey." Beth had hugged him tightly. Her face was pale and her eyes bright but there were no tears, only a steely determination that he recognised in himself and, when she was still alive, in Mia too. "I can't do this anymore."

"Do what?" Luke had demanded. Panic had tightened in his chest like an iron band.

"Watch you risk your lives." Beth had shaken her dark head and she'd looked across at her husband sadly. "I've lost count of how many times I've thought your father might not make it back. I can't be here and watch the same happen to you. I just can't."

Luke had stared at her in utter confusion. The Dawsons were treasure hunters. It was what their family did, what they'd always done. Granted, it was a tough life; he could remember countless times when the family had had to choose between gas for the boat or food for dinner, which meant a lot of time spent fishing for supper. But it was the only life they knew and a good one. Nothing beat the rush of adrenalin when a hunch played out and your dive-gloved hands closed around an item that hadn't seen daylight for centuries. There was always the added excitement that maybe, just maybe, today would be the day when you hit payload. This thought was like crack cocaine to a treasure hunter. Tales of divers who'd found treasure beyond their wildest dreams were what kept you going when the sea was rough, the bank account was empty and your sponsor was being a prick.

Luke thought it was the best job in the world, but he didn't deny that it was a dangerous one. The Dawsons knew that only too well. Eighteen months ago Mia had died when the boat she'd been crewing on had gone down just off Cuba.

"Is this because of Mia?" Mal had asked hoarsely. A muscle had ticked in his unshaven cheek and he'd raked a calloused hand through his hair. "Do you blame me? Do you think it was my fault she died, because I encouraged her? If you do, at least have the balls to say it! For Chrissake! Don't you dare just walk away!"

Luke had found that he was holding his breath. His world was tilting on its axis. Mia's death, too young and too swift, had been one of the reasons he'd decided to quit college and come home. Nobody had loved the sea and the thrill of the hunt as much as Mia. She had been his father's natural successor and her death had left a Grand Canyon of loss in the family. Luke knew that they'd never get over it or comprehend it, but somehow they had to learn to live with it. Coming home to the place and the job his sister had loved had been his way of doing this and honouring her memory. The idea that his decision was now driving his mother away appalled him.

"Mia's death was an accident," Mal had said quietly when Beth didn't reply. "An accident, Beth."

"Was it?" There'd been no mistaking the accusation in her voice. "Maybe, Mal. Maybe. Who knows what happened out there? What risks they took just to find treasure?" She almost spat the word. "All I know is that I've lost one child and I'm not going to stick around and watch it happen again. Encourage Luke if you must, but I'm not having any part of it."

Mal's top lip curled. "Encourage him? He's freaking twenty-one! Old enough to know his own mind."

"Except that he's been brainwashed by you! They both were!"

"Stop it!" Luke had shouted. "This is my decision, mine, OK? And it's what I want to do. Nobody's forcing me. I want to work the *Casadora* with Dad and I want to dive. I'm a Dawson, Mom, and I want to be a treasure hunter."

For a moment Beth Dawson had looked as though she was about to yell back, and she could yell, too – Luke had heard enough rows between her and Mal over the years to know that his mom had a fine pair of lungs and was just as fiery as her husband. Luke had braced himself for some sort of outburst, but the fight seemed to have evaporated from Beth and instead she just shook her head.

"If that's your choice I'm happy for you, sweetie," she'd said at last. "I won't make things difficult for you but I can't be here to live with it. I just can't. If you need me I'll be with Grandma in Miami."

Then Luke's mother had stepped into the taxi and out of her Key West life. Mal had said nothing, but that night he'd hit the bourbon hard and come home with a black eye too, the first of many such nights. Luke had stayed in the family home but the place had felt too big suddenly, and it rang with echoes rather than laughter and footsteps. Gradually Mal had abandoned Beth's elegant sitting room for the kitchen at the back of the house, where he heated up TV dinners, smoked too much pot and worked his way through as much Jack Daniel's as he could lay his hands on. Dust fell and covered Beth's furniture, the vines overgrew the windows and people soon stopped visiting, which suited Luke's father just fine. Sometimes a postcard arrived from Miami, after which Mal would hit the bottle even harder; inevitably, his work began to suffer. No matter what Luke said or did, his father seemed hell-bent on self-destruction.

The memory of this time made Luke's throat tighten and he quickened his pace, figuring that the sooner he had a whiskey the better. Christ. Maybe he had more in common with the old man than he'd thought? Without a doubt, Mal Dawson would be propping up a bar somewhere in town at this moment – not because it was New Year's Eve but because that was his habit now. On most evenings he was out drinking, when really he should be laying off the booze, having an early night and putting out to sea in the morning. It wasn't unusual for him to pass out in a strip joint and be carried home by some of the other skippers, and to wake up only when the sun was high in the sky and another day filled with potential had been squandered.

Professional treasure hunting was a precarious business at the best of times; at the tail end of a global recession it was almost as tricky to find a sponsor willing to take a punt as it was to discover a hoard of gold.

The spoils could be huge but the expenses were even greater. Boats, equipment, crew and dive permits didn't come cheap and *Casadora* drank gas like his father drank JD. Mal Dawson, and those like him, relied on rich sponsors to foot their bills – but these sponsors were a nervous bunch and needed more hand-holding and reassurances than a high-school girl at the prom. Mal's drinking made him tetchy and erratic, and without Beth to charm and schmooze the sponsors, it had seemed inevitable to Luke that they'd soon start to look elsewhere. Time and time again he'd argued with Mal to let him take charge, but his father wouldn't relinquish so much as an inch of control. He was the skipper and that was the way it was staying. For the past twelve months Luke had watched his father make mistakes, get drunk and, worst of all, ignore evidence that Luke knew with all his heart could have led them to success.

The hotel bar overlooked the water, dark now and filled with the reflections of a thousand lights, and bubbles of laughter rose into the air. Inside, fans rotated lazily, stirring the soupy atmosphere while glamorous people dressed in white and taupe sat on bar stools sipping mojitos and chatting. Spotting a gap at the bar and catching the eye of the barman, Luke decided to forego the joys of air con for the sweet relief of being served fast and getting the alcohol to hit his bloodstream.

Yeah, maybe he was far more like the old man than he wanted to admit.

Tumbler in hand, Luke swirled the amber liquid thoughtfully. When on form there was nobody in the business better than Mal Dawson. Instinctive, daring and skilled, he'd been at the top his game for so long that his reputation shielded the truth of the current situation. But this couldn't go on forever. The fact was, Mal had lost his edge and his magic touch – his nose for treasure, if you like – and it was only a matter of time before word got around. He would go down and take Luke with him.

Luke couldn't let this happen. He couldn't.

Just one thing was stopping him from helping his father – Mal himself. Stubborn as the proverbial mule, he refused to listen to his son, insisted on ignoring the research Luke spent hours poring over, and set off instead on wild-goose chases of his own. For a long time, Luke had bitten his tongue and done his best to respect his father, but in the end his patience had worn tissue-paper thin. Things had come to a head three days ago when Mal had ignored Luke's suggested location in favour of his own choice, a decision that had yielded only a wasted day followed by the galling news that a rival boat had discovered a cache of rare coins exactly where Luke had proposed that he and his father should dive. The row that followed swiftly turned ugly. When Mal had yelled that if Luke was such a shit-hot treasure hunter he could go it alone, Luke had decided then and there that this was exactly what he'd do.

"Do it!" his father had sneered, over the top of his whiskey glass. "Let's see how far you get without me, shall we? Womanising and posing on a boat, that's all you're good for. You couldn't even finish your degree."

Luke had clenched his fists. The unfairness of these accusations stung, as did the small grains of truth in them. Yes, he liked women and women liked him. That wasn't a crime. When you lived in the Florida Keys and spent most of your time on the water, you ended up tanned and buff; was it his fault that girls liked that? And as for posing? Luke defied anyone not to look good on the deck of a Hatteras yacht.

The degree was another matter though. He'd abandoned that to come home, to be with his parents and support the family business. After losing Mia, being so far away from home had seemed pointless.

"I'll make it work," was all he'd said, but Mal had just laughed.

"You'll soon come crawling back. You'll never make it without me."

I can and I will, Luke had promised himself, although quite how he'd do this without a boat, a crew or the backing of a sponsor was anyone's guess. Not that this mattered. There was one thing Luke knew for certain: he wouldn't be going back to his father with his tail between his legs. The time had come for him to prove that he had exactly what it took to be the best in the business. He was a Dawson and he owed it to his heritage and his sister's memory, to put that surname back on the treasure-hunting map. No matter what he had to do, no matter what it took, Luke swore that he would do this.

Luke knocked back his drink and held out the glass for another. The bar was filling fast and, as he waited to be served, he glanced around. This wasn't the usual local crowd – they'd all be on a crawl along Duval Street by now – but rather the moneyed second-home owners and those wealthy enough to stay in the luxury hotels. The men tended to be portly and red-faced; they were almost always poured into too-tight chinos and stripy shirts, with Rolexes squeezed onto their chubby wrists. The women, meanwhile, were disproportionately beautiful – all colt-like skinny legs, expensively streaked hair and designer sunglasses. One such specimen caught his eye now, from a little further along the bar. Sensing his gaze on her, she gave him a slow and appraising look. Luke took in the slanting feline eyes, the full sensual mouth and the cascade of platinum-blonde hair, then smiled and raised his glass. The blonde tucked a lock of hair behind her ear, sending several trinket-laden Pandora bracelets slipping down her slender arm as she did so. Her mouth curled upwards, and the invitation couldn't have been any clearer.

Maybe this evening wouldn't be such a washout after all?

"A Jack, no ice – and whatever she's having," Luke told the barman, wincing when he learned that she was on vintage champagne. Since the row with Mal, he'd been sofa-surfing at friends' houses. What little savings he did have wouldn't last long if he spent time with women who drank Cristal as though it were Diet Coke, never mind that he was trying to fund his own dive boat. Still, those were worries for another night, Luke decided as he wove his way through the press of bodies to join her. Tonight he was going to celebrate New Year's Eve in style.

The rest he would worry about later.

Chapter 4

New Year's Day in Cornwall dawned grey, as heavy clouds rolled in from the west and the wind whipped the sea's white horses into a gallop. Even though it was morning the sky was dark; Christmas lights shone valiantly into the gloom, their jaunty colours at odds with the leaden tide and pewter horizon. The rain was spitting half-heartedly, as though it lacked the energy to do much more. In this respect, the weather seemed to be in sympathy with the many villagers who were nursing hangovers and who could do little else but hold their heads and grumble. A few optimistic visitors had left their holiday cottages to brave the world beyond and wander the narrow streets, bobble-hatted and shod in pristine country boots purchased especially for the New Year's Day walk. Most turned back when they reached the cliffs, where the breath-snatching wind flung fistfuls of sea spray up at the path and blew surprised seagulls off course.

Only the toughest, or perhaps the most foolhardy, visitors carried on along the cliff path to the next town. Certainly no locals were out walking on such a raw morning. They were either sleeping in after the previous night's celebrations, or getting ready for the biggest event of the day: Mo and Ashley Carstairs' brunch party.

Since Londoner Ashley had arrived in Polwenna Bay, wealthy, aloof and saturninely handsome, he'd been a subject of intense village gossip and more than a few crushes. Nobody knew much about him, except that he had more money than God. The rumours had only intensified when he'd bought Mariners' View, one of Polwenna Bay's premier properties. Ashley had proceeded to spend a small fortune developing the place and employing most of the local builders and sparkies. Guarded by the giant wall he'd had built, and which the locals had nicknamed the Great Wall of Cornwall, Mariners (as it was known for short) was surrounded by two acres of garden and gazed dreamily out to sea. It was the perfect haven for a man who enjoyed being secretive. Only a select handful of people had seen what he'd done to the interior of the house; the rest could only speculate. Some said Ashley had created a Playboy Mansion style shag pit, while others were convinced that his house was now a minimalistic shrine to modernity that was due to be featured on *Grand Designs*. Betty Jago, who ran the village shop, swore blind that she'd seen Kevin McCloud buying a pasty, whereas the Pollards told tall tales in the pub about how they'd installed pole-dancing podiums and bought leopard-print paint from Trago Mills.

As if all this hadn't been intriguing enough, Ashley Carstairs had then stunned them all by marrying Morwenna Tremaine, the red-headed spitfire who'd opposed all his renovations and generally done her best to make his pet project a headache. Exactly how *that* had happened the villagers weren't certain, but there was one thing they did know for sure: if Ashley and Mo were having a house party then they were all going to be there, hangovers or not. Even the weather, which looked to be closing in fast, wasn't going to stop them walking up to Mariners. What would a soaking from the rain matter if a good look around Cashley's house was at the end of it?

Issie Tremaine had been inside Mariners enough times to know that sadly it contained neither a pole-dancing area nor any leopard print (unless you counted her new brother-in-law, who'd certainly changed his spots for her sister). She, for one, wasn't relishing the idea of a bracing walk across the village and up the steep cliff path. It felt as though a thrash-metal band was playing a set inside her skull, with the drummer currently executing a solo in her left eye socket, and overnight some sadist had fitted a shag-pile carpet to her tongue. As she sat at the kitchen table and attempted to sip the orange juice Alice had put in front of her, the room pitched so violently that Issie thought she was going to throw up again.

She placed her throbbing head in her hands and groaned. Oh Lord. Just how much had she drunk last night? Far too much, of course. Issie's memories of New Year's Eve grew patchy after the fifth, or maybe sixth, tequila slammer. Like a hideous jigsaw, every now and then another piece dropped into place. At least she'd woken up in her own bed, thought Issie with relief, although she had no idea how she'd made it home: the last thing she could remember was dancing around the Christmas tree with Little Rog. Jake had probably carried her back to Seaspray, which meant she'd be in for another heavy-duty lecture from her big brother. Happy bloody New Year.

Hold on, Happy New Year… That rang a bell. Where had she been when the old year slipped away? Issie's brow crinkled and she stared into her orange juice as though it might yield an answer. The church bell had been striking twelve, and she'd been holding someone's hand and watching fireworks whirling above… Or had that been the lights of the Polwenna Bay tree blurring as her head spun from drinking shots all night with Little Rog Pollard? And had she really snogged Teddy St Milton again? *That* had to be the shortest-lived New Year's resolution ever.

Oh God. What else had she done?

Issie's stomach lurched as an awful thought occurred to her.

No. Surely not? She wouldn't have done *that*, would she?

With shaking fingers, Issie picked up her mobile phone and unlocked the screen. Sick with suspense, she scrolled through to the call log, praying that, no matter how drunk she'd been, somewhere in the tequila-sodden depths of her brain there had lurked a scrap of common sense that had prevented her from pressing self-destruct. The relief when she saw that she hadn't dialled anyone or sent a drunken text message was enough to make her want to weep.

Maybe her New Year's resolution should be to stop drinking, Issie thought, pushing the mobile across the table. It was hard enough keeping a firm grip on herself when she was sober; contemplating what could happen when she was drunk and all inhibition had gone out the window was absolutely terrifying.

"Drink that up. It's high time we were off," Alice chivvied over her shoulder. Dressed in a long waxed coat, wellingtons and a headscarf, her grandmother was ready to face the weather and stomp over to Mariners. Issie, who wasn't even dressed yet, felt exhausted just looking at her.

"Can't I stay here?" she pleaded. "I really don't feel well."

"I'm not surprised, given the state you came home in last night." Alice looked pained. "Issie, you can't carry on like this. It's not good for you."

Her grandmother's words reverberated around Issie's skull like reproachful squash balls.

"I know, I know, I know, I know, OK? I'm never drinking again. Honest."

Alice looked at her intently. "I only wish I could believe that. Sweetheart, I can't pretend that I know what the matter is, and when I ask you'll only tell me nothing, but whatever it is you need to sort it out, and soon. You're throwing so much away."

Issie held up her hands. Although she knew Alice only wanted to help, there were some things that her grandmother wouldn't understand and couldn't fix. What had happened with Mark, and the raw pain and shame she still felt whenever she thought of him, couldn't be made better with a Band-Aid and a kiss. If Alice could find a switch in Issie's heart that she could flick to turn her feelings off, then that would be great; otherwise the only thing she'd found that actually worked was alcohol.

"Granny, please don't start the Dropping Out of Uni lecture. I really don't think I can handle it right now."

"I'm not about to lecture you," Alice said, looking hurt. "You're old enough to make your own choices. But I love you and I hate seeing you so unhappy."

"I'm not unhappy," Issie fibbed. "I'm just hung-over."

Pulling herself to her feet, and trying to ignore the listing of her brain inside her skull, Issie finished the orange juice and did her best to look thrilled to be leaving the warmth of Seaspray for the wild weather outside and another party.

Thank goodness it was only Ashley and Mo's bash, Issie thought as she pulled on jeans and a hoody and pinned her braids up onto the crown of her head. There was no need to go mad and dress up for family. Her sister would probably be in jodhpurs, and Ashley only had eyes for Mo anyway. Besides, the green-hued and unmade-up face that was looking back blearily at her from the mirror would do wonders at keeping the likes of Teddy and Little Rog at bay.

By the time Issie was ready to set off the wind was growing louder, roaring through the trees at the top of the village and rushing straight through Polwenna. Alice and Issie found themselves being buffeted and punched by invisible fists as they followed the winding path through Seaspray's gardens, and above them the sky was bruised with storm clouds. When they reached the lane both women looked towards the harbour, their eyes wide when they saw that the waves were breaking over the highest rocks beyond the bay. The storm gate was shut and the quay was teeming with oilskinned fishermen securing their moorings and adding extra bowlines. Davey's Locker was taking the full force of the wind's fury – it was lucky that the shutters had been closed for a few days, otherwise the glass would certainly have been broken. Was it her imagination, wondered Issie, or was the light really fading with each second that passed? Her hand stole to touch the gold coin hanging around her neck and she shivered; this was just the kind of day that would once have been perfect for wreckers like Black Jack Jago.

"This storm's really bad!" she exclaimed.

"It certainly is," Alice agreed. "I've seen lots of them in my time but it looks like this is going to be one of the worst. It's a force-eight gale, Radio Cornwall said earlier, but I think it'll exceed that. That goodness all the trawlers are in."

Mariners' View was directly across the bay from Seaspray, which meant walking down into the village before climbing up and out again. It was a steep walk on a fine day and without a hangover; in a gale-force wind and with thudding temples Issie was ready to collapse by the time she arrived.

The simplistic beauty of Mariners' interior always took Issie aback the moment she stepped inside. Ashley's architect had taken out the internal walls and replaced the furthest wall with glass that framed the seascape, flooding the house with light and creating a living work of art. The scene was ever changing from minute to minute, but today it was at its most spectacular as the waves tore across the bay and dark clouds swelled on the horizon. Who knew what secrets were hidden deep beneath the churning water? As she stood watching the power of nature being unleashed, Issie had the strongest conviction that something incredible was about to happen…

"Hair of the dog?" grinned Ashley, appearing over her shoulder and offering a glass of champagne. "Or would you rather I found some tequila? That's your poison of choice, I believe?"

Issie groaned but she accepted the drink anyway. Sod it; her no-alcohol resolution could begin tomorrow. "Don't tell me you were there too?"

Her brother-in-law laughed. "Christ! You *were* drunk! I helped Nick carry you home. Maybe you ought to stick to orange juice and have a few nibbles?"

Ashley Carstairs' idea of "nibbles" was somewhat more extravagant than most people's. Rather than providing the sausages on sticks, cheese and pineapple and a few bowls of crisps that were the usual fare at village parties, he'd hired Symon Tremaine to do the catering and no expense had been spared. Glancing around the crowded room, Issie was amused to see the most eclectic group of villagers imaginable chowing down on exquisite mini pasties, prawn and chorizo skewers and plates of *fruits de mer*. Granted, Big Rog looked a bit confused by the mini pasties and had combined at least eight in order to equal one of Patsy Penhalligan's bakery-shop versions – and Betty Jago was looking very suspiciously at the caviar blinis – but generally everyone was having fun regardless of the weather. Even Mickey Davey had stopped bragging for long enough to shovel in some smoked salmon.

For Issie, though, any food was out of the question right now. "Not for me, thanks. I don't think I'll ever eat again," she grimaced.

"I thought that was drinking?" Alice remarked drily, joining them and giving Issie a sharp look when she saw the champagne flute in her hand. Kissing Ashley on the cheek, she added, "It's a lovely party, my love. Everyone's braved the weather to come out."

"Of course they have, not that I'm flattering myself it's on my account. They're all desperate for a good nose around Mariners," Ashley said, his dark eyes bright with amusement. Giving Issie a knowing look, he added, "Apparently there was a rumour going around that I'd installed a dance pole. Where on earth could that have come from?"

"No idea," said Issie quickly. Oops. She may have *accidentally* said something like that to Saffron Jago, who had a mouth the size of the Saltash Tunnel. It had seemed amusing at the time to see how long it might take the rumour to get around the village (slightly faster than the speed of the ISS orbiting earth, apparently), but under Ashley's scrutiny it suddenly didn't seem quite as funny. Much as Issie liked Ashley, a man who'd become a self-made millionaire by his mid-twenties probably wasn't to be messed with.

"Where's Mo?" asked Alice, looking around the crowded reception room. "I must wish her happy New Year."

"She's gone to the stable yard because she's worried about the barn roof staying on. Don't panic, Alice, she's not about to start clambering around in the wind. She's taken Little Rog with her and the Penhalligan lads," Ashley told her firmly. "There's no way I'm having Mo climbing ladders in her condition – oh!"

Alice's hand flew to her mouth and Issie nearly choked on a mouthful of champagne. Had Ashley just said what she thought he had?

"Oh dear. Can you forget I just said that?" Ashley asked hopefully. "Silly question. Of course you can't. Damn. Mo's going to kill me. And I've done so well getting over my operation too; what a waste of Mr Oliver's surgical skills."

"Mo's pregnant? With a baby?" Alice looked stunned.

"Knowing Mo she'd probably rather it was a foal," Ashley replied wryly, "but yes, I can assure you that the tadpole we saw on the scan definitely had feet, not hooves."

"That's wonderful news!" Issie cried, her hangover almost forgotten as she hugged him. "I'm going to be an aunty again! Yes!"

"Time to set the new generation an example then," said Alice.

Issie ignored her grandmother. "What a brilliant start to the New Year!"

Ashley nodded. "We think so too. There's a lot to celebrate for us, that's for certain, but could I ask you just keep this to yourselves for a little bit longer? We don't want to say too much until the next scan. You know how it is."

"Of course," Alice assured him. "We can keep a secret, can't we Issie?"

Issie curled her fingers around her mobile phone, tucked deep inside her hoody pocket, and thought that it was as well her grandmother didn't know just how good she was at keeping secrets.

"Sure," was all she said. Some things were better not talked about. Leaving Ashley and Alice conversing in whispers, she wandered to the window and watched the storm gathering power. Rain was battering against the glass now and running down in endless tears. Below, the waves were dashing themselves against the rocks with such ferocity that Issie stepped back, half expecting to feel spray on her cheeks.

There was a trembling in her pocket. Her mobile, switched to silent, vibrated for ten rings before giving up. Issie drew it out as warily as if it were a grenade with the pin pulled; she knew before she'd even looked at the screen who the caller would be.

Mark. Would he ever let her go? And would she be strong enough to allow him to?

With shaking hands, she cleared the call log and switched the phone off completely. Maybe she'd have a digital detox for a while. Cold turkey was probably the only way to get over him. That and another glass of champagne.

Issie pushed the mobile into her pocket and turned back to watch the ocean. This time, she really could feel saltwater on her cheeks, albeit not from the sea.

Chapter 5

Alice Tremaine was observing her grandchildren. It was something she did as naturally as breathing and it never failed to make her proud and worried sick in equal measures. While the party swirled and reverberated with a life of its own, she found a comfortable seat tucked beneath the floating staircase, where she was happy to sit quietly and watch proceedings. Even though little more was going on than chatting and eating, Alice knew her son's brood well enough to be able to tell who was having fun, who was hiding something and who was quietly breaking their heart.

She glanced at Jake and Danny, her two eldest grandsons, and smiled. They were looking relaxed and contented as they chatted easily with their partners and their friends. Danny actually glowed with joy whenever he looked at Jules, his new girlfriend (who also happened to be the local vicar and a dear friend of Alice's). Danny had had such a hard time after being injured in Afghanistan, and he'd suffered more than Alice could bear to imagine, so it warmed her heart to see both him and Jules so happy now.

Then there was Mo too. Alice shook her head in delighted disbelief at the news Ashley had accidentally shared. It was very soon – the couple had only been married a few months and the wedding had been a whirlwind – but she couldn't imagine her fiery granddaughter with anyone else. Ashley challenged Mo and kept her on her toes, which was exactly what she needed with that active mind of hers. Although Mo adored horses and had always maintained that her eventing career came first, the ups and downs of the past year had forced her to change her priorities. Time held a different meaning for the young couple now. Having a new great-grandchild was something to look forward to, even if it did make Alice feel positively ancient. It only seemed like yesterday that she was teaching Mo how to tie her shoelaces; that her granddaughter was going to become a mother herself seemed impossible.

Her gaze drifted across the room. Her son Jimmy was deep in conversation with Mickey Davey and Alice felt a flutter of concern. Jimmy might be in his early sixties now, but he was still a constant source of worry. For what had to be the thousandth time Alice found herself wishing that Penny Tremaine hadn't died so young. Apart from her death being cruel, leaving the children and their father heartbroken, she had been the guiding light that had once brought the wayward Jimmy safely into harbour. Without Penny, his anchorage had broken and Jimmy had drifted ever since, unable to find a purpose. Alice sighed. Penny had been the love of her son's life and without her he just couldn't settle. He was always searching for something to fill that gap, be it a project or a punt on the horses or a crazy jaunt across several continents, but nothing really seemed to work. He gambled, spent too much money and was an easy gull for any shyster with a get-rich-quick scheme – which was exactly what Alice feared this newcomer could be. Her brow pleated. Just who was Mickey Davey? He'd turned up in the village, spent a fortune refitting the beach café (and put the Pollards' noses right out of joint because he'd brought in his own "boys" from Essex to do all the building), but he never seemed to do a day's work. The money for the gold Bentley and all the drinking in The Ship didn't come from baking pasties, that was for sure, and instinct told Alice that he wasn't to be trusted. It didn't bode well that Mickey had made a beeline for her Jimmy.

"Can I get you anything to eat, Alice? Or another drink?"

Reverend Jules interrupted these fretful musings on her way back from the buffet, her plate piled high with seafood and canapés. Seeing Alice look at this mound of food, Jules pulled a despairing face.

"Isn't it terrible? Look at me, breaking my New Year's resolution already. So much for healthy eating and losing a stone. My willpower's useless."

"Symon's food is hard to resist," Alice told her kindly. She knew Jules struggled with her weight and even more with feeling guilty about breaking diets.

The vicar was nodding. "It certainly is. This is my second visit to the buffet. No wonder Sy had such a good write-up in the *Western Morning News* last week. What was it they called him again?" Her brow crinkled. "The next Rick Stein?"

"The *heir apparent* to Rick Stein," Alice corrected. She knew the article off by heart because she must have read it ten times over and had bought every spare copy from Betty Jago. Symon had merely shrugged off all the praise rather than letting it go to his head, but Alice was very proud of her third grandson. His restaurant, The Plump Seagull, was doing exceptionally well and he'd already earned a Michelin star – good going for a young man who was still in his twenties. Yet Symon was a worry too, because he seemed to do nothing except work. Take this afternoon, for instance: he ought to be here enjoying the party with the rest of his family but instead he'd worked solidly all morning to prepare the food and was now back at the restaurant getting ready for the evening's covers. He lived alone, had no girlfriend and seemed to exist for his career and nothing else. And as for days off? If he ever took one it was news to Alice.

It wasn't healthy and it wasn't right. Something had happened to Symon, Alice just knew it, something that had made him retreat from living his own life and throw himself into his career. Professionally this was paying dividends, but there was more to life than work and his grandmother hated to think of him being alone. Sy was a gentle and thoughtful man with a generous heart and a wicked sense of humour. Before he'd left for his training in London, he'd been as outgoing and as sociable as any of her other grandchildren, so shutting himself away like this was completely out of character. Alice had tried talking to him but she'd have found it easier to squeeze a few drops of blood out of the stones on the beach than to get the truth from him. Whatever it was that had changed him so much, Sy wasn't prepared to share it with a soul.

"Alice? Is everything all right?" Jules's sweet face was filled with concern and Alice realised she'd drifted into deep thought. Another sign of old age, she supposed.

"Sorry, my love, I was just thinking about Symon and how hard he works."

Jules nodded. "I can see that just from what he's done today. It's all delicious as always. Did you want me to fetch you anything to eat? Or would you like to join us?"

Alice shook her head. "I'm fine here where it's nice and quiet. You carry on and enjoy yourself. Just look out for Issie, would you? I haven't seen her for a while."

"She's a bit off colour; I think she went onto the terrace to get some fresh air," said the ever-tactful Jules.

More likely she was throwing up in one of Ashley's flowerpots, thought Alice. Outside the gale was raging with twice the ferocity of an hour ago. If Issie was prepared to venture into it then she must be feeling bad.

"You mean she's hung-over," she said bleakly. "I might be old but I'm not stupid, Jules. Besides, I was there when the others brought her home."

"It was New Year's Eve, Alice. I should think most of the people here are drinking hair of the dog today."

But Alice wasn't prepared to make excuses for Issie. There had been far too much of this lately and in her view it wasn't doing her youngest granddaughter any favours.

"You didn't see the state she came home in. Nick and Ashley had to carry her because she was practically unconscious." Alice's hands twisted anxiously in her lap. She'd spent the first hours of this brand new year sitting beside Issie's bed, terrified that her granddaughter might be sick in her sleep and then choke to death. You heard such awful stories. "Oh Jules, this is happening far too often and I'm really worried there's more to it. We need to help her; Issie can't go on like this."

"You're right there," Jules conceded. "Do you want me to talk to her? As a friend, not as a vicar?"

Alice nodded. "If you could I'd be so grateful. She won't speak to me but she might tell you what's wrong."

"I'll do my best," the vicar promised. "Leave it with me."

And with this Alice knew she had to be content. If anyone had a hope of getting through to Issie then Jules Mathieson was that person.

While Jules carried the spoils of her buffet run back to where some of the others were gathered, Alice walked over to the vast window to watch the storm. It was a spectacular vantage point and a crowd was already assembled there, watching as the sea hurled salt water high into the air. The sky was black now and the wind roared like an express train, driving bands of rain across the bay in horizontal sheets and spurring the waves to gallop even faster up the beach.

Alice looked on in awe. In all her years in the village she could hardly recall a storm as savage.

"My missus has just texted and she says the village is flooding!" A wide-eyed Chris the Cod was staring at his phone. "Water's coming into the chippy too, and the drains can't cope with the rainfall. I'd better go."

"I'll come with you, mate. I need to check the café," said Mickey Davey. "I hope that bloody roof holds. Can't have my new floor ruined, even if I did get one hell of a good deal on it."

"There's going to be lots of structural damage. Loads of slates off too, I reckon," Big Rog Pollard remarked to nobody in particular, hardly able to keep the glee out of his voice. While everyone else was starting to worry about their homes, he could only see pound signs tap-dancing through the village. Typical Pollard, thought Alice; his father hadn't been any different.

"Well, there'd better not be any damage to this house or I'll know exactly whose workmanship to blame," Ashley said darkly, appearing behind them all and almost making his builder jump out of his rigger boots. To Alice, Ashley added, "Mo's just called. She's panicking about the barn roof lifting, so Jake and I are going to go over and see what we can do to help."

"Is she all right?" Alice asked. She hated to think of any of her grandchildren out in this storm, but right now Morwenna was doubly precious.

"Don't worry about Mo. I'll keep an eye on her," Ashley promised, and Alice believed him. Even the bad weather wouldn't dare mess with Ashley Carstairs.

Nick was pulling on his coat and wrapping a scarf around his neck.

"I'll go down to the marina and check the boats for you," he called across to Jake, who was already at the door. "Then I'm going to stick some extra lines on the trawler."

"I'll walk down with you, Nick." Summer, Jake's girlfriend, was already in her waterproofs. "No arguments, Jake," she said quickly when her boyfriend looked as though he was about to object. "I want to make sure my parents are all right and that the water's not coming in."

Summer's parents lived in a small cottage alongside the harbour, which right now would feel like it was under attack from a relentless enemy. The basement kitchen of Cobble Cottage was also given to flooding when the drains and gullies, designed to channel water away, blocked up. The Pollards were supposed to keep these clear, and it was a job that the town council paid them to do, but more often than not they "forgot" and then all hell broke loose when it rained hard.

Now Big Rog wasn't looking quite so cheerful…

Jake nodded. "OK, sweetheart. Take care. I'll meet you there as soon as I can."

"Can I come too, Nick? I want to take some photos of the storm!"

This excited cry was from Morgan, Alice's great-grandson, who lived for photography. He'd been busy this afternoon as the official party photographer, but the thought of capturing the big seas was far more exciting than snapping groups of grown-ups eating and talking boring grown-up talk.

"Not down on the quay, mate; it's far too dangerous. The waves are likely to break over the top," Nick told him, and for once his twinkly blue eyes were serious. "You could get swept away if you're not careful."

"I'll be careful. Fact."

Nick looked his nephew straight in the eye. "You're not coming. Fact."

Morgan was hopping from foot to foot with agitation.

"Can I go on the beach then?"

"Absolutely not. It's far too dangerous," said Alice. "Maybe we should go back to Seaspray?" The storm was getting worse and she wasn't relishing the idea of walking back in it. Alice glanced around for Issie but there was still no sign of her. Where on earth had the girl gone and in all this awful weather? Surely she wasn't outside?

Morgan looked mutinous. "That's not fair, Grand Gran. *Issie's* on the beach."

They all stared at him. Alice's heart started playing leapfrog in her chest.

"Morgan, what did you just say?"

The little boy clapped his hand over his mouth. His eyes were wide and horrified.

"Did you just say that Issie had gone to the beach?" Summer asked, bending down and gently unpeeling his fingers from his lips. "Sweetie, if Issie's on the beach you really need to tell us. It's dangerous out there."

"I wasn't supposed to say anything," Morgan whispered. "I promised her. Fact."

"Sometimes you have to break a promise if it means helping someone," Alice told him. "If Issie's on the beach then that's very dangerous in weather like this and very silly of her. She could be swept out to sea."

"Silly?" Jake was furious. "Bloody stupid, is what it is!" He crouched down so that he was at eye level with his nephew. "Morgan, tell me right now! Has Issie gone to the beach?"

Morgan nodded miserably. "Her phone kept ringing and it made her sad so she said she was going for a walk on the beach. She said not to tell anyone where she'd gone because she wanted to be on her own."

"Great, just great," said Jake. He raked an exasperated hand through his thick blond hair. "Gran, can you call her mobile and tell her to come back at once? We haven't got time for this."

"She turned her phone off," Morgan said. "She told me so. Fact."

In spite of Mariners' state-of-the-art under-floor heating, Alice was cold all over. What on earth was wrong with Issie? She knew better than to take risks with the tides and the elements.

Without any warning, the electricity went off, plunging Mariners into an eerie gloom. The lights of the village, which had glowed through the stormy afternoon, vanished instantly and Ashley's Bose music system was silenced. The only soundtrack now was the roaring of the wind outside and the excited chatter indoors.

Alice shivered; the storm felt as though it was a living entity, a predator of some kind. "Where are you, Issie?" she whispered, gazing out at the boiling sea. "What on earth is going on with you? Whatever happened to make you this unhappy?"

"I'll find her, Granny," Jake promised. His mouth was set in a grim line. "And when I do, my little sister is going to wish she *had* been swept out to sea. Fact."

Chapter 6

Far below Mariners, Issie Tremaine was bent double as she attempted to walk along the beach, her body braced against the onslaught and her face wet with rain and spray. Her blonde braids had long since slipped from their hairpins, and now the wind was whipping them around her head and slapping her cheeks. The strength of the gusts had increased even more, and the sea was violent with whitecaps; the sound of the waves slamming onto the sand thundered in her ears, but still she pressed on. It was better to be out here, fighting the elements, than trapped inside and fighting her emotions. Out here she felt alive, and the storm had chased away the last of her hangover. It was as if the storm had been calling her, daring her to be at one with it.

She cupped her hands around her eyes to block out the sand the wind was flinging up the beach. Walking required her total concentration, and Issie was grateful for the challenge of planting one foot in front of the other. She didn't want to think. All the same, her chest tightened as a sudden image came to her, of a young dark-haired woman answering a door with a toddler in her arms and a hugely pregnant belly. This was the wife Mark had claimed was a wife in name only! The same wife he'd repeatedly told Issie didn't love him anymore. The one he was going to leave.

He was a liar. Issie had been in love with a liar.

Don't think about any of it, she told herself furiously. The weight of her guilt was unbearable even all these months on. It had been unbearable, too, to see Mark's name flash up earlier when her mobile had buzzed. Although the phone was switched off now, Issie was sorely tempted to hurl it into the sea, as though its passage beneath the icy water would take her painful memories with it. If only she could leave the whole sorry episode on the seabed, never to be seen again.

If only she had never allowed herself to be persuaded that Mark loved her…

Her face felt raw, although whether from the flying sand or her tears it was hard to tell. As she picked her way across the rocks at the furthest part of the beach, her trainers slithering on the seaweed, Issie sucked in her breath and listened to the hammering of her own heart, almost as loud as the howling wind and beating waves. The more furious the storm the better, Issie decided. That way she couldn't hear the roaring and screaming of her own thoughts.

Polwenna's beach was a sandy half-moon stretching from the foot of the harbour wall to a jumble of snaggle-toothed rocks half a mile away. In the summer the beach was crammed with holidaymakers lazing on stripy beach towels, and the locals wouldn't be seen dead here. They knew that if they scaled the rocks of the first headland and risked slipping on the treacherous slimy green patches, a longer and even better beach lay beyond. There were more rocks there, and as a child Issie had spent many happy hours exploring, with a net and bucket carried across the worm-cast sand. Who knew what mysteries lurked in the cool depths of the rock pools, or what treasures small fingers could scoop out? The Tremaine children had discovered which pools the starfishes lived in and which seaweedy crevasses were home to sharp-pincered crabs and darting shannies. They also knew precisely where the dangerous currents swirled, as well as the exact spots where razor-fingered rocks lurked, lying in wait for the unwary. This beach was beautiful but it was also bleak and deadly.

Issie scrambled up the rocks, feeling exhilarated by the wild elements. This was what it meant to be alive! The wind, the waves and the rain weren't afraid to rage and storm, and they matched her mood exactly. There was no way she could have stayed cooped up in Mariners, sipping drinks and making polite chit-chat while inside her own tempest was raging. Had King Lear sat inside drinking tea, or had he gone out into the howling storm? Then again, hadn't he ended up going mad anyway? At any rate, Issie certainly felt like she was going insane.

She had done ever since her tutor's pregnant wife had answered his front door…

"Come on then! Do your worst!" Issie hollered at the wind, but the storm tore the words from her lips and flung them into the sea spray. Issie only wished she could fling her guilt in too. She was torn between disgust at her own behaviour and despair because, even now, her heart still missed a beat when she thought about him.

Would it ever get better? Or was her punishment to feel like this for the rest of her life? She'd been so stupid, so naïve. Why on earth had she believed him? A bored married man looking for fun with a foolish younger girl. It was the oldest story in the book – and when that man was your university tutor, the story could only have a very bad ending.

Pushing these thoughts away, Issie focused on scrambling up the rocks. The village lay behind her now, and as she perched at the top she looked at the churning sea and marvelled at nature's ferocity. This was Cornwall at its most elemental: granite and salt water and driving rain. A hard and unforgiving place but breathtaking in its wild beauty. Issie loved this location regardless of the weather, but on days like this the county's savage history felt particularly close, as though the mists between the centuries had grown so thin it was possible to pass through. She touched the chain at her neck and felt the warmth of her grandmother's coin hanging hidden and heavy against her skin. Was it fanciful to think that her necklace could detect the echoes of history too?

Issie didn't think so. To her the idea seemed quite plausible, for it was at this very spot that Black Jack Jago had lured his victims to their deaths. Somewhere beneath the boiling water were the secrets he and his men had taken to their graves. This thought made the hairs on the back of her neck prickle.

She turned and began to slither down the rocks onto the second beach. The waves were even rougher here, and for a moment she paused, her instinctive need to escape halted by respect for the power of the tide as it raced up the beach, flinging spray and stones against the shore before falling back and dragging away huge scoops of sand.

Issie's blue eyes widened. She'd lived here all her life but had never known the bay like this. It was both familiar and unfamiliar – unsettlingly so, like a friendly dog she'd played with for years suddenly baring its teeth and snarling at her. The violent surge of water had swept away parts of the beach, uncovered rocks she'd never seen before and revealed what looked like an old tree trunk. How odd. Where on earth had that come from? Had it been washed up from further along? And how come it wasn't moving in the swirling water? Surely it should be floating? Unless she wasn't seeing clearly with all this driving rain, and it was just another rock being exposed?

There was another mighty gust of wind, followed by a wave that threw spray so fast and so hard that for a moment Issie couldn't see. Wiping her eyes on the sleeve of her jacket, she scrambled higher to escape a drenching – but when she next looked across the beach what she saw shocked Issie so much that she almost fell.

It wasn't possible! Surely not?

Issie's pulse began to race. The tree trunk wasn't alone; rather, it was one of several rising out of the shore like the age-blackened ribcage of some prehistoric beast. As the deep sand was sucked away by the greedy sea, more and more ribs were revealed. The unrelenting storm was uncovering something long-buried and half forgotten. It wasn't a rock and it certainly wasn't a tree trunk, and the harder Issie stared the more convinced she became that she knew *exactly* what she was looking at. How could she not? She'd dreamed about this moment for years, had even chosen her degree course because of her fascination with it...

Incredible as it seemed, Issie Tremaine knew with all her heart that she was looking at the wreck of the *Isabella* – or, more accurately, what remained of the *Isabella*. This was the Spanish treasure ship that Jack Jago had lured to her doom, Issie just knew it! What else could it possibly be?

With shaking fingers she pulled her iPhone from her pocket, cursing the rain that instantly rendered the screen slippery, and switched it on. She cursed even more loudly when she saw that she'd had four missed calls from Jake. Great, just what she needed: her big brother on the case. Morgan must have grassed her up.

Ignoring her brother's calls and texts, Issie wiped the screen as best she could and snapped several pictures before an even bigger wave surged up the beach and covered the wreck. The tide must be coming in, she realised with a start, and it was coming in fast. There was a spring tide anyway, and with the added force of the storm it was likely that the water's reach would be far higher than normal. It might even stretch as far as her perch up here. As if the cold spray had brought her to her senses, Issie retraced her steps hurriedly, clambering back up and over the rocks to head back to the safety of the village, now acutely aware of just how treacherous it was on the beach. She slipped several times, grazing her palms and ripping the knees out of her jeans, but even the sting of the cuts and the sad state of her trousers couldn't dim her excitement. If the *Isabella* was here then that meant only one thing: Black Jack Jago and his treasure couldn't be very far away either! Hadn't she always known that the legend was true? And hadn't she sworn that she'd prove it one day?

Her misery forgotten, Issie was skidding down the village side of the rocks when the sound of voices raised above even the howling wind announced the arrival of her brothers, Nick and Jake. Issie groaned. Jake was striding ahead, and even from a distance she could tell he was absolutely furious. The set of his shoulders and the way he shoved his wind-blown hair out of his eyes spoke volumes.

"What the hell do you think you're playing at?" her eldest brother thundered once Issie had slithered down the last few rocks and back onto the sand. "Have you lost your mind? We've been worried sick about you. Granny Alice is in a dreadful state."

Issie struggled to think of an answer, but there was little point because her eldest brother was in no mood to listen to anything she could say. Besides, he was right. For eighteen months or so, Issie supposed that she *had* lost her mind. Not that she could tell him about any of this. She couldn't tell anyone, not even Nick, and she'd always told her twin everything. Her relationship with Mark was her first ever secret and it hadn't been a happy one.

"I just needed some space," she said. This sounded pathetic even to her own ears, and Jake looked as though he was going to combust with anger.

"On the beach and in a bloody gale? I think—"

The wind snatched the rest of the words from his lips, which was probably just as well because Issie couldn't imagine they were complimentary. Looking murderous, he grabbed her arm and frogmarched Issie across the beach at such a speed that her trainers hardly touched the sand. When the tide tore towards them and swirled around their feet she almost fell, and she found herself screaming as the hungry sea tried to snatch her out of Jake's grasp. She realised now that her reckless mood was no match for the wild weather; the storm was threatening and terrifying, and when Jake scooped her up and carried her above the icy waves, Issie buried her face in his neck and clung on for dear life. How had she ever found this exhilarating? Now she wanted nothing more than to be safely at home, warm and snug in Seaspray's kitchen, curled up on the sofa with her family. Wrecks and treasure and Mark were all forgotten as Jake staggered to his knees and cold seawater kisses chilled them both to the core. In the distance she heard Nick call out anxiously about rip tides, and the sheer terror in her twin's cry brought home the danger of what she'd done.

Issie felt sick. She knew better than to take chances with the sea. She had risked both her life and Jake's.

After what felt like an age they reached the steps at the bottom of the harbour wall and Jake set Issie down. Jelly-legged and shaking, she managed to climb up. Once at the top, out of the wind and in a cottage doorway, she eventually found her voice.

"I'm so sorry, Jake," Issie said. "I needed some space so I went for a walk. I didn't realise quite how bad it was out here."

Her brother stared at her incredulously. "You thought it was a good idea to walk on the beach in a force-ten storm? Are you really that stupid? You could have been swept out to sea, and so could anyone looking for you. Did that occur to you, Issie? Did it?"

"I'm really sorry, Jake. I didn't think."

"You never bloody do!" he shouted, and Issie stepped back, shocked because Jake hardly ever got angry. Danny and Mo were the ones with the tempers, but her big brother was usually calm. That he was yelling now was a real indication of just how upset he was.

"I'm sorry," Issie said. "I didn't mean to cause any trouble."

Her brother shook his head. "Well, you have caused trouble and worse than that, you risked my life and Nick's – so just grow up, Issie, will you? Otherwise you're in danger of turning out like Dad."

This barb stung. As much as Issie adored Jimmy, and she did adore him because he was probably the most entertaining and relaxed parent on the planet, she was well aware of his shortcomings. There had been too many broken promises, missed school sports days and forgotten birthdays to count. Issie loved Jimmy Tremaine but did she want to be like him?

The answer to this question was a resounding *no*.

"I'm really sorry," she said again.

But sorry wasn't enough and Jake wasn't in the mood to accept any apologies.

"Save the *sorrys* for somebody who wants to hear them," he said, crossing his arms and glowering down at her. "And if you don't have any regard for yourself, at least try and think about Gran. She's beside herself with worry over you, and not just about today either. You can't carry on stressing her out like this. She's not getting any younger and she doesn't need it."

Issie stared at him. "What the hell is that supposed to mean?"

"Your out-of-control drinking. The endless partying. Messing around with guys like Teddy St Milton. Dropping out of uni. Risking your life by walking on the beach in a gale. Stripping off for charity calendars." Jake was reeling off what was sounding like a very alarming list. "Shall I go on?"

Issie would rather he didn't. None of this sounded good.

"You're having a go at me about the Polwenna Bay calendar? That's rich coming from a man who lives with a glamour model!"

"Don't you dare bring Summer into this!" Jake yelled. "I'm talking about *you*, Issie Tremaine, not my girlfriend. Your partying and your drinking and your stupid, thoughtless behaviour!"

"Like you've never ever got drunk or shagged Ella St Milton," Issie shot back.

"I've done lots of things I'm not proud of," Jake said coldly. "Of course I have, but the difference is that I grew up and stopped behaving like a total moron. The question is, when do you intend to do that?"

And with this he turned away from her, his body taut against the wind while the driving rain turned his hair to darkest gold. Issie gulped back tears. In her entire life Jake had never spoken to her like that and he'd certainly never walked away from her. Her life was spinning out of control and she didn't have the first clue how to stop it. She looked imploringly at Nick but her twin only shrugged awkwardly.

"Jake's right," he said quietly. "You can't go on like this."

Issie stared at him. This was a classic case of the pot calling the kettle black, since Nick's lifestyle wasn't exactly saintly.

"Are you having a go at me as well?"

"It's not a go, Issie. I'm worried about you. We all are. You were so out of it last night and anything could have happened. Now this? I don't know what's wrong but I do know something: you've got to get over whatever it is, otherwise I don't know what's going to happen to you."

And then Nick walked away too, without so much as a backward glance, leaving Issie in no doubt as to just how angry her brothers were.

She shivered, wet and chilled through and utterly miserable. Slumped against the cottage door she watched the rain blow by and tried to gather the strength to walk home. The narrow street was awash, the drains gushing and bubbling just as her mind was now overflowing with regret. Had she been reckless? With hindsight, yes. Did she drink too much? The blanks from the previous night certainly suggested as much. Was she out of control? A memory of kissing Teddy St Milton flittered through her mind and Issie groaned. That was a definite yes.

Today was a wake-up call and one she needed, Issie decided. It was time to turn her life around, put Mark Tollen out of her life for good and do her best to make amends to her family. She'd find a way to make them proud of her – and she suddenly knew exactly how she could do this!

Issie laughed out loud because it was all so obvious. There was a reason why she'd ventured into the storm. Fate had sent her hurtling into the rain and wind. Of course it had. There was no other explanation. This was meant to be.

The galleon slumbering beneath the sand was the key to putting everything right. All Issie had to do was find Black Jack Jago's hidden hoard, and the Tremaine family's fortune would be made. What better way could there be to make them proud and make amends too? She could hardly wait to start looking.

Chapter 7

The storm finally blew itself out in the small hours, and by the time dawn's pink glow stole across the sky the rain had stopped. Although the weather was calm now, the village itself had become a hive of activity; everyone was busy, from the gulls picking through the piles of seaweed to the villagers unhappily assessing the damage.

Big Roger Pollard had been spot on when he'd predicted structural problems. The vicarage roof had taken such a battering that Jules was wearing wellies in her kitchen. Meanwhile, three of the fishermen's stores on top of the quay had blown away completely, and so many slates had slipped that the cottage rooftops looked as though they had bald patches. Swollen with the night's heavy rainfall, the River Wenn raced through the village, foaming white as though whipped up in a blender, and laden with debris washed down from the hills. The water tore under the bridges and burst into the harbour, making the boats dance and the gulls bob about.

As soon as the sun rose, the Tremaine family gathered at the marina, where they checked the boats and the pontoons and began the slow process of mopping up the waterlogged office and workshops. Seaspray had been spared too much damage, save a large tree down in the grounds and a few slipped slates. But just as Summer had feared, the poorly maintained drains and gullies down in the village had been unable to cope with the sudden and vast volume of water, and there had been a great deal of flooding. The houses by the quay all had water in their basements, the main street was awash, Harbour View Café had been cut off by a mini waterfall gushing down its steps, and Chris the

Cod was attempting to sweep the deluge out of his chippy. Funnily enough, neither Big nor Little Roger Pollard was anywhere to be seen.

Issie was mopping the marina office and fighting the urge to abandon the task and tear across the beach, to see if the wreck she'd seen during the storm was really there or just a figment of her imagination. In the cold light of a new day, it was hard to be sure. The pictures she'd taken on her phone had been disappointing, to say the least. Then again, the camera lens had been covered in rain and Issie had been struggling to keep her balance on the top of the slippery rocks, so perhaps it should have come as no surprise that the images were so indistinct. The dark blur in the distance could have been anything.

High tide had come at five o'clock this morning, and Issie was counting down the hours until the beach was clear again and she could venture back for a proper look. Every time she thought about the wreck her stomach did a pancake-flip of excitement. This was the *Isabella*, she just knew it!

"How's it looking in here?"

Jake was standing in the doorway and Issie paused, leaning on her mop. They were just about on speaking terms again after she'd gone home and eaten such a big slice of humble pie she'd not be hungry again until the next New Year rolled around, but she knew he was still exasperated by the events of the previous afternoon. She didn't blame him for being angry. Now that yesterday's high emotion had subsided, Issie was feeling utterly ashamed that her impulsive behaviour had caused so much worry and put her brothers' lives at risk. She was hoping with all her heart that her plan to make up for this would work, and that the wreck she thought she'd seen did actually exist.

She glanced around the office. "It isn't too bad in here. I think it could have been a lot worse. There are a few superficial things we'll have to chuck out, but the electric sockets are high up, so nothing's really damaged – and at least the floor's made of concrete. We can replace the carpet; it was old anyway."

Jake rubbed his eyes wearily. "I guess we should count ourselves bloody lucky. I've just heard that the row of coastguard cottages on Polwenna Hill has lost all its roofing. That would have crucified us if it had happened up at Seaspray."

Issie nodded. Her brother looked tired and drawn. There were purple smudges beneath his eyes, which today had lost their usual twinkle, and his chin was darkened with stubble. She knew he hadn't slept: he'd been up all night trying to staunch the water with sandbags and making sure his customers' boats were safe, before heading to the Penhalligans' cottage and helping out there. No wonder he looked exhausted. And things were already tough enough at Tremaine Marine, without adding flood damage to the list of spiralling costs. How much did a roof cost, anyway?

If she could find Black Jago's treasure, that would solve all their money worries, Issie thought with growing excitement.

As plans went, this one was quite a long shot, but Issie Tremaine wasn't the kind of person to be put off easily. As far as she was concerned, Granny Alice's coin was evidence, and the historical records she'd studied backed up all the stories. Once she went back to check that she really had seen what was left of the *Isabella's* hull, it would be a "fact", as her nephew Morgan might say. All she had to do was put the pieces of the puzzle together and find the loot. How hard could that be?

"I think I'm just about done here." Issie wrung the mop out into a bucket and surveyed the results of her past two hours of labour. She'd rolled up the ancient carpet and dragged it outside to dry, and although the concrete floor was still very damp, at least it no longer resembled a lake. The dehumidifier was chugging away nicely and the small heater was on too, so the place would hopefully dry out quickly.

"You've done a good job," Jake said, perching on the desk and looking around approvingly. Then his blue eyes met hers and he cleared his throat. "Look, Issie, about yesterday? I'm sorry about what I said to you—"

She held up her hands. "Don't apologise, Jakey. You were right, I was only thinking about myself and I was bloody selfish. I'm going to change all that though, you just watch me."

"I was pissed off and frightened when I said all that. You're not selfish." Her brother gave her one of the dimpled smiles that had never failed to melt the hearts of Polwenna Bay's female population. "Well, not all the time, anyway!"

In reply Issie dipped her hands into the bucket of dirty water and flicked some at him.

"Watch it, squirt! Or I'll make you start again!" Jake threatened with a grin. "Or maybe you'd like to check the toilets and see if they've unblocked yet?"

"Gross! No thanks. Can't Nick do that? He's the other one usually in the shit around here," shuddered Issie.

"I think you've surpassed even him," Jake said.

Issie's eyes darted to the clock. It was half past nine. By her calculation the tide would be just far enough out by now for her to make it back to the wreck, but not yet far enough for anyone else to have ventured onto the second part of the bay. She needed to get there soon.

"Much as I hate to miss out on unblocking the loos, I'm just going to have a wander outside and see what's going on, if that's OK?" she said.

Jake yawned and, waving her away, sank onto the driest part of the office sofa. "Go on then. Scoot. Get out of here before I decide to make you do something else." He leaned his head back. "I think maybe I'll just shut my eyes for a few seconds while you're gone."

He'd be out cold in moments, Issie thought fondly. Poor Jake. He worked so hard and worried so much. Thank goodness he had Summer; she always made him smile and did her best to drag him away from the spreadsheets and sums that made his brow crinkle and his mouth droop. If Issie's hunch was right, then maybe Jake's money worries would be over for good. That would be the best way to repay him for all the sacrifices he'd made over the years to look after them all.

Outside the marina office, the world was newly scrubbed and bright sunlight was glaring on the waterways that had replaced Polwenna's narrow streets. High above Issie's head, seagulls were circling and shrieking. All in all, it was a glorious sparkling morning – or would have been, if not for the flooding.

Half the villagers were out in their wellingtons, and as Issie made her way to the beach steps she was stopped countless times and told tales of woe. Silver Starr was almost up to her knees in the water that had poured into her mystic shop. Despite being the local tarot-card reader and clairvoyant, apparently she hadn't seen this disaster coming. Further along the street, Patsy Penhalligan's usual customers were outraged to find the pasty shop closed. Flooding was no excuse, in the eyes of the villagers.

"On a day like this we need our pasties," Big Eddie was grumbling, as Issie sloshed past. "The bloody chippy's flooded and my kitchen's out of action. We're going to starve, maid! I'd even eat some of that posh stuff your brother charges a fortune for, but the bugger's shut."

Big Eddie made Santa look skinny. It would take him a while to fade away, Issie thought with a smile.

"Mickey Davey's opened the Locker. He's doing pasties and cups of tea," called Betty Jago, from the doorstep of the village shop where she was currently marooned. Several seagulls swam past her, looking rather pleased to have another river in the village.

"And charging London prices too, I'd be bound," Big Eddie called back. "There'll be a profit in it for him somewhere!" Big Eddie certainly had the measure of this particular newcomer, but he turned around and made a beeline for the beach café anyway. Issie followed him, amazed by the devastation that one heavy storm could cause. The local TV station had sent a crew down and Radio Cornwall were already interviewing Adam and Rose Harper, who were describing the flood in their cellar.

"Water just rose up from nowhere!" Rose was saying in disbelief.

"Not from nowhere, my lover; it came up through the drains," Adam corrected her gently. "There's probably some underground stream down there that's swollen from all the rainfall."

Issie's ears pricked up. Underground streams and long-forgotten culverts fascinated her. Surely it would have been natural passages just like these that Black Jack Jago and his smuggling cronies would have exploited. Maybe his loot was below the pub? Didn't everyone always say that a pub in a village of hard-drinking fishermen was a goldmine?

The beach was covered in flotsam and thick with kelp that had been ripped from the seabed and thrown high above the tideline. Several people were already beachcombing; usually Issie would have been the first to join them, but today she had more exciting things on her mind than bits of driftwood or nuggets of sea-smoothed glass. Waving at her brother Danny, who was strolling arm in arm with Jules along the water's edge, Issie increased her speed and was soon climbing up the rocks.

The second beach was glistening in the sunshine. Issie squinted into the brightness, shielding her eyes with one hand and holding onto the rocks with the other as she slithered down the far side. The sand had shifted considerably and was far closer to the foot of the cliffs than she recalled. Seaweed was piled high at the shoreline and the remains of a trawl lay tangled over some smaller rocks, but Issie hardly noticed any of these details. As she jogged across the hard sand, all she cared about was the skeleton of what was, without any doubt now, all that remained of a centuries-old ship.

Issie crouched down beside the wreck, her breath coming in gasps – from excitement as much as from exertion. The wood was soft and crumbly beneath her fingertips and oddly warm, as though the ship were alive.

"Oh my God," she breathed, hardly able to believe that she was actually touching the hull of the very ship she was named after. "It's true. It's all really true!"

The exploding seas had shifted sands that for well over two centuries had covered the lost galleon like a blanket. Issie and her brothers had dived the waters around the bay all their lives and explored wrecks – the treacherous Cornish coast was littered with them – but she'd never seen anything quite like this. It was as though she was looking at all that remained of the ribcage of a once-mighty creature. She knew from her studies that the original ship must have been almost two hundred feet long, so this must only be a small section – but even so, what an amazing discovery! Thank goodness she'd set off into the storm yesterday, or she could have missed it. The sand might shift again soon, and it would be as though the ship had never appeared; as the *Isabella*'s hull sank back into the sand, she would sink back into legend.

Issie rested her hand against the soft wood.

"That's not going to happen, I promise," she whispered to the ship. Although it was fanciful, she couldn't help feeling that the old beams understood; the whisper and suck of the waves certainly sounded like a heartfelt sigh.

Issie moved back a little, brushed the sand granules from her fingers and surveyed the delicate wood more carefully. *Isabella* needed the specialist attention of marine archaeologists who'd know exactly how to look after her. Issie bit her lip as her heart twisted with that familiar sense of loss. She'd hoped to pursue a master's degree in marine archaeology after her bachelor's degree, but that dream was now as much a wreck as the once-stately galleon. Of course she'd given up and walked away. What else could she do? Mark ran the department and he'd have supervised her. How could she have coped with spending all that time with him once she knew the truth? And how could she have been near him and not longed to feel his skin against hers?

It would have been torture. Giving up her degree and disappointing her family was nothing in comparison.

She stood up, angry with herself for allowing him to creep into her thoughts. Dr Mark Tollen had no place in her life anymore. He'd lied to her, and all the excuses and heartfelt texts in the world could never make up for that. He'd betrayed Issie, but worse than that he'd turned her into the type of woman she'd always despised – a woman who had a relationship with a married man. A home wrecker.

Her hands clenched into fists.

"Screw you, Mark Tollen!" she shouted into the emptiness. "Screw you!"

But only the shrieking gulls answered. Nobody was listening and nobody cared.

It didn't matter. Her feelings for Mark were as dead as the unlucky crew of this galleon. Or they would be, Issie told herself with great determination, just as soon as this longing for him was gone. Never mind the curse of Black Jack's treasure. Issie wasn't worried about that in the least; after all, what could possibly be worse than the curse of loving somebody you shouldn't?

It was time to move on, and as she snapped as many pictures of the wreck as she could, Issie had the overwhelming feeling that finding the *Isabella* was the first step towards the rest of her life. There was an odd fluttering sensation in her stomach, which for a moment she struggled to identify. When she did, Issie was taken aback. It was hope making her heart lift. Hope! How amazing? How long had it been since she'd felt remotely optimistic about anything?

Still smiling, Issie walked around the remains of the ship, capturing it from as many angles as possible and savouring the fact that, for now, the wreck was her delicious secret. This couldn't and shouldn't last: the *Isabella* was an important find and it had to be documented. And Issie knew with all her heart that this wreck *was* that very galleon. As soon as she was back in the village, she would report her discovery so that things would be done properly, with the care and expertise that were required. The starting point would be to contact the official Receiver of Wreck, even though this particular vessel had sunk many years ago. Salvage law was notoriously complicated. Besides, there were laws to protect wrecks that might be historically significant. It was not for Issie to poke around examining the ship's remains for herself, and she didn't think Jake would be amused if her interest in the *Isabella* landed the Tremaines in court.

Breathtaking as the *Isabella* was, though, it was the lost cargo Issie was more interested in. She was convinced it hadn't gone down with the ship; the coin hanging from her necklace was surely proof of that. If there was even a grain of truth in Granny Alice's bedtime story, then fabulous wealth could be far closer than anyone could ever have dreamt, and finding the wreck was only the beginning.

As she sprinted across the beach and back to the village, Issie Tremaine felt sure that her next discovery would be no less than Black Jack Jago's stolen treasure.

Chapter 8

The fragrance of the magnolia tree drifted on the night breeze, and beyond the window a fat full moon lit the sea. Crickets chirped, the ceiling fan clicked in endless rotation and down on the pontoons engines chugged as fishermen unloaded the day's catch. The hotel bar was jumping with music, and Luke could feel the base beat thrum through the mattress as he lay on the bed. Days on from New Year's Eve, Key West was still poised for action: the bars were heaving, whiskey was waiting and the hot night was filled with possibilities.

So why the hell was he feeling so lethargic? Even pressing the button on the TV remote felt like an effort.

"Come on, baby, we're meeting the others for dinner at eight. You need to get changed."

A slender blonde woman stepped into the room, immaculate in a white shift dress and towering strappy sandals, and narrowed her eyes critically.

"You're not going out like that, are you?"

Luke was wearing board shorts and a black vest. His long dark hair was caught up in an elastic band at the nape of his neck and he was a day overdue for a shave – but then, weren't most guys on Bone Island? He took a swig from the bottle of Bud held loosely in his left hand.

"Well, yeah, I was actually, Stella. Why? Something wrong with this?"

The woman pushed a lock of hair from her forehead, stabbed it into place with a pin, and turned to look at him. Her face was beautifully made up: despite the stifling humidity, her skin bore not so much as a glimmer of sweat. The glittering diamond earrings that swung as she moved her head were matched with a large teardrop pendant, which hung heavily between her breasts – breasts that were significantly younger than the rest of her, Luke had quickly realised. They were as round as twin scoops of caramel ice cream, and displayed to full advantage by a plunging neckline. Not that the rest was any less impressive. Stella de Souza, like most wealthy soon-to-be divorcees, took her personal training and her beauty regime very seriously.

"Sweetie, my lawyer's got a table booked at Zara's, and that place has a waiting list a mile long. I don't want to even think about the strings he's had to pull to get it. So no, I don't think short pants and a vest will cut it."

Zara's was the town's latest be-seen-at venue. In a plum spot right on the waterfront, it seated only twenty or so guests at a time. And there they enjoyed morsels of delicious and, in the locals' opinion, very overpriced food – while their very presence in the place announced to the world just how wealthy they were. It was all bullshit as far as Luke was concerned. In his opinion the fried oyster po'boy sandwich from the bar only metres along the sidewalk was just as good. You could eat that on the pontoon with the same moonlight trickling across the inky water, and what's more you could watch the great dark shapes of tarpon circling beneath. Still, chilling on the pontoon with a takeout and a cold one didn't announce to the rest of the world just how rich you were, did it? And Stella was rich.

Seriously rich.

She was also a great lay. Since New Year's Eve Luke had enjoyed many hours tangled up in white sheets and honeyed limbs in the seclusion of her private guest cottage right on the water. Bored and still waiting for her divorce to be finalised, Stella was in the Keys to blow off some steam. Like many wealthy older women before her, she was more than happy to enjoy some no-strings fun. Stella was hot and totally uninhibited. The champagne had flowed, the sex was good and she'd done a great job of taking his mind off his woes.

She was also very demanding, though. Listening to her now, Luke's temples began to throb.

"Honey, get your ass to the lobby and tell them to find you a dinner suit," Stella was saying, flipping open her Louis Vuitton purse and pulling out a gold Amex card.

Luke grimaced. "What's this? *Pretty Woman* in reverse?"

"You'd better believe it, baby. You're not coming out for dinner dressed like a goddamn bum. Take that earring out too, yeah? It's kinda scruffy."

Ignoring this command, Luke took another long slug of beer. He might be down on his luck but he wasn't any woman's kept man. Stella had liked him enough in board shorts on New Year's Eve – and she'd liked him even better without them. When he'd taken her face in his hands and kissed those suspiciously full red lips, she'd not been thinking about board shorts and earrings.

"And don't tell me you're not hungry," Stella added, crossing to the dressing table and spritzing herself with Opium. "You've been so athletic all afternoon that you must have worked up quite an appetite. You need to eat, honey. Gotta keep your strength up."

As she said this, her feline eyes widened and a naughty tip of her pink, pink tongue darted across her lips. In spite of his lethargy, Luke felt himself harden. God, she knew how to make a guy come to heel. No wonder she was screwing such a huge settlement out of her ex.

"Oliver's worth millions," Stella had told Luke airily that first evening, over a bottle of vintage champagne – which, thank God, she'd refused to let him buy. "He's got so much money the poor bastard doesn't know what to spend it on, which is why I'm actually doing him a favour by going for such a huge settlement."

Luke hadn't followed. "And how does that work, exactly?"

Stella had laid her scarlet-tipped fingers on his thigh, tracing them along his shorts and onto his tanned flesh. All the blood in his brain had instantly migrated south, but somehow he'd managed to take in that her ex was big in hedge funds – and the more he worked, the happier he was. The nearest Luke had ever come to a hedge fund was doing some gardening for his mom, but he knew enough to realise that Stella would be a very wealthy divorcee. Paying her off would only spur Oliver to spend even more time in the office, Stella had said with more than a little bitterness; it would suit him fine, seeing as that was where he liked to be.

Now, as Luke lay on the bed half listening to Stella giving him orders about what to wear, he was starting to have some sympathy for the unknown Oliver. The office was looking like a very attractive place to hide.

"And see if the spa's open: get a haircut, honey," she finished, not even looking at him now but instead smoothing her own hair in front of the mirror. "Put it on my account."

"I'll pay for my own damn haircuts," Luke grated, annoyed now. No matter how sexy and hot in bed a woman was, nothing was worth this.

But Stella just laughed at his irritation. "Oh, don't get all huffy. You sound like my teenagers. When you hit pay dirt, you can return the favour. Until then, enjoy a few treats." She winked. "You've earned them!"

Luke raised his eyes to the fan in despair. He was starting to wish he'd never told Stella what it was he did for a living. At first she'd been disbelieving, then amazed – and now she was determined that she was going to invest in him. This had sounded all very well at four in the morning after a few bottles of champagne and some great sex, but now it was beginning to feel as though the shackles were tightening. As much as a wealthy sponsor was an answer to his prayers, Luke wasn't convinced that Stella was the way forward. On the other hand, there wasn't exactly a crowd of others beating a path to his door.

"I'm outa here." With one final check in the looking glass, Stella stalked to the door and blew Luke a kiss. "See you in an hour, honey. And get yourself sorted, y'hear? Don and Shelly can't wait to meet a real live treasure hunter. Play your cards right and who knows what this year could bring."

Once the door clicked shut, Luke lay back on the pillow and groaned. Christ, he was hopeless. Talk about mixing business and pleasure. Stella was only supposed to have been a fun diversion, but already those "no strings" had turned into golden chains and she was dangling a 24-carat padlock under his nose. This was not the way his New Year was meant to have started.

He stretched his arms above his head and stared up at the ceiling fan again. Around and around it went in never-ending circles, a bit like his thoughts. Here was a beautiful, sexy woman offering him all the funding he'd ever dreamed of. Over breakfast she'd put a proposal to him that would have tempted even Mother Teresa – and Luke Dawson had never pretended to be a saint. In return for a sixty percent share of whatever he found, Stella had said nonchalantly (she'd been pushing her eggs benedict around the plate at the time), she'd provide him with a brand new dive boat, pay for crew and transfer an agreed amount into the business account every month. He'd be functional by February and able to compete with the best.

In other words, Mal Dawson would really be able to see that Luke had known best all along.

Yes, it was tempting.

Yet on the other hand, if he let Stella sponsor him he'd owe her everything. This idea made Luke uncomfortable. Call him old-fashioned, but the thought of being bankrolled by a woman – especially one he'd been seeing – didn't sit well with him. The boundaries were already blurred and if he was feeling this uneasy after three days then how the hell would he feel after a few months?

He groaned. Freaking awful, probably. But what choice did he really have? Fate had sent Stella his way: a sexy, vibrant, rich woman who was prepared to invest in him *and* screw him senseless. Most guys would grab the opportunity with both hands. The problem was that Luke Dawson wasn't most guys. He was proud and honourable and independent to the point of stubbornness. Surely something else had to come up?

He sat up, about to head for the wet room in the hope of clearing his head beneath jets of icy water, when the television on the wall caught his attention. Or rather, the stunning girl on the screen ripped his thoughts right away from showering. Her heart-shaped face was crowned with long honey-coloured braids pinned up with glittery slides, and she was staring into the camera with eyes the exact hue of the Caribbean Sea. A kissable mouth like a fushcia bud opened and closed wordlessly, and her small hands were gesticulating wildly. She was standing on a crowded beach somewhere pretty damn bleak, but even without sound it was obvious she was very excited. Hot as this girl was, though, it was the caption below her that had really grabbed his attention.

Wreck of eighteenth-century treasure ship discovered in Cornwall

Shit. Where was the remote? The TV was on the BBC America channel for some reason. Disinterested in the Brits' grey-looking police series and their peculiar obsession with *Dr Who*, Luke had pressed mute. Now, though, he was desperate to hear what Goldilocks had to say. And where the hell was Corn Wall? Each second that passed felt like a lifetime, until at last his fingers came into contact with the remote control, and surround sound flooded the room.

"…the *Isabella* was carrying two and a half tonnes of gold coins, and was also reputed to be carrying jewels," a reporter was saying, in an accent Luke had last heard when his ex-girlfriend had been watching *Downton Abbey*. "When she was lost, the coins – along with the rest of the treasure – sank beneath the waves."

"But that isn't quite true!" Braids interrupted excitedly. "The ship was wrecked and the treasure was stolen away by a local smuggler. It was smuggled down a secret tunnel. Jonny St Milton from the hotel told me."

"That's nonsense, Issie!" An elderly woman standing next to the girl was looking troubled. "It's just a tall story. Jonny tells lots of them. Always did and always will."

But Issie (as she was apparently called) shook her head defiantly. "It's true. He says he saw the tunnel and was sworn to secrecy."

The reporter turned to face the camera. Behind him, gloved hands waved and pale faces gurned as people pushed forward, all desperate for their moment of fame. Issie remained beside the reporter, a determined expression on her pretty face. Luke was jolted because he knew it was the exact expression his own features arranged themselves into when he was pursuing a lead.

"Shifting sands and currents meant that until this week *Isabella* hadn't seen the light of day for well over two hundred years. Her precious cargo has been missing for just as long, and the mystery of where it went continues. This is Mike Elliott, for BBC News, from Polwenna Bay in Cornwall."

Luke pressed pause on the TIVO control. His heart was racing and he had that sensation in the pit of his stomach that always, without fail, signalled that he was onto something. Springing up from the bed, he tore across the suite and stood so close to the TV that his nose brushed the screen. There he remained for five minutes, staring intently at Issie. Not because she was pretty – which she undoubtedly was – but because of what she was wearing. At the opening of her shirt hung a necklace which, he was certain, proved that her theory was true.

The necklace was in fact a coin on a length of chain. A gold coin. And not any gold coin either, but – and he was pretty sure of this – an eight-escudo piece showing the head of a monarch. Doubtless it would once have been transported across the seas on a ship carrying currency from the New World to the old.

"I'll be God damned!" breathed Luke. If only he could zoom in closer and be certain which monarch… But the LCD screen showed only so much definition and the image was tantalisingly pixelated when viewed this close up. Was it Philip V? It didn't matter. Either way, the feisty Issie was in possession of a coin with a worth that might range from four hundred dollars to over ten thousand – and that coin had to have come from *somewhere*. What was it she'd been saying about a tunnel, before the old lady had cut in with her scathing comments?

Luke rewound the interview and watched it again, his eyes narrowed and his white teeth biting his bottom lip. After viewing it three more times he grabbed his iPhone so that he could Google Polwenna Bay and the *Isabella*. What he read made his pulse race again.

Forget dinner at Zara's, flash dive boats and warm waters. He was going to blue the last of his savings on a hunch that was growing stronger by the second.

Luke Dawson was going to Cornwall, England.

Chapter 9

Alice Tremaine was worried. January was usually the quietest month in the Polwenna Bay calendar. Christmas and New Year were always busy, almost as busy as mid-summer, but once these high points had passed the streets would empty, holiday-cottage windows would darken and most of the gift shops and restaurants would close for a well-deserved break. You could walk from the top end of the village by the primary school right the way through to the harbour without meeting a soul; even the seagulls, deprived of overflowing bins and pasty crusts, were normally subdued during the low season.

This was the time of year when the locals took stock and the village exhaled after all the excitement of the festive period. The decorations came down, the trees were recycled and things went back to normal. Although she enjoyed the bustle and liveliness the visitors always brought with them, Alice always thought that January was when the locals were given Polwenna Bay back for themselves. For those few quiet weeks it was possible to walk the cliff paths alone or have a fireside seat in the pub without having to wait for a group of walkers to finish their drinks and move on. You could even, if you so wished, drive a car through the narrow streets to the marina without having to reverse several times for terrified tourists who'd been lured by their satnavs into the warren of lanes.

Yes, that was what January was usually like – but this year was a year unlike any other. As Alice made her way down from Seaspray with her shopping basket on her arm, she realised that, even six days on from the big storm, the village was just as busy as it had been on New Year's

Day. In fact, she'd go as far as to say that it was busier. The main street bustled with visitors; Patsy's Pasties was doing a roaring trade and Silver Starr's shop Magic Moon was offering half-price tarot readings. Even Davey's Locker was open for business – which wasn't surprising really, since the beach was as packed now as it usually was in August. Apart from the weather being grey and bitterly cold, the only real difference was that these visitors were armed with shovels rather than brightly coloured plastic spades from Merlin's Gifts, and instead of wielding windbreaks they were waving metal detectors over the wet sand.

Treasure-hunting fever had hit Polwenna Bay big time.

Alice sighed. She wasn't convinced this was a good thing. Issie's discovery of the *Isabella* and the widespread press coverage that had followed had caused a surge of visitors to pour into the village, all intent on finding Black Jack Jago's loot. Forget the National Lottery with its odds higher than the International Space Station; everyone was convinced that riches beyond their wildest dreams were just the bleep of a metal detector away. Added to that, some of the national press had managed to tie in pictures of the latest hunky actor playing Ross Poldark, attracting female fans hopeful of bumping into him. Guesthouses were taking bookings, usually empty holiday cottages were full, and the more enterprising villagers were finding creative ways of cashing in on the hype. Today Alice had noticed Black Jack Burgers as lunch specials in the pub, and she'd discovered that Silver Starr's shop was now selling crystals to help find the treasure. There was even an advert in the window of the village shop, offering to rent metal detectors at "reasonable rates". Catching sight of this just as she was about to go in to buy her groceries, Alice tutted to herself.

"If you want to rent one, I'll give you twenty percent off," offered Mickey Davey, peering over Alice's shoulder and almost asphyxiating her in a cloud of Old Spice. "I got a deal on twenty off a geezer I know down Penge Market. They do the job a treat. You'll find the treasure by teatime. Guaranteed."

"I won't, because it doesn't exist," Alice said tartly. Honestly, the absolute brass neck of some people. The man had only been here five minutes and already he was using the village to line his own pockets.

Mickey Davey shrugged the burly shoulders beneath his covert coat. "Your granddaughter doesn't think so, and neither do all those punters on the beach."

Alice was regretting ever telling Issie the story of Black Jack Jago. Unwittingly she'd created a monster. "The whole thing is just a silly bedtime story. Issie should know better."

"Ah, but it isn't just a story, is it?" Mickey's bright and beady eyes lit up like the neon display on a fruit machine. "'Course, they're still waiting for the boat to be carbon-dated, but word is they reckon it's the real deal. Ninety-nine percent confident, one of the boffins who was down here earlier said."

Alice hoped she didn't look as horrified as she felt. "So that just means an old ship was wrecked here. It must be one of hundreds."

"If the boat got here then the treasure did too. I feel it in my water," Mickey said. Then he winked. "Sure you don't want to hire a metal detector? It could be your lucky day."

"I doubt it," muttered Alice as he sauntered off, whistling *We're in the Money*. There was something about that man that set her teeth on edge. It was bad enough that he had her Jimmy delivering crates of pasties to Plymouth, without him encouraging all and sundry to dig up the beach.

At this rate the bay would soon resemble the surface of the moon. And when they realised that the loot wasn't buried on the beach after all, it was only a matter of time before they began to search all over the village…

Looking troubled, Alice pushed open the shop door. She was trying to fight a rising sense of panic. The beauty of Polwenna Bay was its sense of timelessness. Mysterious legends of smugglers and wreckers, saints and sinners, were as much a part of the place as the hard granite cliffs, pounding waves and calling gulls. The thought of several diggers, scores of metal detectors and hordes of visitors greedy for a find made her feel quite ill. This wasn't what Polwenna was about. Some things should remain buried in the past.

Take her history with Jonny St Milton, for example. No matter what he thought, the daft old fool, that was all long over and done with. Heaven only knew why he was so determined to resurrect it now.

"Must be going senile," she muttered. Besides, he'd let her down all those years ago, hadn't he? Just because he was old didn't mean he'd changed.

As usual the shop was full of villagers who'd popped in as much for their daily gossip as for their groceries. Breathing deeply to calm herself, Alice filled her basket with milk, bread and sausages for Morgan's supper later, then hunted for a copy of the local paper.

"None left," Betty Jago told Alice smugly when she enquired where the *Western Morning News* was. "There's a pull-out section on the *Isabella* and the treasure, see, and they've flown off the shelves."

"Everyone's looking for the treasure," piped up Betty's granddaughter Saffron, from the far end of the shop where she was stacking shelves. "The village is full."

"So I see," said Alice. "You'd think people here would have more sense than to encourage such nonsense."

"Issie says it's true," said Saffron. She was a sweet girl but her IQ was on a par with the tins of beans she was lining up; she'd probably have believed Issie if she'd said the moon was made of cream cheese. Not for the first time, Alice found herself wishing that her granddaughter wasn't such a big influence in the village.

"Issie gets carried away."

"It's good for the village, though." Betty crossed her arms over her ample bosom and fixed Alice with a determined look. "My takings have been double what they usually are in January. Lots of the cottages are rented out too. Even old Ed Courtly's place by the cave has been taken. It's got a hellava damp problem too – always did, even before the storm."

Alice couldn't argue with that. Beach Cottage had belonged to an old fisherman who'd barely changed it since Noah was in nappies. That even this tired cottage was rented out in the middle of winter was proof of the current obsession with Black Jack Jago and his hoard.

"I agree. It *is* good news for the village, especially after the flooding," Sheila Keverne chipped in, poking her head around the vegetable display. "Businesses here need all the help they can get."

"Like Pollard and Son Building?" Alice suggested mildly as she handed Betty a ten-pound note. "They seem very busy all of a sudden. Have they fixed the vicarage roof yet, Sheila? Or are they still busy giving quotes for all the storm damage?"

Big and Little Rog Pollard were both claiming that the flooding wasn't anything to do with them; no, according to them it was the fault of the local council for not paying them to clear the drains and gullies last year. It seemed that a sense of civic duty alone had not been payment enough for them to do the job regardless. Big Rog was quite indignant about it all, and Little Rog had almost come to blows with Joe Penhalligan over the flood in Cobble Cottage. In the meantime, they'd picked up lots of extra work caused by the storm; rumour had it that they'd ordered a brand new van. None of this would help the vicar much. Yesterday, when Alice had popped up to the vicarage to see Jules, her poor friend had needed her wellies just to venture into the kitchen to make them both a cup of tea.

"I've asked Mr Pollard to have look," Sheila said huffily. She took her duties as verger and member of the Parochial Church Council very seriously. "I'll ask him again when I see him."

"Good luck with that," said Alice.

"You're in a very bad mood this morning, Alice," remarked Betty, as she counted out the change.

"It's about to get a whole lot worse," Alice muttered, catching sight of Jonny St Milton entering the shop. This was all she needed. He'd been pestering her every day since New Year's Eve by walking up to Seaspray and asking her out to dinner. The silly old fool had a dicky heart and Alice had told him over and over again her answer was "no" and that the climb up was going to kill him. Jonny's only answer had been to shrug and say that he'd rather die in the attempt than take no for an answer.

"Alice!" beamed Jonny, waving at her delightedly. "What a lovely surprise to find you here!"

"It's not a surprise at all. I shop here every morning," Alice said sharply. "Whereas you, Jonny St Milton, have never shopped in the village in the past sixty years."

He laid a hand over his tweed-covered chest. "That's harsh. I often come down to The Ship for a pint."

"Going drinking in the pub doesn't count as shopping," said Alice.

"Technically it does," Jonny disagreed, affably. "I'm buying something, aren't I? Isn't that shopping?"

She snorted. "Beer isn't shopping!"

"Not even in an off-licence?" he asked. "Or in a supermarket?"

Alice thought hard for a moment and was annoyed to find that she was lost for a retort.

"You always did have an answer for everything," she sighed, taking her shopping bag and marching out of the shop.

"Not everything," Jonny admitted, following her. "I got some things really wrong, Ally, and the only answer I have for that is that I was young and stupid."

"And now you're old and stupid!" She spun around, the carrier bag bashing painfully against her calves. "Just go home, Jonny. It's too late and we're too old for this nonsense. You said it before – we missed our time."

To Alice's distress her voice caught as she spoke. Was it possible that even after a lifetime the old hurt was still there? Who was the silly old fool now?

Jonny shook his white head. "It's never too late. I know we don't have much time left but at least we still have *some*, so let's not waste it. Give me another chance and I promise I won't let you down again."

Alice took a breath and was about to give him her usual sharp reply, but was surprised to discover that her heart wasn't in it. Maybe it was because he'd used the long-forgotten pet name or perhaps it was because of the hopeful expression on his lined face. She wasn't sure, but either way the stinging retort she'd been about to volley back had withered on her lips.

Jonny reached forward and took the shopping bag for her, albeit with some difficulty given that he was leaning heavily on his ornate walking stick. None of the standard NHS issue for a St Milton, Alice thought wryly as she watched him trying to balance the weight of the bag without looking too wobbly. Jonny's family never had favoured the ordinary things in life. No wonder he'd married the doctor's daughter. Millicent Jago, with her blonde pin curls and private-school background, had been far more suitable than the daughter of the housekeeper. And as for carrying things – hadn't that been Alice's job? From coal to laundry to saucepans, it was she rather than the son and heir of the house who'd been the one to carry heavy objects.

"Give that back. You'll fall over," she warned as he swayed dangerously.

"Never! I wouldn't dream of letting a lady carry her own shopping."

Alice laughed. "Since when was I a lady? For heaven's sake! Give that bag to me before you fall over and break your hip."

"Only if you'll come and have a spot of lunch with me," Jonny said, sensing her weakening and pressing home his advantage. Besides, he was clearly struggling to hold the bag, and Alice was shocked to see just how frail he'd become. A sudden image of arms holding her close and merry grey eyes twinkling down into hers darted through her memory, so vivid and fresh that it was a shock to see a stooped old man there now – even if the twinkle in those eyes was exactly the same as it had been all those years ago.

She raised her own heavenwards. "If it means we don't have to call the ambulance, then I suppose I don't have any choice."

He passed the shopping bag over. "You may need to take my arm too, just in case I stumble. Or put yours around my waist, if you like?"

"Good try, but I think you'll probably make it," Alice told him. She was laughing as she said this, though, and together they made the short journey through the village to the pub.

It was only noon and The Ship was quiet. A merry fire was blazing in the hearth and for once the chairs next to it were empty. It was the perfect place to sit and look out at the seascape. Or it would have been, if the window hadn't been filled with flowers.

"Have a seat," Jonny said to Alice. "I'll grab us a couple of menus."

He was breathless from the short climb up the steps to the pub, and Alice frowned. She was just about to argue and fetch the menus herself, when Adam Harper pre-empted them by producing two laminated sheets with a flourish.

"We've got the daily specials too," Adam added, gesturing at the blackboard behind him. "May I recommend the soup? It's cauliflower cheese. Rose made it fresh this morning and it comes with a big slab of crusty bread. Or catch of the day is monkfish, if you'd rather."

Jonny smiled. "Crusty bread, eh? Lucky I don't have dentures. That sounds good."

"Certainly does," Alice agreed. "Same for me."

"Two soups," Adam said. "Coming right up."

They settled into their seats and ordered wine too, which seemed rather decadent in the middle of the day. Still, as Jonny said, they were unlikely to develop an alcohol habit at their stage in life, and if they did then so what? As they sipped their drinks and chatted, Alice felt the warmth of the fire spread over her and the tensions of earlier slip away. The whole ridiculous treasure-hunting fad would be over in a week or so and life in Polwenna Bay would go back to normal – and now that she'd agreed to have a meal with Jonny St Milton, he'd leave her in peace too. She was surprised to find that this thought didn't make her as happy as she'd thought it would.

They were each working their way through a huge bowl of Rose's delicious soup when the pub door flew open and something that looked like a triffid bowled in.

"Delivery for Issie Tremaine, again," announced the triffid. "Where shall I leave them? Window, same as last time? Or is here on the bar OK, since you're running out of room over there?"

Before Adam could answer, a huge bouquet of fat pink roses and waxy white lilies was deposited in front of the beer pumps, revealing a young lad dusting pollen from his jacket and grinning.

"See you the same time tomorrow, I guess?" he said.

"I hope not," answered Adam, regarding the blooms despondently. "This is playing havoc with my hay fever." He rubbed his eyes, then sniffed. "Hay fever in January is just taking the mickey."

The delivery boy, halfway out the door now, winked over his shoulder. "Somebody loves Issie Tremaine, that's for sure."

"Well, I bloody don't," grumbled the unhappy landlord. "Aitchoo! Aitchoo! If this carries on, I'm going to have to sack your granddaughter, Mrs T. She's costing me a fortune in antihistamines."

Alice frowned as she glanced around the pub. Goodness, it could double for a florist's. "Are all these flowers really for Issie?"

Adam nodded. "She's been sent a bouquet every day since New Year's Eve." To Jonny he added, "Your grandson's certainly persistent, I'll give him that."

"These are from Teddy?" Jonny asked.

"Certainly are, Mr SM. He's smitten." Adam blew his nose loudly. "I wish he wasn't. Aitchoo! Aitchoo! Issie won't take them home because she says she's not interested in him. She told Rose to bin them."

"Rather harsh of her," remarked Jonny, fixing Alice with a knowing look. "I can't imagine who she takes after."

"Oh dear," said Alice. This was just typical of her granddaughter. Issie's thoughtless behaviour, from talking to the press to kissing Teddy St Milton, was causing havoc. Alice shivered. She had a very bad feeling about all of this.

"It's like Kew bloody Gardens in here, since Rose won't chuck them out. Maybe you could tell him to stop?" Adam asked, looking hopeful.

Jonny swirled his wine thoughtfully. "There's no point doing that, I'm afraid. No point at all."

"Why not?" asked Alice. It seemed a reasonable enough request.

In answer, Jonny reached forward and took her hand. The unexpected sensation of his fingers weaving with hers took Alice's breath away. And she looked up in shock. Surely her stomach wasn't fluttering with butterflies? Not at her age and after all these years? No, it must be indigestion from that rich soup.

"Because," he replied, his eyes holding her gaze just as firmly as his hand held her fingers, "if my grandson takes after me, when he finds the woman he wants above all others, nothing will persuade him to give her up."

He raised her hand to his lips and kissed it. Suddenly Alice Tremaine was a teenage girl again, with her world spinning out of control.

"Nothing," Jonny repeated, so softly that only Alice could hear. "Absolutely nothing."

Chapter 10

"And if you look to your left, ladies and gents, you might just be able to make out the Eddystone Lighthouse. 'Course, that weren't there back in the eighteenth century, and any ships had to take their chance."

Luke huddled into his coat and squinted at the murky smudge that was what passed for the horizon in this strange and small country. He thought he could just about make out a grey blob in the distance, but it was hard to tell because just about everything else was grey too. From the sky to the sea to the faces of the tea-drinking Brits, everything in England was just so relentlessly grey. He had profound sympathy for the Spanish sailors who'd left the hot sun and lemon groves of their own land, only to perish in the icy English Channel. He supposed the one thing worse than feeling as cold and as lost as he did was to be lured into a watery grave by the natives. It was a thought almost too horrible to contemplate.

"We're going to steam a few miles westerly now to where the ship went down," the skipper of the small tripping boat was saying to his passengers. "It's a bit lumpy out here, mind, so best you hold on."

Lumpy was an understatement. The sea was rough and several passengers were already turning green. Taking advantage of those who weren't from local parts wasn't an activity confined to the eighteenth century, Luke thought wryly. Even though the conditions were far from ideal for boat rides, fishermen from this insane village (and it *was* insane, because who the hell had ever heard of a place with roads you couldn't even fit a car through?) were taking groups of tourists out to sea on wreck-hunting trips. Small fishing boats crammed with plastic garden chairs and decorated with handmade signs were vying for trade down in the harbour. They were charging the handsome sum of ten English pounds to take visitors out to sea on what was, Luke was sure, a wild goose chase. So what if the ship had gone down several miles off the coast? The wreck was on the beach. Besides, the treasure had been spirited inland; he was convinced of this. Only curiosity and the desire to see the wild rugged coastline from the water had made him part with a crisp brown note.

As the boat steamed westwards, Luke looked back over the stern, watching the lacy wake peel away and the village grow smaller. He'd never in his life seen a place like this Polwenna Bay. It was like something out of a story book. He had to admit that the place was pretty, with all its quaint cottages, but getting to it had been a nightmare. The United Kingdom's so-called motorways all seemed to be dotted with potholes and lines of cones like some bizarre version of *Grand Theft Auto*. And then there was the jet lag, not to mention having to drive on the wrong side of the road and use a stick shift. As if that wasn't challenging enough, there was the whole business of wiggling a tiny car through winding lanes that left only inches to spare either side of the wing mirrors. By the time he'd arrived at his destination, Luke had been ready to drop.

Maybe Stella was right and this was a ridiculous idea. In the warmth of Key West, Luke had been utterly convinced that he was onto something big – but several days on and a mile out into the English Channel, he was starting to wonder. He couldn't have felt more alien if he'd landed on Mars.

"Honey, have you ever been to England?" Stella had asked when, fired up with enthusiasm and still in his shorts, Luke had bowled into Zara's to tell her his plan.

"No, but I've always wanted to visit," he'd replied. "My mom's crazy about the place. She loves all the history and the royal family."

Luke was pretty crazy about history himself. History had been his major before he'd come back to help Mal. England was full of cool old stuff, Luke had thought with a flare of excitement. Romans. Castles. Ancient buildings. It would be awesome to visit anyway, even without the added thrill of following a hunch.

But Stella had just laughed. "Yeah, I love Hugh Grant and Prince Harry is a hottie, but seriously, honey? England in January? It's gonna be real cold."

"It's cold there even in the summer!" one of her friends had piped up. "You'd have to be mad to go there now. The Brits come to Florida for the winter if they can afford it."

Luke nodded. He knew this was true. Snowbirds from all over the world flocked to the Keys in the winter.

"We're all flying down to Grand Cayman for a few weeks' R and R," Stella had continued, laying her hand on his arm and then running her nails along his bicep. "I need to sort out my accounts and do some business. Why don't you come too? Forget this crazy idea, baby, and just kick back for a week or two. Maybe we can even have a look at getting a dive boat later on?"

Luke had scrutinised her slowly from the top of her platinum-blonde head to the tips of her scarlet toenails. Stella was gorgeous, there was no denying that, and it would be easy to go along with what she wanted. The idea was more than tempting: he'd no longer have to struggle and strive to make ends meet. She was offering him sponsorship and luxury, an existence that would suit most guys to perfection. But Luke wasn't most guys.

The image of a girl with bright blue eyes and honey-coloured braids danced in front of Stella's surgery-perfect profile, and Luke's pulse quickened. While new adventures and endless possibilities existed, he could never chain himself down – even if the chains were made of gold.

"Excuse us," Luke had said to the rest of the dinner party, taking Stella's arm and leading her onto the water terrace. He'd come to say goodbye, and that was what he was going to do. "I'm going to England. There's a ship that's washed up and maybe there's treasure too. I'm going there to give finding it my best shot."

"You want to find treasure? Well, fine. Everyone knows there are countless lost ships off Florida. Let me sponsor you and set you up properly."

"I can't accept that, Stella." Luke had replied steadily.

"Why not? It's what you've always wanted, isn't it?" she'd insisted. Her breasts, swelling beneath the silk of her dress, rose and fell with agitation. "I've not known you long but we've had fun. Why not accept my offer? Why make your life harder than it needs to be?"

He'd shrugged. "I guess that's me all around, making life tougher than it could be. I've enjoyed your company, Stella, and you're a sexy, gorgeous woman, but I'm not going to take advantage of the fun we've had."

She'd laughed and, stepping forward, brushed against him. Luke had felt the heat of her perfumed body through the flimsy dress, and momentarily he was torn between leaving and staying.

"You're sweet," Stella had said. "Do you really think you're taking advantage of me? I'm fifty-one, honey. I'm rich. I'm single and I'm very horny right now. Who's taking advantage of who?"

She was spoilt, pampered and used to having whatever she wanted. That she couldn't have him only made her want him more, Luke realised. The sensation of her breasts against his chest made his head spin, though, and it had taken a great deal of willpower to choose England rather than her.

Even though he'd made his mind up, Stella had insisted on being a part of his new venture.

"I want to do something with all this money," she'd said, when he'd protested. "Stocks and shares are so boring. It'll be fun for me to have a part in something so unusual – and it'll drive my girlfriends wild with jealousy. No strings either, honey. Strictly business. I'll get my lawyers to draw up something official. Sixty percent to me, forty to you?"

He'd smiled ironically. "Nice try. How about sixty to me, forty to you?"

"Fifty-five to you, forty-five to me?" Stella had offered, holding out her hand.

Luke had hesitated but he needed a sponsor; there was no way around that practicality. The dregs of his checking account wouldn't even buy him a bus ticket to Miami. If the deal was official then Luke figured that Stella's dollars were as good as anyone's. Their relationship, such as it was, had moved now from pleasure to business, and this was the way he was determined to keep it. Whether Stella thought the same was anyone's guess, but she'd been as good as her word: the next morning he'd met with her lawyers to hammer out a sponsorship deal.

Stella would pay for the flights and cover his living costs, plus anything else he needed. In return, whatever he found was to be split with her.

He'd not been back to her hotel room. Bored, sexy Stella would have to find her entertainment elsewhere. He couldn't imagine it would be too hard; Key West was filled with young men looking for fun.

So this was how, almost a week on from watching that snippet of rolling news, Luke Dawson was staying in a small Cornish village, renting a very damp cottage that was practically paddling in the sea, and driving the smallest car he'd ever seen in his life. His jaw had almost hit the steering wheel when he'd seen the price they paid for gas here. Jet-lagged and almost seeing double from the effort of driving from Heathrow to Cornwall through the endless rain, Luke had managed to park his car in the allotted bay (narrowly missing the big gold Bentley that some imbecile had parked well into Luke's space), then staggered through the dark and drizzle before finally collapsing through the door of the tiniest house he'd ever set foot in. He'd been too tired to really take in his surroundings; even the musty smell and damp bed linen hadn't stopped him from passing out for almost twenty hours.

Today he'd risen just before lunch, ripped from sleep by squawking seagulls. Pulling open the curtains, he'd seen the village for the first time. It was stunning, if bleak, and for a while he'd just gawped at the view. Florida was pancake-flat, and its sparkling ocean was so bright in the glancing sunshine that the first thing he usually did was reach for his shades. Polwenna Bay was the antithesis of all that. Its steep valley sides rose sharply from the harbour, clad in deepest greens and darkest browns, and dotted with cottages that seemed to cling on for grim death. The sea was pewter and the sun was as coy as a teenage girl; mostly it hid behind thick clouds, although it peeked out every now and again when it thought nobody was looking. Seeing that the tide was in, and alarmed by the amount of people wandering around with metal detectors, Luke had decided he'd better haul ass and start exploring. The remains of the ship would be underwater for a good few hours yet, so the next best thing had seemed like a boat ride along the coast.

Seemed was the operative word. Fifteen minutes into the trip, Luke had come to the conclusion that he wasn't going to learn much from it at all. Sure, the scenery was spectacular in its own kind of fashion, and the big man behind the wheel of the boat was telling some awesome tales about wreckers and smugglers – but there was a frustrating lack of hard facts. The tourists were lapping up the stories (or at least, those of them who weren't leaning over the side of the boat were), but Luke doubted there was much truth in any of these tales.

And he was so goddamn cold!

He'd been in England for less than forty-eight hours, but already he was certain he was getting seasonal affective disorder. Where was the sun? The colours? The warm breezes? Everything was sludge green or mud brown here, and he included the sea in that list. What the hell had the Brits done to it? Luke was used to deep blue water, gin-clear and teeming with colourful fish, but the sea here was murky and freezing cold. If Luke was ever brave enough, or crazy enough, to attempt a dive here, he probably wouldn't be able to see more than a foot ahead anyway – and he'd need to be wearing more rubber than something from a bondage dungeon. And as for girls in bikinis – one of the big perks of working a dive boat – well, they were all wrapped up in jeans and sweaters. Luke didn't blame them a bit; there was no way he'd risk baring any flesh here. He'd probably get frostbite.

Jeez. What a place. Give him Florida any day.

Luke pulled up the hood of his new coat and plunged his fingers deeper into the pockets. He could even see his breath clouding the air, and his nose had gone numb. It was starting to rain again, too. He hoped the trip to the alleged wreck site of the *Isabella* would be worth the effort. The swell he could cope with fine, but catching pneumonia wasn't quite what he'd had in mind when he'd flown out of Miami.

"This is where the ship went down!" announced the skipper, knocking the engine into neutral. Folding his arms over his enormous belly, he surveyed his captive audience triumphantly. "Us Penhalligans have lived here for centuries, and I'm telling you that this is the spot! Over two hundred years ago, the *Isabella* hit rocks no more than fifty yards from here. We call them the Shindeeps because the water's that shallow. We'll go no closer than this. Many a boat's met her end here."

"You don't know that for sure, Dad. There's no proof," pointed out the young man who'd taken the wheel. Clad in a smock, jeans and rigger boots, he was clearly a fisherman too, but one who was taking his father's tour with a big pinch of sea salt. "It could have been within a mile of here," he added helpfully.

The father shot his son a look that should have sent him straight to the seabed. "You wrecked a boat here yourself Joe, my boy. How much proof do you need?"

Joe bit his lip and said nothing. Luke shivered. This was an unlucky place; he could feel it. Having spent most of his life on the ocean, he'd encountered his fair share of watery graveyards. He glanced across the sea. Sure enough, the waves were boiling around a bank of razor-edged rocks that lurked just beneath the surface. The lights of the village were hidden now by the curve of the coastline, but the headland before the bay was in full view. It was easy to see how, if a man had been standing there with a lantern, the crew of a ship might have been fooled into thinking they were safe to approach the land. It was perfectly possible that the *Isabella* had foundered here, and equally possible that several smaller boats had managed to reach her in order to steal her cargo. The wreck could have washed up onto the beach many years later and then been covered by sand over the centuries.

A frown line deepened between his eyes. Yes, the *Isabella*'s treasure might well have made it to shore. The coastline was riddled with inlets and caves – his rented cottage was only yards from one – and any smuggler with a good knowledge of the tunnels beneath the cliffs could have hidden their loot.

His skin tingled again with excitement. Although this place was cold and bleak, there was something about it that made him feel alive.

Now that the skipper had delivered his speech and a fair few passengers were beginning to be sick, the boat was heading back to the harbour. The rolling of the sea and the smell of the diesel were like oxygen to Luke, but he had every sympathy for the unhappy tourists. His stomach was lurching too, except that in his case this was due to hunger: he hadn't eaten since a very glamorous flight attendant had served the airplane meal. Luke grinned at the memory. That was probably the last bit of glamour he'd see for a while, judging by the raincoats and the way the people here walked along with their bodies bowed against the elements. The beautiful people of Florida with their butterscotch tans, micro shorts and designer shades seemed just as unbelievable now as this skipper's yarns of sea serpents and smugglers. Key West was another world.

The rain was easing a little now. By the time Luke had disembarked, weak sunshine was trickling across the village. Smoke drifted above the mossy rooftops and seagulls circled over the harbour. Small boats bobbed lazily in the marina, and at the foot of the harbour wall a small slither of sand was playing peek-a-boo with the waves. Luke checked his chunky dive watch. The tide was on the turn. Maybe in a few hours he could scramble over the rocks and have a look at what was left of this ship for himself. His stomach growled loudly. According to his body clock it was breakfast time – and what he wouldn't give for some pancakes and maple syrup! No hope of any of that here. What was it the Brits liked? A fry-up?

Hell, who cared what they ate here. He needed to find some food. On the way to the boat he'd spotted a pub alongside the quay. He'd find something there, Luke decided as he sprinted up the flight of steps that led to a heavy door, and he could thaw out for a bit in the warmth. Maybe he'd even have a drink.

He pushed open the door and instantly the scent of woodsmoke and stale beer coiled into his senses, mingled with the mouth-watering aroma of home-cooked food. Jeez, his mom would go mad for this place. With its low beams, small windows and crackling log fire, it was everything he'd imagined an English pub would be – and it looked like the perfect place to sit down and enjoy a hearty meal. It would probably take a little getting used to, though. The group of fishermen in the corner were playing a very loud game of dice, and there were dogs roaming about the place too. Luke had already observed that the English seemed to have dogs everywhere. Perhaps that was how they protected themselves in this country, instead of having the right to bear arms. Personally, Luke thought that dogs were preferable to guns anyhow.

A menu board covered in elaborate italic chalk writing proudly proclaimed that tomato soup was on a special and that the alarmingly named Spotty Dick was today's top pudding.

Spotty Dick? Seriously? Was this an example of the famously eccentric British humour?

Luke was stepping forward to take a closer look when he stopped dead in his tracks. The tingling feeling was back and his blood was coursing so swiftly through his veins that it was like a head rush. For a moment he could do nothing but stare. Behind the bar, oblivious to his arrival and wholly intent on pouring real ale, was none other than the girl with the golden braids.

It was her. It was Issie.

And what was more, at her throat glinted the very golden coin that had caught his attention five thousand miles and another world away.

Chapter 11

Issie noticed the stranger the second he stepped into The Ship. How could she not? As the door had swung open, she'd glanced up from the pint she was pulling and almost dropped the glass. Guys like this didn't walk into the pub very often.

In fact, they didn't walk into this pub at all.

For a moment he'd stood framed in the doorway, the sunlight glinting on the ringlets of dark brown hair that brushed his collar. There was an air of quiet strength and confidence about him, and as he approached the bar the man moved with the grace of a panther.

"Who's that?" breathed Silver Starr from her perch on a nearby bar stool.

Usually Issie would have quipped that if the local psychic didn't know then there was no hope for the rest of them, but on this occasion she was rendered speechless. The stranger was staring at her as though he wanted to rip her most guarded secrets from the depths of her soul. Her breath caught in her throat as the greenest eyes she'd ever seen transfixed her.

"My pint!" wailed Big Roger Pollard as frothing Pol Brew foamed over the rim of the glass and sloshed into the drip tray. He made a dive to save it but only succeeded in knocking the glass flying. Seconds later, beer and shards of glass were everywhere.

With a cry of dismay, Issie dragged her attention back to the job in hand and busied herself mopping up beer and sweeping up the mess, while Big Rog grumbled and Adam Harper muttered darkly about docking her wages. Red-faced and furious with herself, Issie fixed her gaze on the dustpan and brush, trying desperately not to feel as though a bolt had gone straight through her. This was ridiculous, Issie scolded herself as she wrapped the broken glass up in newspaper. She was a woman in her twenties, not a teenager. Fancy being distracted just because a fit guy happened to walk into the bar. Pathetic!

Issie lobbed the balled-up newspaper into the bin and took a deep breath before attending to the newcomer. Straightening up to face him, she was met once again by those long-lashed green eyes smiling at her.

"I was gonna order a beer but I'm not sure I can risk it," he said, and a corner of his mouth lifted. "Will you pour mine all over the floor too?"

An American? In the village pub, in January? This was almost unheard of.

"It's an ancient Cornish custom," she told him, flicking her braids back from her face and meeting his gaze head on. "If you think you can handle it, then feel free to order."

"Far be it from me to disrespect ancient customs," the stranger replied. His slow drawl brought to mind sunshine and open spaces, a world away from the jumbled cottages and leaden skies of Cornwall. "As long as it isn't any of that Morris dancing," he added. "I have two left feet."

"Morris dancing is strictly for locals only, I'm afraid," Issie deadpanned.

"Aw hell, I was kinda looking forward to that. I guess beer it is then."

Issie waited for him to make a choice. "Which beer would you like?" she prompted, when no further information came.

"Huh?"

"Welcome to Cornwall. We serve lots of real ales. Pol Brew, Doom Bar, Tinners and Hooky, for starters."

His brow crinkled. "Uh, you lost me at the first one. How about you choose?"

"Pol Brew," Issie decided firmly, reaching for a glass and pulling a pint. "It's the local ale."

"That'll put hairs on your chest, boy," chipped in Big Rog, raising his glass. "Cheers!"

Issie couldn't see the American's chest, but she was certain that it would be muscular and smooth – and warm beneath her fingertips too, if she were to skim them over the tanned flesh. Her face grew warm at the thought; it was just as well the pub was so dimly lit.

Once the drink was poured and safely in the stranger's sun-browned hand, Issie busied herself with the till and tried to calm her racing heart. Honestly! What on earth was the matter with her? She must have been back in the village too long if one good-looking guy was having this effect on her. Besides, he wasn't even her type. Having grown up in a seaside town, Issie was more than used to young outdoorsy guys with tanned firm bodies, slightly-too-long hair and a wicked twinkle in their eye. Her brothers, particularly Nick and Zak, rocked this kind of look to perfection – as did the Penhalligan boys – and it worked wonders with female holidaymakers. The local lads got through girls like Big Rog got through beer, but Issie had always thought herself totally immune. No wonder she'd fallen so fast and so hard for neatly cut dark hair, gold-rimmed glasses and intellectual conversation...

She stole a look from under her lashes at the American, just to reassure herself that he really wasn't her type, and was jolted by a sharp tug of longing. He was seated on the furthest bar stool, one long lean leg swinging idly – and when he caught her looking he smiled, the flash of perfect teeth shockingly white in his tanned face.

"Cheers," he said, raising his glass and tipping back the golden liquid. The muscles in his strong throat rippled and Issie looked away hastily. When she glanced back he was wiping his mouth with the back of his hand, and his nose was wrinkled in disgust.

"Goddamn! This is gross! Your beer's warm!"

There was a ripple of amused laughter from the crowd of locals at the bar.

"We drink our beer warm here," Little Rog told him helpfully.

"No shit." The stranger shook his head in bewilderment. "Why would you do that?"

"I think what you might have wanted was lager," suggested Caspar Owen kindly. "When I was on my book tour of the States I drank cold Budweiser."

"Girl's drink," scoffed Big Rog. "Just right for you though, Cassie!"

Caspar, clad much as usual in a frilly shirt, neckerchief and flowing velvet coat, took this good-naturedly enough, by flipping Big Rog the bird.

"You're in England now! Get that beer down your neck and have a pasty," boomed Eddie Penhalligan, striding into the pub and settling himself onto his usual bar stool. "Or did my trip make you feel too sick to eat?"

"Your boat didn't, but this beer sure does." The stranger turned his wide green eyes to Issie imploringly. "Honey, could you translate for me? What the hell's a *pasty*?"

There was a chorus of horrified disbelief from the regulars.

"Kick him out!" said Big Rog to Adam Harper. "Heathen!"

"Pasties are the food of the gods," said Eddie, patting a stomach that had clearly seen more than its fair share.

"Food of the peasants, more like," sniffed Caspar. To the stranger he added, "It's rather like a pie. It's a kind of pastry filled with steak and potato and turnip, and it's what the miners here used to eat."

"Swede! Not turnip, you blooming emmet! And diced steak with onions!" bellowed Eddie.

"And no carrots," added Little Rog.

All the locals nodded. A carrot in a pasty was a serious issue indeed.

"To be fair, I didn't actually mention carrots," Caspar pointed out. Nevertheless, a very heated discussion soon arose regarding the correct filling of this local delicacy. Before long, Caspar and Eddie were on the verge of having fisticuffs over whether swede and turnips were one and the same thing, and the Pollards had to drag them outside to cool off.

"Carry on and I'll bar you all," Adam called after them.

"Jeez, I'm sorry I asked," said the American to Issie. "Are they always like that?"

Fetching a bottle of Bud Light from the fridge and popping the top, Issie passed it to him and tipped the ale in his abandoned pint glass away. "Pretty much; they just can't help squabbling. Sorry about that anyway. Have this on me as a welcome to Cornwall."

"Hey, thanks! That's real nice of you." He raised the bottle and smiled at her, a cute and quirky smile that made Issie's pulse skitter. "I'm Luke. Luke Dawson."

As if in a trance she let Luke Dawson shake her hand, and a delicious thrill chased a path down her spine. Unused to feeling like this, Issie could hardly think straight. She took comfort from the fact that all the other women in the pub were looking at him admiringly – even her grandmother, who was enjoying lunch with Jonny St Milton for the second time in a week. Whatever was *that* all about?

"And you are?" the American prompted, while Issie stood gazing into those green eyes of his.

"Oh! I'm Issie. Issie Tremaine."

"Nice to meet you, Issie Tremaine," Luke Dawson said. "Thanks for rescuing me from warm British beer."

She laughed. "No problem. Not sure I can save you from pasties though."

The broad shoulders shrugged. "Hey, no big deal. I guess since I'm gonna be staying here for a while I should get to eat the local food?"

"You're staying in the village?" Having had Luke Dawson down as yet another day-tripper here amid all the hype, Issie was both surprised and pleased.

"Sure am. I've rented this damp old place just up from the beach."

"Edmund Courtly's house?" Issie felt sorry for him if this was the case. That cottage might have amazing views across the bay but it made the River Wenn look dry.

He nodded. "Yeah, that's it. Everywhere else was booked. This place is crazy busy."

"We've had an old galleon uncovered by winter storms, so everyone's down to look at it and hunt for the supposed treasure," Issie explained. To be honest she couldn't quite believe the response to the find and was starting to regret opening her mouth on national television.

"Yeah, I know. That's why I'm here too. I saw it on the news."

"It was on the news in America?" Issie couldn't believe it. Seriously? She'd been on the telly in America?

"Sure was. I caught it in Florida, and since I majored in history and I'm real interested in the smuggling trade in eighteenth-century England, I thought I'd have a vacation and do some research."

"No way! I was reading history too, and the local stories about smuggling were what got me interested in it. Are you writing a paper on something to do with all this then? Is it for your masters?"

Luke Dawson paused. "Uh, yeah, something like that."

Issie was on the brink of asking him more about this when Adam Harper flicked her with a beer towel and made a sarky comment about whether or not she actually wanted her job.

"I'll get you fired if we keep talking. Perhaps I should go find one of those pasties for lunch instead. Maybe catch you later?" Luke said, necking his beer and setting the empty bottle down on the bar. "When do you finish?"

"Five," Issie said. Lord, that was three hours away. She wasn't sure how she could bear to stay here all that time now.

"How about I meet you at five then? If you want?"

If she wanted? Like, duh!

"Sure," was all she said. "Sounds good."

Issie pretended to turn her attention to stacking the glass washer, doing her best to look as though she was intent on this task, when in reality she was watching Luke cross the pub with that panther-like grace. He was just at the door when another man blocked his way.

Teddy St Milton.

Oh crap. All the time she'd been chatting to Luke, Teddy must have been sitting in the corner, working his way through his JD and watching them from the shadows. He'd been so odd since New Year's Eve, sending all those bouquets and *accidentally* bumping into her wherever she happened to go. It was almost like having a stalker.

Issie made a mental note not to snog guys who were keener on her than she was on them. Especially if they were used to getting their own way.

"Adam! I think there's going to be trouble," Issie hissed.

"There will be if he sends any more flowers," the landlord muttered. Then his eyes narrowed when he realised what was going on. "Issie Tremaine, I sometimes think having you behind the bar is more trouble than it's worth."

Issie ignored her boss. Over the years she'd had several stints working in The Ship, and Adam had been only too glad to have her back again when Kelly, his previous barmaid, had defected to The Plump Seagull. Issie was good at her job and customers had started coming back especially to see her, which the landlord knew full well. She'd probably been making him a fortune already.

"Excuse me, buddy, but you're in my way," Luke was saying mildly. At over six feet tall and with a muscular build, he made Teddy seem slightly smaller than usual.

"Not nearly as much as you're in mine, *buddy*," Teddy St Milton snarled. He took a step forward and, looking upwards at the tall American, added, "Stay away from Issie, do you hear me?"

Luke raised an eyebrow. "Are you telling me who I can talk to? Are you for real?"

"Bloody right I am. I saw the way you were looking at her."

"I'm not sure I care for what you're insinuating." Luke spoke quietly but there was no mistaking the strength in his voice. "We were just chatting."

"I don't care what you were doing. Just keep the hell away from her!"

"Or what?" Luke asked softly. There was a mocking light in his eyes now. "Last time I looked, buddy, it was the twenty-first century, where women are free to talk to whoever they choose. At least, that's how it is in the USA."

"Or I'll show you how we do things in England!" Teddy threatened.

In answer, Luke Dawson threw back his head and laughed. "Pasties at dawn, is it? Or maybe a warm-beer duel? Whatever. It's all cool with me. Just name the time and the place, buddy."

"I'm not your buddy and you can take the piss all you want. I'm not afraid of you," Teddy blustered, putting up his fists. "How about right here?"

Teddy's raised voice attracted the attention of everyone else in the pub, including his grandfather and Alice, who looked over from their seats by the fire.

Luke's eyebrows had shot into his curly hair now. "Are you seriously asking me for a fight?"

"All right, son, that'll do." Adam Harper stepped forward and laid a large hand on Teddy's Barbour-clad shoulder. "Why don't you step outside and cool down?"

But Teddy shook him off. "Why don't you tell *him* to go outside?"

"Because *he's* not had too much to drink and isn't making a fool of himself!" snapped Issie.

What on earth had she been thinking, getting involved with Teddy? Yes, he was boy-band cute with his floppy blond hair and designer clothes, but he was also spoilt and petulant and, unfortunately for him, paled into insignificance next to a guy like Luke. If she hadn't already regretted kissing Teddy on New Year's Eve, then Issie certainly did now. That was it; she really was giving up the booze.

Adam crossed his arms over his chest. "On your way, Ted, there's a good lad."

Teddy raised his chin. "Make me."

"Excuse me, Adam, but is there a problem?" Jonny St Milton, leaning heavily on his stick, had left his fireside seat and joined them. His face had a grey tinge and he looked exhausted.

"Not if your grandson does as he's told," replied the landlord.

"Edward, come and sit down with me," Jonny said.

"No way!" Teddy's cheeks were bright with anger as he jabbed a forefinger at Luke. "He's insulted me! No one insults a St Milton."

Issie rounded on him. "Well I do! Try this for size: Teddy St Milton, you're a moron! And if I didn't think so already then I certainly do now!"

"Look, I was just leaving. I don't want to cause any trouble between you and your boyfriend," Luke said quickly.

"He's not my boyfriend," Issie said. Furious, she stood herself in between them. "He was never my boyfriend and he never will be. Besides, you're not causing trouble; he is! Stop making an idiot of yourself, Ted! Go home."

But Teddy St Milton, filled with the bravado that comes with several whiskies, was in no mood to listen to reason. If anything, Issie's words had only incensed him further. He lunged at Luke, who neatly sidestepped the punch. Teddy went hurtling into a table. Seconds later he was sprawled across the sticky pub floor, dripping with beer. The eyes of everyone in The Ship were on him now.

"Careful, bud," Luke said mildly. "You're gonna hurt yourself."

Issie couldn't help herself; Teddy looked so utterly ridiculous that she started laughing. Slowly, ripples of amusement spread around the pub. It seemed that everyone was sniggering – with the exception of Jonny and Alice, who looked mortified.

Luke held out a hand to Teddy but his conciliatory gesture was ignored. Instead Teddy picked himself up and marched to the door. With his fingers still on the handle, he turned to stare at Issie – and his black expression made the laughter die on her lips.

"You're going to wish you'd never done that," he told her softly.

Issie swallowed. All of a sudden her grandmother's warning about the dangers of playing with people's emotions was ringing in her ears. Issie had the uneasy feeling that she'd just made a very dangerous enemy.

Luke reached out and took her trembling hand.

"C'mon. I think we should get you the hell out of here."

Without so much as a second thought, Issie twined her fingers with those of this total stranger, and followed him into the chilly afternoon.

Chapter 12

"Who the hell," said Luke, "was that?"

He and Issie stood on the quayside. Their fingers were still tightly laced and as his questioning gaze met hers, Issie struggled for an answer. Lord, this was a tricky one. What exactly was Teddy St Milton to her?

"Forgive me, this is none of my business," Luke Dawson continued, "but if he is your boyfriend you really should think twice, because that dude has some serious anger issues."

Issie shook her head. She was still quite unable to believe the scene Teddy had caused in the pub. He wasn't her boyfriend; at least, she'd never viewed him this way. Teddy was an old friend and, although he'd often been away at boarding school, he was part of the Polwenna Bay gang she'd known all her life. When she'd fled uni he'd been somebody fun to hang out with and a distraction from all the complications of Mark; Issie had never for a minute believed that the time they'd shared was leading to something more serious. Teddy was cute-looking in a One Direction kind of way, had money coming out of his ears and drove a fast car – but there had to be more than that to make Issie want a relationship. She'd truly thought they were just having fun.

But Teddy, it now transpired, viewed things very differently.

"No. He's definitely not my boyfriend. He's just... just..." she struggled for words and was horrified to discover that she couldn't find them. "God, this sounds awful, but he's just somebody I've been hanging out with a bit. It's stupid and I should never have let it get this far."

Luke squeezed her hand and then released his grasp. "You don't need to explain. I've been in similar situations."

Issie stole a sideways glance at him. His face was sun-kissed and his nose was dusted with a cinnamon sprinkling of freckles. But it was his eyes that really drew her, as green as the deepest rock pools along the coast, and glittering with life and energy. Yes, she could well imagine that Luke Dawson understood *exactly* what her situation was. Women would elbow each other out of the way just to be with a man like him. And yet there was an aloofness about him that suggested he held back from getting too close to anyone.

"He's called Teddy St Milton and his family pretty much own most of Polwenna Bay," she told him.

"Kinda used to getting his own way, huh?"

"You could say that. His grandpa dotes on him. I suppose he's a bit of a spoilt brat, but to be honest I've never seen that side of him before."

"So it was all cool before I rocked up." Luke ran a hand through his springy curls. "Jeez. I've only been here five minutes and there's hell up. It doesn't bode well."

"It wasn't your fault. Teddy drinks a lot and he's got a bad temper. Anyway, we were only chatting."

Even as she said this, Issie knew that it wasn't strictly true. Unable to ignore the instant fizz of electricity between them, she'd been flirting with Luke Dawson. She felt a nasty prickle of guilt. Of course Teddy had been upset.

Luke's lips quirked upwards. "This Teddy dude might have been drinking but he's no fool. Say, how about we find somewhere else to chat? Preferably somewhere we won't be in danger of bumping into him again any time soon."

The pub was behind them now and although the door was firmly closed against the chilly afternoon, Issie knew that inside there would be havoc. Adam would be furious that she'd walked out, Alice upset and disappointed, Teddy fuming, and his grandfather making yet more excuses for his bad behaviour. What she ought to do was thank Luke Dawson, apologise to Adam and go back to work.

Yes, that was what she *ought* to do, but since when had Issie ever done anything she was supposed to?

Light rain was starting to fall, stippling the sea and starring Luke's thick eyelashes. It was that Cornish mizzle that seeped into everything; somehow it always managed to get people wetter than the heaviest downpour could. Across the beach the lights of Davey's Locker shone into the gloom as if beckoning Issie and Luke, so they headed over to it for coffee. Tucked into a window seat, their hands wrapped around steaming mugs, they watched the downpour grow heavier.

"Does it ever do anything but rain here?" Luke asked disbelievingly.

She grinned. "Once or twice a year this big yellow thing appears in the sky and everything feels warm. It's amazing."

"Yeah, I know that yellow thing real well. I usually see it every day."

"Must be nice," sighed Issie. "My brother Zak's in the Caribbean at the moment so he sees it a lot. Lucky git."

Luke tipped two sachets of sugar into his mug. "Yeah, the Caribbean's great. Weather's really good. I was working just off Antigua a couple of months ago."

Issie was confused. "You were working? I thought you were a history student?"

"I was crewing on a dive boat for a vacation job," Luke said.

"And you've come here for a holiday when you could be in Antigua?" She shook her head. "You must be nuts."

"I told you, I'm here to do some research into the *Isabella*." Cradling the coffee mug in his strong, tanned hands, Luke glanced out of the window with a faraway expression. "I was kinda hoping to see the wreck today and have a think about what may have happened to the cargo. What the archives tell me is roughly where the ship sank, and I figure it would have taken at least an hour to row to shore. Of course, there are literally hundreds of square miles of where the cargo could be if it went overboard."

Issie said nothing but her hand stole to her necklace, her fingers curling around the coin on the end of the chain. Luke was still speaking, his honey-warm southern tones describing the cargo, but she had the impression that he was thinking aloud rather than wanting her opinion. She listened to him but said nothing, partly because she was fascinated to meet somebody with such detailed knowledge and partly because she was finding it hard to rip her attention away from his full mouth and perfect white American teeth. What would it feel like to have those lips trace the curve of her throat? Or the teeth nip the soft skin of her neck?

Luke leaned back in his chair. "So that's my theory. What do you think?"

Issie flushed. He really didn't want to know what she was thinking right at this moment. "I think you seem to know an awful lot about this ship," she told him instead.

"Yeah, I guess you could say it's my specialist area. I've been looking at the cargo manifest as part of my research too. I started at the national archives in Seville and struck lucky."

Issie stared at him. She'd tracked down the same document as well. In fact, when she'd told Mark about the ship she was named after and how much it meant to her, he'd asked one of his academic friends to help them decipher it. She and Mark had been looking at the translated version together before… before… Well, before everything had fallen apart. That Luke had read it too shocked her more than she could believe. Was it a coincidence? Or was it fate?

"What?" asked Luke when she didn't speak.

"I've read that too," Issie said. "Someone at university was helping me with the translation. I was so excited when I found it; I had to know what it said."

"Cool. Were you doing a paper on it? And how did your degree go?"

She looked out of the window, not seeing the beach but rather the documents shredded all over the floor of her student bedroom.

"Not exactly. And I never finished the degree because I left, but that doesn't matter now."

"Dropped out, huh? That must have been tough." His voice was warm with sympathy.

Tough didn't come close. Breaking up with Mark and choosing to walk away from him had felt like flaying off her skin. Mark had been far more than her boyfriend. He'd been her mentor, her intellectual guide, her tutor, her first true love… and Issie had never spoken of him to a soul. Two minutes with Luke Dawson and she was in danger of singing like a canary. What did Mickey Davey put in his coffee? The truth drug?

"Yeah, well, it's in the past now," she said quickly. "Anyway, never mind the manifest. I don't believe that the cargo went down with the ship."

"What?"

She glanced around the café. Mickey Davey was sitting at the counter talking rapidly into his mobile phone and one of his builders was putting the finishing touches to the new floor, but nobody else was anywhere near. Still, when she spoke, Issie kept her voice low. She didn't trust Mickey an inch; he was just the kind of man who'd have the café bugged. "*Isabella's* treasure made it to the shore. It's here, somewhere in Polwenna Bay."

Fleetingly, she saw a flicker of some undefinable emotion in Luke's eyes. But then he shook his head. "Honey, those crazies on the beach with their metal detectors think the same. It's a cute idea, and I bet it's been great for business in the village, but it's hardly likely."

Issie's reply was to slip the necklace over her head and pass it across the table to him. Luke's eyes widened as he held it up to the light. He gave a low whistle.

"Where the hell did you get this?"

She ignored his question. "What do you think it is?"

Placing the coin between his index finger and thumb, Luke Dawson spun it around several times. When he looked up, his expression was one of disbelief.

"It's an eight-escudo coin. Where did you find it?"

"It's my grandmother's."

Luke held the coin up to the light, shaking his head. "Has she ever had it valued?"

"Not as far as I know. Besides, we'd never sell it. It's been in the family forever."

"I wasn't thinking about you selling it," said Luke, passing the necklace back. "I was thinking of insurance. Some of these coins can be worth over ten thousand dollars."

Issie looped the chain over her neck. The coin slipped out of sight between her breasts, and knowing that the metal was warm from the heat of his fingertips made her quiver.

"Ten thousand dollars? Really?" That would go a long way towards solving the Tremaine's family financial woes.

"Absolutely. Coins from the New World were solid gold. Depending on when and where they were minted, they can be worth serious cash."

"You seem to know lots about this," she said.

"Like I told you, it's kinda my specialist subject." Luke paused. "Where did you say your grandma found it?"

"I didn't."

Issie regarded him intently. The story of Black Jack Jago and his ill-gotten gains was a family legend. In the past Issie had been delighted to share it but lately she was starting to wonder if discretion was the better part of valour. Could she trust Luke Dawson?

"Can you tell me? Or is it a family secret?"

The café was warm, the pattering rain against the window sealing them away from the world, and Issie suddenly found that she wanted nothing more than to share the story of Black Jack Jago with somebody who actually took it seriously. As their drinks cooled she told him everything she knew, from the myth of the cave and the secret passage, to the story of how a handful of gold coins had mysteriously appeared from nowhere. Eventually, she talked herself to a standstill. Luke said nothing; instead, he sat regarding her thoughtfully. Issie couldn't fathom the expression in those emerald eyes.

Did he think she was crazy? Or did he, like her, feel with all his heart that the story was rooted in the truth?

"Go on, say it. You think I'm nuts."

He laughed. "Nuts! That's just such a British expression. No, if you're nuts, Issie Tremaine, then so am I – because I totally believe you."

"You do? Really?"

Luke laid a hand against his heart. "Really. Sift through the myths and the exaggeration and the legends and, sure, there's truth there somewhere. We just have to figure out where."

"We?"

"Was that kinda presumptuous?" Luke asked. "I guess I thought that together we could stand a chance of finding out if there is any truth in the stories? You know this village inside out and I've got some vacation time on my hands. We can help each other."

"You want me to help you with the research for your paper?" Issie felt a rush of excitement. How much she'd once loved doing this kind of thing. There was nothing like following a hunch and looking through old documents for hours in the search of that one sentence, or even word, which could make sense of the whole puzzle. This could be exactly what she needed to do!

For an answer, she jumped to her feet. "Do you want to start now? The rain's easing off."

"It is?" He looked outside doubtfully. "How the hell can you tell that?"

"I can see the far side of the beach. The wreck's just beyond the headland. If we go now the tide will have gone out far enough. I'll show you the cave too."

He smiled. "Sure, that sounds great. No time like the present, I guess."

"I'm just putting off going back to the pub and grovelling to Adam," Issie confessed.

"Will he give you a hard time?"

"He'll try to, but Adam's crap at being angry. Besides, I'm a good barmaid and he needs me. It'll be fine." Issie crossed her fingers behind her back. Hopefully Adam wouldn't sack her. Granny Alice would be extremely upset if he did, and Jake would flip at yet more evidence of her thoughtless and irresponsible ways.

The rain-pitted beach was empty now that today's influx of treasure hunters were sheltering in the pub, so Issie and Luke had the wreck all to themselves. There wasn't much to see now because the sands had shifted again, but even so Luke spent ages examining the exposed section of the hull and taking pictures before they eventually retraced their footsteps and headed to the cave.

"This is the place I was talking about," Issie explained as they trudged towards the furthest crevice, amid the seaweed and scattered rocks. "There was supposed to be a secret passage at the back." It was dank and dark in the cave; seawater dripped continually from its roof like unceasing tears.

"And that was the passage the old dude claims he went through years ago?" Luke shone his iPhone torch up at the piles of granite. "Seems pretty unlikely."

"Granny Alice says he always was a fibber, but I'm not so sure." Issie laid her hand against the cold wet rocks and a shudder ran through her. She'd never liked the cave. It felt unwelcoming and unlucky. "He claims he managed to walk through a section of it when he was a kid."

Luke switched off the torch. "Well, if he did, he didn't get in this end. There has to be another way in."

"That's what I think too," she agreed.

Lost in thought, they walked back into the fading daylight, their footsteps filling with seawater as they crossed the wet sand. From the depths of her pocket Issie felt her mobile vibrate as a text message arrived. She didn't need to read it to know who'd sent it.

Without opening the message, Issie deleted it. She waited to feel the usual tug on her heartstrings, but this time it didn't come and she was taken aback.

"Everything OK?" Luke asked, when her pace faltered.

Issie shoved the mobile back into her pocket and nodded. Now that Luke Dawson was in Polwenna Bay, she had a feeling that things were going to be far more than just OK.

Chapter 13

The box, when she finally found it, was on top of the wardrobe in the smallest spare room and thickly coated with dust. Her fingers could only just reach it even when she was balancing on a chair, and for a few precarious seconds Alice Tremaine swayed on her tiptoes as her hands clawed at the faded cardboard.

"Careful, Grand Gran! If you fall you'll probably break your bones. That's because old people have less calcium," warned her great-grandson, Morgan, who was holding the chair steady and watching her with worried violet eyes. "Old people often break their hips and get pneumonia and die. Fact."

"Thanks for that, my love," said Alice. As if she needed any reminding she wasn't as agile as she'd once been. Not so long ago she'd have hopped up onto this chair, grabbed the box and stepped down without so much as a second thought, but now every movement was laced with potential danger. She was only glad Jake couldn't see what she was up to. Her eldest grandson would go mad – he was such a worrier – and say she should have waited for him to come home to fetch the box down for her. Alice couldn't bear to feel helpless, though.

Or become a burden to her grandchildren.

"Have you got it?" Morgan asked excitedly. As he stepped forward for a closer look, the chair wobbled and Alice swayed perilously.

"Morgan! Sweetheart! Don't let go!"

Clutching the box tightly against her chest, she steadied herself against the wardrobe door while Morgan held onto the back of the chair with all his might. Then, with her heart fluttering against her ribs like a trapped bird, Alice clambered down and leaned against the bed for a moment to catch her breath. The room was whirling and there was a whooshing in her ears. She was afraid that perhaps Jake was right and she really shouldn't take risks. No matter what Jonny St Milton said, she wasn't a young girl anymore. She was seventy-nine.

"Silly old fool," she muttered, although whether she was referring to herself or her determined suitor Alice wasn't sure. Climbing onto furniture to retrieve boxes of old photos wasn't an activity for an almost-octogenarian. She'd have been more sensible to let Morgan do it, even if he was shorter.

"Are your old photos in there?" he was asking, hopping from foot to foot in agitation.

Alice nodded and blew the dust off the lid. She didn't need to cut the string or open the box to know what lay within. The layers and layers of faded images inside were echoes in her own memories and sometimes seemed brighter and sharper than the everyday world around her. Like misty eyesight and wobbly limbs, she supposed this was just another side effect of getting old.

"Can we open it?" Morgan was so desperate to see inside that he looked as though he might pop. Apart from the fact that photography was his passion, he was very keen to work on his school project, *My Family Tree*. When Alice had mentioned that she had some old pictures, he'd been beside himself with excitement. Alice knew she wouldn't have a moment's peace until she'd located the photographs, which was another reason why she'd scaled the wardrobe. Morgan on a mission was a force of nature.

"Why don't we take them into the kitchen and spread them onto the table?" she suggested. This would mean she could sit down and recover with a cup of tea while Morgan sorted out the pictures and worked on his project. Oh dear, since when had everything become so exhausting? It didn't seem so long ago that she'd been perfectly capable of looking after seven children at once, so how come she was so tired just from spending a morning with one small boy?

Doing her best to put these nagging worries out of her mind, Alice carried the box down the stairs to the kitchen and sent Morgan to his room to fetch his school bag and pencil case. Once he was at the table with his scissors, sugar paper and glue organised and she had a mug of Earl Grey in her hand, Alice slipped into the seat next to him.

"Do you want to open the box, love?"

Morgan looked thoughtful. "I think you should, Grand Gran. They're your pictures, after all."

Alice exhaled slowly. These might be her pictures but she'd not looked at them for a very long time. Her husband had been dead for over eight years and this box had been hidden away long before then.

"It's your project, my love. You do it," she said.

Morgan didn't need asking twice. His scissors snipped the string and, moments later, photographs were covering the old kitchen table like an autumnal flurry of sepia rectangles, muted Polaroids and curling black-and-white prints. Half-forgotten faces stared up at Alice, their smiles and their lives frozen in time.

"Where did you want to start?" she asked.

"I wanted to start with Black Jack Jago but there won't be one of him because he's from before cameras were invented," Morgan said sadly as he looked down at the photos. "All the other kids in my class are really jealous that he's in my family."

Alice sighed. She was getting very tired of Black Jack Jago. Not only was half the village obsessed with him, but also the local media kept spinning new angles on the story. And all the while, Polwenna Bay continued to overflow with excited would-be treasure hunters. As for her granddaughter, well, Issie had hardly been able to think straight since the wreck had surfaced. She'd almost lost her job too, after the incident with Teddy St Milton in the pub. Worse, she hadn't seemed at all bothered by this; she'd merely announced that she was going to be running Black Jack Ghost Tours anyway.

"Black Jack Jago is not a part of this family," Alice said firmly.

Morgan looked mutinous. "Issie says he is. Issie says that's where the necklace came from. Fact."

"That is certainly *not* a fact. It's just a silly story."

Alice made a mental note to ensure that Issie returned the gold-coin pendant. Apart from it being valuable, Alice was beginning to feel that it was just encouraging her granddaughter to indulge in ridiculous flights of fancy rather than focusing on the real issues, namely one abandoned degree and a very ill-thought-out dalliance with the volatile Teddy St Milton. Jonny might think the sun shone out of his grandson, but Alice wasn't so convinced. That young man was spoilt, drank too much and had the same nasty streak as his grandmother. They said you shouldn't speak ill of the dead but, even so, Alice couldn't think of anything nice to say about Millicent St Milton…

"Miss Hamilton says I can't have him on my family tree anyway because we can only go back to our great-grandparents," Morgan was saying now, oblivious to Alice's concentration being miles away. He wielded his scissors in a way that suggested he meant business. "Mum's asked Nan and Gramps to send pictures, so I'm going to do you and Great Grandpa Henry first."

"Righto," said Alice, dragging her thoughts back to the present.

"That's him, isn't it?"

Morgan waved a sepia image under her nose, transporting Alice back through the decades faster than any time machine could. A young man stared out from the picture, his mouth set in a firm expression and his eyes daring the photographer to argue with him. He was dressed in uniform and seemed to Alice almost unbearably young. Her heart twisted with loss. Dear, dear Henry. He should never have experienced those horrors at his age, or even at any age. To today's youngsters it was all something from the history books, but her dear husband had relived it every day for the rest of his life. Even now she found it odd to sleep a whole night through without his cries and threshing limbs waking her.

"Yes, that's Great Grandpa," she said quietly.

"He looks like Jake but he doesn't look much like Jim-pa," Morgan observed.

Alice leaned closer and smiled. Jake certainly did share that serious expression and the determined chin – and, like his grandfather, he was a hard worker. Nevertheless, she couldn't imagine Jake being anything near as strict as Henry had been with their son, when Jake and Summer eventually had a family. Her husband had been bitterly disappointed when Jimmy hadn't followed him into the army, but should this really have been any surprise? Jimmy's entire childhood had probably felt like a boot camp. She didn't claim to be a psychologist, but Alice thought she understood why her son behaved the way he did. Although it had been a huge sadness to them both that they'd only been able to have one child, Alice now wondered if perhaps this had actually been for the best. Jimmy hadn't been easy, and even now he worried Alice far more than any of her grandchildren. He was like the Peter Pan of Polwenna. How cruel that he'd lost Penny, that lovely, laughing girl he'd loved so dearly. Jimmy had never been the same since her death.

Alice sighed as she studied Henry's young face, as yet unscathed by the horrors about to unfold in northern France, and her vision blurred. He'd been such a good man, and he'd certainly been her knight in shining armour, but sometimes he'd been too hard on his only son. Henry's high standards had been hard to live with, even for those who'd loved him.

Lord. This family history business was painful. Maybe, like the wreck of the *Isabella*, some things were best left buried?

"Look! That's you!"

Delighted with his find, Morgan held up a black-and-white photo, and Alice laughed to see her younger self on her wedding day.

"I wanted to look like Elizabeth Taylor," she recalled, marvelling at how tiny her waist had been and how thick her once-brown hair was. "My mother spent a week's wages on the fabric for that dress and she always complained that she ruined her eyes sewing by gaslight. I felt like a film star though!"

"You were very pretty, Granny Alice," Morgan told her. "You looked just like Issie, but with different hair."

Alice leaned over and hugged him. "Thanks, sweetheart. I hope I was a bit more sensible than your aunty, though!"

And then, as though fate wanted to remind her that actually no, she'd sometimes been every bit as silly as her granddaughter, a crumpled scrap of paper pinned to a faded square image caught Alice's eye. It was a note attached to a box-camera photo of a smiling girl in a pretty summer frock. Alice didn't need to unfold it to know what was written on the delicate paper; those words were marked indelibly on her heart.

Alice's breath caught. While Morgan chattered and glued and wrote notes, she nodded and murmured in what she hoped were the right places, even though in reality she was a lifetime away...

The woods smelt damp, of mushrooms and mould and rotting things. It was dark here too. Her heart beating fast, she fought her way through the tangled undergrowth. Brambles tore at her bare legs and she felt the sharp kisses of nettles on her ankles. None of this stopped her though, not even when a hawthorn branch ripped the hem of her dress or when her shoes slithered in the mud and she almost fell. The path was overgrown, knotted with bindweed and voracious ivy; it was a long time since anyone had come this way.

Ahead of her a blackbird shrilled in warning, and Alice's pulse skittered in perfect rhythm with its fluting cry. Onwards she went until the waves faded to a whisper and in their place she heard the merry chuckling of a stream.

So she was in the right location! Alice laughed out loud and shook her long brown hair away from her face. In her hand was the note she'd collected earlier from their secret place. It wasn't hard to make an excuse to visit it — all she'd needed to do was tell Ma she was checking the hens and then she could easily run to the garden wall, pull out the loose stone and squeeze her fingers into the small alcove. Alice thought it showed just how much she loved him that she didn't even worry about worms or earwigs whenever she did this!

The sun, peeping through the dense foliage, was high in the sky now and Alice reckoned it must be midday. Unlike him she couldn't afford a wristwatch, but she knew he'd wait even if she were ten hours late.

Noon at St Wenn's Well. I love you x

It was there: held in her hand and proven in writing. He loved her! Alice's lips couldn't stop smiling. He loved her just as she loved him — and now, in this quiet and ancient place, they'd seal their love just as they'd always sworn they would. She didn't think she'd ever been as scared or as excited in her entire life. Before the sun started to slip into the sea everything would have changed. She would have changed.

Her skin tingled with delicious anticipation.

Alice saw him before he noticed her. He was crouching down by the well, dabbling those long, sensitive fingers in the cold water, and wholly intent on his task. Earlier, when they'd met in the cave by the beach, those same hands had cupped her face as he'd kissed her; soon he would hold her close again. For a moment she watched him, drinking in the lean grace of his slight body, the locks of raven-dark hair that fell across his face and the high planes of his cheekbones. He was so beautiful that it almost hurt to behold him.

"Alice!" Catching sight of her, he leapt to his feet. Moments later she was in his arms as he rained kisses down onto her cheeks, her eyes and her lips. "You came!"

She laughed as she kissed him back. He was so tall that she had to stand on tiptoes to brush his lips with hers.

"Of course I came, silly! I had to skive off work, mind, and mother will be pretty angry, but how could I not come?"

He laughed and, stepping back a little, snapped a picture of her with the big square Brownie camera that was the envy of all the boys in the village.

"My God, but you're beautiful," he said, shaking his head. "How the hell did I get so lucky?"

Alice laughed. "I'm the lucky one. Shouldn't I be doing your washing and scrubbing your floors?"

"Never! I should be doing those things for you!" He took her work-roughened hands in his and pressed them to his lips, and she giggled. If only the people at the

big house could see her now! The housekeeper's daughter being treated like a princess by the young master. They'd not laugh then and say she had ideas above her station!

He pulled her close, staring down at her with those grey eyes that were sometimes dove soft and at others the same hue as a stormy sea.

"I love you, Alice Pendeen. I'll never love anyone like I love you."

"I love you too, Jonny St Milton," she whispered.

"Grand Gran! Grand Gran! Are you listening to me? I said can I stick the one of you on my poster?"

Morgan's question snatched Alice back across the years, and for a brief moment she was stunned to find herself sitting at the kitchen table instead of kissing Jonny St Milton at St Wenn's Well. Feeling flustered, and hoping that her face wasn't as pink as it felt, she found herself agreeing that Morgan could glue whatever he wanted onto sugar paper. Oh, what did it matter anyway? Let him cut them up. Nobody else was interested in those old pictures. It was all ancient history and it really should stay that way. Some things were in the past because that was where they were meant to be, locked away in a dusty box and forgotten about. Along with the person who'd hurt you so much that even a lifetime later the scars felt every bit as raw – even if the skin around them was a little more wrinkled than it had once been.

"Like the rest of me," she sighed out loud.

"Like the rest of you what?" Jimmy Tremaine bounded into the kitchen, his grey ponytail bouncing cheerfully. Planting a kiss on his mother's cheek, he didn't wait for a reply, but added, "You couldn't lend us a tenner, could you, Ma? I'm meeting Mickey in The Ship and I'm out of cash."

"There's an ATM in the pub," Alice began, but she knew she was wasting her breath. "Oh, go on, then. My purse is in my bag."

"Jim-pa, have you got any pictures of Granny Penny I can have for my family tree project?" Morgan asked hopefully.

His grandfather looked up from rooting through Alice's bag. "Somewhere, mate. I'll dig them out for you."

Alice knew full well that Jimmy kept a photo of Penny under his pillow and his wedding album tucked behind the bed. Her son was many things but he was certainly faithful to his wife's memory. Was she betraying Henry by spending time with Jonny St Milton and allowing him to slip back into her heart? The thought made her feel uncomfortable.

"You're spending a lot of time with Mickey lately," she said, as much to distract herself as anything. "I'm not sure I'm that keen on him, love."

Jimmy shrugged his denim-jacketed shoulders. "He's all right, Ma. And besides, he's offered me some work."

Alice was most surprised. She couldn't imagine her son making tea in the beach café. "Really? In the Locker? Doing what?"

"Not wearing a pinny and selling scones! I save my pinny-wearing for private time!" Grabbing Alice's apron from the Aga rail, he whipped it round his waist and pranced around the kitchen, making Alice chuckle in spite of her misgivings. That was one of the nicest things about Jimmy Tremaine: he always made you laugh.

"Fear not, I'm only doing some odd jobs for him and a bit of delivery work." Then, having replaced the pinny where it belonged and liberated a ten-pound note from Alice's bag, he made a break for the door.

"I'm not sure about Mickey," Alice warned. "Be careful, love. We don't know much about him."

"Mickey's all right. Anyway, I thought you'd be pleased," Jimmy called back over his shoulder. "I'll earn us some money and make up for my American jaunt. Unless you fancy writing another saucy book and filling the coffers that way? Maybe don't give it all to the church this time?"

Alice flushed. She was never going to live down writing her racy novel. The Kindle royalties might have helped boost St Wenn's finances and buy a few extra groceries, but her brush with literary fame had caused her a whole heap of other trouble, not least because she'd based the hero on her long-ago sweetheart. If she'd had any idea just how many people would read her book, Alice would never have written it.

She was putting this mammoth lapse of judgment down to a senior moment.

"That book was a one-off. I'm never writing another one."

"Shame. Good old Lord Blackwarren was very popular round here. I'll say hello to him if I see him in the pub, shall I?" And blowing her a cheeky kiss, Jimmy Tremaine sauntered out of the kitchen, leaving his mother open-mouthed.

Oh dear. Was it really that obvious that Jonny was the hero in her novel? If so, then Alice was as daft now as she'd been all those years ago. What a silly old fool she'd been to write down her dreams of what might have been between them.

All the same, she couldn't help sliding that faded photo of the smiling girl, her eyes full of stars and her mouth bruised with kisses, into her apron pocket. She would rather die than admit it, but a corner of her heart still belonged to Jonny St Milton, even if, like her, he was stooped and wrinkled and old nowadays.

Chapter 14

"By my estimation the ship went down far closer to the bay than everyone thinks. Looking at the archives and cross-referencing the accounts of eyewitnesses with the charts, it's perfectly possible that the cargo made it to shore."

With his mobile wedged firmly under his ear and against his shoulder, Luke studied the notes he'd made previously and scribbled yet another to himself as he spoke to his investor. If his theory was correct and the wreckers had murdered the *Isabella's* survivors the minute their rowing boats had bumped onto the sand, then the cargo must have made it to the village. The question was, how?

"So you really think it exists?" Stella was thousands of miles and several time zones away, but Luke could hear the incredulity in her voice and it bugged him. Why couldn't she just take his word for it? Still, she was sponsoring this venture. Subduing his rising irritation, Luke forced a light note into his voice.

"Sure, otherwise I wouldn't have come all this way. It's here somewhere. Trust me; my hunches are never wrong."

"OK, sweetie, if you say so – but rather you than me. You really shoulda come to Cayman. It's thirty degrees here and I've already done a sunrise yoga class. We're all off on a boat now to Rum Point."

Luke glanced out of the grimy window. The sun was out today, for a rare change, and the village had been sprinkled with a heavy frost. The rooftops glittered, the sky was brilliant blue and iced spiders' webs laced the bushes in the garden. It was probably thirty degrees here too – in Fahrenheit! Even indoors he could see his own breath and he was wearing both his sweaters and a scarf. No wonder the Brits had a thing about stiff upper lips: theirs were probably frozen. He couldn't remember ever feeling so cold in his life. If Issie hadn't given him the heads-up on hot-water bottles he'd probably have died of hypothermia within his first few days of being in England.

While Stella chatted on about snorkelling and drinking cocktails on Seven Mile Beach, Luke tuned her out and revisited the previous four days. So far he'd met Issie, seen the remains of the ship, fallen out with the rather chinless Teddy, and this morning returned to the wreck site. Today's trip had been far less uncomfortable than his first because Issie had arranged for her brother-in-law, Ashley, to take them in his boat. Far from the tatty fishing vessel Luke had expected, he'd found himself in a brand new powerboat, whose twin engines had made short work of the journey out to sea. He might have only known Issie Tremaine for a short while, but already she was proving to be a useful ally. If he felt bad for not telling her the truth about the real reason for his visit to Polwenna Bay, Luke guessed this was the price he had to pay for getting closer to his goal. What was it they said? All's fair in love and treasure-hunting.

The wind had been biting cold and as they'd flown across the water Luke's cheeks had ached, but the joy of being out at sea had more than compensated for that, as had the stunning views of the coastline. The water here might not be bathwater warm, but in the sunshine it glittered every bit as brightly as the Caribbean, and the cliffs rising from the foaming tide's edge were as breathtaking and verdant as anything in St Lucia.

Once Ashley had realised that Luke knew his way around a boat, he'd happily let his guest take the helm. With six hundred horsepower beneath him, Issie shrieking with exhilaration and the endless blue of the ocean stretching ahead, Luke had felt alive and free – a feeling that had swiftly evaporated when he'd come ashore and discovered two missed Skype calls from Stella.

Luke was starting to think that the money she'd lent him came at a very high price…

"Anyway, rather you than me," Stella was saying again. "I've Googled Corn Wall and it looks very cold and bleak to me."

"It's beautiful," Luke told her, surprising himself. Sure, the weather was as capricious as a stroppy woman, all sunshine and smiles one minute and sulky storms the next, but there was a harsh loveliness to Polwenna Bay that he'd never experienced anywhere else. Yes, it was cold. Yes, it was inconvenient to park miles away and lug everything to the cottage. And yes, pasties were full of fat. But the village was also old and mysterious, and he loved that everywhere he turned there was another story and another slice of history. Key West was old, sure, but it had nothing on this place. Issie had taken him on a walk around the village, and the age of everything had blown his mind. This country had door handles older than the United States.

"Just find that treasure before you freeze to death," Stella ordered. He heard voices murmuring before she added, "Gotta go, sweets; I'm off to brunch. Keep me up to speed, yeah? We need something a bit more tangible than a *hunch.*"

"I'm working on it," he replied, catching sight of Issie Tremaine opening the garden gate, but Stella had already ended the call. She wasn't a patient woman at all, and Luke sighed. Mal had always complained bitterly about his sponsors, hating "dancing to their tune" as he put it, but both Luke and his father knew that the sponsors were a necessary evil. Stella had talked him into letting her help, but in the cold light of a Cornish winter's day it no longer seemed such a bright idea.

Seeing Luke at the window, Issie waved and smiled. He found himself smiling back. Issie Tremaine was real good fun. Mad as a hatter but fun all the same. Bumping into her had been a stroke of good luck, and that she was as sexy as hell an even bigger one. She was as keen to find the lost treasure as he was, too – and her inside knowledge was invaluable.

"I was about to say get your coat and gloves on because we're going for a walk," Issie said when Luke let her in, "but you're ready."

"It's the only way not to get frostbite in here. Haven't you guys heard of central heating?" Luke complained.

"Stop being such a pussy. Central heating's for wimps and incomers," Issie said. "The old fisherman who owns this placed lived here until he was in his nineties without whingeing about central heating. The wood burner did him just fine."

Luke had met the ancient wood burner and, after singeing his eyebrows and burning his fingers, decided that it was best left alone. Ditto the temperamental Aga in the kitchen. So far he was surviving by eating pub food and not moving more than a few inches from his hot-water bottle. He would never reach his nineties if he lived here. A heart attack would get him first.

"It's probably warmer outside anyway," he sighed, pulling on his coat and following her out into the raw afternoon.

"Stop moaning. A good walk will soon warm you up." Issie was already striding ahead of him and out of the garden, before turning right and heading down into the village. Her pink flowery hair slide bounced jauntily. "Come on!"

Luke huddled into his coat. Smoke rose lazily from chimney pots and drifted across the village, while seagulls bickered on the harbour wall. The boats in the marina drifted with the tide's rise and fall, and far away on the beach a dog was barking at the buzz of a metal detector. The sun was still shining weakly but it was much lower in the sky now, slithering towards the horizon. Luke shook his head. It was crazy to think that this watery blob of light was the same burning eye that sent everyone back home running for the shade.

"Where are we going?"

Issie tapped her nose. "Mystery tour."

"Is it far?"

"About three miles. Why? Scared you won't keep up?"

"Hardly. I'm more scared it's gonna rain." He glanced at the bank of cloud that was slowly beginning to roll in from the sea. "Can't we drive?"

Issie laughed. "You know us Brits. We walk everywhere in the rain. Besides, you can't get cars to where we're going. It may have escaped your notice, but Henry Ford didn't exactly design this village. FYI we don't have a drive-through McDonald's either."

That omission hadn't escaped Luke's notice. Although his stomach still felt heavy with the pasty he'd eaten earlier, his mouth watered at the thought of a Big Mac and fries.

"Where *is* the nearest McDonald's?"

"Way too far to visit now. Halfway to Newquay."

"My car's right here. I'm up for it if you are," Luke said. He had no idea where the hell New Key was, but it sounded good to him. Right now he'd walk there if it got him a burger.

They were just passing the private car park where he'd managed to squeeze his little hire car, when raised voices drew their attention.

"That's my bloody space you've parked in and I'm not moving!" bellowed a red-faced man whom Luke recognised as the owner of the beach café. He was standing by a big gold Bentley parked crazily right in front of a blue Volvo, and squaring up to a much smaller man.

"I'm really sorry, mate. I had no idea the spaces were allocated. The holiday-cottage people just said to park here," apologised the shorter man.

"Pricks like you make me sick," the Bentley owner spat. "I've not been able to park in my own bloody space all day."

"It's only been one morning. We didn't arrive until late last night," protested a second man, stepping forward. He was taller than the first and had closely cropped hair. He looked rather upset, too. "We didn't mean to put you out."

"Isn't that the beach café guy?" Luke asked Issie, who nodded.

"Mickey Davey. My brother, Danny, said he saw him this morning trying to shunt that Volvo out of the way with his Bentley. He's a lunatic."

Luke's lips twitched. That Bentley was a sixty-thousand-dollar car. It was official: the Brits were insane!

"I don't give a monkey's about your *sorrys*, son! You bloody did put me out," Mickey Davey was snarling. "So guess what? It's my turn to put you out now. Let's see how you like it."

He pocketed his keys, flicked a V-sign at the visitors and sauntered away, leaving them open-mouthed — and unable to move their car. As he passed Luke and Issie, his pug-like face was bright with glee.

"People get a bit funny about their parking here," Issie explained.

"There's funny and there's totally freaking insane," Luke replied. "Maybe I'll pass on frequenting the beach café in future?"

"Stick to The Ship, especially when I'm there."

He laughed. "Sounds good, apart from your friend Teddy being on the loose. That's one dude I can do without bumping into."

The two men from the car park were staring after Mickey Davey in disbelief.

"The locals aren't all mental, I promise," Issie called to them. "Look, if his car's still there later on, come to the pub and I'll get a crowd of us to bump it out the way."

The shorter man smiled wearily. "Thanks, but I think we'll have to wait. If we move that car he can do us for criminal damage."

"We're here for a few weeks having a fishing holiday, so we won't need it for a while," added his friend. "Hopefully he'll move it later when he needs to go out?"

"Unlikely," Issie murmured to Luke. "Mickey will probably just use his delivery van to spite them."

Leaving the perplexed visitors behind, Issie and Luke headed out of the village and up a muddy footpath, which threaded its way through woodland and up a steep hill. The path was so narrow that Luke had to drop behind Issie. Not that he was complaining; she had a great butt and for a good twenty minutes all he had to do was climb and watch it bobbing in front of him. Even though the hike up made his legs ache and his lungs burn (it was a shock to the system, for someone who was used to flat terrain), there was nothing like a peachy ass clad in tight denim to take a guy's mind off physical discomfort! Luke thought he could probably climb Everest this way.

Finally the path began to level out, and Luke's breathing eased as the track wound through gnarled oaks and withered hawthorns.

"We're here," Issie said. Her face tilted up at him, her wide blue eyes bright with anticipation. "What do you think?"

He glanced around with curiosity. They'd reached a clearing in the woods where a small stream laughed over pebbles. In front of them, a moss-smothered Celtic cross stood guardian over a pool of water surrounded by toy fairies – and little scraps of brightly coloured fabric had been tied to the branches of the ash and willow trees that paddled their roots in the stream. There was an unusual stillness here; although they were deep in the woods, not a note of birdsong trembled in the air. Luke had the weirdest sensation that unseen eyes were watching him.

What was this place? Although the trek here had made him sweat, goosebumps dusted his arms now. It was old, ancient even, and he had never in his entire life been anywhere like it. Sure, he'd visited museums and dived enough wrecks, but this sensation of being suspended in time was totally different. For a few moments he watched and wondered. It was almost as if something from long ago was breathing against the back of his neck.

He shivered and rubbed his arms. "Where are we?"

"St Wenn's Well," Issie said. "It's another mysterious Polwenna place. There are all sorts of myths and legends about it."

"St Wenn, huh?" Luke was bamboozled by the amount of weird and wonderful saints here. As a very lapsed Catholic he sometimes asked St Anthony to help him find things, but his knowledge of saints was as full of holes as a fishing net.

"She's the saint our church is named after," Issie explained, "but there was a well here long before England became a Christian country.

It's a pagan holy well and people still come here to make requests to the water spirits. That's why they leave the ribbons and fairies. They're offerings."

Having spent time in California where whacko ideas were peddled just about everywhere, this didn't sound too odd to Luke. He didn't believe such baloney for a second, but lots of people did. His mom had been a regular customer of the Key West tarot reader.

"If you lean in and make a wish, they say St Wenn will grant it," Issie told him earnestly.

Luke laughed. "Yeah. And Santa too, right?"

"Don't mock St Wenn!" she said. "Go on, make a wish!"

She looked so serious that Luke found himself kneeling at the side of the well, dabbling his fingers in the icy water. In spite of himself he found that a wish was bubbling up from his soul, like the stream that emerged mysteriously from the earth in this peculiar place.

"I'd sure like to find Polwenna Bay's treasure, St Wenn," Luke said.

Issie looked at him in disbelief. "You're wishing for treasure? Wouldn't you rather find true love or something?"

"True love?" Luke rolled his eyes. "I know we're telling fairy tales here, but c'mon. True love? You're kidding, right? At least we know the treasure existed."

Her blue eyes were fixed on his face. "Don't you believe in true love?"

Luke thought of his mom and dad. They'd thought it was true love – and look where that had got them. And Stella and her husband. Jeez. Love was just a myth pedalled by the Hallmark channel.

"Honey, I believe in *facts*."

"Then you've never been in love," Issie said quietly. "Fact."

He shrugged. "Maybe you're right. Or maybe *I* am. Who knows? Anyhow, it's your turn, Issie."

"I've already made my wish here."

"So you only get one? Go on, make another!"

But Issie wouldn't, shaking her head so hard that her pink flowery hair slide flew into the well. Luke's hand shot forward to retrieve it but Issie reached out and caught his arm.

"That can be our offering to St Wenn," she said softly.

Moments later it had vanished into the dark depths of the well. Luke hoped St Wenn liked big pink gerbera hair accessories, otherwise his wish was screwed.

The light was starting to fade so they left the woods and, picking up another track, began their descent towards the village. As the trees became more widely spaced and Polwenna Bay came into sight, Luke realised that the footpath had brought them down to the back of the village and into the graveyard.

"This is awesome," he declared, sprinting forward to check out the lichen-smothered headstones. "See how old these are? Look, this one is seventeenth century," he added, crouching down to examine it.

"Half of them are Tremaines," Issie said nonchalantly. "You should come up here in the daylight and have a good look around. You'll love it, being a historian. There are all sorts of tales about hauntings too, although I reckon those were spread by the smugglers."

He looked up, suddenly alert. "Really? Why would that be?"

She wound one of her braids around her forefinger. "One of the vicars here back in the eighteenth century was apparently the smugglers' ringleader and was storing all sorts of contraband in the crypt. People would've kept away from the place if they were scared of ghosts, though. And the ghost stories would have helped to explain away any odd lights and noises at night."

It made perfect sense, and now a theory was starting to piece itself together for Luke. In this village the truths were as buried within the myths as the roots of the yew tree were hidden in the churchyard soil. Mumbo jumbo and stories were all very well but what he really needed was evidence. As Issie chattered on about the legend of the smuggling vicar, Luke's brain was working overtime.

What if the tunnel under the village wasn't just a story but actually had existed? The cave on the beach and the church could well be linked; that would have made life a lot easier for the smugglers. And what if Black Jack Jago had taken advantage of that very tunnel to move his loot without being spotted? Luke felt the familiar fizzing sensation in his gut which always told him when he was onto something.

"How's the research for your paper going, by the way?" Issie asked.

"Uh, fine." Luke was suddenly even more fascinated by the curling script on the ancient slab of marble. He wasn't proud of himself for not being straight with her, but the girl had ten thousand dollars hanging around her neck, and that coin had to have come from somewhere. How he might be starting to feel about her didn't matter. He would do whatever it took to solve this mystery, because a slice of the fortune buried in this strange village would more than set him up in the salvage game. There was no room for sentimentality.

Luke stood up, brushing grass from his jeans, and stared down at the streets that wiggled their way between clusters of houses. Could it be that a direct route was concealed beneath this haphazard layout? The beach. The cave. The pub. The church. Four landmarks all linked to the legend and, as the crow flew, all in a line. Was it possible? Did the secret tunnel run under the pub and up to the church? And if so, how could he prove it?

He needed to find a way of exploring the pub undisturbed – and maybe, just maybe, the answer was standing right next to him. Perhaps St Wenn was working her magic after all?

"Issie, honey," Luke said, turning and giving her the smile full of sexy promise that had never failed him yet, "are you working in The Ship tonight?"

Chapter 15

Bar work in January was usually an absolute doddle. The Christmas and New Year's visitors retreated back to the cities, the second-homers handed their cottage keys to their cleaners, and most of the locals were too broke to spend any money on beer. At this time of year, an evening shift at The Ship ought to entail little more than perching at the bar with a good book and pulling the occasional pint for the few regulars who'd braved the cold to get here. Now and then it might be necessary to throw a log on the fire or put some glasses away, but generally that would be as busy as the night would get for anyone working behind the bar. It was a cushy number, as Kelly had remarked when she'd learned that Issie was taking on her old job, but it would make up for the summer season when her feet would scarcely touch the ground.

Yes, that was what January was *usually* like in The Ship. This year, however, was very different. If it hadn't been for the cold wind outside and the roaring fire in the hearth, Issie could have sworn it was August. The pub was packed. Rose Harper had been flat out all evening with orders for bar food, while Issie and Adam were run off their feet pulling pints and collecting glasses. All the tables were taken and even the locals had decided to join in, seating themselves in a group at the farthest end of the bar, which was about the only space remaining. In fact, the place was so crowded that Little Rog had been forced to squeeze into the alcove under the stairs, where the coats and waterproofs hung. Every hour or so his empty glass would shoot out from between the oilskins for Issie to refill. It was like dealing with a beer-drinking Harry Potter.

"This is crazy! I can't keep up!" Issie gasped to Adam, squeezing behind him to retrieve mixers from the fridge.

"It's bloody great, is what it is," Adam said. He'd been grinning from ear to ear all evening. "Well done for finding that old wreck, Is! I owe you one."

"Humph," said Issie. She was starting to wish she'd kept her big trap shut about the *Isabella*. So far she'd been worked to death in the pub and not been able to move for *emmets*, all intent on finding the treasure. On the other hand, if she hadn't gone public with her find, Luke Dawson would never have arrived in the village – and that would certainly have been a shame.

She sneaked a glance across the pub to the far window seat. There he was, his tawny head buried in a book, his long lean legs stretched out in front of him and a bottle of Bud held loosely in his tanned fingers. A shiver ran through her as she imagined those same fingers skimming across her naked body...

Sensing her gaze, Luke looked up and smiled, showing a glimmer of white teeth and a dimple in his cheek. Issie flushed and, embarrassed to be caught staring, returned her attention to pulling pints. What on earth was happening here? She was never like this with guys. Until now she'd always been the one to call the shots. Only Mark had ever had the power to stop her in her tracks – and even he had never made her breath catch or her heart gallop like this. It was the strongest physical attraction she had ever known and, for the first time in her life, she didn't have a clue what to do.

Issie checked her watch. It was only ten o'clock in the evening. Ages to go until closing. She and Luke had agreed to meet up once the pub shut, but the minutes until then were really dragging their heels. Praying that time would speed up, Issie busied herself collecting glasses and plates. Mickey Davey and some of his wide-boy mates had left theirs on their table, and as she staggered through the bar with her arms precariously full, Issie wished that people had the manners to help. How hard would it be for them just to put their dirty plates on the bar?

"You can pick ours up next and fetch us another round."

This clipped command was issued by a shiny-faced young man sitting in the corner booth. He was clearly one of the monied set, judging from his blue and white stripy shirt, teamed with chinos and a blue sweater draped across his shoulders – not to mention the expensive Omega watch on his wrist and the fact that he was sitting with Teddy St Milton. Teddy and several of his Hooray Henry mates had been in all night, bolstering Adam's Caribbean holiday fund by ordering champagne and oysters. They'd also been barking orders at Issie non-stop, as though she was just some skivvy there to run around them. Warned by Adam that she had to be on her best behaviour after the last incident, Issie had bitten her tongue so many times this evening that she was amazed it wasn't severed.

"I'll certainly clear the plates, but you'll need to fetch your own drinks," she said.

Teddy's lip curled. "We've spent enough here tonight to have table service. Get us another bottle of Bolly. It's what you're here for."

Issie felt her temper start to rise. "Get it yourself."

"I thought that was *your* job?" Teddy asked, while his cronies sniggered. "Let's be honest, you're from a family of servants, after all, so you should be good at it."

His friend plucked a fifty-pound note from his wallet and threw it in Issie's direction. The note drifted onto the floor.

"Pick it up," he said. "It's the closest you'll get to one of those if you lose your job."

"Are you threatening me?" Issie demanded. Anger was starting to pop behind her eyeballs. She was extremely tired, and she'd had just about enough of having to listen to their snide comments all evening. "You'll be sorry if you are," she said, close to snapping.

"I'm so scared," sneered Teddy, throwing back his head and laughing.

His laughter stopped abruptly when he found himself wearing Mickey Davey's leftover fish pie, though.

"Oops," said Issie. "Clumsy me."

"You stupid bitch! Look what you've done!" Teddy spluttered, dabbing frantically at his Ralph Lauren shirt.

"Oh dear. Maybe you could get one of your servants to wash it?" Issie replied.

"What's going on here?" Having a landlord's instinct that could detect trouble at ten paces, Adam Harper now loomed over the table and glowered at them all.

"I tripped," Issie said. "Honestly, Adam, balancing all these plates is really hard."

"She didn't trip! She bloody well threw it at me!" raged Teddy, still mopping his shirt and oblivious to his mashed-potato hat. "My shirt's ruined!"

"I do hope the stains won't be a *haddock* to get out?" Issie said sweetly. "Being designer, it *cod* be difficult to wash."

"Stop taking the piss!" wailed Teddy. To Adam he added, "Are you going to let her speak to me like that? And assault your customers? After we've spent a fortune here tonight?"

"Issie?" said Adam.

"It was an accident!" Issie widened her eyes, the picture of innocence. "I was coming to collect your plates, like you asked me to, and I tripped."

Adam shot Issie a look that told her he had his suspicions, even if he couldn't prove them. Promising Teddy a substantial discount, he clamped a hand down onto his errant barmaid's shoulder and frogmarched her away.

"Tripped, my arse," he said darkly.

Luke Dawson abandoned his reading and joined them at the bar. He glanced at Teddy and his cronies with utter contempt. "Are they causing trouble, Issie?"

"Nothing I can't handle," Issie answered. Teddy was still glowering at her, his face crimson with rage – but when he saw Luke his expression grew murderous. Oh dear. Twice now she'd humiliated him in the local pub. Recalling Alice's warning that Teddy had a mean streak, Issie felt a quiver of misgiving. Why couldn't she have just ignored him?

"They'll calm down in a bit, now that I've promised them a discount," Adam said wearily. "It'll come out of your wages, mind," he added to Issie.

Great. She'd need to find Black Jack's treasure just to pay for Teddy's champagne and oyster supper.

"Let's get you out of their way for a bit. The Pol Brew's gone, so you can nip down to the cellar and change the barrel," Adam continued. "Don't look at me like that. And don't try telling me it's your worst bar job, either, because right now I don't give a toss about that. Any more trouble and you'll be getting the sack – and I mean it this time!"

Issie groaned. Adam was right: changing barrels was the task she hated the most. The barrels were heavy and awkward to fit to the pipes, and the cellar was a cold and gloomy place. Adam must really want her out of the way.

"I could give her a hand, if that's OK?" Luke offered.

"Be my guest." Adam lifted the hatch to the cellar and a gust of cold, damp air swirled around their ankles. "If you can keep her out of trouble you're a better man than I am."

Like most of the buildings in Polwenna Bay, The Ship had medieval origins. Nowhere was this more apparent than in its cellar, which had been hewn out of the rock below. Here the walls glistened with moisture and it was so cold that even in the summer the bar staff wore sweaters when venturing down to change the barrels. The only access was down a rickety staircase that was missing two rungs, and it was made all the more hazardous by the fact that the light could only be switched on from the bottom. Issie had been working on and off in the pub since she'd left school and knew the quirks of the place, but Luke's feet scrabbled on the rungs; several times during the descent she heard him curse.

"Goddammit! Do you Brits have to do everything the hard way?"

"We think it builds character," Issie said. "Besides, if Hitler had landed, the Nazis would have broken their necks before they got to our beer."

"Nice to know you guys have your priorities right. We sure were wasting our time trying to bribe you with chewing gum and stockings."

"You'd be amazed what some of the girls here will do for chewing gum," Issie said as she flicked the light on.

Luke exhaled, any jokes about stockings forgotten as he surveyed the gloomy space around him.

"Jeez, it's like something out of Edgar Allan Poe. How do you get the barrels in?"

"There's a hatch above and the delivery guys lower them down and pull the empties up." Issie wove her way between the barrels. Where was the Pol Brew? Already cold, she was starting to lose sensation in her fingers. If Adam wanted her to cool off then he'd certainly sent her to the right place.

Shadows pooled in the corners and water drip-drip-dripped onto the rocky floor. It was a dank space but perfect for storing real ale.

"How old is this cellar?" Luke asked, wrapping his arms around himself as his breath clouded the air.

Issie rolled a barrel across the floor. "I reckon it has to be fifteenth century, or at least parts of it are."

"Wow, that sure is old. Here, let me do that." Gently putting his hands on her waist, Luke moved Issie aside and lifted the barrel easily. Minutes later, under Issie's direction the gas was disconnected, the keg coupler had been changed and a new barrel had clicked into place. Luke checked to see whether the float and the gas were working, then winked at her.

"Do I pass the test?"

Issie's waist was still tingling from his touch. Oh yes. Luke Dawson passed the test, all right. He was also pretty good at changing barrels.

"You're a man of many talents," she said. "What else are you good at?"

His face was shadowed in the half-light and his eyes were unreadable. Issie sensed that Luke hadn't followed her down to the cellar because he loved changing beer kegs. Was he going to make a move? And did she want him to?

"Not drinking warm beer, that's for sure." Then he added thoughtfully, "Say, do you reckon the smugglers' passageway could be under here? It's wet and damp and not far from the sea."

Oh. Maybe not then. He was still thinking about history. Surprised by how disappointed she felt, Issie dragged her thoughts back to smugglers.

"If you're thinking that they rolled kegs of contraband all the way to the pub for a celebration then I hate to disappoint you. The Ship wasn't always an inn. I think it was a house back then."

"Even better," said Luke. "It would be far less risky to store that kind of thing in a private house. Say, how about we have a quick scoot about and see if we can find anything?"

"What, you think you're going to find a trap door or something?"

"Sure? Why not?"

He wouldn't be the first person to try searching for one, given that there'd always been rumours about a secret passage leading from the beach to the pub's cellar. Issie had certainly never noticed anything unusual, though. Still, there was probably no harm in having another look. Maybe Luke would spot something everyone else had missed. Issie usually took at least ten minutes to change a barrel. That was why Adam had sent her down her just now, to give her time to calm down. It wouldn't hurt to poke about a bit. Not that they'd find anything.

While Luke examined the cellar floor, Issie checked her mobile. There was another text from Mark, which she deleted instantly. His texts were becoming far more frequent. Once upon a time this would have made her heart sing, but lately all Issie felt was a curious detachment. Mark and Westchester Uni and all the misery of that time felt like another life – a life she was glad to have left in the past. Some secrets were better forgotten.

"What do you think to this?" Luke was in the far corner, looking intently at the cellar floor. "Does it look to you like something's been concreted over?"

Issie crouched down and ran her fingers over the rough surface.

"Maybe? It's hard to tell. People have been using this cellar to store things for years."

His dark brows drew together. "There's another layer just under these barrels. See? If we could push them aside it might give us a better look?"

"You can't do that! You'll disturb the real ale!" Issie gasped. "Adam will flip. If I haven't already lost my job, that's definitely a sacking offence."

The corners of his mouth lifted. "Jeez, I just don't get this obsession with warm beer that tastes like socks. OK, honey. I guess there's no more to see here. Maybe there was an access point to the passage; maybe not. I figure there could be. There has to be a reason they called this place The Ship."

Issie grinned. "You do know that nearly every coastal town in Britain has a pub called The Ship? Still, I suppose you might have a point about the passage being under the concrete. I could always ask Silver Starr, our resident psychic, to bring her divining rods over," she suggested, half serious. "Maybe she could tell us?"

"No, don't involve anyone else. I'll use my own divining rod, thanks," Luke said – and then, as her eyes widened at his double entendre, added, "Why are you looking at me like that? I meant my intuition! What did you think I meant?"

Issie's pale skin flushed rose. "I didn't thinking you meant anything!"

"Fibber," said Luke softly. He stepped forward and took her hand, drawing her against his chest. "Fibber."

Issie tipped her head back to look into his eyes and what she saw there made her heart race. He smelt delicious, of fresh air and salt and a tangy aftershave she couldn't place. She could have drunk him in forever. His other hand cupped her face tenderly. Her pulse was running away with her and she could hardly breathe. Then Luke lowered his head and—

"Issie! Issie! What on earth are you doing down there? Brewing the bloody beer? Get up here now! We're rammed!"

Issie and Luke sprang apart as Adam hollered down through the hatch.

"Nice guy, but his sense of timing sure sucks," said Luke.

Issie nodded. The moment had been well and truly shattered. She felt like screaming. Until a few seconds ago, she hadn't realised just how much she wanted to kiss Luke Dawson.

"We'll have to finish this later," he murmured, tracing her cheek with a tanned forefinger. "How about you come over to the cottage after your shift?"

Issie's heart was pounding now. She didn't think she'd ever been so aware of a man's physical presence in her entire life. Her knees felt watery and it was all she could do to nod.

"Come on then, bar lady," Luke said softly. "Better get back to it."

They crossed the cellar to the rickety stairs. While Luke made his ascent Issie flicked off the lights, plunging the place into pitch black again. It felt eerie now. There were secrets lurking here, she just knew it, just as there were secrets buried deep in her own heart. The question was whether or not they were best left alone. Just how well did she really know Luke Dawson anyway? Dare she trust him with her secrets and maybe even her heart?

As she stepped back behind the bar, Issie was troubled. Luke had only been in the village for a few days, yet already he was closer to her than people she'd known for years. Getting involved with him was madness. He was a total stranger. And yet Issie knew without a shadow of a doubt that the minute her shift ended she would be on her way to his cottage.

Of course she would. Issie couldn't back off now even if she wanted to. The treasure and Black Jack and even Mark Tollen were all fading into insignificance. Kissing Luke Dawson was all she could think about.

Chapter 16

Issie shivered. It was a cold, clear night lit by thousands of twinkling stars, and a chilly breeze blew straight across the sea. It was almost midnight now and the village was still, the cottages in darkness and the seagulls huddled up on their clifftop perches for the night. Apart from a slice of moon smiling down, the only light came from the beach café, where Mickey Davey must be having a late one with his friends.

Thinking of Mickey reminded Issie of the earlier incident with Teddy. She sighed. By the time she'd returned from the cellar, he and his friends had left – but Issie knew full well that the episode wouldn't be forgiven or forgotten. Teddy's sister, Ella, had waited nearly twenty years to get her own back on Mo Tremaine, and Issie had no reason to think that Teddy would be any different. She'd crossed a line with him and Issie knew that she'd better have her wits about her from now on, as well as keeping her temper in check. Pulling pints in the pub wasn't quite the career path she'd imagined for herself; nevertheless, it just about paid the interest on her credit cards and she couldn't afford to lose her job. Adam's patience was running thin and she suspected that if anything else happened she'd be getting her marching orders.

In the meantime, she had more than enough to think about with Luke Dawson and their unfinished business. In a few minutes she'd be knocking on the door of his cottage and then there would be no turning back. Unlike her flirtation with Teddy, this thing with Luke was darker and stronger. Was it fanciful to feel that from the moment she'd first seen him some part of her destiny had clicked into place?

God. Just listen to her. She was sounding like Silver bloody Starr! *Just shag the guy and get him out your system*, she told herself sternly. *Stop mooning over him like a bloody teenager.*

It was a plan, she supposed, and with this firmly in mind Issie dug her hands deep into the pockets of her duffle coat and set off down the beach path. She didn't have far to walk. Luke was renting the last cottage in the village, a small and rather neglected one-up, one-down affair that had been built almost on top of the beach cave. It belonged to an elderly fisherman who'd gone into a care home and who was, according to Ashley, sitting on a fortune in terms of real estate. Issie supposed that with a bit of TLC and some rich city trader's bonus thrown at it the cottage could be very pretty. It certainly had a gorgeous view across the bay, and it was right next to the beach steps.

"Come in, it's freezing out there," Luke said when he let Issie in. "I'm not convinced it's much warmer in here though."

He was wearing board shorts and a soft moss-green hoody that matched the flecks in his eyes beautifully. Tanned, barefoot and with his long curls just brushing his shoulders, he could have just strolled off a Floridian beach. It was hardly the typical Cornwall-in-January look, which tended to include long johns and thick socks. Admittedly, the typical look wasn't exactly sexy, but at least you didn't die of exposure nipping from the living room to the loo.

"Aren't you cold?" Issie asked, stepping into the narrow hallway.

He grinned. "I'm freaking freezing! Cold doesn't even come close. Don't worry, I haven't gone mad. I've found a solution. Come on, I'll show you!"

Intrigued, she followed him to the back of the cottage and towards the kitchen. When Luke flung the door open a blast of warm air coiled itself around Issie like a scarf. The low-beamed room was wonderfully cosy, with heavy curtains pulled against the night and a nest of duvets, cushions and blankets piled in front of the range. Candles wedged into empty beer bottles and flowerpots filled the place with flickering light, while jazz played from his iPhone and a bottle of white wine cooled in the butler's sink.

"You lit the Aga!"

He nodded, looking proud. "I found a load of logs in the little shed outside. The old dude must have been stockpiling them for years."

"I hate to break it to you, but that's probably just one load to get through the first part of the winter," Issie said.

Luke whistled. "Christ. How do you guys do it?"

"We don't know any better? I tell you what though, when the spring comes there's nowhere better than Cornwall."

"Yeah? Do you mind if I take your word for that? I don't think I can risk freezing to death for the next four months while I wait to see if you're right."

He opened the wine and poured her a glass while she made herself comfy on the pile of bedding. Hmm. She'd not been in the cottage five minutes and already she was snuggling up in Luke Dawson's duvet. Pure coincidence? Or was he a smooth operator who'd been planning this carefully?

"Hope you don't mind the bedding," Luke said, settling down next to Issie and handing her a glass of Chablis. "I tried moving the old sofa through, but when I heard scrabbling coming from it I decided to give that idea a miss."

Issie's nose wrinkled. "Mice, probably. The house smells a bit fusty. How come you rented it?"

"It was all that was left – and I only got this because somebody pulled some strings for me."

"Some strings. What have they got against you? Honestly, this place can't have seen new furniture since Black Jack Jago was at school. The Polwenna Bay Hotel would have been way more comfortable."

He shrugged. "I kinda like it. Besides, what I want is right here." He put down his wine glass and, drawing Issie to him, kissed her. Issie's heart was pounding. Luke Dawson's mouth against hers was everything she'd hoped it would be. As his kisses grew deeper, she kissed him back, sliding her hand beneath the fabric of his hoody to feel the warm smoothness of his sun-browned back. Just the slightest touch of his fingertips against her own skin made Issie melt like ice cream.

They fell back onto the soft piles of blankets and cushions. Luke's lips were trailing kisses across her throat and his hands were on her waist as he pulled her closer. All rational thoughts fled when she felt the touch of those strong hands brush her breast, and suddenly all Issie wanted was to feel his body pressed against her, onto her and into her. She never wanted this to stop.

Oblivious to everything now except the man whose lips were tracing fiery kisses along her collarbone, Issie closed her eyes and drowned in the deliciousness of every sensation. The unyielding flagstones beneath her back, his hipbones hard against hers, the cold breeze blowing against her heated flesh, the whisper of the sea…

Hold on! What cold breeze? They were lying by the Aga, which was toasty warm, and there was no way she could hear the sea when they were at the back of the cottage.

"Oh my God!" gasped Issie, sitting bolt upright. "It's here all along!"

"What's wrong? Are you OK, honey?"

Luke's face was flushed and his eyes were bright with passion as he reached out to take her hand. With his tousled curls and bare muscly chest he was drop-dead gorgeous – but nothing, not even over six feet of male gorgeousness, could now divert Issie. Her breathing might be ragged, but Issie's thoughts were crystal clear.

"I can feel air blowing through the floor!"

Luke's brow furrowed. "Is that a quaint British expression for saying the earth moved?"

"No – although it did, obviously," Issie said quickly. "Luke, listen to me. I can feel a cold breeze blowing through the cracks in the kitchen floor and I'm sure I can hear the sea."

They stared at each other and, all thoughts of anything else instantly forgotten, Luke crawled over and laid his ear to the floor.

"Jeez! You're right!"

"I think the smugglers' passage might be right underneath us," Issie said slowly. "The big storm must have cleared a part of it."

"No way! That's one coincidence too far."

"You did ask St Wenn to help you find the treasure," Issie reminded him. Then she frowned. "Anyway, what are the other coincidences?"

But Luke wasn't listening. Pulling on his hoody and straightening his board shorts, he headed to the kitchen sink and began to run the taps. Puzzled, Issie watched as he squirted a dollop of washing-up liquid into the sink and began to sluice it around.

Weren't Americans weird? This wasn't the time to do the dishes.

"Trust me; I haven't lost the plot," Luke promised, seeing her confused expression. Filling a chipped mug with some soapy water, he knelt back down beside her and poured a small amount onto the floor.

For a moment the liquid pooled on the cold surface before trickling towards the cement between the flagstones.

"Wait," Luke said. His eyes were trained on the stone with the same intensity that had been focused on her only moments ago. "There! Do you see?"

Issie did see. For a few seconds a bubble formed; then it popped. Then another. And another. All in a regular rhythm, as though a giant was breathing in and out or waves were pounding on the shore…

"There's a gap underneath this cottage," she murmured.

He nodded. "The floor looks pretty solid though. I didn't notice anything that looked like it might have once opened."

"Let's check the whole ground floor," Issie suggested.

The rest of the cottage was bitterly cold, but Luke and Issie were so busy searching for any trace of what might have been an opening or a sealed-up door that they hardly noticed the temperature. It was only when Issie realised that the tips of her fingers were turning blue that they returned to the kitchen to wrap themselves back up in the duvets and defrost.

"I'll never doubt St Wenn again," said Luke, chinking his wine glass against hers.

"I did tell you."

"So what did you wish for?" he asked.

There was no way Issie was going to tell Luke that she'd asked St Wenn to send her a fit man. He'd think she was a total saddo.

Instead, she said, "So, do you really think there's a possibility that parts of the tunnel still exist?"

"Neatly avoided, Miss Tremaine." He held his glass up to the candlelight, swirling the liquid thoughtfully. "In answer to your question; yeah, I reckon that's a distinct possibility. This cottage is real old, so it'd make sense if the smugglers used it back then. My theory is that whatever loot Black Jack managed to carry with him is buried in a blocked part of the tunnel."

She stared at him. "You really think the treasure exists?"

"I wouldn't have come here otherwise."

Issie frowned. "I thought you came here to do research? For your paper?"

Was it her imagination or did a shadow flit across his face? "Yeah, I did. It's on the wreck and the treasure. That's why I had the manifest with me."

This made perfect sense, but Issie couldn't shake the feeling that he wasn't telling her everything. For a moment she toyed with pressing him for more details, before she remembered that *she* wasn't telling *him* everything either. Luke Dawson had no idea that she'd dropped out of university because she'd broken up her tutor's marriage. She could make as many excuses as she liked about being young and manipulated by somebody in a position of trust, but she'd been over eighteen. She was totally culpable, and what she'd done to Emma Tollen was not Issie's proudest achievement. She'd never breathed a word to anyone about any of this. It was better that her family thought she was a flake than that they knew the truth.

She pulled her thoughts back to the present, and to Luke.

Smiling at her, he reached out and curled his fingers around Issie's gold-coin necklace. As he did so, his hand brushed the swell of her breast and her breath snagged in her throat. Tugging the chain gently, he pulled her towards him until she was just a kiss away.

"This is all the evidence I need," Luke said softly. "But d'ya know what? I'm through with all this for one day. Especially when there's something far more exciting to explore than cold cottages."

And as Luke's mouth claimed hers and he lowered her gently down onto the soft pile of pillows, nothing could have been further from Issie Tremaine's mind than treasure or secret tunnels, or even Black Jack Jago himself.

Chapter 17

"You've got to stop walking up here, you silly old fool! You've got a heart condition!"

Alice Tremaine was nearing the end of her tether with Jonny St Milton. Seaspray was a difficult enough house to reach when you were in your prime – Alice should know, having lived there for most of her life – so for a gentleman in his eighties with angina it was the Cornish equivalent of hiking up K2. Now here he was again, for the third morning in a row, standing on her doorstep puffing and with a face the colour of putty.

"I certainly have," Jonny gasped, holding onto the porch for support, "I've lost it to you."

"Have you been reading Mills and Boon again, Jonny?"

"No, a certain locally written book is more my thing," he replied with a wicked glint in his grey eyes. "I've always preferred facts to fiction."

Alice chose to ignore this. If Jonny wanted to believe that he was the inspiration for her alpha male, then let him. The fact that his assumption was completely right was a secret she was determined to take to her grave.

"You're going to kill yourself making this climb every day," she scolded. "Have a sit-down on the terrace to get your breath back, you silly man, and I'll get you some water to take your pills."

"A couple of lunches in the pub don't amount to a proper dinner with you, you know. I said I'd come up every day to ask you for dinner and I will," Jonny called after her. "I won't give up. Even if it kills me!"

He wouldn't either, Alice reflected as she filled a tumbler at the kitchen sink. Jonny St Milton was stubborn, that was for certain. She suspected it was a trait that both his grandchildren had inherited. It was just a shame he hadn't been quite this determined to win her back when it had really mattered…

For goodness sake! That was a lifetime ago and how old had he been then? Only a teenager. Alice shook her head. That was just a boy, really, wasn't it? Look at her grandsons Nick and Zak for instance. They were in their twenties, years older than Jonny had been, and both of them were still acting like fourteen-year-olds. As she carried the water out to the terrace, Alice understood, with the wisdom of almost eight decades, why Jonny had crumbled: the pressure from his parents must have been immense. Yes, of course she could understand – and hadn't everything worked out wonderfully for her in the end, with darling Henry and the family they'd built together? Alice knew all this, and she could never regret her marriage or the path her life had taken. And yet there was still a little corner of her heart that had been broken by Jonny and never fully mended.

Jonny was sitting on the bench with his white head resting against Seaspray's rippled white wall and his eyes closed. The terrace was a suntrap and even in January the area where he sat was basked in golden sunshine. For a moment Alice watched him, seeing not the snoozing old man but the boy she'd once known. The thought that the Jonny who'd once strode across the cliffs and swept her into his arms to carry her over stiles and puddles could now barely walk up to Seaspray made her heart twist painfully, and there was a knot in her throat. Whatever had happened to the people they used to be? How had the years gone so fast?

"Here, drink this and take your medicine," she said, sitting down beside him and passing Jonny the tumbler.

He did as he was told without protest, popping two tiny tablets under his tongue and then sipping the water. Neither of them spoke; in the quiet, they enjoyed the warmth of the sunshine and the view of the glittering bay. Seagulls circled above and the tide was right out, the wet sand a dark horseshoe against the lapping waves. Out of the corner of her eye, Alice could see the colour returning to Jonny's cheeks, and she breathed a sigh of relief. He might well be a stubborn old fool but she didn't think she could bear it if anything happened to him. Oh dear. Did this mean she still cared?

"You've got to stop pushing yourself like this," she said eventually.

Jonny shrugged his Barbour-coated shoulders, and Alice noticed that they were no longer quite as broad as she recalled.

"I'm happy to die for love."

"For heaven's sake!"

He turned and took her hand. "I mean it, Ally. I'm not giving up. Not this time."

Alice glanced down at their fingers. Their hands were gnarled and spotted with age; a lifetime had gone by since they'd last rested peacefully like this. The annoying lump tightened in her throat.

"Fine. You win," she said gruffly. "I'll have dinner with you if that's what it takes to not have a corpse up here."

He squeezed her fingers. "It's not the most flattering acceptance a man could have, but you've made me the happiest man alive."

"Don't get carried away. It's just one dinner," Alice told him, but she left her hand in his anyway and together they sat in comfortable silence, watching the world below. It was only when her son, Jimmy, sauntered onto the terrace that she slipped her fingers away like the guilty teenager she'd once been.

"Morning, Ma; morning Mr SM," Jimmy carolled, perching on the arm of the bench and pushing his wrap-around mirrored shades up onto his head. "Isn't it a glorious day?"

In his sunglasses, white sailing jacket, skinny indigo jeans and flip-flops, Jimmy looked as though he was about to stroll through the streets of Miami rather than Polwenna Bay in January. It took every ounce of Alice's willpower not to suggest he put some socks on.

"Any calls for me?" he asked with a faux casualness that instantly made his mother suspicious.

"Are you expecting any?" she parried.

Jimmy shot her his cheeky smile. "I always live in hope, Ma."

Alice thought that *living in hope* could be her son's motto – and, thanks to him, *dying in despair* would be hers.

"Actually, we've had three calls this morning but when I answered nobody was there." She frowned. This had been happening quite a lot recently. Were debt collectors after her son? It wouldn't be the first time. "Is that something to do with you?"

"Nope, not guilty. Anyway, I have a mobile if people can't get hold of me on the landline."

"Hmm," said Alice, unconvinced. She'd been sure she could hear breathing and suspected there was probably some lovelorn female on the other end. She'd tried dialling 1471 to obtain the caller's number, but it had been withheld. She was about to question Jimmy a little further about all this when there was a loud boom from the village.

Jonny St Milton jumped, his backside literally leaving the seat. "Dear Lord! My poor heart!"

Seagulls rose into the air, screaming their displeasure. Shouts echoed around the valley and a car alarm began to wail.

"What on earth was that?" gasped Alice. She'd never, ever heard anything like this. Not since Plymouth was bombed, anyway. Just the memory of those dark nights lying awake and hearing the planes drone overhead was enough to make her blood run cold.

"An explosion," said Jimmy, his eyes wide.

"Yes, of course, but *what* was exploding?" Alice stood up. "It isn't anything from the marina, is it?"

"We haven't got any gas there," her son reassured her.

"That sounded to me as though it came from right in the centre of the village, maybe near the green?" suggested Jonny.

"Maybe Ivy Lawrence has exploded? Perhaps the sight of a child playing football on the green or someone having a bit of innocent fun pushed her too far?" Jimmy chuckled.

His mother tutted. "Ivy's much less irritable these days, Jimmy." To Jonny, she added, "I don't know about you, but I'm heading down there to see what's going on."

"Too right. This is the most excitement I've had for ages," he said. "I get a date *and* the village blows up. What a morning!"

Ignoring her son's raised eyebrows about the date remark, Alice fetched her coat. Together, the three of them made their way along the narrow path and into the village where, sure enough, a crowd had gathered on the green. Already a policeman was turning people away, and one of the pretty cottages that backed onto the River Wenn had been cordoned off. Mickey Davey was right at the front of the crowd, craning his neck to see what was going on. Local busybodies Sheila Keverne and Keyhole Kate Polmartin were only inches behind him.

Even Chris the Cod and Symon Tremaine had abandoned their restaurants, and a gaggle of holidaymakers had poured out of the tea rooms and gift shops, keen for a slice of the excitement.

Spotting Issie and the good-looking American boy she'd been spending so much time with lately, Alice and Jonny joined them. Jimmy, newly engrossed in a call on his mobile, wandered away into a side street.

"What's happened?" Alice looked around in confusion. She couldn't see anything untoward but there was an acrid smell that made her nose twitch and her eyes water.

"Some visitors tried to blow up the floor of their holiday let," Issie told her. Her granddaughter's eyes were wide circles of incredulity and Alice was pretty certain her own expression was identical. The cottages on the green were at least two hundred years old and picture-postcard pretty, as well as being listed buildings.

"They did what? Why?"

The American boy sighed. "I guess they figure Black Jack Jago's treasure is buried underneath."

"Oh, for heaven's sake!" Alice couldn't hide her exasperation. She was sick to the back teeth of all this nonsense. If things carried on this way there wouldn't be any village left. "It's just a stupid story!"

"That was daft of them. The tunnel's nowhere near the green anyway," added Jonny St Milton.

Issie's friend didn't miss a beat. "So where do you think it is then?"

But Jonny just tapped his nose and smiled. "That's my secret, sonny."

"You really think you went in that tunnel?" Issie asked him.

"I don't *think* I went into the tunnel, dearest girl. I *did* go into the tunnel."

"So tell me where it is!" Issie begged.

"Maybe I'll give you a clue once your grandmother has dinner with me?" he teased. "That way you'll make sure she doesn't change her mind."

"Hell, we'll drive her to the restaurant for you, sir!" promised the American boy. He held out his hand. "I'm Luke Dawson."

"Nice to meet you, Luke Dawson," said Jonny, shaking it and beaming. "That won't be necessary, though, because we'll be dining at my hotel. I'll send my driver to collect Ally."

"I won't be going anywhere if you keep filling their heads with all your nonsense," Alice warned, crossing her arms and shooting her beau a stern look.

"Ah, well, what *you* say is nonsense and what *I* say is true isn't always the same now, is it, Ally?" Jonny replied, his words loaded. "These young people will just have to make up their own minds."

"I know the coin on the necklace is genuine," Luke said.

Alice was startled. How would he know whether or not it was genuine? Even Alice only had her mother's word for it.

"Luke's a historian, Granny," Issie explained, seeing Alice's surprise. "He's here to do research for a paper he's writing on the history of smuggling in Cornwall."

"Is he, indeed?" Alice found this about as hard to believe as Jonny's imaginary trip through Black Jack's tunnel. "Nothing to do with hunting for the treasure yourself then, Luke?"

He gave her a lopsided smile, which, if she were sixty years younger, Alice might have found cute. He certainly had very white teeth, and those green eyes were compelling. Alice's granddaughter was usually more than a match for most men, but this Luke Dawson was something else entirely. Alice couldn't shake off the feeling that there was more to him than he was letting on. *I hope Issie doesn't get hurt*, she thought.

"I can't deny I'd like to find that treasure, ma'am! Who wouldn't?" Luke said.

"Me," Alice told him. "If it does exist, which I very much doubt, it never brought anyone else any luck – so why should things be different now? Just look at what it's already doing to the village without even being found!"

Her voice was shaking with emotion. Alice could hardly bear to see what was happening to her beloved Polwenna Bay. Holidaymakers blowing up cottages, people digging holes in random places, locals cashing in on the excitement with tacky themed food and tours… The list went on and on. Even as she was thinking this the Pollards sauntered by carrying pneumatic drills – and from what her grandson Nick was saying, the majority of the local fishing fleet was out trawling for treasure rather than fish. Where on earth was it going to end?

"That treasure never brought anyone a moment's good luck," Jonny St Milton agreed quietly. "The curse of disturbing it can last a lifetime."

Luke Dawson's emerald gaze was troubled, but not because of talk about curses. "Do you really think the treasure-hunting will affect the village?" he asked. "Surely it's bringing trade – which is a good thing, right?"

"Ask the villagers who live around Loch Ness and see what they think," Alice said bitterly.

"There's supposed to be a monster in the Loch," Issie explained, and Luke laughed.

"I have heard of the Loch Ness Monster! I'm from America, not outer space."

"Which is a long enough way to come just to research a paper," Alice said. "Why are you really here, Mr Dawson?"

There was a brief silence. Then Luke Dawson put his arm around Issie and pulled her against him.

"Does it matter what brought me?" he asked. "I know what I'm staying for."

Issie blushed and Alice sighed inwardly. Luke Dawson, whoever he was, certainly had her granddaughter on side.

"No wonder Teddy's in a foul mood," Jonny remarked.

Foul mood didn't come close, Alice thought. For the past few days that particular young man had been driving his car way too fast through the village and swaggering round with his arrogant cronies. He was trouble; there was no doubt about that.

Looking Luke Dawson straight in the eye, and reluctantly admiring his unflinching returning gaze, Alice nodded. She'd get the measure of this young man one way or another. There was more to him than he was willing to admit; she just knew it. Her eyesight might not be what it once was, but Alice Tremaine could still see when somebody was keeping a secret – and every fibre of her being told her that Luke Dawson's was something to do with the blasted treasure.

Of course, the American boy already had the greatest treasure imaginable in his arms, but maybe only a daft old fool like her would know that. Young people had to make their own mistakes. Alice only hoped that, unlike her and Jonny, Issie and this Luke wouldn't end up with regrets that echoed throughout the rest of their lives.

Chapter 18

"This is exactly what I need," Issie said, wrapping her hands around the coffee cup and sinking back into her seat. "What a morning."

Luke grinned. "Exploding cottages. And there I was thinking you Brits were anti-firearms!"

"I'm not sure if buying a load of explosives off the Internet and rigging them up to blow a hole in a stone floor really counts as using firearms," said Issie. Her face was white. "Jesus, Luke! What were they thinking? Somebody could have been killed."

The police had eventually sealed off the entire village green and moved the spectators on, so Luke and Issie had retreated to Davey's Locker for coffee and a general regroup. Tucked away in a window seat overlooking the bay and the sparkling sea, they were attacking pasties with gusto and analysing the unbelievable events of the morning. If Issie's head hadn't already been spinning from an incredible night with Luke, it certainly was now. She could hardly take it all in.

"I think we're all more likely to die from the fat content in these pasties," Luke said, forking up a huge chunk of golden pastry and munching it. The expression of bliss on his face made Issie laugh. After turning up his nose to start with, he was now a firm fan of this Cornish staple.

"Mickey Davey does make amazing pasties," Issie acknowledged. "Don't ever let Patsy Penhalligan hear me say that though. Mickey's about as Cornish as you are! No wonder he's selling so many of them. My dad's been driving all over the place delivering for him."

"Your pa sounds fun. Your grandma's pretty scary though."

"She's just protective, that's all."

He quirked a dark eyebrow. "Of you or of the village?"

Issie thought about this for a moment. Granny Alice was no fool; none of the Tremaine siblings had ever been able to get anything past her. Without doubt, the next time Issie was alone at Seaspray there would be a full interrogation.

"Both of us," she decided. "She loves the village so much, and seeing all this chaos is all of her worst nightmares coming true."

"And folks blowing up cottages won't have changed her mind, huh?"

"Hardly." Issie put her fork down. Her appetite had suddenly deserted her. "Luke, what if she's right? What if the treasure *is* cursed?"

"Honey, you know that's all mumbo jumbo to keep people from helping themselves, right? It's no different to the tales of ghosts up in the churchyard."

"I suppose so," Issie said, but deep down she wasn't so sure. There was a palpable feeling of avarice in the village at the moment as locals milked the unexpected trade for all they could and greedy treasure hunters stalked the streets.

"I know so." He reached across the table and covered her hand with his. The mere sensation of his strong forefinger skimming over the back of her hand was enough to turn her legs into soggy seaweed as memories of the night they'd just shared came racing in faster than the turning tide. "Honey, we're so close to finding something really special. I just know it."

She nodded. "You really think that the smugglers' passage ran between the pub and your cottage?"

"I think it did." Finishing the pasty and pushing the plate aside, Luke reached for a paper napkin and took a pen from his pocket. "Here's the cave and here's the pub," he said, scribbling a crude map onto the paper, "and here's the church. As the crow flies they all line up, do you see? I think there was some kind of tunnel taking that path, maybe using an existing river channel."

She shook her head. "I don't think so. There's only one river running through the village and it comes out in the harbour."

"One that we know about. What I can't figure out is where the tunnel would begin. The church is too obvious." He threw down the biro and ran his hands through his hair. "There has to be another place. Somewhere nobody would see. My theory is that Jago was carrying the loot somewhere only he knew about. I don't think he shared the plan with anyone else."

"That would make sense," Issie agreed. After all, the secret of the *Isabella's* treasure had died with the notorious wrecker.

"If only that old dude your grandma was with would tell us what he knows," Luke sighed.

"I don't think Jonny knows anything. He just likes to tell a good yarn," Issie said. "Granny Alice says he's a fibber."

"Hmm. I think your Granny Alice has some issues there. Back home she'd probably be in therapy."

"And if she heard you say that, you'd be needing physiotherapy," Issie grinned.

Still, maybe Luke had a point? Her gran had always been prickly about the St Miltons. While Luke scribbled and frowned and began another sketch, Issie pondered on this and watched the world outside. Dr Penwarren was walking his dog on the beach, weaving in between people wielding metal detectors. The Penhalligan brothers were mending nets by the fish market, and Mickey Davey's powerful boat was coming up alongside the outer pier. Unusually, it wasn't full of Mickey's gin-swilling Essex cronies but instead piled high with shopping bags and boxes of veg.

"Look at that," Issie said to Luke. "Mickey's done his shopping by boat. His car must still be blocking those poor holidaymakers in."

Luke whistled. "What a piece of work. Say, why don't we grab a takeout coffee and get out of here? I'm not sure he's someone I want to be around."

"Couldn't agree more," Issie sighed. "It's such a shame he bought the café. With any luck he'll get bored and sell up. Lots of incomers do."

While Luke went to order the coffee, Issie watched Mickey Davey and her father unload the boat. Jimmy seemed thrilled to be helping – but then, he was always happy. As long as Mickey paid him enough to buy beer and cigarettes, Jimmy wouldn't complain. After all, what more did you really need in Polwenna Bay?

I can't end up like Dad, Issie thought. She had to try to get back to university, otherwise in forty years' time that was going to be her.

It was not a happy prospect.

The ringtone from Luke's mobile, which he'd left propped against the salt cellar on the off-chance of picking up a signal, interrupted her thoughts. She glanced at the phone and grew cold all over when she saw the name illuminated on the screen and the accompanying picture.

Stella

Who was Stella? Not his mum, that was for certain. No son would want a head-and-shoulders shot of his mother that made her look like a cross between Pamela Anderson and Katie Price. Crêpey chest and obviously bleached hair aside, whoever Stella was she was undeniably attractive.

Was Stella his girlfriend?

Abruptly, the ringing stopped and Issie realised she was holding her breath. There was a tight feeling in her chest, which felt horribly like jealousy. Jealousy? That was ridiculous. Why should it matter to her whether Luke had a girlfriend or not? There was nothing serious between them. Yes, the sex had been great (better than great – orgasmically, mind-blowingly fantastic actually), but it was still only sex. It wasn't as though she was in love with Luke Dawson or anything. How could she be when she was in love with Mark?

And she *was* in love with Mark. Of course she was. He was the love of her life. Otherwise what on earth had been the point of all that unhappiness?

"OK, we've got coffee. Let's get outa here." Luke passed a paper cup to Issie and scooped up the napkin map and his mobile. Issie watched closely as he checked the missed call; she was curious to see whether he looked pleased, but not a trace of emotion flickered across his handsome face. Instead, he rammed the phone into the back pocket of his jeans without commenting.

OK. So, whoever this Stella was, he wasn't in a hurry to call her back. Issie wasn't sure if she was relieved about this or not. Did it mean he wasn't interested, or was Luke saving the return call for later on when he was alone?

At this thought jealousy's cold hand really did squeeze her heart.

Furious with herself, Issie strode ahead of him out of the café and sprinted down the steps onto the beach. After the warm fug of Davey's Locker the chilly air hit her cheeks like a slap, and she gasped as the wind snatched at her breath. Still, at least the shock of the elements had distracted her from her thoughts.

"Shit! It's cold!" Luke exclaimed.

"You're not in Florida now!" Issie called over her shoulder. "Come on! Race you to the cave."

Physical exercise was what she needed. The burning of her lungs and the scream of her muscles as she pounded across the wet sand was a million times preferable to the twisting sensation she'd felt in her chest a few moments ago in the café. Running as fast as she could, Issie sped towards the cave, her braids whipping against her face and her footprints filling with water. By the time she reached the beach cave, tears were streaming from her eyes and she was panting like Mo's little Jack Russell terrier.

"That's cheating! I was carrying the drink," Luke protested when he caught her up after taking a more sedate jog across the sand.

"Do you want a rematch?"

He laughed. "Hell, no. You look ready to collapse, honey. Here, have some coffee."

Issie took the proffered cup and sipped what was left of the latte as they stood just inside the cave, droplets of salty water dripping down on them from the granite ceiling. It was dank and still and smelt of mouldering, half-forgotten secrets. Issie shivered.

"This place gives me the creeps," Luke admitted.

She looked up, taken aback that he felt it too. "I've never liked it in here. It feels unlucky to me."

"Yeah. You can really believe somebody was trapped near here and died." Reaching for her hand, he led her deeper into the cave, further and further back until the light began to grow murky and their feet sank into a cushion of wet seaweed. Issie didn't protest; all thoughts of the mysterious Stella and of Issie's dislike of the cave were forgotten the instant Luke's skin touched hers.

"There's nothing to see in here," she said.

"Who says I want to look at anything?" Issie sensed his smile in the darkness before he drew her against him and kissed her. Trembling, she lifted her mouth to his and kissed him back. As his tongue probed hers he reached to cup her breast, teasing her with agonising tenderness that made her quiver. Memories of what had happened the last time he'd kissed her made her quite faint with longing.

Luke broke the kiss first, stepping away slightly and catching his ragged breath. "D'you know? This cave is starting to grow on me," he murmured.

"You really do take a girl to all the best places," Issie said, or thought she did. It was hard to tell above the thudding of her heart.

"I try, ma'am. It's the southern charm." He cupped her face in his hands and brushed his lips against hers. "Sweet Jesus, Issie Tremaine. You are driving me crazy. We'd better get out of here before I lose my mind."

Issie couldn't think of anything she'd like more than for Luke Dawson to lose his mind. Every fibre of her being was aching with desire, but the cave was hardly a private place and, much as she enjoyed risk-taking and the thrill of danger, the thought of being interrupted by a dog-walking doctor or a Pollard wielding a pneumatic drill was not a good one.

"I could invite you back to my luxurious lodgings, but I couldn't get that damn stove to light and I'd hate a lady to freeze," Luke said as, hand in hand, they headed back towards the daylight.

"Hard to resist as that sounds, I'm working in the pub at three." Issie wasn't looking forward to it. If Teddy wasn't there making sarky remarks, then Adam would be moaning or Rose would be demanding that Issie should help in the kitchen too. Oh, to go back to the cottage, burrow under the duvets with Luke and spend hours exploring every inch of that gorgeous muscular body until night drew a veil across the sky and they passed out with exhaustion… "I finish at ten, though, so—"

She broke off. Luke had dropped her hand and was crouched on the cave floor, scrabbling in the wet seaweed.

"No way. Impossible!"

"What? What is?"

Luke straightened up and held out a soggy object. For a moment Issie's eyes struggled to adjust to the dim light – but when they finally did so, her mouth fell open.

He was holding her pink flowery hair slide. The very same hair slide that had fallen into St Wenn's Well.

They stared at each other in disbelief.

"I don't suppose you ever lost another of these?" Luke asked slowly.

"No way. I only had the one. Dad brought it back from San Francisco." Issie took it from him. It was sodden and a bit sandy, but very definitely the same hair slide she'd lost to the well. "How is that possible?"

"I have no idea," Luke shrugged, suddenly nonchalant now that Issie was in possession of the object again. "It's a mystery."

"It's more than a mystery," Issie said. Why wasn't he looking more excited? This was incredible! Somehow her hair slide had made its way from St Wenn's Well to the beach. There had to be an explanation and she knew it was something to do with the smugglers.

Luke, however, couldn't have seemed less interested. He looked at his watch and sighed.

"Honey, there's a few things I gotta do now. How about we catch up later once you've finished work?"

Issie frowned. "What things?"

"Just research and stuff."

"For your paper?"

"Yeah, sure, that's right." But Luke couldn't quite look at her as he said this, and Issie felt a prickle of unease. She opened her mouth to ask him more, but Luke was too busy dropping a kiss onto her cheek and promising to call her later to listen to anything she might have to say. Moments later he was sprinting across the beach to the steps, his mobile clamped to his ear before he'd even reached the top.

Who was he calling with such urgency? The mysterious Stella?

Issie walked back to the village with a heavy heart. The thrill of their earlier kisses in the cave and the excitement of finding the hair slide were seeping away, and anxiety tightened in her gut. Luke was hiding something from her.

But what? Was he with someone else?

Was he playing her?

Had she just betrayed Mark for nothing?

This time when her phone vibrated and she saw who was calling, Issie didn't ignore it. Instead she accepted the call with a shaking forefinger.

"Hello, Mark," Issie said.

Chapter 19

"… so you see, Henry, that's why I said 'yes'. It wasn't because I don't still love you dearly or that I've forgotten all the wonderful times we shared. It just feels like the right thing to do."

Alice Tremaine paused and took a deep breath to steady her nerves. *You're being ridiculous!* she told herself. After all, it wasn't as though her husband could really hear her, was it? Yet over the eight years or so since Henry had been gone it had become something of a habit for Alice to walk up to the churchyard, stand by his headstone for a while and tell him what was troubling her.

In those first dark weeks following his funeral, most days had seen Alice Tremaine walking up Church Lane with flowers in her hand and a heart full of sorrow. Yet as time had passed those visits had grown fewer, as the demands of daily life and grandchildren had filled her days. This was, of course, how these things had to be, but Alice still made a point of regularly visiting Henry's resting place. The headstone was weathered now and the earth softly carpeted with grass. Her grief, like the marble, had been tempered by the passing of the seasons. Alice had discovered that in death Henry remained a wonderful listener, and she never failed to be soothed by spending time here, watching the waves roll across the bay and drinking in the timeless peace.

At least, this was how she normally felt, but today's visit was very difficult. It would sound crazy to anyone else, Alice reflected sadly, that she'd been standing at her husband's graveside for over half an hour, trying to justify accepting an invitation to have dinner with another man. And not just any other man, but the very individual who'd broken her heart so badly that Henry Tremaine had spent a lifetime piecing it together. Was it a betrayal to have these growing feelings for Jonny? Or would Henry be pleased that she finally had some resolution regarding that long-ago heartbreak?

"I'm old, my love, and I understand things more now," Alice said slowly, and no sooner had these words left her lips than the sun slipped out from behind a cloud, casting a slice of lemon-hued light across the bay. It was an apt metaphor, thought Alice, for the years of experience that had illuminated her thinking. "Jonny was young and he was afraid. Goodness, he was just a boy really. He wasn't independent and he had no means of making his own way. His life had been mapped out for him since birth. The right school, then Oxford and afterwards inheriting the family home. He'd been raised to know his duty."

High above a gull cried; it was a harsh and lonely sound.

Duty. What an old-fashioned word that was. Indeed, it was an old-fashioned concept – but it had once meant everything. Young men had willingly sacrificed their lives to do their duty for king and country, and children had dutifully done as their parents bid because that was how it was. You did your duty and there was no questioning whether or not it was fair. It was just the way things were. Was it fair that both her brothers had died? Was it fair that she'd left school to help support her mother by working in the big house? Of course not. She was doing her duty. Jake and Danny might understand the concept, but Alice couldn't imagine that her younger grandchildren would. In this age of celebrity worship, the notion of duty was as alien to young people as a world without electricity or the Internet.

"It was so different back then, love, wasn't it?" Alice sighed. She knew that somewhere Henry would be nodding in agreement. He'd always understood what had happened. Of course he had. He'd been the one to pick her up, dust her down and teach her that love might be lost for the moment, but maybe not forever; it would come again as surely as sunshine followed the rain. First love was the most vivid, the most wonderful and the most painful, but it wasn't always the easiest. And it didn't always last.

Yes, back then duty was everything. Jonny was a St Milton, heir to the big house and the estate, and he'd had a duty to his family. Alas, that duty definitely didn't include having a relationship with the housekeeper's daughter – and Jonny had chosen his family over her. Of course he had. What possible choice was there? He was only fifteen and he knew nothing else. Alice understood this now but she certainly hadn't then or for many years afterwards.

"And he's old now. Old and tired like me," Alice finished sadly. "Lonely too, I dare say, just like I've been. The past is exactly what they say it is: a foreign country. And neither of us are those same people. I can forgive him now, Henry, and I really ought to be thankful to him, because if he hadn't abandoned me back then I would never have met you and had so many wonderful years."

The graveyard shimmered and swam before her, and she dabbed at her eyes with a tissue.

"I really hope you understand," Alice said quietly, "because if it wasn't for you, Henry Tremaine, I'd never have dared to hope love could come more than once in a lifetime."

She kissed her fingertips and laid them briefly against the stone, the lichen crumbling beneath her touch and the marble warm in the weak sunshine. Then she turned away, to begin her walk back into the village.

As she did so a blackbird's song fluttered from the yew hedge, and Alice's heart rose with every trembling note.

A sense of peace washed over her. Henry understood and he was telling her that all was well.

* * *

Polwenna House, as it had once been known, sat at the top of the village, reclining on smooth lawns and gazing out across the endless sea. An elegant Georgian mansion, it had been home to the St Milton family for generations, and in bygone days the big house had been a staple employer for many of the villagers. As the car now swept up the drive, past stately cedar trees and weathered statues, Alice Tremaine felt the same twist of nerves she'd had as a girl when walking up to the house for work. Of course in those days she'd never have dreamed of venturing near the grand front entrance with its huge columns and towering door. That door was strictly for the upstairs people only; Alice, her mother and all the other folks who'd worked for the family entered by the back of the house where nobody would see them.

Out of sight and out of mind, Alice reflected, and they hadn't questioned this because it was just the way things were. Her teenage self would never have believed that one day she'd be chauffeured to the house in a beautiful black Jag, the wheels scrunching over the immaculate gravel as the car neared the foot of the sweeping steps. No, Alice Pendeen was more likely to be found scrubbing those same steps. She certainly wouldn't have been invited inside to dine with the son and heir. Instead she and Jonny had pilfered bread, cheese, apples and ginger beer from the pantry for secret picnics down in the St Miltons' private cove, and nothing before or since had ever tasted as wonderful.

How times had changed. Back then she'd been young with smooth skin and thick brown tresses. Her stomach flipping nervously, Alice checked her reflection in her powder compact and smoothed a strand of her hair back into the chignon Summer had helped her with. Her hair was silver now, and there were a few more wrinkles on her skin these days.

Both of us have altered, Alice thought, gazing up at the house. Although it still looked the same on the outside, it had been converted into a hotel many years ago. The small army of staff had also vanished, replaced now with hotel employees and smart managers instead of housemaids, stable boys and Mr Jensen – the old and terrifying butler. If Alice lived until she was one hundred, she'd probably never get over the horror of being caught by him as she'd sneaked out of Jonny's bedroom. The names he'd called her! And Mrs St Milton's icy fury had haunted her nightmares for years.

Both the butler and Jonny's haughty mother had been dead for decades, but as the car halted and the driver opened her door, Alice couldn't help feeling like a teenager again. She half expected to see her mother scuttling towards her, waggling a finger and muttering. Laughing at her foolishness, Alice alighted from the car and, looking around, frowned. Even for a January evening it seemed very empty here. Where were all the cars for the other guests?

"Alice! Welcome!" Jonny St Milton stood at the foot of the steps, smiling at her and holding out his hands. Her own mouth curving upwards in answer, Alice let him take her hands and brush a kiss against her cheek.

Oh! He still smelt exactly the same, and the giddy rush she felt at being so near to him could have belonged to the same girl who'd once trembled whenever those searching grey eyes looked her way.

"You look wonderful," Jonny was saying, stepping back and admiring her. "Green always was your colour, Ally."

Surely she wasn't blushing? Heat rose in her cheeks as she saw the appreciation in his gaze. Alice was suddenly very glad she'd let Summer persuade her into wearing a pretty green tea dress and cashmere shawl, because Jonny was looking exceedingly distinguished in a dinner jacket and bow tie.

"Thanks," she said. "You brush up pretty well yourself. What a smart suit."

"What, this old thing? I just threw it on!" He offered her his arm. "Seriously, Ally. You look a million dollars and I feel like the luckiest man alive."

Arm in arm, they climbed the steps and entered the grand hall. The fire was lit in the enormous marble fireplace, chandeliers glittered above them and every step on the sweeping staircase was laden with red roses. As Alice stared around in amazement, an employee in smart attire stepped forward to take her shawl and a string quartet began to play Vivaldi. The reception desk was deserted. There was not a sign of any other guest.

She turned to Jonny in confusion. "Where's everyone else?"

"There isn't anyone else." He took her hands in his again. "I closed the hotel for the night. It's just us."

"Jonny! You'll lose a whole night's takings! That's crazy!"

"I am crazy, Ally. Crazy about you."

She raised her eyes to the cupola above them and he grinned.

"Too cheesy?"

"Just a little."

"Well, cheesy or not, I mean it. I am crazy about you, Alice. I always was but I was too much of a coward to do anything about it – and I've spent a lifetime regretting that. What's losing an evening's takings in comparison to losing you?" Then he winked. "Besides, it's January. Trade's slow and Ella wanted a night off!"

But Alice knew this wasn't strictly true. Apart from the fact that his granddaughter was a notorious workaholic, the Polwenna Bay Hotel was always popular regardless of the season. With its award-winning chef, famed wine cellar and wonderful views overlooking the bay, the restaurant was usually booked solid. Closing it for one night must have been a logistical nightmare. Oh dear. He really shouldn't have done that on her account.

"No, protests," Jonny said, seeing that Alice was about to object. "I wanted to have you to myself tonight. Anyway, it's the least I deserve after all that walking up to Seaspray. I thought it was going to kill me."

"So did I," she agreed. "Why else do you think I'm here?"

He looked at her intently. "I suppose I'm hoping you're here because, like me, not a day goes by when you don't think about what we once had and what could have been."

Alice was on the brink of replying that she'd been happily married for a very long time and that although she'd sometimes thought a little nostalgically about her first love, as all women do, it hadn't been a major preoccupation. However, it was at this point that the maître d' joined them.

"Excuse me – sir, madam – but the table is ready for you now."

"Wonderful, Serge, thank you." Jonny released her hands and offered his arm. "Mrs Tremaine, may I have the honour of escorting you to dinner?"

Feeling like a film star, Alice placed her hand in the crook of his arm, and together they walked across the grand hall and through the tall door, which led into the restaurant. The last time she'd been here had been for the annual Christmas charity gala and the place had been full to bursting point. This evening, however, it was dark and empty, the only light coming from hundreds of candles and fairy lights strung outside on the terrace.

"We're eating outside? In January? Won't it be cold?" Alice asked Jonny as two waiters held the terrace doors open for them. Stepping into the chilly night and shivering, she wondered if she could ask for her shawl back.

"Fear not, I've no desire to catch pneumonia. Trust me, you'll not be cold where we're going."

Mystified, she allowed him to lead her along the terrace and then down a flight of worn stone steps onto the main lawn. A marquee had been erected and Alice's hands flew to her mouth. Like a small Bedouin tent it was all red and pink silks, lit with dancing white fairy lights and lined with sumptuous velvet hangings. Heaters filled the space with deliciously warm air and a harpist was playing a heart-achingly beautiful melody. In the middle of the tent, with a breathtaking view of the sea and the stars, was a table set for two.

"Do you like it?" he asked.

"I love it! It's wonderful." Alice was stunned. He'd made so much effort.

"I know it probably seems mad to be eating outside in January, but really I'd wanted to take you to our special cove," Jonny explained, holding out a chair for Alice. Sitting down opposite her and reaching into the ice bucket, he continued, "I had all sorts of ideas about how we could get down there. Boats, quads, even a golf cart, but at the end of the day I couldn't avoid the fact that we'd have had to scramble over all those rocks. I tried to see if I could manage it but my bloody hip just wouldn't make it."

Alice didn't know whether to be moved or furious. "You daft old man! You could have injured yourself."

He nodded. "That's pretty much word for word what Ella said. So in the end I had to admit defeat and plump for this as a compromise. Don't worry though; we've still got bread and cheese for dinner."

"And I suppose that's ginger beer, not champagne?"

"You've got it!" He pulled out the bottle and poured them each a glass. Raising his in a toast, he said, "To old friends."

"To old friends." They chinked glasses and as she sipped her drink the sharpness on her tongue was enough to whizz Alice back across the years.

"And are we really having bread and cheese?" she asked.

"This is a little awkward, Ally, but I don't think my teeth are quite up to a baguette," Jonny admitted. "Just for the record, I still have my own and I'm quite partial to keeping them, so I'm afraid a little cheating has taken place. Are you ready to see?"

"I can hardly wait," she said.

A rich stilton soup topped with croutons was served as a starter, followed by mouth-watering cheese soufflé and then apple tart and clotted cream for pudding. Simple it may have been compared to the usual fare that was prepared in the restaurant, but the thought that had gone into the evening's menu showed that even after all these years Jonny remembered their picnics. Alice was touched. As they ate they chatted easily, the memories flowing like the ginger beer and the years seeming to slip away. The boy she had once loved was still there, Alice realised, but he'd also grown into someone new. Life, with all its joys, heartaches and disappointments, had smoothed away the rough angles and harsh planes to form a man who, like her, had lived long enough to know what was important and what really didn't matter a jot.

Status. Class. Money. Parents. Like boulders washed away from the beach by a storm surge, obstacles that had once seemed insurmountable no longer existed.

Once the plates had been cleared away and they were sipping their coffee, Jonny reached across for Alice's hand.

"I'm so sorry for hurting you back then," he began to say, but Alice shook her head and refused to hear another word.

"I know you are and you don't need to apologise again," she told him firmly. "It was a different world then and we were different people. Good Lord, Jonny! We were little more than children. Of course we made choices that we don't always feel proud of, but we've learned to live with those, haven't we?"

He nodded. "That's true. But it wasn't always easy."

"I've been very happy. I had a wonderful marriage and I have a wonderful family. I don't have regrets or hold a grudge for anything that happened all those years ago," Alice reassured him. "Besides, nothing's black and white, Jonny. As I get old I realise that the past is really a collage of greys. So please, no more apologies."

His knotted fingers squeezed hers. "Thank you."

They sat for a while without talking, each lost in thought. The harpist played on, the waves whispered below and somewhere an owl's cry trembled though the frosty night air.

"Is this our new start?" he asked eventually.

Alice sighed. "I'm almost eighty years old. I don't want to spend what time I may have left looking back into the past. Where's the sense in that? I want to enjoy the present and look forward to the future."

"I couldn't have put it better myself," Jonny said. "Which leads me to something I hope I can put clearly, although I'm shaking so much I'm not quite sure I'll manage it."

Pushing back his chair and holding the edge of the table for support, he lowered himself creakily down onto his knees.

"What are you doing? Get up, you silly old man! You'll get stuck!" Alice gasped.

Jonny ignored her, reaching into his pocket and pulling out a simple diamond ring.

"Ally, I love you. I know I'm old and my heart's a bit dodgy, but it works well enough to know it loves you – always has and always will. Nothing has ever changed that, and I promise I'll love you until the day that dicky old heart stops. We might have months, or we might have years, but one thing I do know is that if you would spend them with me then they'll be the happiest days of my life. So, Alice Tremaine, will you do me the honour of being my wife?"

Alice's hand fluttered to her chest. Never mind Jonny's dodgy heart – beneath her ribs her own was doing a very strange jig.

"I've waited a lifetime to be able to ask you this and I should have done so all those years ago," Jonny said, his eyes holding hers with burning intensity. "So, will you, Alice? Will you marry me?"

Would she? Could she? Her thoughts were whirling with a million fears about being too old or too late for all this, but when she looked into Jonny's eyes Alice saw such love and such hope there that all doubt melted away. What was there to be afraid of? When life offered you a second chance then it should be seized with both hands.

"Yes, Jonny," she said quietly. "Of course I'll marry you."

Chapter 20

As the first pinks of dawn streaked the sky with rose and peach kisses, Luke Dawson slammed the laptop lid shut and slumped at the kitchen table. His eyes felt dry and gritty with exhaustion, yet his system was so wired from a cocktail of black coffee and adrenalin that there was no way he'd have got a wink of sleep even if he'd gone to bed. How could he snooze when every instinct he possessed was telling him that the secrets of the *Isabella* were at his fingertips?

Luke yawned and ground his knuckles into his tired eyes. Bursts of colour every bit as vivid as the galleon's lost jewels danced before his vision. He'd spent the small hours online, cursing the weak internet signal that had made downloading the documents he needed so painfully slow, and reading up as much as he could on the ship, the geography of the village and even the possible origins of Issie's necklace. That coin was all the evidence he'd needed that there was truth in the stories. His expert contact in New York – whom Luke had tried to get in touch with a few days ago and then called again before he'd even left the beach yesterday – had suggested that this one coin alone could be worth twenty thousand dollars. The thought that this might be just one of hundreds was mind-blowing.

He exhaled shakily, unable to dare believe what could be about to unfold. The Polwenna Bay treasure was the sort of find people in his industry spent a lifetime dreaming of. And it had the potential to be his find; it could be the discovery that sealed his reputation and set him up for life. Luke just knew he'd been meant to see that news clip and make the trip to England. Yes, this was the start of something huge.

Stella certainly thought so, and when he'd finally accepted her Skype call at just after midnight she'd been beside herself. She was bored, of course, and it was a thrill for her to have something else to think about other than nail appointments or brunch. Unlike Luke she wasn't experiencing the deep satisfaction that came with knowing that your instincts had been right all along. To Stella de Souza, funding this operation was just another way to spend her ex-husband's money and, Luke strongly suspected, to enjoy spiting him by sponsoring the younger man she was sleeping with.

Not sleeping with, *had* slept with, Luke corrected himself sharply. As far as he was concerned, from the second Stella had put the business proposal to him she'd become his sponsor and nothing more. Whatever they'd had between them previously was well and truly consigned to the past. Theirs was purely a commercial relationship now.

"Oh my God!" Stella had gasped when he'd updated her on the latest developments. "That's amazing! And this girl has part of the treasure? Baby! You just have to find the rest!"

"I intend to." Luke had just about managed not to roll his eyes at this. Jesus. What did Stella think he was going to do?

"And it could be worth, like millions?"

For somebody who already had more money than she could spend in one lifetime, Stella certainly loved green, Luke had thought wryly.

But he'd nodded. "Absolutely. In fact I'd say *several* million, although there are strict treasure-trove laws here just as back home. I believe the Crown also has a right. But there could be a salvage award, based on the value of the find. And imagine the kudos it would bring us!"

"Oh my God!" Stella exclaimed again. Her red-lipsticked mouth was an O of amazement. "The Crown! That's the Queen, right? I love the royal family! Especially Princess Kate! Does that mean that if we find it we get to meet the Queen?"

This time Luke really had rolled his eyes. He was starting to get why the Brits might laugh at Americans.

"I doubt it, but you never know."

But at this point in the conversation Stella hadn't been able to think about much more than garden parties at Buckingham Palace, chatting to William and Kate, and even meeting Hugh Grant (Luke hadn't been able to make that link), so he'd given up listening. The call had ended with Stella deciding that if he was successful, she'd introduce him to a friend of hers who was right up there with Gates and Zuckerberg in terms of wealth and would love to sponsor him in the future.

"This English find is gonna be career-making, honey," she'd promised. "Trust me. You'll never look back once my friend Gerry signs on the dotted line. I swear to God this is the start of big things for you."

Recollecting her words now as pink light crept across the sky and seagulls began to call, Luke tried hard to remind himself what this discovery at Polwenna Bay could mean.

A wealthy sponsor meant a big dive boat. The best crew. His reputation sealed. And best of all he could really flip Mal Dawson the bird. It could be everything Luke had always dreamed of. Wasn't that why he'd come all the way to this damp, crowded and very old island in the first place? Of course it was.

The problem was that a small piece of Luke was feeling decidedly uncomfortable about the unravelling events of the past few days. This niggling doubt didn't make any sense. The search for the *Isabella's* lost hoard was going way better than he'd ever imagined it would, and the start of realising all his dreams was possibly only hours away. This was everything he'd hoped for. Everything.

So why did he feel guilty?

Guilt? What the hell was that all about? Professional salvage seekers didn't feel guilty. Christ, thought Luke as he hauled himself up from the table and went to pour a glass of water, leaving the US hadn't done much for his killer instincts. If he stayed much longer in England he'd be in danger of turning into a proper Brit with all that *after you, old chap* and sporting attitude baloney. That wasn't the American Way, was it? Being frightfully polite and self-effacing wouldn't have won the frontier.

But in Polwenna Bay everyone Luke had met had been polite and welcoming, with the possible exception of Teddy St Milton – and Luke could understand why Teddy been riled. Luke hadn't been here long, but already people said hello to him in the street, Adam in the pub knew to serve him a cold Bud Light, and the pasty shop was putting a large traditional aside for him every lunchtime. The villagers trusted each other and they were friendly. Maybe it was something to do with not carrying guns. They trusted him too, and were happy to tell him everything they knew. Would they all have talked so readily if they'd known why he was really here? Would Issie?

Just thinking about Issie made Luke groan. She was a complication he really could have done without. Getting involved with her was utter madness, but he simply hadn't been able to resist.

He watched the waves roll across the bay, the spray flying as they crashed onto the sand. He saw Issie's face everywhere, in the ripples and the surf, and recalled some old guy in a bar telling him once that there would be weeks, days or even just moments in his life that would have their own kind of intensity, as if the time had been concentrated.

It was true, he realised now: when he'd held Issie in his arms for the first time and kissed her, Luke had passed through such a moment. And yesterday, too, a torrent of emotions had broken over him as they'd stood in that cave together. He'd known then deep in his heart that he should tell her the truth before things became even more complicated. But when Issie had kissed him back, Luke hadn't been able to think of anything else but the closeness of her soft curves and the taste of her mouth against his. He'd been utterly lost.

With a dull ache he knew that soon he would have to tell her why he was really here – and that when he did, the disappointment in those eyes would be more than he could bear. She would walk away for good. Of course she would, because he would have betrayed her.

Luke's hands curled into fists. He hadn't come here to get involved. That wasn't Luke Dawson's way in any case. He was a free spirit. He loved women and he loved the sea. Like the wind, he couldn't be caged. Except that the problem now wasn't that anybody was caging him in: it was that he feared being kept out.

As the kitchen clock had ticked away the hours until dawn, Luke had tried to focus on his research, but instead his thoughts had been full of Issie Tremaine; whenever he'd attempted to read, his mind had insisted on skittering off topic and back to her. Those sparkling blue eyes, the determined chin, the cute tilt of her nose with its sprinkling of freckles… Luke had struggled to concentrate on anything else. The incredible night they'd spent together replayed itself over and over again in his memory, until he'd seriously contemplated making use of the icy cold outdoor shower. Not that he was convinced this would help much.

Issie Tremaine had somehow managed to steal under his guard and straight into his heart. And was it any wonder? Issie was everything

Luke liked in a woman. It wasn't just her looks: she was as much a free spirit as he was, as well as sexy and funny and headstrong. She was fiercely independent and had a mind as sharp as his own. He'd found that he could talk to her for hours on end and yet it would only feel like moments; Luke had never known time to pass so quickly. She was as complex as the Cornish landscape – and, like Polwenna Bay itself, with its lemon-sharp light, harsh granite rocks and glittering water, she was drawing him in and captivating him a little more with every day that passed. If he'd believed in St Wenn and destiny and all that baloney, then Luke would have said that Issie Tremaine was his soulmate.

If only he'd met her somewhere else, under different circumstances. The Luke Dawson Issie thought she knew, the history student and intellectual, had existed in another life, just not in this one. No, this Luke Dawson was a mercenary treasure hunter, and not a wholly truthful one at that. He was starting to fear that he'd used her shamelessly to track down the loot. Beneath her fire and determination, Luke had sensed vulnerability in Issie. Somebody had hurt her badly, and instinct told him it had been a man. Unintentionally he was only going to make things worse.

As the daylight stole across the sky, Luke made a decision. He wasn't going to spend any more time with Issie Tremaine. It wasn't fair. Stella might have urged him to phone the girl and ask her to show him more places where the passage could be, but Luke wasn't comfortable with this. It was lying by omission and he wasn't going to be that kind of person anymore. Issie might be upset at first, but she was a big girl and she'd had holiday flings before – coming from Key West, Luke knew these were a rite of passage for anyone who grew up in a seaside town. She'd put him down to experience and move on. Wouldn't she?

Still, he wondered what she'd thought when they'd found the hair slide. Had she fully understood the significance? Issie had been very pale, her blue eyes huge as they'd stared up at him, and he was certain that she'd made the connection. If only he could have told her the truth rather than having to keep it to himself. If only things could have been different. The idea of searching for the treasure without Issie beside him wasn't nearly as exciting. In fact, if it hadn't been for Stella and her investment, Luke was starting to think he would have given the whole thing up as a bad idea.

"Oh, Goddammit!" he said out loud, slamming his fist onto the draining board. How the hell had it gotten so complicated?

Fresh air was what he needed; he was going stir-crazy cooped up in this tiny cottage. Snatching his coat from the back of a chair and pushing his feet into the country boots that had swiftly replaced his flip-flops, Luke let himself into the new day.

It was a biting cold Cornish winter morning, so sharp that it snatched the breath from Luke's lungs and made his nose and ears tingle the moment he stepped outside. The sky was pink and gold now and the sea an oily blue. A trawler was steaming out of the harbour and another was being filled with ice, but apart from that all was still. Even the gulls seemed to have given up. Frost had iced the grass and made the village sparkle like something Stella would wear for jewellery, except that no diamond would ever come close to the beauty of this place.

Hey! Slow down buddy, Luke told himself. What on earth was he thinking? Steep valleys, sharp rocks and hoar frosts weren't what he found beautiful. No, he was all about palm trees and deep blue water and sunshine. That was what Luke Dawson loved: the warmth of Florida. England was damp and cold and not for him.

Right?

Still, whether or not it was damp and cold here, seeing the sun rising over the hill and the mists hovering over the top of the village was something else. There was a sense of something ancient slumbering beneath the surface, and Luke felt that familiar prickling sensation. The lost cargo was so close he could almost smell it.

He was heading for the small church that stood halfway up the hillside as though it was watching over the village. It was certainly a good vantage point: from St Wenn's the view across the valley was uninterrupted. Anyone standing in the churchyard had a perfect eagle's-eye view into the narrow lanes that wiggled between the tightly packed cottages, as well as being able to watch any goings-on from the beach. In other words it was the ideal place for a smuggler to keep a lookout. From the beach to here to that strange little well in the woods would be a direct line as the crow flew, and Luke suspected there was an underground stream running directly to the cave. His theory was that, over time, the stream had carved out a passage that Black Jack Jago and his ilk had exploited for their own ends, at least until a rockfall had thwarted their activities. This was how Issie's flowery hair slide had found its way into the cave, and it meant only one thing: the big storm on New Year's Day had shifted something in the tunnel and there was now a way through. How long this would remain the case he couldn't tell. The English weather was as unreliable as the heating in his cottage, and another storm could blow in at any moment.

Time was of the essence.

Luke didn't have a plan in mind. Tired and emotionally torn, he was making the climb up to the church as much to clear his head as anything else. Maybe he'd have some inspiration; maybe not. At home he would have put on his sneakers and taken himself off for a run – but no way was he trying that here, not with roads that were practically vertical and covered in ice. A walk seemed the next best option. After all the pasties, he figured he could do with some exercise. Treasure-hunting wasn't foremost in his plans for the morning.

So when he passed through the lychgate and into the small churchyard, only to see Issie pacing across the grass with a look of fierce concentration on her face, Luke was taken aback at first and then impressed. She'd worked it out too then? Of course she had. She was Issie Tremaine, wasn't she? Smart. Determined. And more than a match for him.

Just one look at her was enough to banish all Luke's earlier resolutions; they melted away just like the frost in the sunshine, and with a wave and a smile he strode across the grass to join her.

Chapter 21

Luke! Whatever was he doing up here so early? Issie hadn't expected to see him this morning – and especially not in the churchyard. He'd been so odd yesterday too, charging off like that and not even calling into the pub later to see her; she was starting to think he was having second thoughts about what had happened between them. If so, he wasn't alone. Talking to Mark even for a few minutes had flooded Issie with so much guilt that she'd thought she would drown in it, which was ridiculous because *she* was a free agent. As soon as she'd taken his call, Issie had known it was a mistake.

She didn't love Mark anymore, she realised with a start. When he'd spoken, she'd found that her heart wasn't doing its usual fluttery thing and her throat wasn't tightening with the usual knot of grief for him. Nor had she found herself longing to touch him. Rather than any of that, she'd felt a sense of irritation that he hadn't once asked her how she was, but instead had launched into a tirade against his wife. Emma didn't love him. Emma didn't care about his work. Emma didn't understand him. The words had turned Issie cold. Had he always been this weak and this selfish? And if so, why was it only now that she could see it?

Was it because Luke Dawson's slightest touch had burned through her like wildfire, and just the brush of his mouth against hers had been enough to make her melt with longing? She yearned for him to pull her against his hard body again and to the feel the corded muscles of his arms as she leaned into his chest. It was as though the bliss of being close to Luke had driven out all that had gone before; her feelings for

Mark, which she'd once thought so powerful, had crumbled into dust. He was a weak man, she realised – the kind who would without so much as a second thought betray the woman who loved him if he felt there might be something better elsewhere. How had Issie been so stupid to fall for his lies? She was supposed to be clever, and yet when it came to men it seemed that Issie Tremaine was something of a dunce.

Teddy was turning into a liability. Mark was pathetic and a liar, and Luke Dawson was probably regretting what had happened between them. Maybe she should ask Jules about how to become a nun?

But seeing Luke heading towards her now, with his white smile dancing against his tanned skin, was enough to send her hurtling into confusion. He certainly didn't look like a man who was having regrets.

"I don't need to ask what you're up to. You've figured it out too, haven't you?" Luke drew alongside her and brushed a kiss against her cheek, his lips just missing the corner of her mouth. His cheek was unshaven, and dark stubble rasped against her skin.

"I think the tunnel ran up to St Wenn's Well," she said slowly, and Luke nodded.

"At some point there must have been a way down from the well and the village. It makes perfect sense. The church crypt would be the ideal hiding place, especially if the pastor was in on it too."

"We call them vicars here: St Wenn's is Church of England. My brother's dating our vicar, Jules, but I don't think she'd be big on smuggling. Only if it was packets of chocolate biscuits," Issie told him.

"Pastors. Vicars. Priests. Whatever you call them, they would have been right in the middle of it all. Probably spreading all those stories about ghosts. That would've kept the villagers away at night when they were moving the contraband."

"Then from the church, through the tunnel and up into the woods," Issie concluded. "That way, everything could be carried away quietly, day or night, and nobody would be any wiser. Black Jack could have made use of that same route to move his spoils from the wreck." Her hand stole to Granny Alice's necklace. "That could explain how the coins appeared in the family cottage. Some of his loot was siphoned off straight away – just a handful, before he went back again for the rest later with something to carry it all in."

"But he never made it from the beach back to the well, because somewhere along the way the tunnel collapsed and he was trapped," Luke finished.

They stared at one another.

"Which means he really is still in there," Issie whispered.

It was a grisly thought and she shuddered, recalling how the story went that the treasure was cursed. Granny Alice always said that some things were best forgotten. Was this one of them?

Luke's eyes were bright with excitement. "Somewhere here there has to be an entrance to that tunnel. It'd be sealed off and overgrown, but it'll be here somewhere. I just know it." He reached out and took her hand, tugging her after him. "Come on. Let's see what we can find."

In the early morning sunlight, Issie and Luke scoured the churchyard. They examined gravestones, paced out the distance from the gate to the church porch, got scratched by hedges and yew trees, and even found themselves hiding from Jules when she left St Wenn's after matins and returned to the vicarage. Issie felt bad for keeping things from the vicar, who was a friend as well as Danny's girlfriend, but for now what they were up to was Luke and Issie's delicious secret. Every glance from him and every brush of his fingers against hers promised wicked delights to come.

Finally, after over an hour of fruitless searching, Issie and Luke paused for a breather on the churchyard wall.

"I can't believe we didn't see anything," Luke said.

Issie glanced around. "It's here somewhere. It's just a question of where."

They sat in thoughtful silence for a while, listening to the gulls and the trickle of water flowing from an old horse trough on the lane.

"What is that thing?" Luke asked eventually.

"A watering trough for the horses in the village. It was donated by some long-forgotten benefactor." To be honest, Issie had never paid much attention to the trough. It was something she'd seen most days since she was born, and was as much a part of the village's background as the seagulls and weathered Celtic crosses.

"Here?" He jumped up to look more closely. "Were there that many horses at the church? The land doesn't go anywhere else, does it?"

She shrugged. "Maybe the horses got thirsty while people were in church? I don't know. You're asking the wrong sister. Horses are Mo's thing, not mine."

"And across the lane from the trough is a drain, supposedly for any overflowing water. But *is* it actually a normal drain?"

Luke shot out of the churchyard gate and crouched beside the drain. It was choked with weeds and leaves, and covered with a corroded grille.

"I've never noticed that before," Issie admitted, joining him.

"That's the point. Nobody would." Luke tried to rattle the grille, but it wouldn't budge. "There's water flowing under there and I don't think it's anything to do with that horse trough. My guess is that's just a diversion. Your benefactor, whoever he was, was covering his tracks."

"He did a good job. Polwenna's full of drains and gullies; it's a pretty wet village. I don't think anyone's looked at these for years." Issie could hardly keep the excitement out of her voice. "The Pollards are supposed to keep it all clear but they don't really bother too much. That's why we had all the flooding." She peered closer at the grille. "This looks really old. I bet Old Rog put that down years ago just to stop people falling in and nobody's touched it since. Big Rog and Little Rog would've just left it, I expect."

Luke grinned. "Well, there's warm beer to drink and pasties to eat, so why bother?"

"And the war was probably on when Old Rog stuck this on it. I guess anyone would just assume that the water down there feeds into the Wenn," Issie replied.

"It's echoey." Luke straightened up. "I think that could have been the entrance once. It's blocked now, for sure, and there's no way anyone could fit through. But my guess is it courses through the village and down to the beach. If we follow the pattern of drains that were made to divert water into that channel, I think we may have the path that the tunnel used to take."

It was so simple that Issie couldn't believe it hadn't occurred to her before. Maybe it had taken the fresh eyes of a stranger to see what had been in front of her all along. Polwenna was a village that ran with water all year round, and over the centuries its residents had worked hard to find methods to divert the flow out of the houses and into the river. Except that there were *two* rivers, the River Wenn and the hidden stream that ran from the well and trickled through the cave, before slipping secretly into the sand.

Sure enough, as they walked down Church Lane and into the village, a series of grates and small holes at the side of the road funnelled away the rainwater and run-off from the valley sides. Many of these were choked with leaf litter and mud, causing miniature rivers to flow overland, but nevertheless they seemed to follow a straight line. It was only once they reached the final houses in the village, the last of which was Luke's cottage, that the drains stopped. Nothing seemed to go any further.

"That's it. There aren't any more. The trail stops here," said Luke.

But Issie wasn't so sure. The drains had certainly stopped, that much was true, but there would still be water below. Water was everything here. People fished it, drank it, brewed beer from it, used it to wash in, used it for their sewage... Their sewage... Surely not? For a moment she could hardly breathe. The answer seemed obvious to her now. If she was right, then it was somewhere nobody in their right mind would ever want to look.

"I think I know where an entrance to the tunnel might be," she said slowly.

"Seriously?"

"There's a shed behind your cottage, isn't there?" Her heart was starting to race as she said it.

"Sure, there's a woodshed. I told you, remember? That night we..." He gave her a wicked grin and her pulse skittered all the more. "Well, you know what I'm thinking about. I'd lit the stove after dragging a load of damp logs out of it."

"It's not really a woodshed," Issie told him as together they walked to the back of the cottage to examine the ramshackle building. "It was the outdoor privy."

Luke's brow crinkled. "It's an outdoor what?"

"A privy. Loo? Bathroom? John? Khazi? Bog?"

He held up his hands. "Jeez! You Brits and your toilet obsession. I get the gist, OK? And just in case you're wondering? It's called the restroom where I come from."

"I don't think anyone would want to rest long in here." Issie pushed open the door and they peered in, their eyes adjusting to the dark and their noses wrinkling with the smell of rot and mouse. Something scuttled deep beneath the mouldering woodpile, and fat black spiders lurked in corners. Old scallop dredges rusted silently in the shadows, neglected furniture was piled up like an abandoned game of Jenga, a bicycle with flat tyres listed drunkenly against one of the slimy walls, and bin liners bulged like putrefying corpses.

Luke whistled. "No way! This is seriously the restroom?"

"It was once. Long before indoor plumbing. Even the old man who lived here used the indoor loo instead. He was a recluse though and a bit of a hoarder."

"You figure? Hey, Sherlock Holmes should be real scared!"

"Yeah, CSI Polwenna, that's me." Taking a breath and doing her best not to gag, Issie stepped into the gloom. Oh God. She didn't even want to think what that might be crunching beneath her feet. Luke, just behind her, put a hand on her shoulder and squeezed it.

"You're doing great, because this is totally gross," he said.

It certainly was gross, but Issie knew that she'd have to ignore the urge to spin around and get back into the daylight, if she wanted to find out whether her hunch was right.

"Personally I wouldn't have wanted to make use of this either, unless I *really* needed to go," she said. "To be honest, most of these outdoor privies were either knocked down when people got decent plumbing, or turned into sheds, like this."

"Honey," Luke drawled, "I have never in my life seen a shed like this. Thank the Lord!"

"Anyway, historically I don't think it was uncommon for people to have privies that were little more than holes in the floor, positioned over a stream. The stream would have carried the waste away out to sea. Basic but effective."

"So what you're telling me is that the entrance to the tunnel is through the toilet?"

"Don't I take you to all the best places?" Issie said.

Together, they began the unpleasant task of moving piles of rotting junk aside. Before long they were almost accustomed to the smells and strange scurrying sounds; their growing excitement had lessened their revulsion, and the closer they came to exposing the floor the more likely Issie's idea seemed. Finally all that was left was an enormous paving slab at the furthest end of the shed. When Luke and Issie heaved it aside, they saw that there was nothing underneath except for a hole. Below that, there was gaping darkness. From the marks on the floor it looked as though there had been some kind of toilet over the hole once upon a time – a large box-like structure that would have featured a seat in the middle, presumably – but this had been ripped out long ago and lazily sealed with a slab. How long it had been like this was anyone's guess.

"That's our entrance," said Luke. His expression was hard to read but there was determination there and a harder emotion Issie couldn't quite identify. Her stomach clenched with sudden nerves. Did she really want to do this?

Luke was certainly right that they'd found a way into the smugglers' passage. Whether it was one she fancied exploring, Issie wasn't quite so sure.

But before Issie had time to consider the matter, Luke had switched on his iPhone torch and was lowering himself down. Toilet or not, he wasn't worried. Nothing, it appeared, was going to stop Luke Dawson's hunt for Black Jack's mythical loot.

"It's a narrow tunnel with a small stream," he called up, his voice echoing and seeming far away. "There's only just room for me to stand up, but you might find it a bit easier. Come on, I'll catch you."

The dark and the damp were one thing at ground level. The thought of venturing below into somewhere confined and unknown made Issie hesitate. What if she got stuck? Or the tunnel collapsed on them and they suffocated? Or…

Come on, she scolded herself, *you've wanted to prove this story's true for years! Now's your chance!*

She positioned herself carefully, took a deep breath and lowered herself into the blackness. Luke's hands caught her waist and she felt the warmth of his body as he slid her gently against him until her feet touched the rocky floor. As her eyes adjusted, Issie made out a passage little more than three feet wide. Its green walls ran with moisture, and to the left of them rocks had fallen and blocked the way. But, just as Luke had told her, a little stream trickled merrily over the rocky floor.

"It exists!" Issie gasped. "Oh my God, Luke! I can't believe it really exists!"

He kissed her fiercely and held her close. "Of course it does. You always knew it. You even said so on—"

He stopped and Issie waited for the sentence to finish, but instead he just shook his head. "Anyway, never mind all that. It looks like there's only one way we can go, so how about we explore?"

With the torch casting eerie shadows that leered and leapt at them, Issie and Luke began to walk in the footsteps of Black Jack. The only sounds were their ragged breathing and the burble of the stream. The narrow streets of the village were above their heads, but although now and then a finger of daylight prodded at the darkness through a distant grille, Polwenna felt like another world. Issie could hardly believe that she was really in the same tunnel that Black Jack Jago and his henchmen had used all those years ago. The tunnel really existed!

Granny Alice would be stunned if she could see Issie right at this moment – and not just because her granddaughter was creeping through a secret tunnel, but because Jonny St Milton had been telling the truth all along. Yes, Issie thought, *that* was what would really throw her grandmother. To think that for all these years she'd been calling him a fibber!

They made their way along the tunnel a few inches at a time. In some places Luke had to crawl on his hands and knees because the roof was so low. Eventually Issie had to do the same, and soon her jeans were sodden and her hands aching with cold.

"Dammit!" Abruptly, Luke stopped. He was shining his torch up and down what looked like a sheer wall. The tunnel was inky dark here, except for the torchlight, but as Issie shuffled forward she saw that they'd reached another rockfall. It was blocking almost the entire diameter, from the wet floor to the dripping roof of the tunnel. The stream trickled its way between the crevices and cracks, but for anything bigger than a mouse there was no hope of accessing the tunnel beyond.

The sense of disappointment was overwhelming.

"This must be the rockfall Jonny St Milton was talking about," Issie said, trying to come to terms with the fact.

Luke nodded. "This is as far as we get today."

"Today?" Issie was confused. "How can we go any further?"

"We bring down diggers and specialist equipment, of course. Hey, the hardest bit is done. We've proved the tunnel exists. With that and your grandma's necklace too, there's enough evidence to explore even further. No one's gonna doubt that there's something pretty special buried down here."

"I'm not sure about that, Luke. Won't it cause havoc?" Issie was alarmed. Diggers and excavation? What would that do to the village? Suddenly Alice's warnings, which until now Issie had dismissed as an old lady's paranoia, seemed all too real.

"Hey, it'll be cool. Don't worry, honey, I've handled loads of things like this before. The main thing is to find what's really buried down here and then figure out how to get it out."

Issie was confused. "What do you mean? How have you handled stuff like this before? I thought you were just doing some academic research?"

But Luke wasn't listening. He was busy trying to squeeze his hand through a small gap between the rocks. Swearwords echoed around them as his knuckles rasped against the granite.

It was clear that Luke's hand wasn't going to fit. He turned to Issie and passed her his phone. "Issie, honey, see if you can squeeze your hand through and take a picture. I've put the flash on. It's a long shot, but you never know."

Issie glanced down at the water. It was flowing towards them as well as downhill, and judging by the way it was rising and then falling, this was more than just the stream. The tide was starting to rise; it was seeping in through the cracks at the back of the cave, and at the moment Luke and Issie were squeezed into the narrowest part of the tunnel.

Shit. This could be bad. Wasn't the treasure cursed? And wasn't Black Jack supposed to have drowned in the tunnel when he was trapped?

Her mouth dry with fear, she tugged his arm. "Luke, I think the tide's coming in. We need to go."

"Take the picture, Issie, and then we're out of here." He turned to face her and Issie was taken aback by the determination in his eyes. Where was the happy-go-lucky guy with the honey-warm drawl and laid-back attitude she'd fallen in love with?

Hang on. What was that thought? Had she just entertained the idea that she was *in love* with Luke Dawson?

"Issie! Hurry up!" Luke was urging, glancing down at the water swirling around them. "The phone's all set up. Take it! Take as many as you can, but quickly!"

This was no time to be pondering her emotions. Moving forward, her thumb positioned over the side of phone, she forced her hand through the small gap, wincing as the rough stone scraped her skin. Her wrist was slender and, unlike Luke, she was able to wiggle her hand right through and press the button several times. Pictures of nothing, obviously. Were they really risking their lives for that?

"It's done," she gasped, drawing her hand back through and passing the mobile to him. "I've taken some. Now let's go."

But Luke didn't move. He was staring at the phone.

"Luke!" Issie gave him a shove. The water was definitely rising. "Come on!"

"We're going, honey, I promise. But just look at this quickly and tell me what you see. Tell me it isn't my imagination."

He held the phone out. The screen glowed brightly in the darkness and for a moment Issie was dazzled before her eyes adjusted. When they did she rubbed them once, twice and then three times, just to make sure that she really was seeing what she thought she was.

"I'm not imagining things, am I?" Luke said quietly. His eyes slipped to the rockfall and her own gaze followed.

It was as though the rising tide and the darkness had receded.

"No," she whispered. "It's not your imagination. Unless I'm imagining it too?"

She looked again at the phone's screen, but this time there was no doubting what it showed. The shot Issie had taken, although blurred and dark, had revealed the top of a human skull.

She and Luke had found the last resting place of Black Jack Jago. And there appeared to be something else too. Something that had caught the camera light and glinted.

Chapter 22

Luke didn't remember much of the journey back through the tunnel; his thoughts were such a kaleidoscope of excitement, disbelief and plans that he barely noticed the water swirling around his ankles or the rough passage walls scraping the skin from his hands as he lifted Issie out and hauled himself after her. Even the sight of her gorgeous butt just a few tantalising inches above his head barely registered.

He'd found the *Isabella's* lost cargo. Holy shit! He'd really gone and done it! Just as his instincts had told him, riches beyond imagination lay beneath this quaint little village, hidden for years by legends and fallen rocks, but there nonetheless. That one blurry image on his mobile phone was going to change everything for him and he could hardly wait.

"What are we going to do?" Issie was asking. Her face was pale and she was trembling, although whether from cold or excitement Luke wasn't sure.

He took her icy hands in his and raised them to his lips, an arrow of tenderness shooting through him. Issie was so clever and brave, and without her he would never have got this far. If he hadn't seen her on the TV, he wouldn't have known about the coin necklace and realised that there was truth in the legend. Folding her in his arms, Luke kissed the top of her golden head. Black Jack's loot had been hidden in the tunnel for well over two hundred years. It wouldn't hurt to leave it there for a few more hours.

"We're going to get you warm and dry, that's what we're going to do," he told her. "We're going to worry about the treasure later."

She stared up at him and her blue eyes were dark with worry. "I wasn't thinking about the treasure. Luke, there's a body in there."

Luke squeezed her fingers. He'd dived wrecks more times than he could recall, and coming across human remains was par for the course. All the same, he still remembered the first time he'd come face to face with a skull. Those empty eyes and the leering grin had haunted his dreams for months.

"Honey, I think we know who that is."

"Black Jack," Issie whispered.

"I'd put money on it. He must have been on his way back up to the woods when the tunnel collapsed and he was trapped. The rising tide probably drowned him," Luke replied. A shudder ran through him. Jeez. What a way to go, pinned down in the dark as the brine seeped into your mouth, your nose, your eyes. He wouldn't wish that on his worst enemy.

"The treasure's supposed to be unlucky," Issie reminded him as they made their way into the cottage. She bit her lip. "What if it really is?"

He laughed. "C'mon, honey. You're smarter than that. You don't believe all that horse shit. It was made up to stop the likes of Black Jack trying to steal it."

"Well, whether or not that stuff about a curse was made up, that treasure didn't do him any favours," she pointed out.

"Ill-gotten gains tend to have that effect on the people involved with them," Luke said firmly. There was no way he was having Issie freak out on him now. "I bet there are lots of modern-day drug smugglers who feel pretty cursed when they're banged up or executed."

Issie nodded, but didn't look convinced. While Luke filled the kettle to make tea – Jeez, was he turning into a Brit? – she leaned against the counter and gnawed her thumbnail.

"Maybe we shouldn't say anything?" she said quietly.

Luke was so taken aback that he barely noticed the tap water reaching the top of the kettle and starting to overflow.

"You think we should just keep quiet?" he asked incredulously, finally turning the tap off. "Honey, this is the discovery of the century. I thought you were desperate to find the treasure and prove the story?"

She bit her nail again. "I was but I didn't get it then. It wasn't real."

Ah. Issie had made the mistake of letting it in; Luke totally got that. To succeed in his business you had to harden your heart to the human tragedies and the suffering that invariably led to wrecks. When you explored a dive site you had to remain dispassionate and keep a level head. The moment you realised you were actually plundering a mass grave was the moment your career was over. He'd seen it happen to other people. Emotion was fatal.

He took a deep breath. "This is history and it needs to be documented. We have a duty to do that. We can't just leave it there because you're worried about a load of old mumbo jumbo."

Her gaze, clear and honest, met his. "The manifest exists and the cargo is documented. You already have all you need to write a paper, surely? And the main thing is that we know we were right. So why can't we just leave it where it is?"

Luke couldn't meet her eyes. The truthful answer to her question was that Stella was expecting a return on her investment, and Luke needed this find to set himself up properly. But how could he possibly tell Issie this when he'd not levelled with her in the first place?

"Don't you want people to know you were right?" he asked.

Issie laughed, but it was a harsh sound and nothing like her usually merry giggle. "Are you trying to appeal to my vanity? Yeah, sure there's a nasty part of me that would love to stand on the quay and yell *I told you so* to everyone, but where would that really get me? I know the truth. Do I really want half the village dug up and even more visitors coming in the hope of finding more loot somewhere else as well? Granny Alice is right: Polwenna Bay will be ruined."

Luke ran his hands through his curls. His brain was whirling as he tried to put counterarguments together, but he knew that Issie was talking perfect sense, at least in the context of their original plan. She just had no idea how much he needed that find. His entire future was staked on it.

"That treasure is worth millions," was all he could say. He knew it sounded lame.

"So it all comes down to money? That's all you care about?"

"Money's pretty damn important!"

She swept her arm towards the window and the view of the bay beyond. "More important than this?"

The day was a cold bright blue, and beyond the golden sickle of sand the waves danced. Across the bay, cottage windows glittered in the sunlight and the valley was vivid green. Smoke from chimneys drifted lazily and a small fishing boat chugged out of the harbour gate. The scene was stunning and timeless, and to his horror Luke felt a sharp tug at his heartstrings.

"More important than us?" she said softly.

Torn and confused, Luke Dawson couldn't reply. What the hell had happened to him? He'd only been in this strange place for a short time, but somehow its magic had crept under his skin and into his heart. The harsh beauty and racing clouds, the scoured light and broad seas thrilled him and captured his imagination, just as this determined girl filled his waking thoughts and excited him with her every touch. He'd come to England with one express purpose, and that was to find the *Isabella's* lost treasure. Falling in love with the place and with Issie had never been part of the deal. Some no-strings sex? Sure, he was up for that, like any guy would be. But anything else had never been on the table. It still wasn't.

Luke Dawson didn't do commitment. Ask Stella. Ask any of the girls in Key West. He certainly wasn't about to start now, not when his whole future depended on it. He just had to hold firm. In a few weeks' time this would all feel like a dream.

The million-dollar question (literally) was, did Luke want Issie Tremaine to be a dream? Or did he want every moment to feel as real as all the moments they'd spent together so far?

The cottage was so quiet that it felt as though the whole world was holding its breath in anticipation of his reply. Then Issie's iPhone shrilled and the mood was broken.

"I'd better take this: it's my sister and she never calls," Issie said with a frown as she took the call. "Mo? Are you all right?"

The Tremaines were a tight-knit clan and Luke envied them that. They were the opposite of his splintered family unit. After all, his parents were estranged, his sister was dead, and he and his father weren't speaking. The Dawsons were the original good old screwed-up American family. The Waltons they were not.

"Everything OK?" Luke asked as soon as Issie ended the call. She hadn't said much during it but there had been a lot of gasping, followed by a few exclamations. Now the call was over Issie seemed even more shell-shocked.

"This has to be one of the weirdest days of my life," Issie said, looking stunned. "Mo's just told me that Granny Alice is getting married. Granny Alice!"

"Cool," said Luke. "That's good news, right?"

"I suppose so. It's just a bit of a shock. Mo says Granny wants us all at Sy's restaurant for a celebration lunch. You're invited too, by the way, which means she thinks you're all right."

Luke felt a prickle of guilt. Alice wouldn't think he was *all right* if she knew why he was really in the village…

"Her fiancé's that old dude, Jonny, right?" he said quickly, to cover the sudden feeling of unease.

"Are you psychic? Yes, Jonny St Milton. How the hell did you know that?"

He laughed. "It was obvious something was going on."

"Not to me, it wasn't," said Issie. Then she groaned. "Oh bollocks. I'm going to be related to Evil Ella and Terrible Ted. Kill me now. Do you think they've gone senile? Maybe I can stop this before it's too late."

"Just because they're old doesn't mean they don't have feelings. And besides, there's history there," Luke said.

"You're right. I'm happy for them both; it's sweet. And I'll take your word for it about them having a past, since history's your thing." She smiled up at him, the first real smile he'd seen since they'd returned from the tunnel. It felt to Luke as though the sun had come out from behind louring clouds, and his heart melted. There was such trust in that smile that he felt winded. Christ. He'd do anything to see Issie smile.

Maybe even step away from a fortune?

Yes, he'd even do that. God help him. He was smitten. Totally and utterly smitten.

He stepped forward and took her face in his hands.

"*You* are my thing," he said – and as he kissed her, Luke Dawson knew what his decision was. He just hoped he had the stones and the strength of will to stick to it.

* * *

Jonny St Milton might be old but he certainly did things in style, Luke thought admiringly. Although this was incredibly short notice to organise an engagement lunch, he'd managed to pull it off – albeit that the lunch was slightly later in the day than usual. Symon Tremaine's seafood restaurant was the perfect venue. Low ceilings, small windows and soft lighting created an air of intimacy, and great care had been put into the seating arrangements so that everyone was with their nearest and dearest. Sitting beside Issie, with her fingers woven with his, Luke didn't even need to drink his glass of Taittinger for his head to start spinning; the events of the day so far had already had that effect. After all, it wasn't every day you discovered a king's ransom in lost treasure and decided to turn it away. And it wasn't every day that he realised he was in love.

He was in love with Issie Tremaine. *That* had never been on the agenda, but somehow this small, determined girl with the face of an angel and the courage of a lion had found her way into his heart. As the chatter rose around him like the bubbles in his champagne flute, Luke glanced at Issie and knew he was making the right choice. Where this was going he hadn't a clue, maybe nowhere, but giving up without trying to find out wasn't going to be an option. That he wanted her more than he wanted the treasure surely told him all he needed to know about the strength of his feelings?

Issie's family were out in force for Alice's engagement lunch: the sister with the wild red hair who was married to Ashley with the boat; the oldest brother with his stunning model girlfriend; the injured soldier brother with Jules the vicar; and then Symon, who owned the restaurant and was popping in and out of the kitchen whenever he could. Only two of Issie's brothers were missing, one being out fishing and the other abroad. But even the soldier's ex-wife was present with her new doctor partner, and there was a great-grandchild too, enthusiastically taking pictures. They all clearly adored each other and were having a wonderful time in each other's company.

In direct contrast to the gaggle of noisy, happy Tremaines, Jonny St Milton's family consisted of just two grandchildren – both of whom looked as though they were sucking acid drops and sitting on itching powder. Luke's old adversary Teddy couldn't have glowered more if he tried, especially whenever he looked over at Luke and Issie. Meanwhile Teddy's sister, a sulky skinny blonde, could barely bring herself to look up from the tablecloth. Whenever Alice tried to engage her in conversation, the blonde merely shrugged her bony shoulders.

"That's Evil Ella," said Issie, seeing the direction of his gaze. "Might be beautiful but she's total hell. Hates Mo and Jake with a passion, and not too keen on the rest of us either."

"Neither Teddy or Ella look thrilled by any of this," Luke observed.

Issie laughed. "No shit, Sherlock. Probably think we're going to steal their inheritance when dear old Jonny pops his clogs. That's how their minds work, because that's *exactly* what they'd do. All those two care about is money."

Luke got this. In his world it was all about the green: nobody looked down at people for wanting money, making money or flashing it about. In fact, the bigger your car, the flasher and newer your house, and the more your wife dripped in diamonds, the better. Throw in a boat and a jet ski and it was job done. In England things seemed very different. Take Jonny St Milton for instance. The guy was obviously seriously rich but he was dressed like a tramp, walked everywhere and lived in an ancient house. Even Prince William looked like he could do with a trip to Saks.

No, Luke thought, *I don't get it. Brits are way odd.*

Jonny St Milton stood up, cleared his throat and struck a wine glass with his butter knife until the room became quiet.

"Thank you all for making it here at such short notice," he began, beaming around at them all. "I can imagine that this has come as quite a surprise for many of you—"

"A shock, more like," Ella St Milton muttered, but her grandfather chose to ignore her, pressing on valiantly.

"…but I'm thrilled to say that today I am the proudest man alive because Alice has agreed to be my wife."

Alice, who was sitting beside him, blushed. Luke thought she looked years younger. There was a sparkle in her eyes and she couldn't stop smiling. Happiness was obviously the best anti-ageing product out.

"Senile old fool," Teddy spat, but luckily his vitriol was drowned as everyone clapped and called their congratulations. Looking mutinous, Teddy shoved his chair back and stalked out of the room without so much as a glance in his grandfather's direction.

"Nasty, aren't they?" Issie whispered to Luke. "Poor Granny, inheriting those two. I hope Jonny kicks them out."

Luke was on the brink of replying when the door of the restaurant swung open and a man strode in. Slight in stature, with floppy dark hair and designer wire spectacles, he didn't look anything like the golden- or red-haired Tremaines, or the sharp and spiky St Miltons.

Which party does he belong to? Luke wondered idly, his thumb tracing small circles on Issie's palm. Maybe he was with Ella? From the way this guy's intense hazel eyes were scanning the room, Luke reckoned he must be searching for a woman.

"Issie! There you are my darling!" His face breaking into a smile, the man waved delightedly across the restaurant, apparently oblivious to the celebrations around him.

"Oh my God." Issie's fingers slid from Luke's, in synchrony with the colour sliding from her face. "I don't believe this. No way."

"I had to come." The man was opposite her now and still smiling. "Darling, I'm so sorry I didn't let you know I was coming, but after our call I couldn't think of anything else. I just had to be with you. None of the other things matter. We can work through those, I promise. You were right all along and I should have listened. What matters is that we love each other."

Luke felt as though all the blood in his body had frozen. He waited for Issie to demand to know who this crazy man was and what the hell he wanted, but a part of Luke already knew this wasn't going to happen. Judging by the shocked expression on her face, Issie knew exactly who this was. This man was no stranger.

He was far from that.

"Mark, what the hell are you doing here?" Issie exclaimed.

The man beamed at her. "Exactly what I should have done months ago. I'm telling you how I feel, Issie. It's over with Emma, long over. I love you and I know you still love me. I should never have let you leave. Christ, I'm an idiot, but it's going to be all right now, my darling. We can be together properly."

Issie's mouth was a little o of surprise. She seemed stunned. When the man reached for her hands she let him take them as though in a dream.

"I love you, Issie," the newcomer repeated. "I'll never let you down again. Please come back with me. Marry me. Come back to Westchester like we agreed the other day."

Luke had heard enough. It was pretty damn obvious what was going on. This was Issie's boyfriend, a boyfriend he'd had no idea existed but with whom she'd obviously been in contact. And she wasn't in a hurry to send this man away, either.

He pushed back his chair and without a word turned and walked out of the restaurant. He heard Issie call his name but Luke ignored her; there was no way he was going to stay and look like an idiot. His heart was black with anger. She'd played him, and like a fool he'd fallen for it. Christ. It was the oldest trick in the book, wasn't it? Make the ex jealous by hooking up with somebody else – and in this case it had worked a treat. She'd set the whole thing up. It was obvious.

It was as if a stingray had shot a barb straight through his heart.

Issie Tremaine wasn't the only one who could keep secrets, Luke thought furiously. He had a few of his own too, and somebody who would just love to hear them all.

Thankfully Symon's restaurant was tucked down a quiet side street, and all was calm outside it. Luke leaned against the building and took a deep breath. The narrow road was in shadows, the low winter sun already starting to sink behind the cottage rooftops, and the air was cold against his hot face. Afternoon here was morning in the Caribbean. Back home people would be up and breakfasting in the sun or already lazing by azure pools. In any case, Stella would be awake – and what better way to start her day than with some good news? Pulling his iPhone from his pocket, Luke scrolled through to the Skype app. He was about to have a very interesting conversation. A conversation that was going to change his life forever. Screw anything else like sentiment and scruples. Just look where those got you. Taken for an idiot.

Issie Tremaine needed to learn that some secrets really shouldn't be kept.

Chapter 23

When Issie was a child Granny Alice used to say to her *be careful what you ask for because you might just get it*, and Issie used to laugh because this sounded like complete nonsense. Surely everyone wanted what they asked for? Sweets. Ice cream. Staying up late. Like, duh!

But now, and at the grand old age of twenty-two, Issie finally understood: her grandmother had been trying to warn her that sometimes what you *thought* you wanted and what you *really* wanted were two very different things.

Take finding the treasure, for example. Ever since she was a little girl listening to the legends of the wreckers and the smugglers, Issie had longed to discover Black Jack Jago's loot. When her school friends and siblings had laughed and told her this was just a story, Issie had stamped her foot in rage and sworn that one day she'd prove them wrong. When the wreck had appeared on the beach, which felt like a lifetime ago now, she'd been filled with excitement and her thoughts had been preoccupied with the search for the lost cargo. So she ought to have been ecstatic when she and Luke had seen that sea-washed skull. It should have been all her dreams come true, but it hadn't been like that at all. Instead, Issie had had an overwhelming sense of misgiving, and every fibre of her being had been shrieking that she had to turn tail and run. That treasure was cursed; there were no two ways about it. Men had been murdered for it and others, overtaken with greed, had willingly sacrificed their lives. It was best left buried.

And now there was Mark, yet another perfect illustration of her grandmother's wise words. Not so long ago he'd been Issie's entire world. She'd adored him, and her every waking moment had been filled with thoughts of him. In lectures and tutorials she'd hung on his every word, living for a smile or a kind remark, and unable to believe her luck that he'd singled her out. When she'd discovered that Emma was still very much his wife, Issie had thought her heart would never mend. She'd loved him for almost three years, her three most impressionable years, and stepping away had been excruciating. Not sitting her finals – and disappointing her family because of that – had been nothing in comparison to losing him. How many hours had she spent gazing out to sea and longing for him to appear in Polwenna Bay, even though she knew it was wrong to wish for another woman's husband? To have Dr Mark Tollen, dark and handsome Mark Tollen, sweeping into a big Tremaine family gathering and claiming her for his own would have been all her dreams come true.

And now this was happening for real: Mark was here declaring his love, and she couldn't have been more horrified. The irony of it wasn't lost on Issie. Fate certainly had a sick sense of humour. As he held her hand and gabbled on about how he'd missed her and couldn't live without her, it was all she could do not to snatch it away and tear after Luke. The look of betrayal on Luke's face had cut her to the quick, and she couldn't bear to imagine what he must be thinking.

"Why didn't you call and tell me you were coming?" Issie asked, interrupting Mark in full flow.

An expression of annoyance flickered over his sharp features, then melted away under the brilliance of his smile. Oops. All of a sudden Issie remembered how much he'd always hated being disturbed when in the middle of making a Very Important Point. Very few people ever interrupted Mark Tollen or, God forbid, challenged him. He was used to having hordes of admiring undergraduates hanging on his every word, and they very rarely disagreed with him or corrected him. Which, thinking about it now, wasn't exactly conducive to their learning.

A year on and a year wiser, Issie was starting to understand why a man like this might find his wife, and his equal, *critical* and *not very understanding*.

Emma Tollen probably understood her husband only too well…

Crap, thought Issie now. *Why didn't I realise all this before?* All this time, she'd been eating her heart out for nothing. It wasn't a pleasant discovery. On the other hand, it was surprisingly liberating to look at him and feel nothing but faint annoyance that he'd hijacked her grandmother's engagement lunch to make this unwanted and quite frankly way-too-late declaration of love.

"I wanted to surprise you, sweetheart," Mark said, sitting down in Luke's seat without even being asked and helping himself to a glass of champagne. "After we spoke the other day I missed you so much and I knew there was no point being apart anymore."

Issie stared at him. If only she'd stuck to her guns and not answered that call. She'd only spoken to him out of jealousy because she'd been convinced Luke had called the mysterious Stella. This was what you got for game playing; she really should have learned her lesson after all the drama with Teddy.

Mark leaned over to kiss her cheek. He smelled sour, as though he hadn't washed for a day or two, and he was more stubbly than usual.

"I could tell how much you missed me," he murmured.

He could? Issie racked her brains for anything she might have unwittingly said to make Mark think this, but she drew a total blank. In fact, as she recalled, hadn't he ended the call rather abruptly? A sure sign in the past that Emma had walked into the room.

Aware that her family were doing a very bad job of pretending not to be listening in, Issie stood up.

"We need to talk and this isn't the right place," she told him.

Mark peered at her over the champagne flute. That it had originally been Luke's made irritation flare deep inside Issie. This was typical Mark. He assumed that everything was his by right and there for the taking. Including naïve undergraduates. God. Why hadn't she noticed any of this before? Talk about love being blind. It must have been deaf and dumb to boot.

"We can talk here, sweets. We don't have to hide anymore. Your family is going to get to know me soon anyway."

Issie shook her head. Not if she could help it. "It's too late, Mark. I don't want you here. It's over."

"You don't mean that, Issie. You love me. I know you do. That's just your guilt talking – and it doesn't have to anymore, because Emma and I are over. I've left her. It's not been right for years and she doesn't appreciate me or love me. You know that; she was always the same. I only stayed for Sammy anyway."

The ease with which he dismissed his wife was breathtaking. Who was Dr Mark Tollen? Certainly not the man Issie had believed she was in love with. That man didn't exist. He was just a façade, concealing the selfish shallow creature that Mark really was. And she, silly inexperienced girl that she was, had fallen for it.

"You do know I saw her, don't you?" Issie said slowly.

That day would be etched in her mind forever. It was the reason she'd packed her room up, handed back the key to her digs and then run home to Polwenna Bay and gone travelling soon after, instead of staying for the rest of the academic year and her finals.

Desperate to see Mark, who hadn't answered any of her calls, Issie had broken the cardinal rule and taken the bus to his house. She'd known it was a bad idea. After all, hadn't Mark told her a thousand times that she mustn't ever contact him at home? Emma was volatile, he'd said, and he never wanted Issie to have to face her. Almost three years into their relationship and frantic to see him, Issie had finally plucked up the courage to visit his pretty terraced house. Telling herself that since Emma was a wife in name only (Mark's words, not hers) and that there wouldn't be a problem, Issie had walked up the neat path and pressed the doorbell.

The tired woman who'd answered the door, hugely pregnant and with a toddler in her arms, had known exactly who Issie was and why she was there.

"Oh God, not another one," she'd said wearily.

Issie had stared at Emma Tollen's distended stomach and her legs had buckled. This was not a woman who was a wife *in name only*. Feeble and incoherent with distress, Issie had somehow found herself on Emma's sofa, drinking sweet tea and sobbing while her boyfriend's wife comforted her resignedly. The two women had talked for several hours and by the time Issie had felt strong enough to walk away, she'd known that the relationship with Mark was over. How could it be anything else? He had deceived her right from the very beginning.

"And no doubt she told you a pack of lies," Mark sighed, the very picture of a wronged man. "Issie, my love, how many times do I need to tell you? It's over with Emma. I've left her because it's you I want to be with."

And suddenly Issie understood. It was so obvious that she couldn't help laughing.

"What?" Mark asked, looking offended. "What on earth can be funny?"

"You!" Issie gasped, pointing at him. "You with all your big gestures and your *I love yous*! What a load of rubbish! She's kicked you out, hasn't she? That's why you're here in yesterday's clothes and without having a shave."

"That's rubbish! I left her! I left her for you!"

But he was lying, and his gaze slipped away from hers like butter from hot toast.

"Go home, Mark. I don't want you here," Issie replied.

Two red spots appeared on his cheekbones. "I don't believe you. You don't mean it!"

Issie's fists were clenched with frustration. "I do. I really do. It's over, Mark. Please go."

"I don't know who you are, but you heard my sister and you need to leave." Jake had joined Issie, placing a hand on her shoulder.

"Or else we can always help you on your way," added Danny, stepping forward so that both brothers were flanking her. With his stern, scarred face and severe military crop, Danny looked exceedingly menacing.

Mark blanched. Throwing his weight around with eighteen-year-olds was one thing, but the two eldest Tremaine brothers were quite another. There was a sheen of sweat on his face, and a look of fear.

Once upon a time Issie would have felt pity for Mark – but not now. He was a weak, treacherous man who'd never thought of anyone but himself. If there was anyone she felt sorry for then it was Emma and her children.

Tossing a black look in Issie's direction, Mark rose from his seat. He was doing his utmost to look dignified, but haste made him clumsy and he knocked the champagne all over his trousers. As he stood there huffing and puffing and looking like he'd wet himself, Issie realised that this was the real Mark Tollen, the one who hid behind his status as a tutor and who preyed on vulnerable undergraduates. Urgh. He was utterly pathetic.

"You're making a big mistake," he told Issie coldly. "You'll never find anyone else who loves you like I do."

"I do hope not," Issie said fervently. "Go home, Mark. Make it up with Emma – if she'll have you – and for God's sake don't ruin any more undergraduates' education."

Mark looked like he was about to reply, but with the eyes of everyone in the room on him he thought better of it. Instead he turned his back on Issie and stalked across the restaurant. All was quiet until the door clicked shut behind him, and then excited chatter bubbled up, filling the room. Issie waited for the stab of regret, but she only felt relief. She was free. Loving Mark had been nothing but a burden of guilt, and only now that it was gone did Issie realise how heavily it had weighed on her.

She was exhausted.

"I'm sorry, Granny," she said to Alice. "I had no idea he was coming. I wouldn't have spoilt your lunch for the world."

Her grandmother smiled. "It takes a little more than a man declaring undying love to put me off my lunch."

"I'll be declaring undying love for you every day, so that's just as well," added Jonny, and laughter rippled through the restaurant.

"We'll talk about this later," Alice said, in a tone of voice that told Issie there would be no escaping the grandmotherly inquisition. "I think I understand now why you quit your degree."

Issie hung her head. "I'm so sorry, Granny. I couldn't tell you what had happened. I was too ashamed. I've been so stupid."

"Stupid? Never, my love. I'm proud of you for sticking to your morals."

Issie stared at her grandmother. "Really?"

"Really," said Alice firmly. "But now isn't the time to get into that. Maybe you should go and find Luke? He seemed pretty upset."

Of course. Luke! What must he think? Horrified, Issie nodded.

"I haven't a clue who that was, but I can guess – and it explains a lot," Danny said to Issie, once the waiters had begun serving the starters and the excitement had died down. "Shall I go and give him a good kicking? It might be hard with only one arm and a dodgy leg, but if he's hurt you I'm more than happy to give it a go."

She laughed at this because in spite of his injuries her brother was easily stronger than Mark, and would no doubt terrify him. "Oh, Dan, I've been such an idiot."

"Who hasn't?" Danny said gently. "We love you, Issie, and I wish you'd told us what had been going on with you. Now get out of here and go and tell your friend Luke that he's not just been dumped – because judging by the look on his face when that tosser Mark came in, that's exactly what he thinks."

Issie didn't need asking twice. Poor Luke. She certainly had her fair share of explaining to do and she only hoped he would understand. She sprinted into the street, then looked left and right to make sure Mark wasn't lying in wait with another deadly guilt trip. Having reassured herself that he'd gone, Issie was heading in the direction of the harbour when an arm shot out from a doorway and a hand fastened about her waist. The sweet smell of cannabis mingled with Bleu de Chanel gave the identity of her assailant away in an instant.

"Get off me, Teddy," Issie snapped, shaking off his clammy hand. She really hadn't got time for this. What was up with all the men in Polwenna Bay today? Was there a weird full moon or something?

"Chillax, Is," drawled Teddy. Even in the gloomy doorway she could see that his pupils were huge. Great. Teddy, stoned and belligerent. This was all she needed.

"I only wanted to give you a warning because I care about you. Christ knows why," he continued.

"Yeah right," scoffed Issie. Since his quarrel with Luke, Teddy had been vengeful and resentful; there was no way he'd want to watch out for her now. She didn't trust him an inch.

"I'm serious." Teddy drew on his joint, the tip glowing scarlet, and breathed out a puff of sweet smoke that made her nose wrinkle. "Here I was in this doorway, quietly skinning up and minding my own business, when who happened to pause right here but Captain bloody America?"

"Big deal," said Issie scornfully.

"Ah, but I haven't finished. Our Yank pal then made a very enlightening phone call to a woman. Stella, I think he called her? They seemed very... close."

Issie's face gave away her shock, and Teddy laughed. "I can see that's got your attention. Want to hear the rest?"

Her mouth had dried but, like a rabbit mesmerised by an adder, Issie couldn't have stepped away even if she'd wanted to. Teddy genuinely had heard something. How else could he have known about Stella?

"I don't really understand what he was talking about," he said thoughtfully, inhaling again and blowing smoke rings into the afternoon air. "It's not that I'm totally mashed, Issie, more that it didn't make any sense to me. Whatever have you two found that's worth so much money? What did he mean by," with the joint wedged firmly in the corner of his mouth, Teddy made inverted commas in the air with his fingers, "*hitting pay dirt?* And why is this Stella going to set him up with a boat and a dive team in Florida?"

Blood was racing around Issie's body now, and she steadied herself by laying a hand against the door.

"If I didn't know better," Teddy continued slowly, enjoying every malicious moment of his revelation, "I'd say that your new best buddy isn't quite who he says he is. In fact, I'd say that he sounds just like a professional treasure hunter over here for the express purpose of finding Black Jack Jago's loot. He seems none too scrupulous how he finds it, either. Just the sort of cynical manipulator who'd sleep with a girl who was silly enough to tell him everything he wants to know. Somebody's taken you for a ride, Issie Tremaine, haven't they? They've used you. Led you to believe one thing and then done another. It doesn't feel very nice, does it?"

Issie didn't wait to hear any more. With Teddy's mocking laughter echoing in her ears she was running through the village as fast as she could, through the narrow streets, past the green, over the bridge and then past the harbour and up towards the last few cottages. Even though her lungs were burning she didn't stop; neither did she pause to intervene in an argument between Mickey Davey and the two men in the car park – presumably still blocked in by the belligerent café owner. All she could think about was reaching Luke and finding out what he was playing at. She needed to know who Luke Dawson really was. He'd said he was here to research a paper on the smuggling trade, and he'd certainly had a great grasp of the subject. It had seemed plausible. Yet several times he'd said things that had taken her aback, and for an academic he certainly had a good tan. And his knowledge of handling boats had even impressed the notoriously tricky Ashley. Issie had just assumed this was all part and parcel of growing up on the Keys and living in the sun, but now she was starting to wonder.

Had a cynical and mercenary treasure hunter really taken her for a fool? It didn't seem possible when the time they'd spent together had been so magical. Surely Luke couldn't have faked that?

"What the hell's going on?" Issie demanded when Luke finally opened his cottage door, which she'd been pounding with her fists. Barging past him into the small hallway, she spun around, her braids flying. "Who the hell is Stella? And who the fuck are you?"

Luke closed the door. "While we're playing a game of who the fuck is who, why don't you tell me who Mark is? Or were you planning to keep your boyfriend a secret?"

"Oh no, you needn't think you're getting round it that way." Hands on hips, Issie glowered at him. "Let's not bring my ex into the equation."

"Your ex? Didn't look much like an ex to me."

"If you'd stuck around instead of storming off in a huff you'd have been there to see me send him away," Issie retorted. So Luke was jealous of Mark? That was interesting.

He looked at her long and hard. Was it relief she saw flicker in the depths of those jade eyes? "So you're not in love with him then?"

"No, not that I need to justify myself to you. Are you in love with Stella?"

Luke threw back his head and laughed. The strong muscles in his throat rippled. "Hell, no! It's nothing like that. Stella's my sponsor."

"For that paper you're researching?" She was clutching at straws here, but Issie wanted so much for her worst fears to be nothing more than Teddy's malicious lies. The thought that Luke might have used her stung like a lash.

But his answer was to shake his burnished curls. "I'm gonna level with you. There is no paper and there never was."

"You're not a student?"

His dark brows drew into a line. "Not anymore. Like you, I dropped out. I wanted to join the family business."

"Treasure hunting," she said bitterly. "Don't bother to deny it. I can see the truth written all over your face."

Luke sighed and held up his hands. "OK! I'm a professional treasure hunter. Google Mal Dawson and you'll find all you need to know about my family. It's what we've done for generations. We're salvage experts."

"So you lied to me." It wasn't a question, and tears she was too proud to shed blurred her vision. "You used me to find what you were looking for."

"And you lied to me," he shot back. "You never told me about you and this Mark."

"Because there was no me and Mark!" She stamped her foot in frustration. "Like there's apparently no you and Stella."

"Since we're being honest, you should know that there was a time when we were more than just business partners," Luke confessed. "That's over now though."

Issie glared up at him. "And Stella knows this, does she?"

"Sure, she knows. She's funded my trip here as an investment in the business, and business only. A very good investment as it's turned out."

Issie's heart plummeted. "You've told her about what we found, haven't you?"

His silence was all the answer she needed and Issie's fight drained away.

It was too late. The secret was out and nothing she might say could change that. There weren't words enough in the world to express just how betrayed she felt. Mark Tollen, her lost education and the pain he'd caused her were as nothing in comparison.

"What have you done?" Issie whispered. The tears spilled over her cheeks; she didn't even try to hold them back now. "I thought you cared about Polwenna Bay. I even thought you cared about me, but it was just a pack of lies, wasn't it? People like you only care about money. It doesn't matter to you who gets hurt or what beautiful things are ruined in the process. As long as you have your cut then so what? Me, the village, everyone who welcomed you: we're all expendable."

"Issie, I swear it wasn't like that—"

He stepped towards her and she recoiled. "Don't touch me! Don't you dare! You make me sick, Luke Dawson." Her words were sobs now. Love and hate wrestled in her heart, but most of all she was furious with herself for being stupid enough to have trusted him in the first place. She'd handed a complete stranger the power to destroy the quiet village life that was her sanctuary and that of so many others, whether they lived here or not.

What had she done?

With a strangled cry, Issie shoved past Luke and fled down the path. She hoped with all her heart that she never laid eyes on him again.

Chapter 24

To say that Luke Dawson felt awful was an understatement. In fact, as he watched Issie run away through the cottage garden, he felt like a total bastard. Single-minded, determined and ambitious he might be, but Luke was also being brutally honest with himself now. He knew without a shadow of a doubt that he was in the wrong: he should have told Issie from the outset exactly why he was in the village and what it was he really did for a living.

He hadn't been straight with her. Damn it, he'd as good as lied to her. There was no point sugar-coating it now, by leading her to believe he was a history student with a purely academic interest in the *Isabella*. He'd deliberately sought Issie out because of her connection with the coin and the legend, and he'd used her local knowledge in order to make contacts and follow leads that otherwise might well have evaded him.

No wonder Issie was so angry. After all, she was right wasn't she? He *had* used her. Intentionally at first, which he wasn't proud of, but then he'd pushed that to the back of his mind. As time had passed, Luke had found that he genuinely enjoyed Issie's company. She was fun to be with, intelligent and as passionate about the treasure as he was. Every moment with her had flown. Her knowledge of the village and its history, not to mention the warm welcome of her friends and family, had made his stay in Polwenna Bay special. He knew that it would have remained in his memory forever, even if he hadn't found the lost cargo.

Or fallen in love.

"Dammit!" Consumed with frustration, he slammed his fist into the cottage wall, barely noticing when the stone skinned his knuckles. Physical pain was preferable in any case to this dull ache in his chest. What did a bruised hand matter? Issie's feelings were more than bruised, and seeing the hurt in her blue eyes and knowing that he'd caused it had been unbearable.

Should he have told her the truth earlier than this? Probably, if he'd been smart, but he'd got caught up in the romance of this quaint place and then made things ten times more complicated by becoming too close to Issie. That this hadn't been part of some dastardly master plan was something he knew she was never going to believe. By the time he'd wanted to tell her the truth – and there had been several occasions when a confession had dithered on the tip of his tongue, like a nervous diver standing on the edge of the top board – it had felt too late and there'd been far too much to risk.

He realised now that his feelings for her were stronger than he'd ever imagined. The full extent of them had only become apparent when the unknown man had walked into the restaurant and claimed Issie. That guy was clearly no stranger to her, and the expression on her face had told Luke everything he needed to know. They were lovers. Of course they were. The second Luke had seen her reaction, loss and rage had knifed straight through him.

Issie had lied to him. She was with somebody else. She'd played Luke for a fool. Maybe *she* was the one using *him*.

Prompted by white-hot fury, Luke had barely recalled leaving the restaurant. His anger had been sharpened by self-loathing because, in a moment of weakness fuelled by his feelings for her, he'd decided to give up his dream of uncovering the treasure. Like an idiot, he'd almost put a woman above his career.

Almost.

Before he'd known what he was doing, Luke had called Stella. It may have been morning in the Caribbean, but his news had soon put paid to any objections she had to being woken up. As he'd described the find, she'd shrieked so loudly that he could almost hear her without Skype. Barely a few minutes later, Stella had decided to fly to London and meet up with him. There they would complete and send off the relevant form to register the discovery with the Receiver of Wreck, before deciding what to do next.

"You do have proof?" Stella had asked. "I'll need proof."

"Hell, yeah. I have pictures."

"Great! So email them already."

He'd laughed at this. "Honey, if you were me would you send out a copy of evidence like that? Who knows how secure emails are? I'm not saying I don't trust you but—"

"You don't trust me." Stella had laughed too. "Smart guy. I wouldn't trust me either, in your shoes. Or anyone else, especially if you've found what you think you have. Keep the proof close, huh? That's cool. I can wait a little longer. Does anyone else know about this?"

"Nobody who'll say anything." Of this, Luke was one hundred percent certain. Issie's first reaction had been concern about the consequences for Polwenna Bay. She wouldn't want to tell anyone. Unlike Stella, Issie couldn't have given two hoots about the money; she only cared about the village. In spite of his anger with her, Luke had felt another twinge of regret.

Christ. This wasn't a good time to start developing a conscience.

When the call had ended, Luke had walked back to his cottage. He was still fuming after Issie's betrayal, but the thought of his own dive boat, a professional crew and a massive budget had gone a long way towards calming him down. Returning to the sunshine was also a welcome thought. Hell, back home there would be plenty of gorgeous girls in bikinis to take his mind off Issie Tremaine. Screw her anyway. He was made and his future was secured. This visit to England had been a big success, even if right now it didn't feel that way.

Once back in his cottage, Luke had cracked open a celebratory Bud, although he didn't feel much like drinking it, and had made a start on his packing. He'd figured there was nothing to stay for now, so his best bet was to drive to London. Provided no maniacs in gold Bentleys had blocked him in, of course. Jeez. This was a crazy place full of lunatics; the sooner Luke was gone the better.

He'd already put his bag by the door, and was only minutes from leaving, when Issie Tremaine had come storming up the path to turn his world inside out and upside down. In hardly any time at all she'd scaled the walls of his carefully constructed self-justifications, knocked down the arguments that moments before had seemed so solid, and sent firebombs of guilt into the carefully defended depths of his heart.

Alone now and with her words still ringing in his ears, Luke paced the kitchen. He knew in his gut that she was right.

He *had* lied to her. He *had* used her. Luke couldn't deny these accusations, even if his feelings for her had changed somewhere along the way. No wonder Issie was so angry. And – just to make everything even worse – now that Stella knew the truth, the way of life in Polwenna Bay was about to change forever. All because of him.

Beyond his window the village was basking in wintry sunlight, and above the cottages the January woods were dressed in russets and browns. The cool breeze drifting into the kitchen smelt of salt and damp earth and rotting leaves; smells that Luke knew would for the rest of his life send him hurtling back to this place. Polwenna was a world away from the brazen sunshine and bright citrus hues of Florida, but it had an aching beauty all of its own. Like Issie Tremaine, it had managed to steal into his heart and soul.

Luke grabbed his coat and was striding down the path and through the village before he'd even made a plan. Issie's words had cut him to the core and all he could think about now was trying to make amends. The sun was still shining down but he was barely aware of it, or of spring's promise in the air. There was nothing for him but the bleakness of a future without Issie. Life was a bad joke, wasn't it? Now that he'd found the very thing he'd thought he wanted the most, Luke Dawson suddenly realised that it was meaningless. Black Jack's treasure could remain hidden forever for all he cared: Luke only knew that he had to put things right with Issie. He tried her cell phone, but there was no answer, so Luke turned and made for the cliffs. He figured she must have headed for Seaspray, the Tremaine family's big house that stood sentinel over the village.

The climb up dragged the breath from his lungs but Luke hardly noticed this, or the dizzying view of the village falling away below him. Ignoring the doorbell, he hammered on the door with his hands.

"Issie! Issie! We need to talk!"

But there was no answer. Luke knocked again and then, shielding his eyes against the sunshine, stepped backwards to crane his neck up at the house just in case Issie was looking out of her bedroom window.

"She's not there."

A tall figure stood at the top of the path, outlined against the blue sky. As soon as the person had stepped out of the brightness, Luke recognised that it was Issie's brother-in-law, Ashley Carstairs.

"Where is she? Where's Issie?" Luke demanded. He didn't intend to be rude, but urgency was robbing him of the ability to make small talk.

"Calm down. She's with Mo up at Mariners," Ashley said. His dark eyes were keen as they regarded Luke. "I don't know what's happened between you two, and I don't want to, but she's pretty angry."

Luke sighed heavily. "She's right to be. I've messed up, Ashley, messed up real bad. I'll go find her."

But Ashley shook his head. "Not a good idea, mate. First of all, I'm not having my wife upset under any circumstances at the moment, and secondly I'm afraid you're the last person Issie wants to see. As I said, I don't know what's happened between you, but she's made that part very clear. Right now the women are deep in discussion, and I suspect you're the hot topic of conversation."

Luke would have put money on it. "I can't stay away. I need to see her. I have to explain what happened."

"I'm not having Mo upset for anyone, do you hear me?" There was an edge of pure steel in Ashley's voice; this was not a man to be messed with.

"I won't upset your wife," Luke told him. "I just need to talk to Issie."

"Unfortunately, I don't think she wants to hear anything you have to say. From what I overheard, she thinks you're just another man who's betrayed her trust," Ashley replied.

"But I have to make her understand!"

Ashley lifted his hands in an expressive gesture. "Can I give you some advice, my friend? As someone who knows the Tremaine women a little better than you?"

Luke felt defeated. If Issie didn't want to speak to him and wouldn't take his calls, what else could he do? "I guess so."

"You can try and explain all day long. It won't make any difference." Ashley stated. "I know that sounds bleak, but there's no point my softening the blow and letting you waste your time. Issie's like Mo. Once they make up their minds about something it's bloody hard to persuade a Tremaine to change their mind. Mo changed hers about me, thank God, but it certainly took some doing."

Ashley was a multimillionaire. He'd probably smothered Mo Tremaine in jewellery, Luke thought bleakly. Of course, the irony was that Luke could use the same tactic, now that he'd found his fortune. Not that it would help.

"I'm not talking about buying presents," Ashley remarked, correctly reading Luke's thoughts. "That would be easy, but women like Mo and Issie don't care about *stuff*. They're worth more than that. They can't be bought." His lips twitched. "Believe me, I've bought a lot of perfume and shoes in my time. That was easy and usually very effective. When I found a woman who preferred eau de horse and whose idea of shoe-shopping was to have the farrier visit, I was really stuck. Issie might not be horse mad, but she's a lot more like her sister than most people think."

"So what did you do?"

"I had to prove to Mo that my love for her was real," Ashley said. "It really is true that actions speak louder than words – and rather than chasing Issie Tremaine halfway around the village and shouting, you need to show her how you feel. You need to do something that will prove to Issie beyond all reasonable doubt that you're genuine."

Luke nodded slowly. Yes, that made perfect sense. He'd lied to Issie and betrayed her trust. Why should she believe another word that came out of his mouth? She'd think everything he said was another cynical ploy, and who could blame her when he'd misled her from the moment they'd first met?

Ashley kept his eyes fixed on Luke. "I have a pretty good idea why you're really here and what you really do," he said softly. "From what I saw, you certainly seem to know how to handle a boat. And as for your intricate knowledge of exploring wreck sites, well… I'm afraid something just doesn't add up. My guess is that you're not working on an academic project at all. I can also imagine why you and Issie have fallen out."

Silence fell for a moment.

"You don't miss a lot, do you?" Luke said.

"You don't make millions in the city by going around with your eyes shut," Ashley answered. "But this isn't about me, is it? This is about you and how you can put things right. If you really want to, that is."

"Oh, I want to," Luke affirmed, his voice charged with emotion.

"Then take some advice from someone who really knows what he's talking about here," Ashley said. "There are some things in life worth far more than treasure and money. There are riches beyond your wildest dreams if you only know where to look."

Luke exhaled. It was clear to him what Ashley meant by this. Luke had already found treasure, hadn't he? Before he'd even arrived in Polwenna Bay, fate had given him the biggest clue as to where the real treasure was to be found – only he'd been too blind and too greedy to realise it.

Luke Dawson knew exactly how to prove to Issie Tremaine that she could trust him. After that, whether or not she wanted to be with him would be entirely down to her.

Chapter 25

As if in keeping with Issie's mood, the weather had decided that it was time to forget bright sunshine and clear skies and instead empty the heavens onto the village. The day following Alice and Jonny's engagement lunch had dawned grey and sodden; sea and sky merged with mucky sand and dark slimy rocks, until the whole scene resembled a single leaden smear. Any Tremaines at home were having a quiet day. In Seaspray's cosy sitting room Alice and Jonny were making a list of wedding guests; Jimmy was using the laptop and Nick was slumped on the sofa sleeping off his Sunday lunch. Even Symon was having a rare afternoon away from the restaurant, and was currently relaxing in a chair by the fireside, flicking through the papers.

From her curled-up position in the window seat, Issie tuned out the family chatter and watched the pewter waves chase one another up the beach while the rain trickled slowly down the glass. Nobody was out treasure-hunting today, and even the gulls were silent. Perhaps everyone had given up and life in this small Cornish fishing village in the depths of winter was starting to return to normal.

She drew a heart in the condensation on the big sash window, then scrubbed it off viciously with the heel of her hand. Normal? Nothing was going back to normal. Nothing would ever be normal again now, thanks to Luke bastard Dawson. She'd been so stupid to be taken in by him. How he must be laughing right now. She'd told him everything he wanted to know – and he hadn't even needed to try that hard to get the information from her. One smile from that full sexy mouth, one twinkle of those gorgeous green eyes, and she'd been putty in his hands.

Yes. Issie could just imagine how much Luke Dawson and the mysterious Stella were crowing over her gullibility. For a while – for the sweetest and most blissful interlude she'd ever known – Issie had really thought she was falling in love with him. She'd even thought that maybe, just maybe, Luke felt the same way too. To know that she'd been played from the very beginning was so intensely painful that she couldn't bring herself to tell anyone, not even her sister.

After leaving Luke's cottage yesterday, Issie had fled through the village, little caring about the tears streaming down her cheeks for all to see. Bumping onto Ashley and Mo, who'd been on their way home because Mo was feeling sick, Issie had found herself being scooped up by them and taken into their care. She'd spent the afternoon up at Mariners sobbing as though her heart would break.

"Please, Issie, talk to me. Tell me what's happened," Mo had said, clearly worried. "This isn't like you."

It was true. It wasn't like her at all. Issie was usually so proud; she almost never cried in front of other people, and she wasn't given to sharing the innermost secrets of her heart. Even when she'd been in pieces about Mark, Issie hadn't breathed a word of it to anyone. Yet Mark, the man she'd once believed herself so in love with, faded into nothing when compared to Luke Dawson.

Poor Mo was green with morning sickness but had gathered Issie into her arms and rocked her gently while she choked out the story of how she'd been betrayed by Luke. At some point Ashley had made himself scarce by going to Seaspray to fetch an overnight bag, since the alarmed Mo was adamant that Issie should stay with them. There was no way she was letting her little sister out of her sight in this state. Wine had been opened and tissues had been fetched, and gradually Issie had calmed down and her weeping had subsided. Several glasses of wine later and totally exhausted, she'd fallen into a heavy sleep on the sofa. It was where she'd woken up this morning, toasty warm beneath feather duvets and with Mo's dog Cracker lying on top of her ankles, cutting off the circulation to her feet. Turning down breakfast (which usually came with the condition that she helped Mo muck out her horses), Issie had returned to Seaspray with red and heavy eyes, and an even heavier heart.

Luke Dawson held the future of Polwenna Bay in his hands. What he would choose to do with it was anyone's guess.

Far across the bay the mouth of the cave was a big black yawn. Despite the warmth of the fire in Seaspray's sitting room, Issie shivered to think of the narrow tunnel snaking beneath the village; a tunnel hiding the bones of a long-dead thief.

For as long as Issie could remember, she had adored the story of Black Jack Jago. As a child she'd begged Alice to tell it over and over again. She'd loved imagining the wreckers high on the cliffs with their lanterns, luring innocent ships onto the snaggle-toothed rocks. Mo had been sick of this bedtime tale, *Black Beauty* being more her style, but Issie had never been able to hear it enough times. Although the gold-coin necklace technically belonged to Alice, it was Issie's proudest possession; she'd always dreamed that one day she would find the other riches that had accompanied it. When the wreck had washed up and at last people had begun taking the story seriously, Issie had hardly been able to contain her excitement. Yet seeing the skull had suddenly made everything real, and the dream had melted like frost in sunshine. She realised now that all of her grandmother's warnings were justified: already, the village was flooded with people intent on finding the cache and, worse, excavating it. Besides, there was a body trapped in there with the stolen treasure. Issie shuddered at the idea of disturbing Black Jack's final resting place. She was certain the hoard was cursed, and it seemed unwise to go unsettling things that ought to remain buried. As she'd stared at the photo on Luke's phone, Issie had been struck by an overwhelming sense that they must leave well alone. She and Luke knew the truth and they'd proven that the tale was true. Surely that was more than enough?

She'd never imagined for a second that Luke might not agree. That he'd believed her and shared her passion for the tale was something she'd truly thought of as a link between them, a soulmate's bond even. The notion that he'd simply exploited her for her local knowledge was unbearable. For Luke, finding the lost treasure wasn't about uncovering the past, as it was for her. No, everything he'd told her was a lie. He was a professional treasure hunter, bankrolled by a sponsor and only here for the money. He didn't care about the history, or the village or about Issie. Luke Dawson only cared about the loot.

And Issie hated him.

This morning she'd Googled his family and felt sickened with stupidity. The evidence was right there in front of her. Blue skies, blue water, tanned people with white smiles, Luke and his father beaming at the camera from the deck of their dive boat... It was endless and she'd shut the laptop lid with a howl. She'd been too trusting.

Was this her punishment? Issie wondered now. Emma Tollen must have felt betrayed and heartbroken when she'd seen Issie at the door. It didn't matter that Mark had lied and that Issie had genuinely believed his marriage to be over: Emma must have known this twisting, turning pain that Issie was feeling now; no doubt she'd wept until her eyes were sore too. Seeing Mark yesterday had been a shock, yes, but it had also been liberating. At least Issie knew now that she felt nothing for him. In fact, she'd seen him for the weak man he really was – somebody who lied to everyone, himself included, and who abused his position in order to feel admired and special. He wouldn't have left Emma of his own accord, Issie reflected. Hopefully his wife had seen sense at last and kicked him out. He'd only fled here because he'd nowhere else to go. He didn't love Issie. He never had. There was only one person Mark Tollen loved, and that was himself.

God, but she was an idiot.

"Can't I just pick them?" she said bitterly.

"What was that, sweetie?" Jimmy Tremaine asked, peering up from the laptop. He was busy booking another trip to the USA; unlike the last time though, Jimmy was paying for this with his own money, earned by running errands for Mickey Davey.

"Nothing," Issie muttered. She knew there was no point trying to talk to her father about what had happened. Jimmy would be the first person trying to dig up the village if he thought there was a chance of money. As for discussing her broken heart, well that was never going to happen. Judging by the amount of silent calls they were getting and the Skype history he'd forgotten to erase from the family computer, Jimmy was busy breaking his own share of hearts. There was probably a trail of sobbing women all along the west coast of America. The latest went by the moniker of *Emerald SanFran* and didn't look a day over twenty.

Was it any wonder her love life was such a mess, with Jimmy Tremaine as a role model?

"Can I come to America with you, Dad?" she asked hopefully. A break from Polwenna Bay was just what she needed; that, and a bit of winter sun. Maybe she and Jimmy could do Route 66 and have a bit of father–daughter time? The idea made her spirits lift. It could be fun.

Jimmy didn't seem thrilled by this idea. "Not this time, doll. I've got things planned."

"What things?" Issie asked, knowing full well that it wasn't a case of *what* so much as *whom*. It was typical of her father that he'd rather chase a total stranger than spend time with his own daughter. Issie didn't remember her mother, but she did have vivid memories of Jimmy Tremaine taking off and leaving them. Mo had cried for days.

"Just things, baby girl. We'll go another time. I promise."

Issie wasn't going to hold Jimmy to this. As far as she was concerned her father was just another man in a long line that had let her down.

"You're not still upset about what happened in the restaurant are you, love? I can imagine it was very distressing for you," Alice said, with a worried look.

Issie sighed. Loved-up her grandmother might be, but she still had a nose like a bloodhound when it came to her grandchildren. "It's fine, Granny. Mark's just an ex. I just wasn't expecting him to turn up, that's all, and certainly not at a family lunch and make a scene. We've been finished for ages."

"Just because people are apart doesn't mean that the love has gone," remarked Jonny St Milton, peering at her over his half-moon glasses.

"I don't think I ever really loved Mark in the first place," Issie admitted.

Jonny fixed her with a searching grey-eyed look. "Who says I'm referring to this Mark, hmm? He wasn't the only young man to make a dramatic exit."

Issie screwed up her nose. "If you mean Luke Dawson, he's gone and I won't be seeing him again."

"That's a shame," said Alice.

"I didn't think you liked him?"

"I thought he was very charming, and certainly you seemed happy spending time with him, which was nice to see," her grandmother replied thoughtfully. "I suppose I just didn't like the idea of strangers being so keen to explore secrets that I feel should remain hidden."

"You were right. He's not from here, and Polwenna Bay's past has nothing to do with him," Issie said hotly. "The village's secrets should be left alone. And you should have this back too." She slipped the necklace over her head and held it out to Alice.

Alice was taken aback. "But, darling, you love this necklace."

Issie shrugged. "I don't think I feel the same about any of the Black Jack Jago legends anymore. You're right: it'll ruin the village if people keep coming here trying to find his gold."

"I really shouldn't worry about the village," said Jonny with a wink. "Polwenna Bay can keep a secret or two."

"Meaning what exactly?" Issie asked.

He tapped the side of his nose. "Let's just say that sometimes things that are found have a way of being unfound again. All will be well, that's the *bare bones* of the matter."

Her mouth fell open. Was Jonny saying what she thought he was saying? Had he found the skeleton and seen the gold too, when he was a boy? He'd always claimed to have discovered the tunnel, but she'd never once heard him mention a skeleton or anything else in there. He winked at her again before returning to selecting wedding stationery, and the moment was lost.

Issie glanced outside again. Luke's cottage was in darkness now, and the only evidence that he'd been here at all was the clawing sensation in her chest. In spite of everything, she missed him dreadfully and her mood matched the bleak weather. She was trying as hard as she could to erase the memory of his touch, but whenever she closed her eyes she relived the moments they'd spent alone and her heart beat faster. Her reflection floated before her in the glass, pale and strained. There were dark rings around her eyes too. If this was love then you could keep it.

The shrilling doorbell was a welcome distraction from her gloomy thoughts.

"I'll get it," Issie said, slipping out of the window seat and making her way to the hall. A small pathetic part of her was hoping that when she opened the door she would find Luke there, if only so that she could have the satisfaction of slamming it in his face. But unfortunately it was only Mickey Davey on the doorstep, in a very bad temper.

"I want a word with your brother! Now!"

Issie was not in the mood for bullies. What was he going to do? Park his Bentley across the Seaspray door and block them in to starve?

She raised her chin. "Just the one? I've got five, although it might take a while to fetch Zak from Antigua."

Mickey was puce in the face already from the steep climb up, and now he was turning purple.

"Don't get clever with me, love! You know exactly which one! Is your father in on it? Was this his idea?"

"In on what?" asked Issie, totally confused.

"My delivery!" Mickey's eyes were bulging as he advanced on Issie. "He's stolen my delivery and I want it back. I don't have time for this. I've got the builders in."

"Again?" Issie was surprised. Mickey was always having builders from up country in to work on Davey's Locker – it was a constant source of upset for Little Rog – but whenever she went to the café it always looked exactly the same. There was a new floor and a heavy front door, but apart from that it was pretty shabby. Even the Pollards would have done a better job.

"I think it's me that Mr Davey's looking for."

Symon joined Issie at the door, and instinctively Mickey took a step back to size him up. Tall and slender Symon might be, but Issie's brother had a stillness about him that reminded her of a big cat poised to spring. With his deep-red hair, high cheekbones and piercing blue eyes, he certainly had something of the tiger's latent danger about him.

"Your delivery was left on the doorstep of my restaurant. The driver was looking for a Mr Tremaine, my father I presume, but he was directed to me instead. Your delivery's in my kitchen. Tara should be there soon to open up. She'll let you in."

Mickey narrowed his eyes suspiciously. "Why would they leave it there?"

Sy raised a shoulder. "I'm Mr Tremaine too. It was a reasonable assumption, although I can't imagine ever needing so much flour. Nor can I imagine why you'd think anyone might want to steal it."

"People will half-inch anything, son," Mickey said over his shoulder, already on his way back down to the village. "You can't trust anyone around here. Mark my words."

"Ain't that the truth?" Sy said to Issie as they shut the door. "What an idiot that man is. Throws his weight around, runs the worst café in the village and is obsessed with making pasties. There's something about him I don't like."

"He's a nasty bully," Issie said. "I saw him blocking some holidaymakers' car in with his Bentley, just because they'd parked in his space by mistake. He loved every minute of watching them squirm. He's not moved it for ages, either."

"Sounds about right," said her brother. "I get tossers like that in the restaurant all the time. I wish Dad wasn't so involved with him, but you know our father; a free drink and a tenner and he's anyone's."

"Well, he's off to San Francisco again next week, so that should keep him out of trouble."

"Ah yes, the mystery woman. Good luck to her," grinned Sy. "Pa's certainly been very secretive about it all. She's probably a pole dancer or something."

"She certainly looks very young," Issie said. "About nineteen, I'd say."

"About the right level of maturity for Pa then!" her brother quipped.

But Issie wasn't laughing. She had a very bad feeling about her father's visit to San Francisco, and an even worse one about Mickey Davey. But most of all she was worried sick about what Luke Dawson was going to do next.

Polwenna Bay's future was hanging in the balance and there was nothing anyone could do about it – and it was all her fault.

Chapter 26

Alice Tremaine sat on a bench overlooking the bay and watched the waves running up the beach. As had been her way for decades, Alice had come here to find peace of mind; she drew comfort from the knowledge that this same scene would be here long after she was gone. The view of the village, with the sea and sky stretching out beyond it, somehow made her worries seem smaller and more manageable. This was the magic of Cornwall and of Polwenna Bay in particular, and Alice hoped and prayed that nothing would ever change this.

It seemed ironic that, despite having reached a point in her own life when she had so much to look forward to, Alice was also worried sick about so many other things. She glanced down at the diamond ring on her left hand and felt the warmth of true contentment. It wasn't the biggest or the flashiest engagement ring, but it was classic and pretty, and when Jonny had slipped it onto her finger Alice had cried with pure joy, because this was the ring that a lifetime ago she'd dreamed he'd put there. So much had happened since then – loves had come and gone and whole lives had passed in what felt like the blink of an eye – but his love for her was as strong as it had ever been. Alice knew she was truly blessed to have this second chance of happiness.

Happiness. Was there anything more important than that? If there was, Alice couldn't imagine what it might be. Her ring sparkled in the light, a glittering reminder that although the union it symbolised was the true wealth, there were plenty of people for whom the diamond itself was the thing of value. There were all those visitors who'd flocked to Polwenna Bay in search of treasure, for instance, and the villagers who'd been only too willing to take advantage and make money from them. The Pollards were driving a new van, Betty Jago had booked a cruise and, judging by the hammering and banging from the beach café, Mickey Davey was having yet more work done. The digging on the beach and the destruction of listed cottages didn't seem to bother any of them. Alice sighed. Of course it didn't. Peace and beauty wasn't a currency you could pay into the bank, was it?

The treasure-hunting fever had died down a little as the winter weather had tightened its grip and as people returned to work after Christmas and New Year, but Alice feared this was only an interlude. While there remained a possibility of discovering the lost cargo, people would continue to search for it. Fact, as her great-grandson might say. For some this would just be a bit of fun on a summer's afternoon, a dig in the cave followed by an ice cream, but others wouldn't be nearly as scrupulous. It was only a matter of time before somebody worked the puzzle out and excavations began in earnest. What then of the soul-soothing quiet and the way of life that had gone unchanged for generations? Who would care about that if wealth were at stake?

This was the age of vast lottery wins and of bankers with bonuses that bought entire houses. Everyone dreamed of being rich. *Big Brother*, *The X Factor* and the lottery show dominated the television schedules with their promises of fame and fortune, and they made Alice feel very tired and very old in a way her aching bones never did. She was so out of step with it all because, to her, none of this mattered. Perhaps it was because she'd lived through a world war. Losing a beloved husband and daughter-in-law had certainly put life into perspective too. As far as Alice Tremaine was concerned, she was looking at the true treasure of

Polwenna Bay right now – and once that was plundered, it would be lost forever. Why could nobody else see this?

Well, she'd said her piece and made her views clear. When she'd talked to dear Jonny, he'd merely shrugged and promised her that the village would keep its own secrets. He didn't seem at all worried. She would have to take his word for it, Alice decided, because there was nothing more she could do.

A chilly gust blew and Alice pulled her scarf tighter and huddled into her coat. Seagulls rode the wind, calling raucously, and the rooks in the woods shouted back. A boat's engine chugged into life and on the quay Big Eddie was yelling something over the noise. This was the soundtrack to her life, Alice thought, and she felt comforted.

So she would take Jonny's lead and try to put her fears for the village out of her mind. That left her free to turn her attention to Issie. Alice was so worried about her granddaughter's wellbeing at the moment that her old concerns about the hard partying and the waste of Issie's considerable intellect now felt like minor niggles. Issie, usually a whirlwind of energy and trouble, had been so quiet and withdrawn lately that Alice was alarmed. Her granddaughter had scarcely left the house for two days and she hadn't eaten either, which was particularly disturbing given that Issie normally had a huge appetite.

Did Issie and Luke fall out because of the strange events at my engagement lunch? Alice wondered. *That* had certainly made sense of Issie's hasty and hitherto unexplained exit from university. Alice might be old but she'd correctly read the situation within moments. She knew exactly what kind of man Dr Mark Tollen was. He might be smooth and good-looking, but it was in a groomed way that suggested he was only too aware of his own charms and spent a great deal of time and money on them. No doubt he was arrogant enough to believe he only had to snap his fingers for women to come running. Everything about him had made her hackles rise. Only the gentle yet firm pressure of Jonny's hand on her arm had kept Alice from getting to her feet and sending the interloper packing.

"Careful, Ally," he'd said quietly. "This is Issie's business, not ours. She needs to deal with this in her way, not yours."

He'd been right; of course he had been. One of the things Alice had always loved about Jonny (although it drove her mad, too) was that he was rarely wrong. In general he was not a man to impose his views on others, and so when he did say something it was well worth listening to. Knowing this, Alice had bitten her lip.

Alice could guess exactly what had happened between this Mark person and Issie – it was hardly an original scenario – and her fingers had itched to give his handsome, smug face a hard slap. Actually, Alice would have liked to have made that two slaps. The first would have been for abusing his position of trust as a tutor and ruining her granddaughter's education, and the second would have been for betraying his wife, because Alice knew there *would* be a wife in the background. Men like him, with their ironed shirts and air of contentment, always had a wife somewhere whom they never chose to leave. His had probably just discovered another infidelity and thrown him out – and so he'd come running to Issie, because such men always needed a woman to bolster their weak egos.

Yes, all these thoughts had raced through Alice's mind, but she'd kept her counsel and said nothing. Instead, she'd been proud of her granddaughter's quiet dignity. Issie hadn't crumpled or allowed herself to be persuaded by him, but had sent him packing – just as he deserved. Whatever his hold over her had been, it was clearly over.

Issie had never spoken about her reasons for quitting university, but Alice had long suspected that a broken relationship was the cause. Her granddaughter might be wild at times and headstrong, but she felt things deeply. Once she gave her heart, Issie gave it entirely; that was the Tremaine way. How painful it must have been for Issie, to have had those feelings betrayed. Alice understood now why her granddaughter had become so superficial and so foolhardy lately when it came to relationships, distracting herself by flirting with holidaymakers and the likes of Teddy St Milton. None of these were Issie's equal though, and Alice had hated to see her wasting her time when she deserved so much more.

The mysterious American, however, was something very different. He was undeniably handsome, but Alice had also sensed in him a single-mindedness and a determination that were equally present in Issie. They had that rare potential to work together as a couple and as a team, but only if they were honest with one another. That Mark's existence had been a shock to Luke was obvious, and probably explained why Luke had left so abruptly – but the American was keeping secrets too, of this Alice was certain. What they might be was between him and Issie, but what a waste! Maybe it was her age, Alice thought as she rose carefully from the bench, but she couldn't bear people not grabbing life and all its opportunities with both hands. The years went too fast and what might seem desperately important when you were young was as nothing when you had sixty more years behind you. If Issie felt half as much for this young man as Alice suspected she did, then Alice hoped with all her heart that they could manage to sort their differences out. What she wouldn't have given to see Issie behaving in her usually lively, daft way again.

It was fortunate that Alice was still holding onto the bench while she hauled herself up, because out of the blue there was an explosion so strong that it shook the ground beneath her feet. Glass splintered, the smell of smoke filled the air, and flocks of outraged seagulls rose screaming into the sky. Down in the village people ran into the streets, shouting and calling to one another, and the fishermen sprinted to the quay wall to discover what on earth had happened. Alice's heart was crashing against her ribs and her legs were trembling so badly that she crumpled back onto the bench. The explosion had been so loud that it had made the previous holiday-cottage incident sound like a faint pop. Her ears were still ringing.

For a few terrifying seconds Alice struggled to breathe. If she didn't know better she'd think somebody had detonated an old mortar shell. The fishermen sometimes dredged them up in their trawls, but they were all experienced enough to throw the things back in and hope for the best. Even Nick wasn't daft enough to bring one home.

"Blooming emmets!" she heard Big Eddie Penhalligan holler from the quay. "They'll be treasure-hunting for Black Jack's bloody loot again!"

But Big Eddie was wrong. Treasure-hunting holidaymakers couldn't be blamed this time. Today's explosion had less to do with rogues from the eighteenth century and far more to do with rogue builders. Now that the shock was receding and her breathing was under control, Alice gazed out from her vantage point and saw exactly where the blast had come from – and she gasped. Where the beach café had stood for the past forty years there was nothing left but a pile of matchsticks.

Tongues of orange flames licked through them and within moments the place was ablaze.

Thank goodness it was Monday, the one day of the week when the café was closed. Alice felt quite faint when she thought about how busy Davey's Locker would have been at any other time, especially in January. It was one of the few cafés that hadn't remained shut for the winter. She watched, still stunned by the event, as a host of locals began a bucket chain to douse the flames. She prayed as hard as she could that nobody had been inside. Mickey Davey was a nasty piece of work and Alice didn't trust him an inch, but even he didn't deserve this. And what about his builders or anyone who worked for him? Could they have been inside?

Her hand flew to her mouth. What about Jimmy! He worked for Mickey, didn't he? What if he'd been in the café? Alice had no idea quite what it was her son did – delivering pasties and helping haul Mickey's crab pots, as far as she could tell – but could he have be inside doing repairs or painting? Feeling sick with terror, Alice knew she had to find out. No matter how peculiar she felt, there was no way she could sit here – she had to know whether her son was safe.

Still shaking, Alice began the steep descent. Nothing mattered apart from reaching the café. When she got there at last, she was frustrated to find the area already roped off. A crowd had gathered by now and speculation was rife as to what might have happened. Retained firefighters had arrived at the scene, and the Polwenna Bay Dragon, the ingenious pump that sucked seawater up to douse fires a conventional fire engine could never access, was hard at work.

"Jimmy!" cried Alice, elbowing her way to the front of the crowd. She was desperate to see her son. Oh, she'd never complain about him again if he were only safe and well. "Jimmy! Jimmy!"

"You can't go through there, Mrs T! It isn't safe." Chris the Cod stepped forward, his burly form blocking Alice's progress.

"But I need to find Jimmy," she gasped. "He could be in there!"

"He's not, Mrs T. The place was empty," said Big Rog, mopping his sweating face with a hanky. "I promise. The boy and me were first on the scene and the place was locked."

Alice spun round, frantically. "But he could be inside with the door locked!"

"Alice, don't panic. Jimmy's safe. I've just seen him — he's helping to pass the water buckets along." A comforting arm was around her shoulders, and as the gentle tones of the Reverend Jules seeped through Alice's panic she caught sight of her son through the billowing smoke. His face was smeared with smuts and his eyebrows looked singed, but he was very much alive. Alice felt weak with relief. Jimmy was safe. Her feckless, silly, generous son was safe. Nothing else mattered.

"Do you know what happened here?" she asked Jules, still unable to believe what she was seeing.

The vicar shook her head. "I've no idea. It's caused a huge amount of damage though. The cottages near the beach all have smashed windows."

"There's been a massive rockfall in the cave," said Chris the Cod's wife. "And the explosion really shook the chippy, didn't it love?"

"Certainly did," agreed Chris the Cod. "Ketchup bottles fell off the shelves. It looks like the set of *Saw 3* in there!"

"But what's happened?" Alice paused to catch her breath, still unable to comprehend quite what had taken place. Buildings didn't just explode, surely?

"There must have been a gas leak in the café. Somebody said the cooker's been moved; I bet a pipe fractured. The electrics must have ignited it somehow. You can't be too careful in these old buildings," said Big Rog Pollard, enjoying his newfound role as expert.

"But he's had so much work done. There was always somebody in working on the place," said Adam Harper.

"Was it done properly, though?" asked Little Rog Pollard, struggling to keep the glee from his voice. "These things happen when you don't employ professionals. Don't they, Pa?"

"That's right, my boy, that's right," his father nodded, trying to look sorrowful and failing completely. "Mickey should have asked me if he wanted that old gas stove moved. I know my way around a gas cooker, I do."

"That's not what Ma says," said Little Rog, earning himself a cuff on the head. He didn't seem upset though. In fact he was giggling like an idiot and his father was laughing too. Even Alice's own head felt a bit swimmy and odd, and for some reason she wanted to laugh out loud. She supposed this was probably a reaction to the shock. Maybe she should go home and have a cup of sweet tea. She was about to suggest this to Jules when Mickey Davey shoved his way past.

"My café!" he cried, his eyes wide with disbelief at the scene in front of him. "My bloody café! My floor! Out my way, you morons! Let me through!"

He started to push his way under the cordon, but Chris and Big Rog held him back.

"Let me through! Get off! That's my bloody café," Mickey snarled, trying to shake them off.

"It's not safe, mate," said Adam. "It'll take a good few hours before that fire's out. They're doing their best, but it's going to take time – and a fair bit of water."

"They can't flood it with water!" Mickey was practically screaming now. "Of all the stupid idiots! No water! Turn that bloody hose off! I said no water!"

For a man whose livelihood was burning down before his eyes, Mickey was behaving rather strangely, thought Alice. It was almost as though he didn't want the fire put out.

"Not the floor," he wailed, clutching his head. "Not the floor!"

There was something very odd happening. The smoke was thick and yellow, and the strangest smell hung heavy in the air. Alice's nose wrinkled with the pungent scent. Thick and bitter, yet sweet too; it was oddly familiar and reminded her of a fragrance Jimmy sometimes wore. Goodness it must be strong! Her head was spinning!

"Ally! Thank God, there you are. I was worried!" Jonny, his face taut with concern, had joined them. Pulling Alice close, he kissed the top of her head before sneezing violently.

"Good Lord, it smells like the sixties down here! Whatever was the café made from?"

"Wood?" said Jules.

Jonny laughed. "Obviously I'm not speaking from experience here, Rev, but I'd have said cannabis, not wood. The whole village smells like a hippy commune!"

"Cannabis?" echoed Alice. "As in drugs?"

It was as though she'd uttered a magic word with the power to unfreeze Mickey Davey. He was spinning on his heel, about to make a speedy exit, when two young men left the bucket chain, ducked under the rope and marched up to him. Alice recognised them as the two holidaymakers who'd been trying desperately to liberate their car from Mickey's space. They'd been in the village shop, sounding most upset, and had even asked Jules to intervene. Mickey had certainly done his best to make their fishing holiday an utter misery and Alice understood they were angry, but did they really need to yank Mickey's arms behind his back like that? And goodness, were those handcuffs? What on earth was happening?

"Michael Davey, you do not have to say anything, but it may harm your defence if you do not mention, when questioned, something which you later rely on in court. Anything you do say may be given in evidence against you."

"Get off me!" Mickey yelled, trying to wrench his shoulders away from them. "You can't nick me because I've blocked your car in, you tossers!"

"No, sir, but we can arrest you for possession of illegal drugs with intent to supply, and for storing them in a secret bunker under your café," said the taller of the two men, politely.

Mickey's eyes were bulging. "You fucking what? You can't arrest me. You're emmets!"

"We might be emmets but we're also police officers," said the taller man, snapping on the handcuffs, "who just happen to be on a surveillance job with a bit of fishing thrown in as a nice bonus."

"We're actually CID, if you want to get technical," added the other one.

Mickey stared at them in disbelief. "You're having a laugh!"

But the two CID officers were too professional to laugh, although Alice could imagine they might feel like it.

"I'm afraid not. You've been on the radar for some time," said the first detective to his stunned prisoner. "Although, you've made our job so much easier by blocking in our car and not going anywhere in a hurry. Surveillance has never been so easy. We even got some fishing in too."

Mickey's jaw was swinging open and all his bluster had vanished. As he was marched away the gathered villagers watched in shock, dazed by the events of the past few minutes as well as the potent aroma of cannabis. It just didn't seem possible! Explosions? Dope hidden underneath the beach café? Sleepy Polwenna Bay, a hotbed of international drug smuggling?

The only person who didn't seem surprised by any of this was Jonny St Milton.

"See," he said to Alice, kissing her hand as his grey eyes twinkled at her, "didn't I tell you that the tales of smugglers in this village were true?"

"In the eighteenth century! Not today!"

He winked. "The date's just a technicality. The point is, I was telling you the truth. So doesn't it stand to reason that I've always told you the truth about everything else too?"

Alice nodded. She couldn't argue with that.

"So trust me," he said, gently, "when I tell you that everything is going to be just fine."

Jonny was right. Polwenna Bay would keep or reveal its secrets when the time was right. That was the way it always had been and always would be, and Alice knew that she could trust him completely. She was willing to believe that all was not yet lost for the village.

Chapter 27

"Issie! Issie! Wake up! It's all going mad! The police are here and they're taking Dad to the station for questioning!"

Issie opened her eyes and saw her brother Nick sitting on her bed. He was fully dressed, bright-eyed and looking full of beans, whereas she felt as though she'd only been asleep for a few minutes. Her head was woolly, her mouth was dry and her eyes were still swollen from crying late into the night.

The excitement of events at the café and of the police raid that had followed had barely registered with Issie: all she could think about was Luke's betrayal. She kept telling herself she hated him, but her heart didn't want to listen. It leapt whenever her treacherous thoughts strayed to his kisses and the thrill of feeling his skin against hers. Last night, when most of the villagers had headed to the pub to discuss the café drama, Issie had stayed at home. She'd worked her way through what was left of the Christmas sherry, before passing out.

And the worst thing of all? After going to all the effort of drinking herself into oblivion she'd even dreamed about him…

"Why aren't you at sea?" she croaked. Her brother was dressed in his customary smock, jeans and rigger boots – but he was usually long gone by dawn, and the light stealing through the curtains suggested it was way past this time.

"None of us can go, because the police are searching all the boats. The quay's off limits," said Nick. "But never mind all that. Didn't you hear me? Dad's had to go to the police station to help with enquiries, and Granny's frantic. So come on, get up!"

Her brother whipped off the duvet and the arctic blast of air jolted Issie awake. Her brain felt as though it was swivelling in her cranium, and for a moment her every cell screamed out for coffee. Then the shock of Nick's words sank in.

"The police are questioning Dad? But why? This is nothing to do with him!"

"He was working for Mickey Davey, wasn't he?"

"Delivering pasties and helping him haul crab pots, not smuggling drugs. Jesus, Nick! Dad's daft but he'd never be involved in anything like that!"

"Not intentionally, but apparently Mickey was smuggling the cannabis out in pasties," Nick told her, a grim expression on his face.

Issie stared at him. "The pasties Dad was delivering?"

"You've got it. It gets worse. Apparently a boat was dropping the cannabis out at sea in crab pots – and we all know who was helping to haul those, don't we?"

"But that's just coincidence!" Issie cried, although even with a pounding techno beat in her skull, she could appreciate that the situation didn't look good.

"Of course it is, but just to make things worse he's been smuggling cocaine too. It was disguised as flour, apparently. Sy took a delivery by mistake the other day, so I bet they'll question him too," Nick continued. "And we've all used the café as well."

"Everyone in the village uses the beach café," Issie pointed out.

"*We* know that, but you must admit it doesn't look so great for us this morning. Council of war in the kitchen in ten, OK? Now move your arse!"

Issie dragged herself out of bed and somehow managed to have a shower. By the time she'd made her way into the kitchen, dressed in jogging bottoms and a tee-shirt, she was starting to feel slightly more human. The coffee Summer had brewed was helping to revive her too, although Issie still felt as though she was having an out-of-body experience.

With the noticeable exception of Jimmy (and Jake, who'd driven his father to the police station in Bodmin), the extended family had gathered around the kitchen table. Alice was in her usual place by the Aga, but for once she was sitting down and letting Mo and Summer sort out toast and tea. This was a sure sign that Alice was worried; usually, nothing could keep her from running around after her family. Jonny St Milton was here already, holding her hand and murmuring soothing words. Even Jules had arrived, straight from early-morning prayers and still in her cassock. Issie really hoped she had a direct hotline to her boss, because if anyone needed divine intervention right now it was Jimmy Tremaine.

"I've called my lawyer and he's on standby if we need him," Ashley Carstairs was saying to Danny, who nodded.

"Thanks, but let's hope it doesn't come to that. Two minutes with Dad and any copper with sense will know he's totally clueless. Mickey just used him."

"Mickey used the whole village," said Alice bitterly. "He's not the first and he won't be the last. Cornwall's always been a magnet for smugglers."

Honestly, thought Issie as she curled up on the sofa by the Aga, she was sick to the back teeth of smugglers, dead or alive.

"It's a magnet for the press right now," said Jules. "It's gone crazy down there. When I came past the green the Pollards were talking to the BBC and Caspar was being interviewed by Radio Cornwall. I even overheard Ivy Lawrence telling Sky TV that she'd never trusted Mickey."

"Ivy doesn't trust anyone," Alice remarked. "Besides, did any of us trust him?"

As the discussion turned to how everyone had always known Mickey was bad news, Issie helped herself to a couple of the day's newspapers and began to read. With every word she was more astonished. No wonder a swarm of reporters had descended: this was already being hailed as one of Britain's biggest drugs busts. Once again, Polwenna Bay was in the national press because of a smuggler.

It certainly made a good story. Issie read on, hardly able to believe that all this had been happening right under her nose – quite literally, at times. Whoever could have imagined that there was over a tonne of cannabis hidden beneath the café floor? Or that it was being smuggled out in the pasties? It was like something out of *Midsomer Murders*. According to several reports, the floor of the café had been hollowed out to make a small bunker. All along, the modern-day equivalent of Black Jack Jago's activities had been taking place only metres from Black Jack's tunnel.

As Issie was trying to take this in, the phone rang. It was Jake, calling to let them know he was on his way back.

"With Jimmy?" Alice asked. She was gripping Jonny's hand tightly and looked close to tears.

"With Jimmy," confirmed Ashley, who'd taken the call. At this, Alice slumped against Jonny with relief.

"And that's it?" Mo said. "He's in the clear?"

Ashley nodded. "He's been released without any further enquiries. He made a statement and apparently that's it. Jake says it was very apparent he really didn't have a clue."

"About the drugs or just in general?" muttered Danny, and Jules shot him a warning look.

"That's fantastic news," Jules said warmly, to the others. "I'll make us more tea and toast, shall I?"

"How about some pancakes?" Nick asked hopefully. "With bacon? And maple syrup?"

Just the thought of frying bacon was enough to make Issie's stomach curdle. Leaving her family to it, she slipped out of the back door. Some fresh air and a walk along the cliffs were what she needed to clear the remnants of her hangover. Mending her broken heart was another matter entirely.

* * *

While Polwenna Bay came to terms with its new infamy as the scene of one of the UK's biggest drugs hauls, Luke Dawson was grappling with the idiosyncrasies of the London Underground and doing his best to negotiate Piccadilly. Jeez. London in the rain was hard work. The Brits might have the whole thing down to a fine art as they swarmed out of the underground stations with their umbrellas and scurried along the greasy pavements, seemingly oblivious to the red buses swishing by only inches from their elbows – but Luke was struggling. Icy water trickled down his collar, he'd almost lost an eye to a rogue umbrella spoke, and trying to navigate using his cell phone had proved impossible with the rain blurring the screen. By the time he stood dripping in the foyer of Stella's hotel, Luke was cold, pissed off and longing for Florida. England could keep her cups of tea and royals and god-awful weather: give him sunshine and Starbucks any day.

Stella's suite was on the sixth floor. As Luke rode the elevator, or *lift* as they insisted on calling it here, he did his best to dry his face and hair with his sweater. A glance in the mirrored interior made him wince. He looked like a bum. His chin was dark with stubble, his curls were tight with damp and his clothes were creased from sleeping in the car. He hardly fitted in with the clientele of this elegant boutique hotel. Small wonder the concierge had looked a little surprised when Stella had affirmed he was meeting her.

Luke guessed he could have spent the night in a hotel if he'd wanted to – albeit nowhere near as plush as this one, with its ankle-deep carpets and original artwork. But since even staying in a Travelodge would have meant using some of the funds Stella had given him, there was no way he would do this. He wouldn't accept another cent from her, and he fully intended to pay back everything she'd advanced him. As far as Luke was concerned their business relationship was over.

Now all he had to do was make this clear to Stella.

Luke pulled his cell phone from his pocket and scrolled through the photo gallery, until he reached the images Issie had snapped in the tunnel. Even in the warmth of this luxurious city hotel he shivered. He would never forget that experience and what they'd discovered resting beneath the village. The images were dark but, even so, when Luke had zoomed in on them, there was no mistaking the evidence: at least some of the lost treasure was visible in that underground passage, along with the remains of the man who'd stolen it. Black Jack had died for that gold – and so had others, if the legends were to be believed. If Luke didn't stick to his guns now, who knew what other tragedies might unfold? Already Luke had lost the one woman he'd ever truly cared about, and that seemed bad enough.

He shook his head. On previous explorations, he'd been deep beneath the ocean, encased in a mask and breathing through an oxygen tank; he'd always felt somewhat removed from what he was looking at. The discovery in the tunnel had been immediate and shockingly real. This job didn't feel the same as the others had done. It felt like grave-robbing. His finger hovered over the screen before selecting all the images and deleting every last one. Then, for good measure, he double-checked that there was no remaining trace of them anywhere.

That was it. For better or for worse, the evidence was gone.

Abruptly, the elevator doors hissed opened and Luke stepped out into a palatial suite, so blindingly white that for a moment he blinked. Sheesh. You could lose a polar bear in here.

"Luke!" Stepping out of the whiteness was Stella, clad in a pristine bathrobe. She held a champagne flute in her tanned fingers and was smiling at him, her eyes shining with excitement and promises. Stepping forward and rising onto her immaculate red-nailed toes, she brushed her lips against his cheek.

"I was expecting you *last* night. Still, I didn't fly in till late, so maybe it's just as well, huh? You wouldn't have had the best of me. Come and have some champagne. We've got some celebrating to do."

She swished her way over to the ice bucket and lifted out a magnum of vintage Taittinger. Luke watched her helplessly.

"Stella, we need to talk."

"And we will, once we've had a glass of this and caught up! Fetch a champagne flute from the bar there, will you? We need a toast. This is a celebration. You've found the treasure!"

This was it, the point from which there could be no turning back. The recognition and success he'd always wanted was at his fingertips, but it wasn't enough anymore. He'd be selling out, no more his own man this time around than he had been with his father – and he'd be betraying Issie too. There was no way he could ever tell Stella what they'd really discovered. The price of success was far too high.

"There's nothing to celebrate, Stella."

She laughed. "Of course there is! You've located the *Isabella's* cargo! You told me yourself. We're rich, honey! I'd say that's something worth celebrating."

He shook his head. "No, we're not. I made a mistake."

She stared at him. "I don't understand."

"I was wrong. The things I found weren't…" He struggled for a minute, hating to lie but even more reluctant to give the slightest thing away. "I guess it wasn't what I thought it was. I was mistaken."

"What do you mean, mistaken?" She took a step back, her kitten-like playfulness vanishing in an instant.

"I don't believe you," she said slowly. "You're hiding something. You were so certain. You even said you had evidence."

"I thought I did, but I was wrong."

Stella's eyes narrowed. "You didn't sound as though you had any doubts when you called me. You sounded one hundred percent certain. *Evidence that proves everything*, was what you said, so let me be the judge. Where are the photos you told me about? Or are you keeping them and the find for yourself? Is that it? Are you playing me for a fool just because I let you screw me?"

Luke was horrified. "Christ, Stella, I'm not that much of a bastard. What we had and our business arrangement were two different things."

"Yeah right," she said bitterly. "How like a man."

Luke shook his head. "I'm real sorry, Stella, but I guess it was all a wild goose chase. I was wrong about the treasure. That happens sometimes in this business. It's risky, but you knew that. I did warn you."

In answer she knocked back her drink, and this time when her eyes met his they blazed with anger.

"Screw your warnings! You *promised* me that you'd found it. You told me there was evidence."

"I know and I'm sorry but—"

"Don't you *dare* try and apologise to me!" Her voice was a screech of fury. "Not when I've done everything to make this work for you! Have you any idea what I've been putting in place or how hard I've worked?"

Luke spread his hands. "Stella, this is how it goes in my business. Sometimes a lead plays out and sometimes it doesn't. That's the gamble."

But Stella wasn't listening to him. She poured another glass of champagne and began pacing the suite, tense with rage.

"Goddamn you, Luke! How could you do this? I thought you were a professional?"

That stung but Luke knew he had to take it. "This was just a lead that didn't quite play out. It happens in this game. Ask any of the guys."

"I'm not sponsoring them. I'm sponsoring *you*, and you told me this was a certainty," Stella hissed, rounding on him like a cobra. "For Christ's sake! I've pulled in big favours here for you! I've got a billionaire flying over on his Learjet to set up a sponsorship deal, and my friend in PR has been in touch with all the nationals and they're desperate for an exclusive. I've set up a big press conference this afternoon – it was what I was about to celebrate with you."

"Stella, I'm sorry, but I never asked you to do any of that. Nothing's ever certain in this game until there's actually something tangible recovered."

"You said there was evidence! You told me you'd found it! How did you manage to screw that up so completely? Are you fucking incompetent?"

Her words were like a lash and Luke winced. His reputation and his ability meant the world to him. He'd even sacrificed his relationship with his father to protect his professional name. It would have been the easiest thing in the world to tell Stella the truth and throw Polwenna Bay to the wolves. He'd be made. Everything he'd always wanted would be his.

The problem was, Luke didn't want those things quite as much anymore. His obsession with finding treasure and making his name felt like they belonged to another life. Ashley Carstairs was right: riches weren't always in the places you expected to find them.

"I even cancelled my holiday," Stella said bitterly.

Luke looked at her in disbelief. He'd told her to stay in the Caribbean but she'd insisted on catching a flight anyway. As for all the publicity she'd sorted? He'd never wanted or asked for that. Usually there were all kinds of legalities to deal with first before the salvage team had any claim. She'd more than jumped the gun; she'd run the race before the gun had even been loaded.

"I'll take all the blame," he told her quietly. "I'll come to the press conference and I'll tell them all it was my mistake. I'll apologise to your friend as well. Everyone will know this was my error and not yours."

"Damn right they will." She folded her arms across her chest and glared at him. "I'm not having my name dragged through the dirt. You've made an idiot of me, Luke Dawson, and no man does that and gets away with it."

"If I did that then I never meant to. I appreciate everything you did to help with this and I'll pay you back every cent," he told her.

She gave a resentful laugh. "You'll need every cent you've got by the time I'm through. I'll make sure your career's over; you can bet your life on that. By the time I'm finished nobody will hire you to drive a goddamn pedalo!"

"Go ahead," Luke sighed. "Do whatever you need to do, Stella. I won't argue with you."

This was probably the least he deserved for letting her down. So he'd seem like an idiot and his career would be in tatters, but at least he could hold his head up and look the world in the eye. Whatever else he might have done, he wouldn't have sold Issie and Polwenna Bay out to further his own ambitions – and that was all he cared about now.

Leaving Stella snarling into her cell phone, Luke stepped into the elevator, his heart a thousand times lighter than it had been on the journey up. Where he might go from here was anyone's guess, but he would be going there with his self-respect intact.

It really was true: there were some things in life you couldn't put a price on. He just hoped he wasn't too late to make that clear to the only person who mattered.

Chapter 28

The tide was right out, leaving the beach glistening in the morning light. Its jagged rocks were no longer submerged beneath the waves, but now resembled darkened teeth rooted in the wet sand. Although the quay remained cordoned off while police searched the trawlers and the fishermen's stores, the beach was still open to the public. A few die-hard visitors were already hard at work with their metal detectors and shovels. Everyone else was gathered as close to the café as possible, taking selfies and craning their necks to be in the shot of a news broadcast. Bobby and Joe Penhalligan looked as though they were trying to inhale whatever fumes might be lingering from the fire, which made Issie laugh. Mickey Davey hadn't intended to give the village a free high, but even her grandmother and Jonny had giggled for most of yesterday afternoon before raiding the fridge. Pensioners with the munchies. You couldn't make it up!

Life in Polwenna Bay was many things but dull certainly wasn't one of them.

Today had dawned steel grey with rain clouds hanging heavy on the horizon, and there was a sharp easterly wind. It was a typically bleak January day and it suited Issie's mood perfectly. Digging her hands deep into the pockets of her coat, she sprinted down the beach steps and jogged along the tideline until she drew parallel with the cave.

From the outside everything looked just as it always had. The mouth of the cave yawned dark and vast, and the smell of rotting seaweed made her nose wrinkle. How odd to think that at the far end of this cave the lost tunnel had begun, twisting its way under the village all the way up to St Wenn's Well. It was even stranger to think that, in the shadowy depths, the remains of Black Jack Jago guarded his unlucky loot. Stepping into the cave made Issie shudder. Alice had been right: the treasure was cursed. What if Issie's meddling was the reason Jimmy had been caught up with Mickey Davey and almost implicated in the crime? Was this her fault? And when Luke revealed the truth about the tunnel, would there be worse to come?

Issie knew she was being ridiculous – but in the blackness, where the only sounds were her own breathing and the drip, drip, drip of water, it was only too easy to be superstitious. She was unlucky in love too. Was that another sign of the curse? After all, how many twenty-two-year-olds had grandmothers with love lives in better shape than their own?

Issie attempted to step forwards, but cried out as her knee slammed into solid granite. This couldn't be the back of the cave, could it? It had been far deeper than this before. Something must have changed. Issie pulled her iPhone from her pocket and switched on the torch, then gasped.

"No way!" she whispered to herself in shock. At least half of the cave was now blocked.

Yesterday's explosion must have destabilised the rocks. There'd been falls in the past – many of them, judging by the state of the tunnel – but never anything quite like this. Water still trickled through the cracks, but apart from that there was no chance of anything or anyone being able to get through now. If the beach end of the smugglers' passage had been obstructed before, then it was well and truly sealed now. It was as though the village was doing its very best to guard the secrets that lay within.

Her hangover forgotten, Issie raced back across the beach and up the steps. A thought had just occurred to her and all she could think of now was seeing whether or not she was right. After all, what was it that Jonny St Milton had kept telling them all? *The village keeps its own secrets.* He'd said it over and over again, and now Issie knew why: Jonny had found the treasure years ago. His stories of exploring the tunnel weren't stories at all – they were true.

The cottage that Luke had rented was empty now. As she walked up the path, panting for breath and with an agonising stitch in her side, Issie tried her hardest not to think about the time she'd spent with him there. Luke had to be put out of her mind. He'd been a lapse in her judgment, a mistake, a fling, she told herself sharply. He wasn't her soulmate or her missing half; Luke Dawson had been nothing but a confidence trickster, and she'd been a gullible idiot to be taken in by him so easily.

The outhouse was just as gloomy as Issie remembered, but at least this time there was no need to move a decade's worth of rubbish and piles of rotting wood. Dragging the heavy slab from the opening of the old privy took some effort, and a couple of annoyed spiders scuttled out, but within minutes Issie realised that the explosion and the rockfalls in the cave had altered everything.

She crouched down and peered into the darkness, her eyes wide when she saw water swirling by only inches below the aperture. The rockfalls further downstream must have blocked the tunnel significantly and the water, unable to flow as freely as before, had backed right up.

Black Jack, his treasure and the smugglers' tunnel were entirely hidden now. Did this mean that she'd escaped the curse? Was that why Jimmy had been released without any further trouble?

Issie laughed. These thoughts were absurd, of course, but even so she felt a huge sense of relief. There was no way any other treasure hunters would be able to come across the lost cargo now. The secret was safe with her.

Except it wasn't just her secret, was it? Luke Dawson knew everything, and Issie could only imagine that in his industry a few fallen rocks and some fast-flowing water were just minor inconveniences. Nothing was going to stop Luke. Look at all the effort he'd gone to already. And worse, he had those pictures on his phone as evidence. With a wealthy sponsor and his ruthless determination, he wouldn't rest until he'd returned for the treasure. The passage might be blocked for the time being, but nothing had really changed: the future of the village and the slumbering secrets beneath it were still in his hands. Luke had been gone for three days now, more than enough time for him to set the wheels in motion. He was probably shacked up in some luxury hotel with the mysterious Stella, swilling champagne and having a right laugh about how stupid English girls were.

Deflated, Issie made her way back into the village. The police were still in evidence and the quay remained out of bounds, but the locals had moved on – probably to the pub, since it was coming up for lunchtime. She decided she might as well join them. If the hair of the dog didn't make her feel better, then a big plate of cheesy chips certainly would.

"Aha! The wanderer returns! We missed you last night!" said Adam Harper when she pushed the door open.

"I had a night in," Issie said, hopping onto a bar stool and indicating the scrumpy pump.

"A night in drinking, by the look of you." Adam poured the cider and then rubbed a chalk mark off the tally chart on the beam above. "Six left, Issie."

"I'll buy you another," said Little Rog quickly, holding an empty glass out. "Half for me, Ad, and put a scrumpy in for Issie."

Great, she could get drunk again for free, flirt with Little Rog and afterwards stagger back to her grandmother's home and pass out. Then she could do it all over again tomorrow. And the next day. And maybe the day after that too. Seeing her life panning out this way made Issie feel quite depressed. She had to do something to change it or she'd end up being the mad old drunk in the corner nobody wanted to talk to.

The answer was obvious, and it wasn't one that could be found in the bottom of a glass: Issie had to go back to university. Mark Tollen couldn't influence her future anymore. It was time to take charge of her life.

"Delivery for Miss Isabella Tremaine? The Ship Inn, Polwenna Bay?"

Issie looked up in surprise. A deliveryman stood at the bar, glancing around at the motley collection of locals, who in turn were eyeing him suspiciously. Even The Ship's most loyal customers weren't in the habit of using the pub as their fixed address.

"That's me," Issie said, intrigued.

"Great. Here's your parcel," the deliveryman replied, placing a rectangular package on the bar. Now, if you'd just sign here?"

But Issie was confused. "I'm not expecting anything and, if I was, I wouldn't ask for it to be delivered here."

"We're a pub, not the bloody post office," Adam huffed.

The deliveryman laughed. "You'd be amazed at some of the places we deliver to. Haven't you see *Castaway*?"

"I thought that was FedEx. But either way, being marooned on a deserted island without the missus and this place sounds good to me," sighed the landlord, returning to polishing glasses.

Once Issie had provided her signature and the deliveryman had bid them farewell, the curious locals gathered round to see what was in the parcel.

"Go on then, Issie. Open it. Don't keep us all in suspense," Adam urged.

"I've no idea what it is or who's sent it," Issie said, turning the parcel around as she studied it. The return address was the same as the delivery one – somebody was certainly determined that she got this parcel. She felt rather nervous. What if Mark had sent something? Wasn't it odd that for months she'd longed for a romantic gesture from him but now she couldn't imagine anything worse?

"Only one way to find out," Big Rog said.

"Quicker with these too," added Adam, passing her some scissors.

"God, you lot are so nosey. Get a life," grinned Issie and, taking the scissors, she snipped through the packaging tape.

"Yours is so much more exciting," Adam sighed. "Nobody sends me secret presents."

"Is it something personal?" Little Rog asked hopefully, peering over her shoulder.

"It's not from Ann Summers if that's what you're hoping, you sad person," Issie said, rolling her eyes. Still, just in case, and to the disappointment of the lunchtime drinking crowd, she took the parcel over to a quiet window seat to open it in private. If Mark had gone mad and sent some sexy underwear, unwanted or not, the last thing she needed was the Pollards perving over it.

The outer packaging contained a box filled with bubble wrap. Frowning, Issie eased this out. Slowly she unravelled it until she was holding a beautiful ship in a bottle. The glass was old and thick, filled with bubbles and swirls, and the neck was sealed with a thick cork. The vessel inside, sailing on a blue-glass sea, took her breath away. Tears filled her eyes because there was only one person in the whole world who would have sent this. The ship in the bottle was a stunning miniature galleon, perfect in every detail and proportion, and on the bow, written in gold script, was the name *Isabella*.

Issie felt as though someone had just cut all her strings. A rolled-up parchment rested just inside the neck of the bottle and, as though in a dream, she pulled out the cork and retrieved it. Holding her breath, she unrolled the document slowly and smoothed it out on the table, then placed on its corners whatever paperweights came to hand – the salt cellar, the pepper, the vinegar and a bottle of ketchup. And when she finally saw what was on the parchment, she laughed out loud.

The document was a hand-drawn map of the village. It was sketched out in an amateur fashion in crayon and ink, and yet it was accurate in a way that was deeply personal.

Treasure of Polwenna Bay, declared the map's heading.

The map showed the wreck, the cave, the old cottage privy, the church and all the locations in between, from shops to houses to the special places where the events of the past few weeks had happened. It must have taken hours to draw and had been crafted with such loving attention to detail that Issie could only shake her head in disbelief. This wasn't the work of someone whose only thought was of money and glory. This didn't make any sense at all. Unless… Unless…

Unless the person who had sent her this map was trying to give her a message that only she would understand?

Where wishes bring true riches, read the script on the map.

There was no X marking the spot, and there were no more clues – but Issie didn't need them. She knew exactly where she had to look. It was obvious and always had been to her.

But could the person who had sent this to her really feel the same way? And, if so, could her heart learn to trust again? Overflowing with questions and full of a hope she hardly dared acknowledge, Issie left the pub and set off on a new treasure hunt.

Chapter 29

Issie stopped dead at the top of the footpath. Her breathing came in sharp painful gasps, plucked from her lungs after running most of the way up from the village to the woods at the top. Here it was still and eerily quiet. There was no birdsong, no shrieking of seagulls, and even the wind seemed to have stilled. As always there was the strange sensation that time was holding its breath here. Stepping into the dim hollow, it was as though the outside world had ceased to be; there was nothing else except the trickling of quicksilver water onto the dank earth.

St Wenn's Well. It had to be. Where else in the village would you come to make a wish – and not just any wish, but a wish for true love? It was here, back in the autumn, that Issie had dipped her fingers into the icy water and done exactly that. Although she'd quipped about finding a sexy millionaire, the yearning that had sprung from her heart had been for a soulmate, her missing part. The place had a brooding, watchful air that made Issie's arms ripple with goosebumps. It was a strange and magical location, and whenever she visited she couldn't help believing that something old and timeless had been listening to the longing that had filled her that day.

Later, when she'd come here with Luke and told him the legend, he'd laughed and said that his wish was to find the treasure. St Wenn had certainly granted that, hadn't she? Riches beyond Luke's wildest dreams had been within a fingertip's reach – and still were, if he chose to come and get them. So why hadn't he returned to claim his fortune? After all, wasn't this what he'd always wanted? She'd Googled the Dawsons and knew they lived and breathed treasure. Some of them had even died for it.

She knelt down and dabbled her hands in the cool water, marvelling at the mysterious journey it would make down through the rocks, past gold coins and tide-washed bones beneath the village, before joining the vast seas beyond. The clear water would keep its secrets. Would Luke?

"Making a wish?"

It was him. Issie didn't look up; she didn't need to. Her heart knew it was Luke. He was the one she'd wished for all those months ago, and deep down she'd always known that.

"I made my wish a long time ago," Issie said quietly.

"And did it come true?"

She continued to stare down at the laughing water. Her fingers were tingling with the cold.

"Did yours?"

"You heard me wish I'd find the treasure." Crouching beside her, Luke dipped his own fingers in the water and swirled it thoughtfully.

"You did find it." Issie knew she had to be strong now, not just for herself but for everything she loved. She turned to him, her eyes taking in his strong profile, the full generous mouth, and her heart fluttered. Whatever the outcome, she had to know the answer. "Is that why you're back, Luke? Have you come for the treasure?"

In answer, his fingers slipped through the water, lacing with hers, and then pulling her to her feet. Then his cold hands cupped her face, tenderly stroking her cheeks, before his lips paused just a kiss away from hers.

"I did," he said softly, "but I didn't need to ask St Wenn for help. I'd already struck gold. I was just too stupid to realise it." His green eyes held hers, earnest and full of an emotion she hardly dared name. "And yes, I've come back for that treasure, because *you're* the true treasure of Polwenna Bay, Issie. I was just too goddamn blind to see it before. I had something so precious in my grasp and like an idiot I let it slip through my fingers. So yeah, I'm back here for the treasure – if that treasure will have me, of course?"

Issie's eyes widened as the meaning of his quiet and heartfelt words sank in. For a moment she quailed, hurt so badly in the past that it felt as though it would take an enormous leap of faith to trust again. But then sun slipped out from behind the clouds and dappled the grove with dancing light, as though St Wenn herself was giving her blessing. Issie's breath caught in her throat. There was nothing left now but honesty. She ached for him to kiss her, but there was something she needed to know first, something on which the future of everything seemed to depend.

Issie stepped back and looked up at him. The sunlight glinted on his broad shoulders and burnished his curls to the colours of autumn leaves. She was mesmerised by the sheer beauty of him and the intensity of his jade-eyed gaze, just as she had been when she'd seen him for the first time. She hadn't imagined the chemistry between them: it was as real as the dancing light, the damp earth and the blood running through her veins. Yet before she could tell him that yes, she wanted him more than she'd ever thought it was possible to want someone, there was a question that had to be answered. She'd imagined a thousand times what she would say to him if she ever saw him again, and in those conversations there hadn't been words bad enough to make it clear how hurt and angry she was – but now that the moment was actually here, Issie just felt sad. The treasure really was cursed if it had destroyed the magic that had been between them.

"It's not just about how I feel," she told him. "This is about more than us, Luke."

"You mean what am I going to do about what we found?"

"You used me to find it."

He nodded. "At first, I guess I did, and I'm not proud of that. It wasn't something I'd intended either. I'd watched the TV broadcast and yes, I'd seen you already and I could tell you knew more than you let on."

"You said you were a history major."

"That bit was true. I am, or maybe more accurately I was. I dropped out to help my dad when Mom left." He smiled ruefully. "I didn't think you'd be nearly as happy to spend time with me if I said I was a professional treasure hunter."

"So you kept it a secret from me."

"Guilty as charged," he said, visibly wincing at the accusation. "But hey, you kept a secret too. I had no idea about your past either."

This was true and Issie nodded. "Mark was married. He was my tutor and it's a long story and I'm ashamed of it all. I really liked you, more than I was ever expecting to like anyone again, and I suppose I didn't want you to judge me," she confessed.

Luke smiled. "Ditto. You blew me away, Issie Tremaine, and I was never anticipating that either. I thought I'd come here, find the lost cargo and then it would be job done. My name would be made." He dipped a feather-soft kiss onto her mouth. "I just never expected to fall in love."

Issie's heart was hammering in her chest. "Luke, I can't... I..."

"You need to know what I'm going to do?"

She nodded. She was falling in love with him too – maybe had fallen already, and harder than she could ever have imagined – but everything that could be, that she longed to be, depended upon what he said now.

"I love you," he told her, staring into her eyes as though willing her to believe him. "Nothing else matters. So, in answer to your question, I'm doing nothing."

"Nothing?"

"I've deleted the pictures and I've told Stella I made a mistake about the treasure," Luke said. "As far as anyone else is concerned there never was any cargo. It was all a hoax."

Issie could hardly believe what she was hearing. "But what about your reputation? And the sponsorship?"

He shrugged. "I guess I can kiss goodbye to both of those. Stella organised a big press conference and, man, she was pissed. The last I heard she was out to crucify me. She's perfectly within her rights to be mad. She put up the money to fund all this, after all. But I'll work my butt off to pay her back. I'll even sell my ancient Boston Whaler. It's not worth much but it'll be a start."

She blinked. "Luke, you can't do that! And what about your career?"

But Luke just laughed. "Do you know what? I realised none of that matters a damn if I don't have you. Everything I care about is right here."

His words were like a caress and, as Luke pulled her close, Issie knew he meant every one of them. She felt the muscles of his arms tighten around her and as she leaned her head against his chest, Issie sighed with happiness.

Luke was right. Some things were worth far more than gold and silver, and all the treasure in the world couldn't buy the joy that filled Issie when he finally kissed her. Deep below the ferny floor a king's ransom slumbered in peace, while the nearby stream chuckled and the sunbeams stole through the trees and stroked the couple's blissful faces.

THE END

Epilogue

Six weeks later...

Studying in the sunshine was hard enough, Issie thought, with the lure of the cool ocean just a dive away – but it was even more difficult when the pages of your notebook kept sticking to hands that were sticky with sun cream, and when there was a gorgeous man on the deck wearing nothing more than board shorts and a smooth butterscotch tan. Doing her best to ignore Luke, whose every sinew was outlined and gleaming as he pulled himself out of the water, Issie shoved her shades up her nose with her forefinger and returned to her textbook.

Eighteenth-century politics was definitely far more exciting than swimming in the Gulf of Mexico, she tried to tell herself. Who wanted to snorkel with stingrays and parrotfish when they could be reading all about mercantilism and making notes on Adam Smith? Issie gritted her teeth and tried to focus; if she stood any chance of catching up on her lost studies then she needed to immerse herself in the 1736 Act of Indemnity rather than deep blue waters. At least she was able to toast her limbs while she swotted up for her university interview. That way she wouldn't look too much like an out-of-place Brit!

Issie flipped the page and tried her hardest to concentrate on long-ago Parliamentary Acts. After all, she reminded herself, these might seem a world away from the vibrant colours and heat of the Keys, but it was from such paradises that Black Jack's smuggling trade had begun – and the history of the New World was so tightly woven with the Old World of Polwenna Bay that it was almost impossible to see the joins. Her world and Luke's hadn't been so far apart either, and the values they shared had turned out to be in perfect harmony, just like their hearts and souls. The misery and angst of the months with Mark were like a bad dream, and Issie shuddered to think how her life could have been if she hadn't found the strength to walk away from him. She hoped that Emma, wherever she was, was happy too.

Applying to resume her studies in Florida so that she could be near Luke was a no-brainer, and Issie didn't think she'd ever been as happy as she was now. Every morning she woke to the whir of the ceiling fan and the sounds of the boats coming to life, unable to believe that she was really in Key West. Eyes still tightly closed, Issie would stretch out her foot beneath the crisp white sheets to touch Luke's bronzed leg with her toes, a smile of delight curling her mouth when she realised anew that this wasn't a dream. She really was waking up in the US of A with her gorgeous boyfriend. Did life get any better?

Boyfriend! Issie sighed contentedly. It still sounded so strange. Luke was far more than a boyfriend. He was her best friend, her soulmate, her diving buddy, her intellectual sparring partner, her lover…

She looked over the top of her sunglasses and her smile widened at just the sight of him. Studying with Luke around was easier said than done. He was rinsing out dive gear at the back of the boat now. He looked so sexy in his board shorts, with his mop of hair springing into long ringlets that brushed his shoulders, and rivulets of salt water running down his sculpted chest, that she needed to dive into the ocean just to cool off. Well, either that or hose herself down with the deck wash… How could she possibly concentrate on history books when she was longing to trail her fingers across his chest and feel the tautness of his muscles beneath her fingertips?

Issie yawned and stretched her sun-warmed limbs. Maybe studying could wait until this evening? Her interview with the history department wasn't for another week and she already had a killer case study to wow them with, after all. The past was great but the present was far more interesting!

And the future? Well, she had a feeling that was going to be even better...

"How's that chapter going?" Luke asked sternly, glancing over and seeing her looking distracted. "Ready for me to test you yet?"

She grinned. "You can *test* me any time you like!"

"Oh, I fully intend to," Luke assured her, his green eyes dancing with promise, "but before we think about anything more *exciting*, you need to be up to speed with your interview preparation; we owe that much to your gran."

Luke was right and Issie nodded.

"I know, and I won't let her down. I'll get my place on the course and make her proud."

When Alice had announced that she'd sold the gold coin and wanted the proceeds to help complete Issie's education, her granddaughter's first impulse had been to say no. That money belonged to Alice and the family – heaven only knew they needed it to help with the boatyard and subsidise Jimmy's spending now that his days of innocently delivering cannabis pasties were over – but Alice had been adamant.

"We both know you could have easily claimed a whole lot more," her grandmother had said firmly. "Luke too."

Issie had stared at her in surprise. She and Luke had sworn never to mention their find to anyone – they were in perfect agreement that this was the only way to keep the secret safe — so however could her grandmother possibly know?

Seeing Issie's confusion, Alice had laughed. "You're not the only one to have secrets, love."

"Did Jonny tell you?" Issie had asked. "Did he know all along?"

But Alice had merely maintained an innocent expression and wouldn't be pressed any further. Like the lost treasure, she was keeping her secrets close.

"But the coin belongs to you," Issie had protested.

Her grandmother had frowned. "It was never really ours, though, was it? If the story's true it was stolen from the ship and is part of the original cargo. I think using it for a good purpose is the right thing to do. That treasure has brought enough misery in the past. Maybe now it's time to use it for good?"

It wasn't a fortune, but the sale of the coin had raised enough for Issie to look at university courses in the USA and for Alice to donate a sum to charity. With her future suddenly wide open, Issie had started to make plans. Westchester was never going to be a possibility after all the heartache she'd experienced there. Besides, it felt good to be starting again with a clean slate. Where better to have that slate than Florida, and close to Luke too? Like the undiscovered wrecks sleeping in the deep blue depths, their relationship was unchartered territory — but Issie was looking forward to exploring it. Her world, once full of despair and regrets, was suddenly a treasure trove of possibilities. Nothing would ever be the same again for Issie.

This wasn't true for Polwenna Bay, though. Once the excitement of Mickey Davey's arrest had died down and the news had spread that Black Jack's treasure was just a hoax, life had soon settled down. The

Pollards had given up with metal detectors and returned to building (and sometimes clearing drains). Meanwhile, without boatloads of tourists to exploit, the fishermen were back at sea. Even the holiday cottages were empty again for now. Life would return with the buds and warm winds of the spring, but until then everything was as it should be. Polwenna Bay had slipped back into its old and familiar rhythm.

Yet for Issie Tremaine, everything had changed. When Luke had flown back to the States she'd known that her path was going to take her far away from the village she loved and the world she'd always known. She was taking a risk, but wasn't life all about taking chances? Wasn't that really living?

Issie had only been in Florida for a couple of weeks, but already her limbs were golden, her hair was bleached several shades lighter and her heart, like the Keys, was filled with sunshine. Luke, who'd sold his boat to start paying Stella back and was living in a small beach shack, was worried that he had little to offer now – but to Issie his love was the greatest wealth imaginable. For the time being he was working as crew for other dive boats and attempting to build bridges with his father (who was still drinking heavily, as far as Issie could see), but Luke still dreamed of having his own business. The discovery of Black Jack's hoard beneath the village could so easily have made his dreams come true, but the fact that he'd sacrificed these to do the right thing told Issie all she ever needed to know about him. Some things were worth far more than money.

A text alert sounded on her phone and Issie glanced down at it, squinting against the glare.

"Tell Luke I like a man who knows what's really valuable," the text read, in true cryptic Ashley Carstairs style. "Call me. I have a proposal he might be interested in."

Interesting, Issie thought. She'd no idea Luke had made such an impression on her brother-in-law, but she'd pass the message on. A little knot of excitement tightened in her tummy. Could Ashley's proposal be about sponsorship? This was just the kind of venture her speedboat-loving brother-in-law would relish.

Pushing her books aside, Issie crossed the deck and joined Luke, winding her arms around his neck. Ashley's intriguing text message could keep for a moment, though, because she no longer needed to go treasure hunting. Luke Dawson's heart was made of pure gold and his love made Issie Tremaine the richest girl in the world.

The treasure she'd been searching for was right here in her arms.

Ruth Saberton is the bestselling author of *Katy Carter Wants a Hero* and *Escape for the Summer*. She also writes upmarket commercial fiction under the pen names Jessica Fox, Georgie Carter and Holly Cavendish.

Born and raised in the UK, Ruth has just returned from living on Grand Cayman for two years. What an adventure!

And since she loves to chat with readers, please do add her as a Facebook friend and follow her on Twitter.

www.ruthsaberton.co.uk

Twitter: @ruthsaberton

Facebook: Ruth Saberton

Made in United States
North Haven, CT
06 April 2024

50962930R00193